Sorrow

Sorrow
The Sorrows Trilogy Book 1
© 2017 Pitbull Publishing

This book is protected under the copyright laws of the United States of America. Any reproduction or unauthorized use of the material or artwork contained herein is prohibited without the express written permission of Pitbull Publishing.

Published by Pitbull Publishing 73 Eagle Road, Orangeville, PA 17859 USA | 1 (570) 458-5890 | www.getsomebite.com | sales@getsomebite.com

All characters and events portrayed in this book are fictitious. Any similarity to real persons, living or dead is purely coincidental, and not intended by the author.

Sorrow concepts and all characters by Zachary Weaver
Cover and interior design by Michael Weaver and Zachary Weaver

ISBN: 978-1-970018-01-1
ISBN: 978-1-970018-03-5 (ebook)
ISBN: 978-1-970018-04-2 (Kindle)

Cataloging-in-Publication data is on file with the Library of Congress.

Visit our web site at www.SorrowsTrilogy.com

To my parents and little brothers: thank you for staying involved in the chaos of my creations. Your patience has paid off, and I will never forget your time, love, and dedication. Success, has many forms, and this is only one of many to follow. Thank you also for always giving me a way to relieve my stress, even if that's by kicking your butts in video games or wrestling in the rec room. This is all for you.

To my grandmother: I have no words for how much you've helped me gain an understanding of the type of person I am, and for that, I will be forever thankful. No words can describe the long talks we've had on terrible business ideas and corny jokes, but each little bit contributed to the long road ahead of me. P.S. I think you've waited long enough.

To my brother-in-arms: No war would I ever wage without you watching my back. Years of success lay ahead of us, and in many hidden forms. Thank you for the long chats, the hours on hours of competitive gaming, and most of all, your friendship. Now go pay some taxes.

To my editor: years of hard work have finally reached a culmination, and for most of the critique, frenzied ideas, and long conversations, I have you to blame. Thanks for sticking by my side through thick and thin, version after version.

And to every other countless individual who won't fit on this page: Your help is not diminished or forgotten over time. I never would have gotten this far without the help of a select number of individuals. You have all contributed to helping me in various ways, and for that, I thank you all.

Devoid, I suppose, is how I would describe my soul: the black phantom in my heart fusing pain to my thoughts and emotions. Every one of them is an unbearable agony, these unattainable ideals adding yet another scar to my already shattered heart. Every time I look back at them, I feel wicked, cruel tears cutting through my sightless eyes. This misery is my curse, bound to me by an unseen contract deep within my skin.

I am a mask; A ghost.
A terror whose every last shred of spirit has been devoured by a fire of antagonistic memories. I die with the fading embers of my sanity.
I am a nightmare. A disease. The predator to all the prey in the world.

I am Sorrow.

Lines
Jalix

    Intently listening, I closed my eyes as the first note was struck. It resonated for a moment, reverberating in the acoustical balance of the room before drifting off into a brief pause. Immediately, her fingers began moving lithely between the keys, striking each one at her will. My heart twisted erratically, chasing the melody. Her black hair swayed with her body as the chords rang out in perfect harmony with her hands. I smiled in the dark, letting the beauty fill my mind and ears. As I took a deep, shaky breath, the vibrations in the air saturated my lungs and infected my body with a purifying sadness. The tempo slowed, and the notes gradually grew quieter until they were nothing but a whisper. A silent crescendo ended the composition, and she smiled.
"Beautiful." I said quietly, just loud enough for her to hear. She giggled in the dark as I put my hands around her waist. "You are flawless," I whispered in her ear. She leaned into me, the aroma of rose petals intoxicating my senses. I ran my hand through her silken jet hair, letting the strands fall through my fingers.
"I love you." She whispered, turning around.
    The darkness shrouded her, blinding me from everything she was. Still, without seeing her eyes convey their desire, I knew she spoke the truth. Moving her gently, I laced my fingers with hers and leaned back, pulling her onto the bed with me and away from her position

on the piano's bench. She sighed, falling into me and meeting my lips with hers. The sensation of her body resting against mine was nothing other than perfect, our breathing, though ragged and uneven, feeding into our mutual desire. I knew that neither of us wanted to be anywhere else. She paused, running a hand through my unkempt hair and breathing an ecstatic sigh.

"I never thought I'd end up here. With the man I love." She whispered, her lips brushing against mine with every word.

"End here?" I replied, tracing a finger along the edges of her face.

"Here isn't the end. It's the beginning." She smiled, her heartbeat anxiously fluttering against my chest. Her mouth moved to my neck, each kiss she placed leaving raw ecstasy on my skin. It was an indescribable feeling, to know that the image of perfection was so purely, so unconditionally taken with me.

"You know that you're perfect, right?" I smiled, caressing both of her cheeks in my hands. She grinned, taking the remark lightly despite my seriousness.

"I'm far from perfect, my love. But I'm glad you see it that way." She sat up slowly on the edge of the bed, her back facing me.

"Help me get undressed? I should get a shower before we leave." I pulled off her shirt to expose her snow-white skin, obscured slightly by black lace lingerie. Unhooking her top, I kissed her neck before sliding her clothes down to the bed.

"I'll be out in a few minutes." She turned her head and smiled before sauntering to the bathroom. Looking at my alarm clock, I realized how early it was. I picked up her discarded sleepwear and placed it in the laundry basket before hearing the shower turn on. I felt bad for waking her up so early, despite her prior warnings that she would have a long day. I opened the bathroom door quickly and closed it behind me, so the heat did not escape.

"I'm sorry for waking you up, Kara. I had no idea it was so early or I would have went out to the couch."

"Why are you apologizing? I got plenty of sleep. And I know how old scars feel." She remarked, pulling back the shower curtain to look at me. My eyes wandered over her body at her sheer beauty, the few minor scars she bore catching my eye.

"Sometimes I forget you've never needed much sleep." I replied, looking into her bright, silver eyes. She smiled, her perfect teeth almost masked by the steam.

"And I'm a light sleeper. I'm glad I got up, anyway, I was having...freaky dreams. And it's almost six. It's not *exactly* early."

"Still." I said, rubbing my chin thoughtfully. "Want to go get coffee before you have to go for the day?" She tilted her head and batted her eyelashes.

"A date? My goodness, how could a girl like me say no?" I grinned and reached over, lacing my fingers with hers.

"God, I love you." As I took a step toward the shower, she laughed and kissed me gently. She stared at me with her beautiful silver eyes before biting her lip and closing the shower curtain. The shower turned off and the curtain was thrown back once again.

"You should go get dressed." She winked at me before stepping out and putting her wet arms on my shoulders.

"I'll be done in just a minute." She grabbed a towel from the rack next to me and ran it over her leg. My eyes lingered on the elaborate tattoo of thorned roses, embellishing the length of her thigh.

"I'll go get dressed." I distracted myself and made my way into our bedroom, throwing the closet open and flipping through my assortment of suit jackets. Dressing for a day of comfort, I picked out a black blazer and a pair of dark jeans before reaching into my nightstand and removing the small black box inside.

"I don't suppose that today's the day you tell me what you do for a living, is it?" I called, asking the same question I did weekly. Tossing it lightly, I contemplated whether today would be the right day to propose.

"Umm...how about serial killer this week? No, wait. Professional women's basketball player." I laughed quietly, placing the box in my pocket and checking myself in the mirror. I looked over as the door opened from across the hall.

Kara strode out of the bathroom, the steam creeping out behind her, quietly stalking each barefooted step. Her full, red lips stood out against her pale complexion, but her eyes stood out against everything. Her irises were bright silver, outlined with black and with lashes so long, that when she looked down, they touched her pale cheek.

"Someday soon, Jalix. Just not today." I nodded, content with her response. Rain outside tapped against the window quietly as she slipped on a stiletto.

"I get it. But busy day today, right?"

"Yes, Jalix." She chuckled, putting her hands on her hips. "But I think I've got time for coffee."

***

We sat down at a small table near the window. The raindrops fell from the sky slowly, setting a sad tone that contrasted our moods. I gazed at the movie theater across the street for several minutes with no interest in it whatsoever. The energy she radiated from across the table was contagious, melting away the stresses of a normal day. I could not be bothered with the menial thoughts of the impending meeting I would attend, or the worries that my payment would not go through in time for her engagement ring. The feeling of muted contentedness was shared, indicated by her quiet smile and wandering eyes. Kara's fingers intertwined with mine underneath the table as the strong, bitter scent of fresh coffee reached our table. She smiled and laughed quietly.

Sorrow

"Plan on getting coffee anytime today, or just sightseeing?" She bit her lip in the cute, girlish way she knew I liked.

"I'm so sorry, my fair lady. I had no idea that you were in such a hurry." She laughed and pushed me gently before standing up. I had an arm around her waist as we walked up to the counter. The people behind it were busying themselves with cleaning, but one stopped long enough to look at me.

"One vanilla cappuccino and one black decaf, please." She nodded and scampered off to get our order.

"I have to use the bathroom. Be right back." Kara's black heels clicked as she strode down the hallway towards the restroom.

"Here's your order, sir." The server from behind the counter said. I thanked her and walked over to our table. The television in the far corner of the room was set to a news channel, where they were covering a story about the war in Afghanistan. The images were unfortunately familiar, but the news remained positive, indicating that American troops were leaving for the most part. Interrupting the memories of my former career, my phone vibrated. I tapped the screen to open the text message from my boss.

"Jalix. I hope I didn't catch you at a bad time. Please call me when you can. Concerning the Raven deal." I immediately hit the call back button.

"Jalix?" He said. He sounded like he was smiling.

"Yes, sir. What can I do for you?" He laughed on the other end.

"Don't call me sir, anymore. You just got promoted." My heart stopped for a split second, but I let him continue. "The medical company went public with the deal. They're up a hundred points from last night. Your pay? A twenty thousand dollar bump."

"Upwards?" I asked shakily. I knew the answer.

"Yes, indeed. Good job, as per usual, Jalix. I mean that. Congratulations. I have to go; I can't talk for long, but one more thing.

Their CEO is going to be here today for the press conference. Two hours. You miss it, you're fired."

"Yes, sir. Thank you." He chuckled at his own joke before hanging up. I sat in astonishment for a moment, completely bewildered. The money was of minimal consequence, but the success was unprecedented. I had to tell Kara. I looked around as she walked out of the bathroom and anxiously ran a hand through her hair. Sitting down at the table, she finished her drink in a matter of seconds, taking no time to enjoy it.

"Are you okay?" I asked her. She sighed.

"Yeah…yeah, I'm fine. I have to go sooner than I thought, unfortunately." I stroked her arm reassuringly.

"Before you do that, I have some news…" I said, smiling at her. She raised her eyebrows.

"Oh, really? And this would be concerning what?"

"My job." She rolled her eyes.

"Jalix. I thought this was your week off. You even said-"

"I got promoted. The medical contract went huge. They want a press conference to confirm and to make it official. Kara. It's an extra *twenty thousand dollars.*" She gaped for a moment, and then beamed before hugging me tightly.

"When's the conference?" She asked, holding my hand. "And do you want me to come with you?"

"No, it's okay. You just said you have to leave. And it'll be boring, anyway." She put a finger under my chin and kissed me.

"I'm proud of you. I'll wait in the car." Confused as to why she did not wait for me, I followed her.

"Are you sure you're okay?" I asked as I started up the car. She nodded.

"I'm fine, Jalix. I just need to head into work early. I'm fine. And I mean that literally. I really am okay."

Sorrow

"I know, but it's just…" I sighed. "You're right. I just worry about you… I'm here if you ever need to talk." She shook her head.

"It's okay, it's just…" She paused and looked out of her window, the rain pattering against the glass. "I've always had to look after myself. And sometimes others. I'm not used to someone…watching out for me. I'll call Alice and have her pick me up at that theater over there. I don't want you to be late, and I need someone to vent to." I took one hand off the steering wheel and put it in hers, interlocking our fingers.

"If that's what you want. I'll always be here to watch out for you. Okay?" I pulled into the parking lot across the street and stopped to let her out. She walked around the car to my side and opened a red umbrella, the same shade as her dress.

"I love you." She said, tracing one black fingernail along the edge of my face.

"I love you, too. More than anything and everything."

"I'll call you when I'm out." She waved a goodbye as I put up my window.

She slowly vanished from sight as I backed out of the parking lot and onto the turning lane for the highway. I sat for a brief moment, the blinking light of my turn signal fading into the rain.

   A sudden screech from behind me gathered my attention and I adjusted my mirror to see it. Too late, I realized it was a car moving much faster than mine was. It slammed into the rear door on the driver's side of my vehicle, catching the edge of my rear bumper, smashing it into pieces. My entire body slammed backwards, then forward with all my weight. My forehead and cheekbone hit the wheel before bouncing off brutally. Our cars slowed to a stop and hissed angrily. I immediately took off my seatbelt and tried to open my door. It was crushed inwards, and would not open. I tried to kick it, but to no avail. I slumped backward against my seat, quietly letting the blood trickle down my face for several moments. My vision was

Weaver

blurry, and my ears were ringing for numerous seconds before I heard anything. The sound of sirens grew closer and closer until it was almost deafening. I instinctively started assessing myself, so I could best explain to the medics what had happened. Disoriented, I felt the area of my face that hit the steering wheel. Warm liquid confirmed my suspicions of bleeding. I lightly pushed on the area, testing for broken bones.
"Sir, can you hear me?" A voice called from outside the car.
"Yeah, I can. I'm not hurt too bad. Just a little banged up. Take your time." I tried not to laugh at how ridiculous that sounded. The sounds of a tool bag hitting the ground preceded that of shearing metal. The frame of the vehicle's door slowly pried open. I took the advantage and slowly started to make my way out of the wreckage.
"Sir, don't try to move. You could have a neck injury."
"I'm okay." I mumbled, standing up and walking into the rain. Everyone around me was shouting orders and trying to sort things out. "I'm okay." I said a little more confidently to the medic attending to me.
"Ok, sir, but we have to run a few tests and clean up your injuries." He walked me to the back of an ambulance, but kept the engine on and the door open. Off in the distance, I saw a girl with long, black hair running towards me. Kara. I doubted she had even made it to the front door.
"Let her through. Please. It's my girlfriend." I said to the medic. He looked at me strangely, but I pointed to her.
"The girl in the red mini-dress? Wow. Sure, we'll let her through." He put a cotton ball to my head and began to sterilize my injuries. Kara ran up to the ambulance crying. I ignored the medic who was obviously and awkwardly staring at her.
"Jalix! Are you okay? Oh my god, there's so much blood…" I nodded slowly, my vision swimming.

"Yeah. I'm okay..." She groaned quietly into the back of her hand as the medic nodded.

"He'll be alright. There's no concussion as far as I can tell, which is borderline incredible. His pupils aren't dilated. And he's only bleeding so badly because of this vein." He pointed to a spot on my temple. "He's actually extremely lucky. I'm just going to give him a non-narcotic painkiller." He put a syringe into a glass bottle and began to extract a liquid. Police were putting up yellow tape off in the distance and trying to quarantine the area. I looked at the bottle's label briefly.

"Can I see that?" The medic shook his head.

"No, sorry. Policy." Kara put a hand on his shoulder.

"Please? He's not going anywhere with it..." She beckoned to my bleeding. He sighed and handed me the bottle. I focused my eyes on the label. The logo of a black bird clutching a globe read *'Raven Pharmaceuticals.'* I laughed and handed it back to him.

"I just finished up an investment deal with that company. I'm on my way to the press conference." I briefly looked at my watch, but groaned because of the pain in my skull.

"I *was*, anyhow..." He rubbed my arm with an alcohol pad and Kara twitched.

"Wait, the one that's all over the news?" I nodded, though my head felt like it was going to split in two. He smiled.

"You're that Jalix guy. Jalix Kane. I thought it was you. I watched the CNN special. They were talking about you and how you saved the investment with that negotiation in Egypt. With those sick kids. A lot of people admire you, you know. Including the hospital I work for. They all use Raven meds and equipment." He pulled out the needle and put it into a biohazard trashcan.

"I'm going to tell the police to give you an escort. You'll get there on time." Kara nodded and smiled through her tears.

"One thing, though. Where's the other driver?" She asked. The medic shrugged.

"Probably took off. We saw empty needles in his car, like, syringes or something, so he was probably on drugs. We'll send a cruiser out to patrol the area, see if we can catch him. We'll call you for questioning later, if that's all right. In the meantime, we'll take care of towing your car." He walked off to talk to the police officer that pulled into the parking lot as Kara hugged me gently. I looked over her shoulder, the rain pounding against the hissing ruins of my car.

"Jalix, you're lucky the fire station was right there. You could've really bled…" She examined my stitches briefly before letting out a breath. "Alice would be proud of these. They did a good job." We sat in silence for a moment before she hugged me again.

"Kara. I really…really need to get to this conference."

***

The guards followed behind me into the building to find camera flashes exploding in our faces. Reporters swarmed us, asking questions about the accident and trying to find out what I was doing now. The guards pushed some of them back long enough for me to get into the conference room. My boss, a few quiet reporters, and the CEO of Raven Biomedical were sitting down at the table. Kara looked around awkwardly.

"It's okay, they don't bite." I said quietly, laughing.

"And if we do, we have a medicine to treat it. Robert Schillinger. CEO of Raven." Kara chuckled nervously and shook his hand before we sat down. Her eyes were strangely fixed on him, as though she were studying him.

A young woman was standing behind him and decided to step forward, shaking my hand daintily. She seemed like a bossy, bratty woman, a perfect tan and matching body flaunted by an expensive cocktail dress.

"I'm Raven. Robert is my father." She looked into my eyes and smiled, one corner of her mouth turning up more than the other. It was an uncomfortable, flirtatious smile, and not one that a businesswoman would normally give under watching eyes. She flipped her short, black hair behind her shoulders and looked at Kara.

"You must be his newest plaything." She giggled and shook Kara's hand as well. Kara feigned a smile, more of a grimace, her jaw locked in an angry position. She kept a light hold of Raven's hand, although as soon as she let go, Kara clenched her fist until her knuckles were white. As she turned around to walk away, I saw Raven's backless dress expose the tattoo of a large black bird spread from shoulder to shoulder.

"Okay," My boss said, gathering up papers. "I'm Gregory Hartman. President of Syndicomp, Incorporated, and I'd like to start off with some off-the-record conversation." The reporters took their hands off their laptop keyboards and leaned back. The little red light on the camera turned off. He looked at me and my heart dropped to the floor.

"Jalix Kane. You...are an incredible man. First, you save a hundred or so kids with malaria in Egypt and Iran, and now you arrive five minutes *early* to a press conference...after a car crash. How do you do it?" I looked at Kara.

"You do crazy things to impress a girl," I said chuckling. Everyone laughed except for Kara, who blushed. "Besides, I'm *supposed* to be getting a bonus." I said pointedly to my boss. He laughed and clapped his hands together.

"You work the camera in our favor and I'll personally write the check, kid." Gregory laughed and looked at Robert, who nodded to the camera operator. The red light came back on. Robert stood up calmly, looking directly at the camera with unparalleled composure. He was a few years older than I was, extremely intelligent and spoke with a formal British accent.

"Hello. My name is Robert Schillinger. I am the CEO of Raven Biomedical, and today, the business partner of Gregory Hartman." They stood up, shook hands, and Robert sat back down.

"Thank you, Robert, but today I would like to focus on a very special member of Syndicomp, Incorporated, Jalix Kane. Jalix, our executive for foreign affairs, was in a car crash…" He looked at his watch and laughed. "About a half hour ago. He's still bleeding from it. And God bless him, he's what every company needs. A man willing to bleed for his cause. Tell me Jalix, what makes you so sure about this investment?" The camera swiveled to me and I stood up, taking a discreet, deep breath. Surprisingly enough, I would have been more nervous telling Kara something inspirational than a million random people. The lack of nerves was apparent in my calm, open stance and the natural rhythm of my voice.

"Mister Gregory, my boss, is right. I *was* in a car crash. And as you can tell from the wounds, it was fairly severe. However, there was one thing that I couldn't help noticing. When I was in the ambulance, I was given a shot of *senaerafin*, a drug created, tested, and developed by Raven to ease my pain. Not moments after a life-threatening accident, Raven was there for me. And that is why I believe in this investment. Because Raven saves lives. They saved *my* life, they saved the lives of thousands in Egypt and Iran, children, women, and soldiers, and they will continue to help people until the day Raven dies." It got quiet for a few seconds. "And Syndicomp is not about to let that happen." Thunderous applause broke out in the lobby as the small red light on the camera turned off. I smiled as Kara hugged me. "Jalix, that was amazing."

"Well done." Robert shook my hand, a neutral expression on his face.

"Thank you, Mister Schillinger." I nodded to him. Gregory shook his head.

Sorrow

"No. Thank you." He slipped a check in my suit pocket and winked. Every reporter was on their cell phone, giving me brief, smiling glances. I took Kara by the waist and kissed her passionately, overcome with the emotional proportions of the moment. She giggled quietly.
"Jalix." Raven cooed from behind me, interrupting the intimate moment with Kara.
"Raven. Hi. What can I do for you?" Kara's hand twitched in mine, something I normally would not have noticed.
"Oh, nothing. I just wanted to thank you. My already diverse stock portfolio is probably skyrocketing at the moment. I noticed you're not exactly an investor, despite your success." I was slightly taken aback by the casualness of the conversation until she continued. "We should get a drink sometime and discuss some investment options." I fumbled to find the right words for the situation, a mixture of bewilderment and discomfort silencing my voice.
"Actually, Jalix and I prefer to put our investments in a federally-backed system. With the economy recovering, private corporations like these are volatile, and it seems as though if Jalix left the company for a better position, the stock price, as well as certain people, would be...bitterly disappointed. Besides, in the long term, a federal system has a more steady, and predictable, rate of return. But we appreciate the generous offer." Kara's brief monologue left Raven and I equally stunned for a brief moment.
"Well...that's...certainly understandable. The offer stands, Jalix. If you're ever interested, let me know." She flashed a brief smirk at me before leaving, a discontented scowl on her face.
"I..." I started, leaving the conference room and pushing my way toward a cab. "Am so in love with you. Beautiful *and* intelligent? Luckiest guy on the planet, right here." The noise of the crowd outside was muffled as I closed the door.

"Del'tonio's." I said to the driver, turning to Kara. "If that's okay for lunch. Unless Italian food isn't your thing." She kissed me on the cheek and leaned into me.

"Putting that raise money to use already? Sure. I could go for some pasta. And wine. Lots and lots of wine." She giggled and put a hand on my chest, but sat up quickly.

"What's the hard thingy in your pocket?" My face became red as I realized what she was talking about. The black box. Immediately, my mind combed over objects of a similar shape and size. The suddenness startled me and I stammered.

"Oh...that's the garage door opener. The new one. The company sent me a new one. Because the old one was broken. And I put it in my pocket so I didn't forget it."

"Oh...okay." She laid her head on my shoulder as we coasted onto the highway. The response seemed to satisfy her. "I love you." She mumbled. I ran a hand through her hair as the scent of roses floated up to me.

"You smell...and look...beautiful. Words truly can't describe." She smiled.

"You're such a sweetheart. Any other man..." She slid a hand around mine. "Would have gotten sick of me by now."

"Impossible." I whispered, stroking her cheek. We pulled into the parking lot slowly and cruised into the space in front of the lobby.

"I couldn't get enough of you if I had forever. We're here." I said, lifting her head gently. The valet opened my door and I handed him a twenty-dollar bill. The sparkling chandelier of the carport sent twinkles of light rippling over Kara's dress as a waiter approached us.

I winked at him and mouthed 'balcony', pointing to the beautiful tables outside. He nodded, looking at Kara.

"Hi, and welcome to Del'tonio's. If you'll follow me." He turned and led us to a quiet, private table off to the side of the restaurant. It was

quiet and serene, the white marble and soft glow of the candles creating an extremely romantic atmosphere.
"Two glasses of Ele` Perion. Bring the bottle." I told the waiter. He smiled and walked away quickly to get the bottle of red wine. Kara smiled at me and shook her head.
"No need to impress, Jalix. I can deal with a cheaper wine. Although... I do love a glass of Ele`." She laughed and smiled at me.
"That's okay. You deserve it. Besides, *I* got a raise. Remember?" She looked up from the tablecloth and smiled wider at me.
"I hate your company name." She smiled through clenched teeth. "No matter how rich they are."
"Yes, Kara. Syndicomp, Incorporated is a stupid name. But we help a lot of businesses with loans and investments and things like that. A name doesn't matter when you help people."
"Like those kids in Egypt. What was that one boy's name? Omar, I think. He was so close to dying. But you saved him." I nervously chuckled and fingered the black velvet box in my pocket. I was sweating, I was shaking, and I felt like someone was watching me, even though I was on the balcony with her alone.
The waiter arrived with the expensive red wine and left quickly, obviously realizing my plan. I pulled the black box out of my pocket and set it on my lap just as I took a deep breath.
"Kara." She looked up after a sip of wine. "I want to say that... No matter what, you are always there for me. And that's the kind of person that I want to be with for the rest of my life. Kara..." I got down on one knee and opened the box. Despite my confidence, my vision narrowed to a thin tunnel. "It's a little sudden. And it's a little soon...but I can't help how hopelessly in love with you I am. Will you marry me?" The beautiful diamond ring inside glistened as if winking at me.
"Jalix! I... " She stared at the ring as if it were magical. There was a long pause of silence, the shock ripping through her mind.

"Jalix... you're the only one I've ever felt so deeply and so truly for. Yes." She sobbed. "Yes. Of course I want to be with you forever!" With that, I took the ring from the box and slid it onto her finger. It slipped on easily, a perfect fit, and I knew that she liked it. She looked into my eyes.

"I will never leave you. You are the best thing that has ever happened to me."

"I love you. More than everything and anything." Her face shot forward and her lips were on mine before I could say anything further.

"Jalix," She began. "I have never been happier. Not once in my life have I been as content as I am now." I smiled knowingly.

"Just wait. It gets better." I reached down into my suit pocket and pulled out two plane tickets, sitting back down in my chair, across from her energetic form.

"I took the week off for a reason. And if it doesn't fit your schedule, I can move the dates, but-"

"Where to?" She asked excitedly, deciding whether she wanted to stare at the ring or get up and hug me again.

"Pennsylvania. The Pocono Mountains. I had a business trip there once, but never got to see the more romantic side of things. I have a suite booked at a resort right next to the casino." She wiped the tears from her flushed face and sighed, cocking her head and gazing into my eyes.

"You're such a romantic, Jalix. You're like something out of a dream. You know that?" Seeing Kara emotional was extremely unusual, but she radiated happiness as I smiled at her.

"Congratulations, you two. You both look so happy." The waiter said, walking up to the table with two menus. "I'll come back in a few minutes for your orders."

"Who the hell cares about food? I'm getting married!" Kara exclaimed giddily.

Sorrow

***

"Spending that bonus already?" Kara murmured sarcastically as I set down my cards.

"I have to lighten my pockets a little. How else will I know you're not just marrying me for my money?"

"And if you win?" I chuckled as a portion of my chips were taken, marking the loss of another hand.

"That hasn't been a problem so far. Royal flush takes all. So unless I get that, I have a feeling it'll be a short night."

"I can't watch this. Have fun." Kara laughed, walking away.

"Go be a jinx somewhere else, then." I called. She turned her head to smile at me before disappearing into the crowd behind her.

I turned around to face the green, felt-covered poker table and sighed contentedly. There were a few other people gathered at the board, but not as many as there were at other tables.

   The cards I received for the next hand were nothing special, so I avoided doing anything rash. A large Russian man bet a large amount of money and bluffed his way to a win on the first hand. I managed to win the second hand, only being against the other three players for that round. One was an Asian man, and the other two were a couple that mimicked each other's moves. The Asian man bluffed his way out of ten thousand dollars in the first five hands. The girl managed to last longer than her boyfriend who, when he lost, headed to the bar. It was just us three now.

   The dealer gave us all two cards again. I looked at my two, and to my cheerful surprise, I received two aces.

"Five hundred." I tossed in five chips. Both other players said the same. The dealer put three more cards down. Queen, King, and ten. All suited to my ace of spades. My heart started to pound in my head. *Could I really receive the best hand in the world of poker tonight?*

Weaver

I didn't want to overdo it, so I threw another five down. The man closest to me, the girl's boyfriend, folded, but the Russian smiled. He raised more and I matched it. The dealer put down a two of hearts. *Uh- oh. All or nothing.*
"One thousand." I said. He chuckled.
"You terrible bluff." He said with a thick Russian accent. "I go all in. You do same or fold." Of course, I was confident. Maybe a little arrogant. Blind to the subtle hints around me. His hand shifted to his outside pocket, where it seemed like he was hiding something. He switched his footing, so he was not facing the table anymore. He was facing me. And his eyes dropped behind dark sunglasses to a faint scowl.
"All in."
I thought my heart would implode from the suspense. With an intensely trembling hand under the stress, the dealer put down the last card. It was a Jack of spades. Just to be sure, I looked at my cards. There was no way that I got a royal flush. I took a peek. Ace. King. Queen. Jack. Ten. Of spades.
"Yes!" I said triumphantly. I almost didn't believe it. The Russian man looked at me and chuckled.
"Lucky draw, right?" I nervously smiled and laughed. "But, like they say, you should quit while you're ahead. I can only get so lucky" I said. He stood up.
"Lucky. You are not that lucky. You cheat against me. You cheat in hell." He drew a pistol out of his leather jacket and pushed it to my chest.
"Umm, you want the money? Take it. I don't care." I said worriedly. He laughed.
"I don't want money. I want your brains on this floor. I want to watch your fiancé writhe in pain after seeing you headless. What *I* want, mister Kane…" He raised the pistol and pressed it to my forehead. It was shockingly cold, but forced sweat onto my brow. I stared back at

him, completely unaware of what to do. I tried to recall some of my hand-to-hand training from the Army, but found myself unable to think at all.

"I want Kara...to see-"

He couldn't finish his sentence before being jolted with a thousand volts of electricity.

I looked up to see the dealer holding the other end of the stun gun. His face was pale, but he held a firm glare.

Security came out of the room nearby and immediately put him in handcuffs, a strong knee in his back. They looked bewildered at the fact that he got a weapon past the guards. Unfortunately, he was still conscious. He laughed again, a hoarse, raspy snicker.

"Nice scars, Jalix. Car accident? Luckily for you, Kara was there..." The guards picked him up and dragged him off the playing floor, ignoring his speech. I, on the other hand, could not. He knew my name. He knew Kara. And he knew about the car accident.

"Jalix! Oh, thank God you're okay." Kara threw her arms around me, taking me by surprise. I sighed and hugged her back halfheartedly.

"It's not like I got shot or something." I said, a half-attempt at humor. I was more worried about her.

"He knew us, Kara. He was big, and Russian. I don't know what his name was, but he knew about us. How?" I asked, looking over my shoulder. He was gone, but everyone else was gathered around. Some of them recognized me and whispered things amongst themselves. She shook her head and did not say anything.

"I have no clue. Maybe someone from another business. A different company that hates Raven. Or just someone out to bring down your company. I don't know. But you're a celebrity. Anyone could have said what he did, I suppose." I nodded, still speechless. A security officer walked over to me with a notepad and wrote something down.

"Good evening, Mister Kane. I'm so sorry about what happened." Kara nudged me gently.

"See? Even this guy knows your name." He nodded.

"Yes, ma'am. We had the press conference on as it was happening. We were all watching. Raven runs the hospital down the street." I nodded, but stayed quiet. I had no clue what to say.

"Anyhow, sir, I have to ask you a few questions. Uh...first off, have you had any threats over the last year that you can remember?" I shook my head.

"Can you remember any specific incidents that may have put your life in danger over the last year? And I already wrote down the car accident from the day before yesterday." I shook my head again.

"No offense, mister Kane, but I'm supposed to get you to talk to me. To make sure you're alright."

"Yeah, I'm sorry. I'm fine. I'm just confused and...Just confused." He scribbled something down and looked up at me.

"I understand. We're going to keep a guard posted down the hall from you, so you'll have no more trouble tonight from anyone, paparazzi included. The manager said drinks and room service are on the house for the duration of your stay. We're talking to him now."

"Thank you. We're just going to head back to the room and open a bottle of wine." Kara said, wrapping her hands around mine. I nodded, strongly agreeing with the idea of alcohol. I turned around and started trudging toward the exit of the hall, still unsure of what to do.

Would I be asked more questions? Was that really the end of it? Who was he?

"I'm sorry everything was such a disaster tonight, Jalix." Kara said, turning onto the stairs.

"It's not your fault. I just don't know what to do now. I guess just enjoy the rest of our trip. If I can."

"Jalix." Kara said as she unlocked the door. It swung open silently and we stepped in. She looked sad, more than anything. Without a word, she leaned in, her breath smelling like the sweet softness of wine, and

kissed me. It was gentle. I could almost sense that she was too cautious, too careful. I kissed back, and she got more intense. Now it was like a deep, blazing fire was set through my body. Cradling my head with one hand, she closed the door with the other and pushed me onto the bed. Now she was forceful. I could feel my body merging with hers like liquid. Her hands fell down to my chest to unbutton my shirt, slid down my warm chest, then around my waist.
"I love you." She breathed heavily before leaning into me once more. Her tongue explored desirously, almost entrancingly. I reached behind her and pulled down the zipper on her dress, tugging it away from her shoulders. I traced my finger down her back and up around her neck. She shivered from the feeling and giggled. My hand caressed her face as I held her in my arms. The dark room hid many of her finely chiseled features, but I did not need light to kiss her. She paused.
"I want to be with you forever." My lips brushed against hers, and for a moment, our hearts seemed to stop in perfect synchronization.
"You will be." Once more, our lips met, her bottom lip gently quivering.
"Tell me how much you love me." She whispered quietly.
"Perfectly. Purely. Absolutely." She smiled and buried her face in my chest.
Her fingers wrapped around my back and she laughed.
"Easy, Kara." I chuckled nervously. She giggled again before rolling me off the bed, hitting the floor with an exceptionally loud thump. I couldn't tell if it hurt or not.

    Her passion was nearly overwhelming. She was hungry, lost in her own lust. The small pains of her teeth and nails were all but ignored, the bliss of her perfect devotion washing over me. She was infectious. I grabbed her by the arms and pinned her to the floor, alternating between bites and kisses on her shoulder. Her nails dug into my back like claws, drawing me closer to her heated figure. Quiet moans echoed from her throat into the room, the only interruption in her shallow breathing. Her lips met mine again, this time with a harsh bite.

"Ow." I whispered quietly, a hand wiping away the blood I knew was there. "Easy, Kara." The sound of her breathing quieted a moment, as though she was holding her breath.

"Are you bleeding?" She whispered, tracing a fingernail along the curves of my chest. Her touch was tantalizing, sending shivers across my entire body.

"I think so. It's alright." I smiled and went to lean in, but her hands lightly pushed against my chest.

"Let me go grab something for it. It'll only take a minute." Her voice was uneven, almost scared. She went to sit up, but I pushed her playfully down again.

"I *said* I'm fine, love." She shook her head, the only indication being her hair gently whipping against my arm.

"It'll only take a second." She repeated, standing up before I could protest further. I sighed and sat down on the edge of the bed, finding a way to blame myself.

"Kara, really. I'm fine. You, on the other hand...I mean, I don't mind, but...you really wanted it rough, huh?" The silence in the room was deafening. "You can turn on the bathroom light, Kara. It won't bother me." A quiet rustling came from the bathroom, as though she was rooting through her handbag. I sat quietly, eagerly waiting for her to return. All too quickly, she wrapped her arms around me and embraced my shoulders in a tight hug.

"I'm so sorry, Jalix."

"Kara. It was a little bite. To be honest, I kind of liked-" A sharp twinge in my back interrupted my confession, triggering a sharp inhale. "Ow. Damn, what was that?" She leaned back, looking into my eyes.

Sorrow

"I need you to stay really calm, okay? Whatever you do, don't panic. I love you. I always will." As she spoke, the edges of her face blurred and a metallic taste overwhelmed my mouth.

"What…" I couldn't get more than the single word out of my mouth, a massive lethargy sweeping over me. Gently, she leaned into me and lowered my frame onto the bed.

"I love you." She repeated.

Weaver

Sorrow

Accessory
Jalix

I silently studied my environment as I awoke, attempting to keep my breathing slow and steady. I was laying on my side on a soft surface, presumably a bed. There was distant noise, like the bustling of a crowd, but nothing nearby. No telltale signs of human breathing or movement permeated the still air around me. Deliberately, I opened one eye just enough to see my immediate surroundings.

I pushed aside my stray thoughts, analyzing the objects immediately to my front. My eyes fell on a white picture frame; a photograph of Kara and I occupied its window. An empty cup, a closed novel, and a single metal fork were scattered on the surface of a nightstand. Alarmed, I realized that the nightstand was neither Kara's, nor my own.

"I know you're awake, Jalix." Kara's customarily soothing voice shattered my deception as I jerked upward, frantically scanning the room. Kara sat cozily on a chair, several feet to my right. The room was in the style of an apartment, but no windows offered hints as to where I could be. I glowered at Kara, awaiting some form of explanation or meaningful contribution. Her eyes were fixed at her feet, curled into the chair as she nervously gauged my response.

"Speak." The command escaped my throat hoarsely, and with more force than I had intended, but I felt no remorse at being uncouth. Her eyes dimmed ever so slightly, as if offended by the single word.

"I will. I promise. Take a moment to recover. A few deep breaths."
"I'm recovered. Speak." I hissed, trying to understand the situation. Past experience dictated that I should have attempted to subdue her, so she couldn't pull another trick to knock me out. However, something in her eyes told me that she felt ashamed, almost mortified at what she had done.

"Okay, Jalix. I will." She took a quivering breath and looked into my eyes, the penetrating silver of her irises captivating me as they normally did. "First thing's first, I want you to know that at any time after I'm done explaining, you have the option of going home. No strings, no attachments. You can...wash your hands of me and be done." Her voice was firm, but pressed. She didn't want to say the things she did.

"Tell me what is going on, Kara." She smiled at me remorsefully, the red precursor of tears fading into view.

"I'm sorry for not telling you everything. It was the only way to protect you." I grew more concerned as the seconds passed.

"Are you behind it? The attacks against me? Are you some kind of...contract killer?" A single, silent laugh escaped her lips. She shook her head.

"I wish it were so simple. No, Jalix. The truth is that the men who went after you were trying to get at me. They know I'm too skilled at fending for myself. So...they went after what was closest...and most vulnerable." She tilted her head apologetically. "You."

"Why are people after you?" I started to calm down somehow, my fists slowly unclenching and my jaw creating more space between my teeth.

"I run an organization. Literally *and* figuratively, underground. These people are unique. It's too much to explain all at once. They have a genetic distinction onset by a virus that's been around for a long time. A virus that, last night, I passed to you. But don't worry." She said hurriedly, watching my visage as my face assumedly grew pale. "It's

not a sickness, per se. This virus has given us certain abilities. The things we can do-"
"Okay, seriously, what's going on? I'm not in the mood for mind games."
"I wish I *was* kidding, Jalix. This virus coexists in our bodies. We feed it, we nurture it, and in return, it prolongs our lives and keeps us healthy, gifted...beautiful." The tightness in my chest increased as I attempted to comprehend her words.
"You cannot be serious. It's not possible. There's no way that what you're saying is real." Her head slowly fell against the back of the chair. Letting out a sigh, she continued.
"I *am* serious. I know you don't believe me. No one ever does. I've helped hundreds of people get introduced to this life...I just never thought I'd have to do it for you." Her voice grew more unsteady as she went on, filled with a mixture of grief and conviction.
"Okay. You *are* the most beautiful woman I've ever seen, but aside from that, how the hell am I supposed to believe that anything you just said...*might*, possibly, somehow, bear any truth?" I asked in earnest, hoping that my argument would dismantle her hoax. A long pause followed my question, awkwardly filling the room with silence.
"Hand me that fork." She responded quietly after another sigh. I warily handed her the utensil. Slowly and deliberately, she pulled on a single strand of her hair until it came free, and then handed it to me.
"Hold it up against the bed's headboard." I hesitated, unsure of where the situation was going. I did as she said, pinning the long strand of hair against the wooden bedframe with a single finger. The slightest twitch of her fingertips preceded the fork hurling through the air and cleaving the lock in two, burying the implement up to the base of its handle.
"O-kay!" I exclaimed, standing up and placing my hands on the top of my head. She removed herself from the chair and took a step toward me.

"Jalix, you have to understand that this is normal for me. I know it's weird for you, but I promise it doesn't take long to..." Words spilled from her lips in a flurry, echoing against the walls and falling onto deaf ears.
This is not real. You are dreaming. You are sitting in your car right now at the accident, waiting to wake up.
"Kara, let me go now. I can't handle this. It just can't be... it's just... a dream." I said finally, unable to form a coherent thought. I punched one of the walls, apparently concrete, to try to wake myself up. I gave up with a last attempt as I slumped against the ground, putting my head between my knees.
"Jalix, it'll all be fine, and we-"
"It will not be fine!" I screamed at her as I looked up. "The- the...vacation was supposed to be relaxing, and now *I'm* getting attacked, and *you're* some sort of superhero...how is any of this fine?" She sat down next to me, as collected as one could be.
"Our love is real, Jalix. And because of that, you know that you believe me. But-" I cut her off again.
"No! I can't believe you. I don't even know that you *do* love me. What if it's fake? What if it's all a lie?" She replied hesitantly, an obviously hurt look smeared across her face.
"Jalix..." She sighed, distancing herself by a fraction of a foot. "The reason you're here is that I love you. The ones that we usually convert are...outcasts from society. Orphans. Terminally ill. We select people; we *choose* people to be like us. It's not something lightly shared. I chose *you*, because for the first time in my entire life, I fell in love." She gripped my hand lightly. I neither returned the favor, nor did I pull my hand away.
"Your entire...*prolonged*...life, as you mentioned. How old *are* you, exactly?"
"Three thousand years." She quipped quickly. My jaw didn't have time to fall before she returned with an apology. "I'm so sorry, that's

horrible. I'm not that old. I'm used to doing this with humor. I'm three hundred." I stared at her, waiting for a secondary joke to expose itself.

"As if...that's...any better." I muttered, sinking my head into my hands. I heard Kara chuckle for a moment, realizing that what I said was true. I couldn't help but to smirk, finding the slightest bit of humor in the situation.

"Jalix. You're going to be okay. Worst-case scenario, you're going to go back to your old life with some perks. You'll never...have to see me again, if you choose not to." She gritted her teeth silently, fighting off an impending breakdown.

"I need some time, Kara. I need to let this...sink in."

"I know. This room is...well, technically ours, but I'll stay somewhere else so you can have it to yourself. I'll probably just be down the hall-" She stopped herself and inhaled sharply as my head snapped to look at her.

"Down what hall...wait." The realization swept over me. "Where am I, Kara?"

"Okay, yeah. If you want, I can show you that, too. I just need you not to freak out and try to murder a bunch of us out of panic." A long pause followed her statement.

"You impaled...a fork...into solid oak from ten feet away. I have a feeling I shouldn't try to piss you off." She smirked.

"That's the Jalix I know and love." She stood and grabbed my hand, helping me to my feet. Her motions were characteristically fluid, but noticeably more powerful, as if she had been holding back her strength. "Let me call Val first. I'm sure he can share some insight as we walk around to show you the place. Things I might forget." As she pulled her phone out of her pocket, I recognized the name.

"Your brother? He's one of these superheroes, too?" The phone rang quietly, pressed against her ear.

"We're not superheroes. The name is Vampyres, but it's not one that we exactly- hey, Val." She casually picked up the conversation with her brother, ignoring the fact that she just referred to herself as a mythical creature.

Looking around as she began her conversation, I began to appreciate my circumstances. The room was nice, reminding me heavily of the apartment we shared. Crisp white linens and a chocolate brown comforter completed the elegant bedspread, complemented by Kara's chair: a rich auburn leather recliner. Several bookshelves rested against the wall, littered with old manuscripts and piles of notebook paper.

"Yeah, he just woke up. Come down and say hi. We're going on a tour. Make sure Krystal is…occupied." Pretending to look around casually, I watched her eyes dart briefly in my direction. "Yep. Bye." She hung up and replaced the phone in her pocket.

"So…" I continued. "Vampyres."

"I knew I would get that reaction. Yes, society gave us that name a long time ago to put a name on what we were. We couldn't get rid of it, so we stuck with it, and prefer the original spelling."

"Okay…" I began, passing over the fact that a single grammatical difference was of any importance. "Any similarities to the stories?"

"Well, not in the traditional sense. Garlic, wooden stakes, silver, sunlight, that's all a load of crap. The only real relation is the…" She bit her lip gently. "Fangs." I waited.

"Fangs."

"Yep." She failed to elaborate for a moment. "They grow and shrink like cat's claws. They only come out when we're hungry. Or…aroused. They're not even fangs, really. Just extended canine teeth."

"So-"

"Yes, you turned me on, I bit you, and now you're a Vampyre. That's what you get for falling in love with me." She smirked and shook her head.

Sorrow

"So do you have them because you need to drink blood?"
"Yes and no." She retorted thoughtfully. "We *did*. A long time ago. Keeps the virus happy. It feeds on components of your blood, which is why we needed to either consume it or die. But it only needs those very certain components. So we engineered a medicine to keep it at bay. We take a shot once in a while. That's it."
"I *wish* that was it." I muttered under my breath, striding over to one of Kara's bookshelves.
"No, it really is. That's the sum of it all. No more surprises, no more revelations. Aside from seeing the city, you know everything." Heavy footsteps drew near the doorway behind Kara. Stepping away from the bookshelf, I turned to face the door.
"And the city is frickin' awesome." Val stepped into the room, a bear of a man with a broad, vivacious smile. "What's up, Jalix?" He strode over and casually shook my hand.
"Hi. Kidnapper number two, I take it?" I jested.
"How many kidnappers do you know that offer to give you a tour of their underground hideout?" He looked at Kara and shook his head. "The guy's kind of a dumbass. You sure you want to marry him?" She chuckled and held out her hand.
"Yes. Provided he still...wants to." Her eyes darkened and the smile on her face disappeared as I took her hand. "But we can talk about all that later. Let's walk."
"Jalix, this is my favorite part of doing this: showing people this place. It's huge. It's happy. Everyone knows each other. One big family, man." He led the way through the door to Kara's room, then briskly down a short hall.
"So this is all underground?" I asked no one in particular. The concrete hallway was more open that it would have seemed at first glance. Smooth masonry and apparent care created a spacious atmosphere.

"Yes, right outside Salem. Her name is Aerael. I can give you the whole history of the city someday." Kara sounded either pleased or proud at her knowledge.

"Yeah, she *loves* talking about the old days, carving trails into the west, settling down in Oregon, creating a 'new Salem' before realizing that the first one was home." Val spoke dismissively of Kara's past, although I desired to hear more. He opened a door for the two of us, but I stopped walking and shook my head, trying to wrap my head around his last sentence.

"Wait. Kara. Are we talking about *the* trail out west to Oregon? As in, the Oregon Trail?" She nodded, the ends of her hair dancing across her hips.

"Yep. It's a long, long story. I could fill a book. We'll talk about it all later. Focus on the city for now. It'll be enough to keep you busy." She strode through the doorway, still holding my hand, and gently pulled me with her.

Entering the giant cavern of a hall, the sight before me took my breath away. A bustling crowd of seemingly normal people roved the corridor, engrossed in their own business. The ceiling of the room was at least a hundred feet, reaching several stories above our heads and culminating in a bright array of lights.

"It's a bitch to change the light bulbs here." Val retorted as my eyes fixed on the boundless ceiling.

"This is the main hall, Jalix. Think of it as a mall. Food, clothes, anything you need…is in here."

"How has no one found this?" I asked, bewildered.

"One or two have. Surveyors and the like. They live here now." She laughed as if joking, but declined to change her answer.

I watched, speechless, while the crowd passed by, hardly giving our small group a sideways glance. I mulled the scene over in silence, trying to pick out distinct features. Distant fast food restaurants and clothing outlets littered the strip. It was an entire hidden culture, tucked away from the rest of humanity.

"Why don't they just live with the rest of us?" I asked, turning around. Val and Kara were facing each other, and I had failed to notice that they were whispering. "Hi. New guy here. Care to share the conversation?" Kara shook her head.

"Nothing important." She looked at Val once more. "Just make sure she stays out of sight."

"She's down at the strip club. Trust me, she's not going anywhere." Val disregarded her mystery concerns, turning toward me. "So, Jalix. You like what you see?"

"I mean, it's pretty incredible. What's the catch?"

"No catch. We're all smart, and we're all dangerous. So no crime here. Aside from the occasional drunken, frenzied mess that comes out of the club. It's great here. That's why people stay here instead of going back to civilization to deal with obnoxious, whiny, violent humans." The look on my face apparently merited an apology. "Sorry. No offense." He added.

"Alright, let's recap." I rubbed my chin before continuing. "My fiancé decided to infect me with a virus that will turn me into a superhero-"

"Not a super-"

"Basically a superhero, drugs me, kidnaps me, and brings me into an underground mall filled with what basically looks like half the population of Salem, Massachusetts."

"So-"

"I'm not done." I interrupted Kara, the need to voice my situation aloud overwhelming my desire to hear her elaborate. "I'm currently standing in an underground city, surrounded by people that could kill me with a snap of their fingers, and their biggest concern is whether or not they want fries with their meal. Do I have it about right?" The siblings looked at each other for a moment before Val shrugged.

"Pretty much, man. I mean, we have some people you should meet-"

"Yes, great! Let's go meet people!" I exclaimed, a false sense of positivity becoming the most helpful coping mechanism of the moment.

"Sweetie. Take a breath." Kara sighed, putting her forearms on my shoulders and leaning into me. Somehow, even in the toxicity of the moment, I managed to find her beauty breathtaking. Knowing that she was still close to me was a comfort. Everything from her smell to her wide, mirror-grey eyes told me that I was safe. I drew in a deep breath.

"Okay. Breath taken. Just a little bit in shock, I guess." Kara smiled and kissed my cheek. For the first time, I did not know how to react. Everything about her still seemed so perfect, despite every instinct telling me to run from her.

"Val's right. We have some people you should meet. You already know a few."

"Are all your friends Vampyres?" I recoiled at the words that came out of my mouth, never having expected to utter them in my entire life.

"Pretty much." They both responded simultaneously. I smirked.

"You know, I get that you're in a bit of shock right now, but I'm a little surprised that you're not angry." Kara continued.

"I have no idea what would even make me angry right now. I'm more nervous and confused than anything." I rubbed my neck awkwardly, realizing how vulnerable I sounded compared to my normal, confident tone.

"I don't know. Doesn't it make you angry that I kept this from you?" I shook my head.

"Not at all. This is a pretty big secret. And as a matter of fact, I have no idea what made you do it now."

"How about the fact that I'm three hundred years old?" She said plainly. My smile shrank, but it still did not make me angry. "Jalix,

Sorrow

there's a lot I haven't told you. One of these things is going to piss you off."
"Somehow I doubt that. Why do you want me angry anyway?" She smirked, seeing my first statement as a challenge.
"I don't. But I need to gauge your reactions to make sure that you're handling the situation properly. Some people can't take the stress. Anger *should* be natural." Val smiled and crossed his arms before leaning against the wall, as though preparing for a show.
"Jalix, sweetie. You know I've killed people, right? A *lot* of people."
"Sexy. Keep going; I like this. It's like couples' therapy but cheaper." She bit her bottom lip in irritation, maintaining her smile.
"I'm literally older than your great, great, great grandmother."
"Gross, but that doesn't make me angry." Her smile disappeared. It actually seemed to irritate her that she could not make me upset.
"I like to torture people. Sometimes for hours on end."
"I can tell. You're doing a great job."
"Sex with you is always disappointing."
"How do you think I feel? You gave me a virus I can't get rid of." Val roared in laughter, pressing Kara to try harder.
"Your cooking sucks."
"I know."
"The SUV you picked out is terrible."
"The storage capacity is nice."
"Your job is basically sitting at a desk all day sending emails."
"Kara, according to the IRS, you don't even exist."
"Your proposal was generic."
"Your tears called, they said you're a bad liar."
"This isn't going to work, is it?" She sighed, exasperated, yet grinning. Val was gasping for air, struggling to hold himself upright.
"Not a chance." I smiled, knowing she was utterly defeated. The playful banter reminded me of the previous months. Our relationship

was built on an unusual brand of humor, and despite all of the chaos, it was something we still shared.

"I like you, Jalix." Val chuckled, wiping tears from his eyes. "We're going to get along. Maybe I won't kill you for marrying my sister."

"Yeah, thanks. So. Where next? Who do I have to meet?" Kara looked down thoughtfully for a moment.

"Probably Alice, but I think she's busy, so-"

"Nah, she's bartending down at the club. Probably bored." Val interrupted. Kara's jaw tightened.

"Yes, Val. But I really don't want to go down there right now."

"Look, he's going to have to meet her at some point. We can try and keep her away, but it's only going to work for so long." Kara shook her head.

"Who am I not supposed to be meeting, Kara? Secret boyfriend?"

"It's a girl, dipshit."

"Secret girlfriend?" Kara sighed exasperatedly and threw her hands in the air.

"Fine. We'll go try and meet up with Alice. Hopefully we can avoid Krystal completely. And no, before you ask again, *not* a secret girlfriend."

Val stepped into the crowd, followed by Kara. I stayed close, avoiding the urge to venture out into the hall further. We passed by specialty shops and vendors of all sorts, spanning nearly the length of a city block. Muffled music grew closer, shielded by both the noise of the crowd around me and the approaching set of large oak doors. The entire environment reminded me of nothing less than a normal city, the only indication otherwise being the massive cement walls curved graciously upward into an arced apex. A mild claustrophobic sensation arose, but quickly subsided as Kara stopped in front of the doors to what I assumed was the nightclub referred to by siblings.

Sorrow

"Stick close. It's probably packed in here. Val, take Jalix into the break room in the back. I'll grab Alice from the bar and we can introduce them." Val nodded, smiling slightly.

"What's so funny?" I asked.

"Nothing. This is Archangel. I love this place."

Kara pushed the doors open, and immediately, my senses were engulfed in an amalgamation of bizarre sensations. Faint smells of smoke, sweat, and liquor bombarded my nostrils. It was an apt accompaniment to the pulsating vibrations of loud dance music. Walking inside, I could almost taste the haze of artificial fog hanging in the air. I was nearly pressed against Val's massive figure as Kara broke off from our group and headed in a different direction. He yelled something I couldn't hear, smiling at me and pointing to the obscured stage, several yards away. Graceful dancers spun on suspended rings high above the floor. Their bodies arced in unnatural, yet elegant poses, transfixing and captivating the high-spirited audience. Like something from a dream, they swung from ring to ring, three of them trading places effortlessly above the ground. It was entrancing. Val stopped to let me watch for a moment. They were all extraordinarily attractive, far removed from any human beauty I had ever seen. They seemed to be flawless, each perfect curve covered by a thin veil of lace and every inch of exposed skin immaculately smooth. Without warning, one dancer fell several feet, catching herself on a tall pole and easing down onto the stage. The crowd erupted in applause.

Val patted my shoulder and continued to walk, moving parallel to the stage. He reached a door, painted black to match the walls, and pushed it open to reveal a well-lit room. I entered, closing the door behind me. Cold air moved around me, cooling the beads of sweat on my brow. Kara and another woman sat at a table, talking quietly.

"I told you this place was awesome." Val laughed, motioning towards the female sitting across from Kara. "Jalix, this is Alice. You might remember her from a double date we went on a few months ago." I recognized her as Val's red-haired girlfriend. She stood up and shook my hand, grinning. Her bright green eyes gazed directly into mine, studying me.

"Hi, Alice. I do remember, actually. How are you?" I cleared my throat, realizing that my meekness was obvious. She laughed, sitting back down at the table.

"How am I? The question is, Jalix, how are *you*? I understand you've only been introduced to this lifestyle for about an hour." I hesitated, unsure of how to respond.

"Honestly? Nervous as hell. Freaked out. But dealing with it, I suppose. There's only so much panic you can have." She nodded, maintaining eye contact.

"That's completely understandable. I've helped a lot of people deal with integrating into our society. Normally, that's my job. I sort of work as Kara's right hand, keeping this place running when she's not here. My main profession is the lead doctor in the infirmary. I handle surgeries and more complex medical tasks. I also usually deal with new people, but Kara wanted to handle you personally, for obvious reasons. And by the way, congratulations on your engagement." She smiled at Kara before continuing. "I'm so happy for you two."

"Thanks." We both said simultaneously. There was an awkward silence, as though I was supposed to say something.

"What exactly is my role going to be here? I mean, am I going to have to take a shift bartending, or-"

"*If* you decide to stay, and of course that is entirely up to you, you would just have to assist Kara with what she does."

"And that is…"

"Not much." Val mumbled immediately after my inquiry, provoking glares from the two women.

"Kara is the boss down here. She runs the show. She decides who gets to join us, she keeps us hidden and protected from watching eyes on

the surface, and most importantly, keeps everybody in check." My eyebrows furrowed in confusion.
"I thought Kara said you guys didn't have a problem with crime down here." Val stepped forward to explain.
"We don't. But there are certain...things that we have to deal with. We'll explain more later. It's unimportant for now. But essentially, what Alice is trying to say is that sometimes the people down here need a guiding hand. And Kara takes that role." His seriousness displayed an unintended respect for Kara. Alice nodded in agreement.
"While flattering, they do exaggerate a bit. Sometimes, I do have to give a speech or two, but my basic role is to keep everyone happy. There isn't a single person down here that doesn't deserve a normal life. People like Alice and me want to make this place a safe haven. It's not a cage for some wild animals to live in. This is a home." She spoke with passion, clearly swelling with pride at the noble society she created. "That's why we give everyone the option to leave, but once they see this place, they don't want to. Everyone fits in. And of course, you can have it both ways. Plenty of people do. They have normal jobs on the surface, but a family down here. They still go out and see the world, but they know their true home is with us. It's a place like no other. That's why I brought you here. As much as I want to marry you and have a life with you, this is my home. And I needed you to see this before..." Her eyes roamed away for a moment, trying to find the right words.
"Kara, I love you. If this is your home, then this is your home. I get that. I'm not angry with you. I'm just confused. Bewildered, I guess. It's a lot to take in all at once. Sure, if I look at it from the outside, this is amazing. A completely new world to explore. On the other hand, now it's something else I have to adjust to. I swear this all feels like an insanely realistic dream." I shook my head in disbelief, still comprehending the gravity of my situation. "I want to be a part of

your life, whatever that takes. But I need to know everything." The three of them exchanged a nervous glance before looking back at me. I rolled my eyes and crossed my arms in annoyance. "What *now*?"
"Like Valterius said, Jalix, we'll tell you everything. Just not all at once. Adjust a little bit at a time. It makes things easier." Alice reassuringly put a hand on my shoulder. She seemed like a very caring individual, almost motherly.

   The music outside the door stopped, and commotion atypical of a party crowd came from the nightclub. Our heads turned to the door when a single voice distinguished itself among the rest in the form of pained screaming. Val threw the door open and charged through, pushing people aside. I followed him with Kara and Alice close behind me. The patrons had created an enormous cluster around a girl, clutching her stomach and rocking back and forth on the ground. Her screams turned into gasping shrieks as the seconds passed. Alice pushed her way past me and crouched next to the girl.
"Come on, sweetie. Let's get you some help." She picked up the girl, nearly Alice's size, as if she were an infant, cradling the body against her chest.
"Move!" Val bellowed, scattering the crowd away from the door.
"What's wrong with her?" I asked, looking at Val.
"Probably pregnant. Vampyre pregnancies aren't like humans'. The virus infects the fetus at around only a few days old. It works like a catalyst, either destroying the cells or maturing them in a matter of minutes, draining what it needs from the mother. It's fast as hell, unbearably painful, and almost always fatal without the right medical care." He explained, walking toward the exit to the club. I followed, continuing the conversation.
"I'm assuming pregnancies aren't as common for you guys?"
"I mean, they're not rare. But it's not a drawn-out thing like with humans, waddling around for nine months. If a couple suspects a pregnancy, the female usually lets Alice or one of the other doctors

know so they can be nearby. This one got lucky that Alice *was* here."
A sharp voice echoed from the room behind us.
"When did *you* get back?" It hissed, angry and demanding. Val and I turned around, but Kara remained where she was, facing the door with a scowl.

A woman distinguished herself from the crowd, standing at the forefront with her arms crossed. She was strikingly beautiful, her sky blue eyes veiled by chin-length hair of the same hue. Despite her thin frame, she had an aggressive, intimidating aura. I couldn't help but to stare uneasily, a deep blue cocktail dress conformed to every curve of her body.

"Recently, Krystal." Kara replied without turning around. The answer didn't satisfy her.

"And you were planning on telling me when, exactly?"

"I don't answer to you, Krystal. And I have better things to do right now." Kara continued walking, with Val and I close behind. The noise of the crowd slowly increased as we left, accumulating distance between the scene and ourselves.

"I told you we needed to keep some distance." Kara muttered through clenched teeth to Val as we once again conformed to the mass of people walking down the long hall. Val said nothing in return.

"Is she usually a problem?" I asked, provoking a wide-eyed shake of the head from Val, indicating that I needed to stop speaking. Kara disregarded the question, instead choosing to enlighten me in regards to our destination.

"We're going to head to the armory next, and after that, you and I can take a break from the tour to get something to eat and explore." I nodded silently, taking in the scene around me. Laughing couples sat in the café next to us, drinking coffee and casually carrying on conversation. The image of normality was briefly comforting.

"Hey, Jalix?" Val jeered, shoving an elbow into my side.

"What's up?"

"So you remember those dancers back at the club? I was stalked *relentlessly* by this chick, Maria. Man, she would do some crazy shit to break up me and Alice. One time, I confronted her when she showed up at the house after her shift, so she was still dressed all...slutty. When Alice came in, I thought she was going to kill me. Totally thought I was cheating on her. Frickin hilarious." He laughed, patting Kara's arm. "You remember that?" She nodded, smiling.
"Maria...*really* liked you."
"She was crazy. Bona fide, asylum crazy. Alice nearly lit her on fire chasing her away." I stopped walking as we approached a set of metal doors.
"Wait, so your girlfriend nearly set her on *fire*, but this Maria was the crazy one?" I asked, smirking. Val nodded vigorously.
"Yeah, Alice has a thing with fire, so that's pretty normal. That's one of those things we'll explain to you later. But this chick? She was...something special."
Kara pushed open the doors, exposing a small, caged room. On the opposite side of the bars were two men arguing, along with an assortment of firearms gathered into neat stacks along the wall.
"This is the armory. Tony and Eric are the-"
"Hack! How's it going, man?" Val bellowed happily, rushing to a small window in the cage and shaking the hand of the man behind it. He looked young, maybe twenty, with thick-rimmed glasses and shaggy brown hair.
"Hi, Val." He said meekly, shaking Val's hand. "What are you guys up to?"
"Hey, Eric. This is my fiancé, Jalix. He's new. I wanted to introduce everybody." He shook my hand, introducing himself.
"Hey, Jalix. I'm Eric. Some people call me Hack. How are you?"
"Confused. You?"
"I'd be doing a lot better if *someone* would believe me when I said I didn't screw up any paperwork." His passive voice gained a hint of

belligerence as he shot a look at his partner, quietly busied in a stack of papers. The second man responded quietly.
"You did your inventory wrong." Eric shook his head and apologized. "That's my brother, Tony. He's irritated right now. Ignore him. Miss Sorrow, would you like us to get him fitted today?" Ignoring the odd name, Kara turned to me to explain.
"Along with weapons, these two deal with keeping us protected in a much greater sense. They make body armor for those of us going into dangerous situations." She turned to them, answering his question. "Not at the moment, but we'll be back tomorrow if Jalix wants to stay."
"Aw, come on, Kara. Look at this guy. He loves it here!" Val's optimism was likely a sharp contrast from the bewildered look on my face. Looking around, I recognized several styles of weapons behind the cage.
"You're pretty well-armed. Where do you buy these? Black market?" Eric's pride was obvious as he answered.
"We make them, actually. Everything in here is hand-tooled and machined by us." Tony remained silent, glancing back and forth between two sheets of paper.
"Everything okay?" Kara asked quietly, stepping toward the window.
"Yeah, it's fine. Tony thinks there's two pistols missing for some reason. I told him I locked up before I left, and I haven't issued anything in a week."
"I do the inventory every day. The one day that I'm not here, the records are short by two nine millimeter pistols." Tony announced softly.
"It's fine, miss. We'll have it figured out by tomorrow."
"Eric, I've told you to call me Kara. Literally a thousand times."
"I know, miss. Old habits and all that." Kara turned away from the counter and stood in front of me.

Weaver

"That's everybody for now, Jalix. Let's go back to the room and talk for a little while."
"Alright. It was nice meeting you guys." I waved a goodbye as Kara took my free hand in her own and led me out of the room.

***

I took a large gulp of coffee and stared at the dwindling group of people in the hall. My stomach felt empty for the first time in hours, rather than twisted and contorted into nervous knots. The silence was blissful, allowing me to process the chain of thoughts in my head without interruption. Kara sat across the table patiently, sipping on her tea and busying herself with her phone. I was calm, for a change. "You have things you need to tell me, right? All the little *I'll tell you later* details? I think it's about time to know those." Sighing, she placed her phone facedown on the table.
"Okay. You need to hear me out, though. Whatever I have to say." I nodded, taking another long drink of coffee. She continued. "Well, the most important thing, I suppose, is that we're at war. Our way of life is threatened by two groups." She paused, gauging my reaction. I had only assumed that there would be a threat to a society so great, but I kept my mouth closed and awaited further details. "One group was called the Pyrates. Several hundred years ago, they broke away from the initial group of Vampyres. Their mindset was that they were superior to humans, and wanted to replace them as the *superior species*, as they called it. Before they could massacre humans in the way they wanted, we killed them. At least, most of them. There are still a few that survived, biding their time until they find the resources to make a stand again. They're not much of a threat anymore." Silently breathing a sigh of relief, I asked a question. "Were they actual pirates?"

"They started that way. A merchant ship gone missing was a meal for them, and a mystery to the rest of the world. It wasn't questioned, and it was low-profile crime." I nodded, indicating she could continue. "The head of that organization is Kilkovf Strevieg. The guy that attacked you at the casino. The other faction is called Shift Company. Company as in, a company of men, not a corporation. Their focus is genetically perfecting Vampyres to create a new world order. Naturally, the two groups get along. With that being said, Shift is more science-oriented, focused on the virus rather than the people. They want to refine its flaws and create a new race. An obedient race, mind you. They're very well funded, God knows how, and extremely well hidden. They're the current threat, but they also have Pyrates working for them as security and foot soldiers." She took a breath and a sip from her tea, allowing me to comment.
"Let me make sure I have this right. Pyrates: crazy Vampyres. Big Russian dude in charge. Shift Company: mad scientists. Big Russian dude also in charge?"
"We're not sure. We have some...speculation. But nothing solid, yet."
"Alright. Anyone else trying to kill you?"
"Nope." The nonchalance with which she made the remark was unexpected.
"What else do I need to know?" She grimaced.
"Remember when you mentioned us being superheroes? Some of us actually do have different...peculiar abilities." She lifted her hand and made a casual motion with her hand. My coffee lifted from the table briefly, hovering for a moment before setting down.
"That's mine."
"Okay, that pretty much defies physics. How the hell does it even work?" I grew angry that, once again, I was being presented with a situation that seemed to defy common sense.
"It's actually *all* physics. We haven't researched it fully, but from what we can tell, we can use electromagnetism to interact with things in

different ways. Control their energy levels to manipulate objects. Alice gathers nearby energy from other objects and increases it, setting things on fire most of the time. Krystal does the opposite. She draws the energy *out* of the object and basically freezes it. Everything from the moisture in the air to solid brick, we can interact with." She looked away for a moment in disbelief. "This actually does sound crazy, I'm so sorry."

"It's fine. It makes sense...sort of."

"It's all about the virus. It wants to stay alive for as long as it can. Poison dart frogs evolved to be toxic to live longer. Imagine something that lives inside you, able to change your body to suit its needs. Having hundreds of years to do so. Humans shaped the world to make it more livable; the virus did the same thing to us."

"Wait, do I get superpowers?"

"They're not superpowers." She sighed again, smiling.

"They're totally superpowers."

"They're not superpowers. And I don't know. Not many people do anymore. It was more common when there were only a few of us and we were fighting things all the time. Alice, Krystal, and myself do. Some have abilities that aren't like this. We call Eric Hack because he basically speaks computer. He can read binary like it's English, write computer code fluently. There's a girl named Violet that can hit a grain of sand from a hundred feet away with a knife. We all evolve differently, as individuals. It's quite something."

"Yeah, it's definitely something. So you can make things float?

"I can move things. The heavier, the more difficult. The more intricate the movement, the more difficult. Making a coffee cup float is easy. Folding origami is a little trickier." My head was swimming with questions I was too afraid to ask, knowing it would only complicate the already convoluted situation.

"What else?" She slunk back in her chair, thinking.

"Honestly, those were the two biggest things. If that makes you feel any better." I inaudibly exhaled a large breath, glad that the worst was over. "I should tell you about Krystal, though. Since you're bound to run into her again."
"Yeah, you seem to have a very complicated relationship with her." She winced.
"I wouldn't use that word. She has a...an involvement with me. She's drawn to me for some reason. I trained her when she first started developing her abilities. She was young, a teenager. She became a sociopath. She became...a lot of things. And I care about her so much, but..." She looked away again. "She's changed. She's not who she used to be. Just be careful around her. She's not going to hurt you or anything, but she's...addictive. Her recklessness, her sense of moral direction...sometimes they're misguided."
"That was her, at Archangel, I presume? The one with blue hair?"
"Yeah, that was her."
"Why the blue hair?"
"It's actually natural. Kind of. It was from a medicine she took when she was a child. Wait. *That's* your question right now?" She seemed alarmed at my composure.
"I have a lot of questions, Kara. How did you build this place without humans finding out? How have the bad guys not found you? Why did you pick me for this? How did-"
"Pick you?" She interrupted, tilting her head. "Jalix, I fell in love with you." Her statement startled me, and for a moment, I had no idea how to react.
"You're three hundred years old-"
"Three hundred and forty."
"Whatever. You're old as hell, you've seen the world move, you're a superhuman freak, and you fall in love with *me* of all people?" Her eyes grew wide and her face widened after I stopped talking.

"I'm...I'm not a freak." She didn't know what else to say, and I regretted my choice of words.

"That's not what I meant. I mean, you're better than every other girl out there. And I mean that literally. You're not only better than every human, but you're in charge of everyone that isn't. You are the epitome of perfection, and yet you chose boring-ass me. How?" Her eyes were starting to tear up, but she closed them and inhaled slowly. "I'm *not* perfect, Jalix. I've been through hell and back with the scars to prove it. It took its toll. But for all that time, I never stopped to think about settling down. No one was good enough. But you? You've seen war at its worst. When I ran into you at the hospital, I knew you were special. And meeting at the bar an hour later? It can't have been a coincidence. You're smart. You're funny. I think you're perfect too, Jalix. And I *am*..." She playfully glared at me, taunting me for my choice of words. "...old as hell. So I've met a lot of people. You're perfect for me." She reached across the table to hold my hand. I pulled on her arm, jerking her across the table to kiss her. She tried not to smile as our lips met, but failed. Pulling away, I looked into her eyes.

"Then I guess I'm staying." Her smile grew again, inadvertently inflicting the same on myself.

"Jalix, I know there's a lot about me you don't agree with. And hopefully someday you'll know everything about me. But you know just as well as anyone that good people have to do bad things occasionally. That good person is me. I *promise* I am who you think I am. But who I am and what I do are different. You're the same way. Your military career sent you down a lot of grey paths. But at the end of the day, you're a good person. I just need you to see that." She took my hand in hers quietly and looked into my eyes. I understood what she was saying, and although I was confused and nervous, I felt just as in love with her as always.

Sorrow

"I know, Kara. It's just a lot to take in all at once. You know? You're not human. That's tough to accept. However long ago this happened to you, I'll bet you felt the same way." Her eyes darkened and lowered as she opened her mouth to say something. Her bright red lips had trouble forming the words she wanted to say.

"My circumstances were a little different. It wasn't a choice for me. And it also wasn't as easy. There was no civilization when I was infected. There was no one else like me. I felt alone. I had one person in the entire world that knew what I was going through. And..." Her voice cracked, but she remained strong and resisted the overwhelmingly obvious urge to cry. "And I lost her. Right before I met you. We had to go through these changes alone. And yeah, Jalix. I was scared. Because when it happened to me, it wasn't a favor. It was a curse. It was genetic rape. It was something that I wished for hundreds of years would be taken from me. But it wasn't. And finally, when I met you, it all seemed to make sense. Like it was all worth it."

I sat, speechless as I tried to find the right words for the situation. She continued, pushing through the sadness and appearing a little more comfortable the longer she spoke. "That's why, when you proposed, I wanted you to know why I was saying yes. So many people tried to get close to me...But when I knew I had to watch them die, and I would continue living...it wasn't worth it. So you're the first person I've ever opened my heart to. And that's why I wanted to marry you."

 I was quiet for a moment, trying to take in the emotional depth of her statement. I had no idea what to say, but attempted to make her feel better.

"Kara...I love you. That's it. Nothing else to be said. We're going to be married; we're going to fight these...bad guys. Pyrates. And then we're going to live long, happy lives together." She beamed, the tears in her eyes finally falling. I felt odd saying it. It was as if I was lying, despite the fact that, to the best of my knowledge, I wasn't. "I feel like a kid saying he wants to be an astronaut." I confessed. "I want this for us, but I have absolutely no way of being able to say that with certainty. I want to help make this happen, but I don't know enough about this lifestyle yet. You're going to have to help me."

"Of course I will, Jalix. You can take the role of whatever you want around here. I think for now, we can call it a day. But whenever you're ready, we can introduce you to more." I nodded, glancing at the hall once more. The lights were dimmed slightly, as though they were mimicking a setting sun.

"Yeah. Let's get some sleep. I have a feeling it'll help."

***

    I awoke at the same time Kara began speaking, catching me off-guard and startling me.

"Good morning. I made coffee." The pungent, smoky aroma of fresh coffee endorsed her casual statement. Stretching, I sat up to see Kara seated in her chair, warming herself with a hot mug. Her appearance was almost cat-like, curled into a comfortable position with almost no intention of moving.

"Thanks. How did you know I was awake? Hell, I didn't know I was awake until you said something."

"Humans have slight changes in their breathing patterns before they wake up." She took a long gulp of her drink before continuing. "And you stopped snoring."

"I don't snore." I defended, almost instantly stressed by her nonchalant use of the term 'human.' I shook my head to discard the thousand thoughts racing through my mind, running a hand through my hair and groaning.

"Did you sleep okay?" She asked.

"I feel tired. So probably not. But then again, I probably needed far more sleep than normal after yesterday." She glanced over her shoulder at the clock mounted to the wall, too far away for me to read.

"You were out for twelve hours. I think you'll be fine." Standing up, I fixed my crooked pajama pants and walked to the coffee maker. My lethargy was swept away rather quickly as I moved through the room that wasn't my own. "What would you like to do today?" She continued. I stopped.

"Kara. I think that's going to be your call. It's not like I'm going to suggest we go to the movies or something."

"Alright. No need to be cranky." I sighed, leaning against the countertop and taking a deep breath.

"Don't mind me if I seem irritable. I don't like new things. And I don't have much of a choice in backing out of all this. Not saying I want to, necessarily, just that...basically, I know I'm going to have a long day." She nodded, her eyes shifting down to my midsection.

"You know...I don't tell you this often enough, but you *do* remind me frequently of what a good choice I made." I looked down, realizing I had forgotten to put on a shirt. I smirked.

"Thanks, I guess." We sat in silence for a moment. "When did you get up?"

"I didn't. We don't need sleep often. Once or twice a week is usually good enough. I usually take some sleeping pills just so I have an excuse to cuddle with you."

"So what did you do while I was asleep?"

"Talked to Alice and Val a bit about what we could do for you today. Set some things up. I checked on the girl that collapsed in Archangel."

"Oh, yeah." I realized I had forgotten about it, despite the fact that it was extremely alarming when it happened. "What was wrong with her?"

"Pregnant. The baby's healthy, and she'll live."

"She'll *live*? Is that really how bad it gets?" She paused, finding the right words.

Weaver

"Yeah, to be honest. It's dicey sometimes. Normal pregnancy tests can catch it in time for the mother to know. But after that, it's a gamble as to when everything will happen. Sometimes a week, sometimes two. It all depends." A flurry of concern went through my mind for Kara, but I stopped distressing myself, realizing that we had a long way to go before we would decide something like that.

"So what *is* the plan for today, if you three already came up with ideas?" She smiled, placing her cup on the end table and sitting forward on her chair.

"Well, we have a few options. There are still some areas you haven't seen. The training room, conference room, stuff like that. We can introduce you to some more people that you'll run into frequently. Or we can go back to your apartment and you can take care of anything you need to. I already have some clothes for you, along with a toothbrush and some less important stuff, but if you need to take care of anything work-related-"

"The company can take care of itself for a few days. According to them, I'm on vacation for another week. I would like to get more acquainted with things around here. After that, it's up to you." She smiled.

"Sounds good. Here." She reached to grab some clothes from the table next to her chair before tossing them to me. "We have quite a few places we can explore. Anything in particular on your mind?" As I considered several answers to her question, I slid on the plain black shirt and pair of comfortable jeans.

"Not really. Can you give me some options?"

"Why don't I show you around a little more? We'll go visit Alice and she can tag along." She moved to the door and opened it, inviting me to leave with her. "She's in the armory right now, which is pretty close to everything else I was planning on showing you."

"Speaking of the armory..." I closed the door behind me as we began walking. "The one guy called you something weird yesterday. Miss

Sorrow

Sorrow? What was that all about? Are you a dancer at the nightclub or something?" She laughed and shook her head.
"No, Jalix. I'm a lot of things, but a stripper isn't one of them. When this city was first started, we all chose identities to hide behind. It started with me, unfortunately. I didn't choose the name. It was a way for us to communicate with each other without revealing any family ties, who we knew, things like that. When no one knows your name, you're a lot safer." We entered the main hall, and again, my eyes roamed over the scene in admiration. "Sorrow was given to me by an old friend. Hers was Spirit. From there, a core group went by our own identities instead of our given names. We decided it would be safer until things were more established."
"So does everyone here have one?"
"No, only a few of us do anymore. And none of us uses them, at least not frequently. The core group that created the city, we all had those unusual abilities, were known by their aliases, so it became a symbol of respect, more so than an identity. Alice was Pyro. She picked that name almost sarcastically. She wasn't a fan of the whole idea. She thought we would be safe enough as it was. Val was Bones. You'll meet Jared later. His was Morph."
"What about Krystal?" I wanted to avoid talking about her because I knew it was distressing for Kara, but at the same time, I felt like I needed to learn more about her. Kara responded the same way she did to the rest of my questions, deciding not to show any significant emotion.
"Krystal played a large role in helping the city become what it is today. But she refused to change. She believed that people should respect, or fear, whoever you really are. That we should be sentient, and not lose sight of the fact that we were more than symbols. She was...oddly right. I think it was the first time I saw some of her rational side. She saw the world for what it was and decided that being an individual was more important than being an icon." She was

quiet for a moment as we walked, making our way through the crowd. "Some of us took names that didn't have abilities because they wanted to escape from wherever they came from. That's why Eric chose Hack. Tony's was Hammer. And you'll meet a really special girl later. Her name is Violet. It became a way for people to leave their past behind. But then, over time, we stopped using them. We felt like it was finally a safe haven for us. Mine is the only one people still cling to for some reason. It's just a measure of respect, I suppose, although I wish they would leave it in the past." We approached the familiar metal doors of the armory, already wide open with several people inside. They carried on quiet conversations, oblivious to our presence.
"Why do you keep so much tradition alive here, but want to throw away your title?" I hit a nerve with something I said, her facial expression clear in that regard.
"Because I didn't choose it." Her tone changed, now almost angry. "Because it's not who I am anymore. I'm not Sorrow. I'm Kara. I'm not a machine or a mindless being. I want an identity. I want to be more than the sum of my actions." She sighed, realizing I regretted my words. "I'm sorry. You don't know any better. One of these days, you'll understand. Now's not the time for all this negativity. It's all in the past."
"Don't be sorry. I asked a question, you answered honestly. It's good that I know these things." She smiled and kissed me briefly.
"Hey, lovers!" I head Alice's voice call from within the armory. Kara smirked.
"Hi, Alice." We took several steps into the room, and the individuals that I didn't recognize decided to leave. Alice, Kara, Eric, and I stood in a small circle in front of the protective cage.
"Hi, Alice." I echoed Kara, giving her a small wave.
"Jalix! How are you?" She unexpectedly gave me a warm hug, reinforcing the feeling that she was no one to be afraid of.

Sorrow

"I'm decent. Kara said you would be accompanying us on a more thorough tour?" She nodded, handing a clipboard to Eric.
"Yeah, of course. Kara forgets the little details sometimes, so I like to tag along and fill people in. If you want to stick with just being the two of you, I have no problem with that." Kara shook her head.
"No, we'd love to have you. Is everything taken care of from yesterday?" Eric immediately spoke up.
"No, it's not. Tony is being a complete ass and decided to lock the cage before I could get in this morning. And I have no idea where he is. He's insisting that those two guns went missing, and I know I didn't issue anything. So now, no one can get in, and I'm going to be backed up on paperwork." He took a deep breath, containing his irritation. "But I'm sure he has his reasons. And luckily, we keep our measuring equipment out here, so I can still get Jalix fitted today." He gestured to a small box, filled to the brim with measuring tapes, rulers, levels, and other miscellaneous measuring equipment.
"Eric, you're busy. We'll come back later to-"
"No, he's fine, Kara. Besides, sooner rather than later, right?" Alice interjected. Eric reached into the box and pulled out a cloth measuring tape. I looked at Kara blankly, unsure of what to say.
"Alright, go ahead." Eric smiled.
"Jalix, if you can step forward, just stand with a normal posture. It'll be quick." I stepped forward and watched as he wrapped the tape around my arms and waist.
"So, Jalix. You have a very unusual name. Can I ask where it came from?" I smirked, answering the question I had been asked dozens of times before.
"Mom wanted Jasper, dad wanted Alex. They found a middle ground."
"That's neat. I was named Eric after my grandfather." He wrapped the tape around my upper torso and asked another question.
"Do your parents live in Salem?" Like a partially healed wound, I felt a familiar twinge of pain at the question. Kara inadvertently took a

sharp inhale, and Eric stopped moving, realizing it was the wrong question to ask.

"Um...they used to live in Boston. They...died when I was twenty. My girlfriend at the time worked in the World Trade Center, and they went to visit her one day. They were going to take her out to dinner; she was going to give them a tour of her work. I was in college at the time, so MIT knew about the towers pretty much as soon as it happened." Alice's mouth was open in shock, and Eric was frozen. "A week later, I was leaving for military training." I concluded, hoping it would end the subject.

"You poor thing. I'm so sorry." Alice whispered putting a hand on my arm.

"It's been fourteen years. The scars have healed pretty well. It's fine." Eric tried to recover himself, taking the measurement for my inseam and asking another question.

"So...what made you leave the military?" Kara groaned aloud and once again, Eric found himself trying to recover from the awkwardness.

"I was a special forces officer. So my team, twelve guys, went into some pretty bad situations. We were in Afghanistan trying to find someone that was supplying terrorists with rockets and small arms. We ended up in an ambush and I was hit pretty badly. I was separated from my team and left in the heat for a few days by myself. After that, I decided I had enough adrenaline for one lifetime."

"Okay, Eric, you're not allowed to ask any more questions." Alice reprimanded sharply, embarrassed for the both of them.

"It's fine, Alice. I'm a part of your society now. I have nothing to hide. It's in the past." I looked at Kara as I realized what she meant a few minutes ago. "And it can stay in the past. I have a chance at a new life, and Kara is doing an amazing job at helping me create the one I want."

"Well, I'm done. I'm going to go write these down and start on his stuff." Eric muttered before scampering away with his toolbox. I wanted to apologize to him as he left, but had no idea how to say it. Sighing, I looked at Alice.
"Well, that's done. What's next on the list?" Alice immediately spoke up.
"How about the conference room, Kara?"
"It's a conference room. If you ever need it, it's around the corner and has big glass doors." Her statement bordered on sarcasm, trying to lighten the mood. "How about you show Jalix the infirmary?"
"Yes. Great idea. Let me lock up first." Kara took my hand and guided me out of the room as Alice closed and locked the doors to the armory. "Well, the infirmary is right next to the training room, so after we're done there, we can show you how we hone our skills." She smiled at me and we stepped into the hall, skirting along the wall and avoiding the crowd. "The infirmary is our little hospital. We're fully equipped to handle basic surgery, lab tests, and emergency prenatal care."
"What about the fundamentals? Are you supplied with antibiotics and basic medicines?"
"We don't get sick. So there's no need for lesser medicines like that. Most of our supply is either painkillers or sedatives. We also have a healthy supply of blood, plasma, and scanning equipment." I raised my eyebrows.
"Do you guys really find yourselves using these things often?" Kara answered my question instead of Alice.
"No, but it's better to be prepared. We can't go to surface hospitals because our needs are different, not to mention that a simple blood test would raise alarms that we weren't like most humans." We stopped in front of a massive glass wall, supported by metal struts and revealing a hospital-like interior. Doctors sat with patients, carrying on conversation while nurses scurried around. The scene

was characteristic of any hospital, the only difference being a sparse population. No loudspeaker or series of ringing phones detracted from the serene environment.

"We don't need to go inside unless you want to, Jalix. There's nothing significant you have to see. It's just good to know where the place is."

I found myself captivated, unable to look away.

"This is amazing. An entire race, hidden away. A whole civilization, secret." I turned to Kara. "I suppose the training room is next, right?"

She nodded, pointing to a cut-out section of the wall a hundred feet from where we were.

"It's through there. I have no idea who's in there right now, so be on your guard for people asking you questions."

"It shouldn't be a problem." Introducing me repeatedly seemed like a trivial problem to have. Alice decided to chime in.

"Is there anything you need while you're down here, Jalix? I know it's too soon to decide if you want to stay, but I can always pick some things up for you if need be." I smiled at her generosity as we walked to the training room.

"I appreciate it, Alice, but as long as I can eat and sleep, I'll be just fine. Thanks, though."

The first thing I noticed when we entered the massive room was the enclosed, oversized boxing ring. It was set up like an armored cage, with steel bars and padded cushioning surrounding the entire system. Krystal and another girl were inside, sparring with the utmost sense of frailty. It was obvious after a moment that Krystal was training the girl. I looked around the room at the other features. Rows of lockers were stacked against the far wall, indicative of moderately heavy use. A rack of dummy weapons was neatly organized outside the cage.

"Well, this is it. The main attraction is the cage. Not much use for gym equipment here. Most of our skills come from our heightened senses.

Sorrow

We can see small movements, predict where someone is going to hit, and we can counter that."
"Is there ever training conducted with weapons? You guys have guns, don't you ever practice with them?"
"Think about what target practice involves. Steady breathing, body positioning, acquiring a good picture with your sights. All of that comes naturally. So we just have classes on how the weapons are used." Krystal heard Kara's response to my question and walked to the edge of the ring, wrapping her fingers around a metal bar. She had fighter's gloves on, a navy blue color with black trim.
"Some of us don't *need* practice, either. Some of us just like to grapple for fun." Her taunts were apparently directed at me, her eye contact unnerving and merciless. "Why don't you step into the ring, new blood?" Kara replied without hesitation, forceful and clearly livid.
"Why don't you go screw yourself, Krystal? He's new. I don't want him to get the wrong impression of the city."
"I will if you watch." She bit her lip and smirked at Kara in response to the first part of Kara's statement. "And what's to be impressed about? It's an underground mall. New York has, like, five. Ours just has bedrooms."
"Say one more word, Krystal. I dare you." Kara grew increasingly irate, her fingers curling into white-knuckled fists.
"Or, what, princess? What are you going to do? Come in here? Show me a good time?" Kara's breathing was frightening, akin to that of a large bull. Without a word, she stormed off to the corner of the room where the lockers resided, vanishing from eyesight. Alice sighed.
"Krystal. You're my sister. I love you. But Jesus Christ, you get on people's nerves. Can you not just...be you for a day?" Krystal grinned, her eyes darkening in an evil smile.
"You all wouldn't make it a day without me being who I am." Her gaze turned from Alice to me, bearing down on me as if I were a meal.
"And *you*. You think you're so special? You think you're Kara's little

pet? I've been around a *lot* longer than you have, and let me tell you something, Prince Charming." She knelt down to almost eye level. The irises of her eyes were a pale, snow-white, and her skin radiated a fine, icy mist that chilled me to the bone. "You? You don't stand a chance around here."
"And what makes you so sure of that?" Kara's voice rang out from across the room, and all of our heads snapped to look for the source. Kara stood wearing a pair of short athletic shorts, a sports bra, and a pair of gloves that matched Krystal's in everything but color.
"Kara, no. Now's not the time-" Alice attempted to make an argument and failed, resulting in Kara's sharp tone criticizing her.
"Alice, not now. If your sister is so set in believing that she's the boss, I'll give her a shot at proving it." Krystal turned to the girl she was training.
"Violet, sweetie, go wait by Alice. I'll be out in just a minute." Her cocky tone only served to increase Kara's apparent rage. I was frozen, unable to argue with either side and helpless to stand between them. Alice sensed my unease and turned to me, spewing apologies.
"Jalix, I'm so sorry you have to see this. You should go wait in the armory or Kara's room until this is over. I really don't think you need to see-"
"Oh, trust me, Alice." Kara said, placing a mouth guard between her teeth. "He needs to see this." Kara threw open the cage door, allowing the young girl to run out and take her place by Alice's side. As Kara stepped in, she closed the door behind her and turned a large latch, effectively locking them in the ring.
"H-hey! Jared!" The young girl was turned around, facing the exit and yelling at someone walking by. "Krystal and Kara!" She struggled to raise her voice to that volume, her tone ostensibly quiet and reserved. The man turned around to the hall and bellowed, surpassing the volume of the crowd in its entirety.

Sorrow

"Kara and Krystal are in the ring!" He ran into the room, grinning from ear to ear. Alice rolled her eyes and turned to him.

"Morph, do you really think that was necessary?" He turned to look behind him as a flood of people crowded into the room, yelling and jeering.

"I mean, kinda." He shrugged, his massive shoulders struggling to stay within his shirt. He was close to twice my size, his frame nearly casting a shadow over mine. Val pushed his way to the front, yelling the entire time.

"Move! Get out of my way!" The crowd grew quiet as he shoved his way into the front of the group, stopping once he was a few feet from the ring. "I'm her brother. I deserve the best seat for the show." He remarked defensively, inciting a rowdy cheer of agreement from the crowd. Alice buried her face in her hands, shaking her head.

"I'm so sorry." She repeated, staring into the ring. Kara and Krystal were circling each other slowly, like vultures competing for the same meal. Kara's eyes were dark and drawn, as though she was already planning her moves several moments in advance. Krystal was speaking, but the crowd behind me was so loud, I couldn't hear her.

Kara lashed out first, throwing a low hit with her left arm, and then following it with a forceful shot to the face from her right. The first blow landed, but Krystal moved aside to avoid the second. Without a break in movement, Krystal threw a kick to the side of Kara's head, missing by a matter of millimeters. Kara was already underneath Krystal, using her advantage in height to hoist Krystal off the ground and slam her into the mat. The crowd went insane, cheering louder than at any fight I had ever watched. I turned to Val, who had an approving grin on his face.

"They're not going to get seriously hurt, are they?" I yelled to Val.

"God, I hope so!" He retorted, shouting over the noise. "Krystal doesn't quit until she's broken or knocked out!" A sinking feeling grew in the pit of my stomach as I turned back to the fight, quickly increasing in pace. The movements seemed to grow faster, as though the first few were a warm-up. Kara moved almost blindingly, changing positions and throwing punches faster than I could keep track. Krystal was putting up a fair fight, as well, taking her time and waiting for a good opening. Without warning, Kara staggered back several feet after a hard hit, bleeding from a cut on her brow. Krystal smiled and shook her hands, small ice crystals falling to the mat. The crowd booed loudly, inciting Kara to move forward again.

"Alice, they're going to kill each other!" I yelled, turning to face her. She remained quiet, shaking her head. A slight smirk crossed her face and she pointed, mouthing the word 'watch.' Krystal lunged to grab Kara and failed, recovering gracefully on the far side of the ring. She moved forward again, retaliating and attempting the same move. Kara rolled to the side, simultaneously locking her ankle in the back of Krystal's knee and pulling her down. In a single, effortless move, Kara spun around with a kick, connecting with Krystal's chest and forcing her to crumple to the ground. The mob erupted in cheer, throwing their fists in the air.

"Sorrow! Sorrow!" The crowd chanted, clearly appeased with her victory. Kara spent no time celebrating in the ring, unlocking the door and quickly moving to the lockers, once again disappearing from view. The crowd began to dissipate, eagerly and excitedly involved in loud discussion. Val approached me, as well as the man called Jared and the young girl. The noise began to fade.

"Well, Jalix. Now you know. My sister. Your fiancé. Our badass. *Never*, and I mean *ever*, piss her off." Val chuckled and looked at Jared. "By the way, you can pay up now." Jared shook his head vehemently, crossing his arms.

"No way, dawg. You said Krystal would get *knocked out*. She's still conscious." He pointed to the ring, where Krystal was seated against the wall, groaning quietly.

"Didn't you see that last move? Kara did that on purpose. She *let* Krystal walk away from this one. She totally could have-"
"But she didn't."
"Is this because you're broke again?"
"I ain't broke! It was one time, and Maria-"
"Yeah, I know, she took all your money for lap dances. How many times are you going to tell me this story?"
"She said I was her favorite." Jared grumbled. Val put a hand on his shoulder.
"She says that to everyone, buddy. Now pay up."
"I might be a little broke."
"God dammit." Val gave up with a sigh, turning to me and shaking his head disappointingly.
"Jalix? Never make a bet with this guy. He's got all this money to go to Archangel, buy everyone drinks, get lap dances, and enough champagne to get the whole city drunk, but when it's time to settle a bet? Nothing." Alice shook her head.
"Boys, settle this later." She put a hand on my shoulder. "This is Jalix, Kara's fiancé." Jared extended a massive hand.
"I'm Jared. Some people used to call me Morph. Others call me Father. I run the chapel." Alice snapped her fingers.
"The chapel! That was the other thing I wanted to show you. Sorry, Jared. Continue." He shrugged.
"That's all I got. Come see me when you're ready to get married." He turned around to leave, calling back to Val. "I'll buy you a beer, later, Val!" Alice shook her head again.
"You two and your bets."
"I don't lose often, do I?" He remarked, smiling. Alice turned to the girl standing behind her.
"Violet, this is Jalix." She waved timidly.
"Hi. I'm V-Violet." I waved back, waiting for her to say more. Instead, she walked to the cage and spoke to Krystal. "K-Kryssi. Are y-you

okay?" Krystal failed to speak, but smiled at the girl through her pain and nodded.
"Shouldn't we help her?" I whispered to Val.
"I'm...fine...new blood." She hissed, hearing my hushed tones from several feet away. "Since you...couldn't...fight me yourself." She struggled to breathe, her ribs probably broken.
"You'll get your chance, Krystal." Kara's voice called as she emerged from the lockers. She was wearing her normal clothes again, a pair of dark, fitted jeans smoothing over the perfect curves of her legs. "He only has another day or so before things kick off."
"What kicks off?" I asked, almost dreading the answer. She explained carefully, simplifying the details.
"The virus is changing your body slowly. Any faster, and it would be extremely painful. Right now, even though you can't tell, it's repairing all the damage your body has accumulated over time. It's cleansing you, essentially. Once it's done, it'll get to work on your senses. You'll feel sore all over for a few days, but your eyesight, your hearing, it all starts to improve. You'll also start getting cravings. Your fangs will come out and you'll feel an odd appetite, like you need to eat and drink at the same time. We'll give you an injection to kill the craving, and then you're one of us."
"Aren't you going to say anything about what just happened?" I asked, motioning to Krystal.
"There's nothing to be said. Someone asked me to spar with them and told me not to hold back. So I did what was asked. Her ribs will heal in a matter of hours. She'll be fine." Krystal's head was bowed, her sky blue hair covering her face. "And speaking of healing." She wiped her brow, indicating that the cut she suffered was all but gone, a light pink line tracing the upper edge of her forehead.
"I'm going to hope that this was my daily dose of weirdness." I said quietly, hoping to move to activities that are more normal. Kara

Sorrow

chuckled and left the room, the group of us trailing behind her. The hall loomed before us, open and awaiting our arrival.

"I told Jalix we could go see the chapel." Alice added helpfully. Kara nodded thoughtfully, gazing inquisitively at a small group of people.

"We can go see the chapel." Her words lacked focus; she was distracted and distant.

"Kara...you okay?" I asked hesitantly, placing a hand on her shoulder. She smiled and turned to the group, facing away from where she was looking.

"Don't look, but something really weird is going on across the room. I don't like it." She maintained her smile to give an appearance of casual conversation. Alice's eyes darted to the location Kara was referencing, nodding once.

"I see them. It's Tony and two other residents. What's so weird about it?" Kara stood in silence for a moment, thinking.

"I don't know. But I don't like it. Who are the residents?" Val shrugged, taking a quick look before realizing the answer.

"Oh, they're new. Alice and I brought them in about two months ago. They were terminal cancer patients, husband and wife. I really doubt there's anything wrong." Kara shook her head slightly, convinced that they were suspicious.

"Stay here." She said quietly, returning the smile to her face and walking away. The three of us stood uncomfortably, feigning conversation.

"Is this a regular occurrence?" I asked Alice, clearly troubled.

"No. It's not. Kara rarely has concerns about residents." Her brow furrowed. "And even less often is she wrong."

"I don't like it. Wasn't Tony missing this morning?" Val asked.

"Yeah. He locked up the weapons cage before Eric got there today. Didn't say a word as to why." She turned to me. "Jalix, you should go back to your room. If there is something wrong, I don't want you caught in the midst of it all."

"I'll be fine." I defended, sorely disliking the implication that I was helpless. Val shook his head.

"No, Jalix. No offense, but if you get hurt, say a broken leg, you're out for what, six weeks? Eight? For us, it's a week. You can't afford to be out of the fight for that long." I looked over at Kara, engaged in conversation with the group. Her body language indicated that she was no less relaxed than the moment before.

"She's my fiancée. Soon to be my wife. I'm staying."

"Jalix, that's a beautiful sentiment, but-"

Without warning, Kara shoved Tony to the side forcefully, driving him back several feet. The couple leapt back and drew handguns, concealed in the waistbands of their jeans. I had enough time to take a step forward before Val grabbed my arms and threw me in the same way that Kara had done to Tony, moving me out of the line of fire. I sat up as soon as I hit the ground, watching Kara move effortlessly around them and snapping the woman's neck. Too late, her finger twitched and a gunshot rang out across the hall. A majority of the crowd screamed, and rushed in a mass to the opposite end of the hall. The man spun around and fired two shots in her direction, missing before her arms were wrapped around his neck. He slowly fell to the ground, struggling. I lurched up and ran towards her with the intent to help.

"Jalix, stay back!" She yelled. I stopped in my tracks, her voice commanding and powerful. Alice ran to her side, collecting the weapons and grabbing ahold of Tony by the throat. I took a few steps closer to gain a better view of the situation.

"What the hell is going on, Tony?" Alice yelled, pinning him against the wall.

"They stole the guns." He croaked, straining for air. She relaxed her grip, letting his feet touch the ground.

"And what were you doing talking to them?"

Sorrow

"He was helping me." Kara said calmly, allowing the limp body in her arms to fall to the ground. She approached Alice and put a hand on her shoulder.

"Let him go. You okay?" She turned to Tony, coughing and clearing his throat.

"I'm fine. But I was right." Kara gritted her teeth and shook her head.

"Dammit. I didn't ask you to help. You could have gotten killed."

"I know, ma'am. But others could have, too." She sighed and bowed her head, clearly distressed.

"These two were working against us. For which faction, I don't know, but I asked Tony to track down the missing weapons this morning. They were stolen by these two." She motioned over to the bodies as she explained. "Eric used his skills to get into their computers, and found messages implicating that they were going to attack us."

"Are you okay?" I blurted.

"I'm fine, Jalix. Luckily." She looked down at the bodies. "And so is the man. He's alive, but unconscious." The crowd began to surge into the hall once again, filled with noise and unease. Slowly, a horde of the city's inhabitants gathered around the scene, yelling questions and demanding answers.

"Shut up!" Val bellowed, quieting the crowd. Kara stepped forward.

"I'm sorry." She began, letting her words hang for a moment before she continued. "I'm sorry that something has happened to mar the beauty of our sacred city. These walls have kept you safe for so long...but clearly, they're not as safe as they once were." Hushed gasps echoed across the cavern. "We have kept you sheltered. But we cannot guarantee your protection any longer. Too often, we find ourselves so immersed in the beauty of what our civilization has become...that we lose sight of what keeps us here. We are at war." Her words were more than enthralling, our eyes fixed on her compassionate visage and devoted to every word she spoke. "Now, more than ever, our war, our fight has reached a point where we cannot falter. We have no choice but to strike back." She began to walk in front of the crowd, looking at its individuals as she resumed. "I will not ask you to fight. If you have a home on the surface, please...go home. If you have a family, if you have friends...go to them. Create a haven for yourselves on the surface until we can win. And we *will* win." Several people yelled approvals. "I would not ask you to fight. But for some of you? This is the only home you have. This is your *true* home. Your city, your family here...is under attack. For those that have no place to go, for those who choose to stay, I do not ask you to fight." She grew quiet for a moment. "But we will take every warrior we can get." She looked at me apologetically, a distinct look of sorrow overcoming her expression. "This cannot wait any longer. For those of you that will...leave now. For those of you staying?" Her expression transformed into a firm conviction, her eyes alight with anger. "We will fight."

***

"Kara, I said no. I'm staying."
"I don't give a *damn* what you said, Jalix!" Her protests rang out uncontested in the empty hall as she carried the body of the unconscious man. "You need to be kept *safe*."
"I *am* safe!" I roared, turning on her figure and subduing her sense of authority. "You think I'm here because I'm weak? You think I'm here because I'm fragile? I'm here because I am where people *go* when they want to be safe!" Everything around me slowed to a stop as I unleashed my emotions, infuriated with the global appearance of fragility. "Karalynn, I spent three days bleeding to death in Afghanistan without food or water. I spent September 11 watching my friends and family die. If you think for a damn second I don't belong in the worst fight this world has ever seen, you need to take another look. War is my home!" She stumbled as the body on her

shoulders fell to the ground with a dull thud. My figure towered over hers aggressively, a sense of understanding overshadowing her face.
"I don't want you to die." She whispered fearfully. I recoiled, realizing how hostile I seemed. "I need you alive, Jalix. Because you *are* that strong. I need that."
"And I will be here to provide that, Kara. But you need to understand that I need *you*, as well. I have no idea how this change is going to work. I need you to guide me through it. Then I can be so much more than I am." I felt a hand on my shoulder as Val approached me from behind.
"She's just looking out for you. We treat all new Vampyres the same way. I guess we all forgot that if Kara chose you...you've got to be special." I felt flattered, relaxing another inch.
"I need to stay and fight, guys." I looked around, realizing Krystal had slowly ambled her way into the circle. "I can't sit in my apartment and wonder what the greatest conflict between two species entailed. I can't wonder if I could have influenced the outcome. And I don't want to know that anyone died when I could have stopped it. Especially the woman I fell in love with." Kara picked up the body again and smiled, continuing on her way.
"I fell in love with you for a reason, Jalix. I have a feeling that time will tell why that is." I smirked, catching up to her.
"Speaking of time, we don't have long until he wakes up. Where are we going?"
"There's another part of the city you're going to see. You'll be one of the first, actually. We keep it tucked away because...well, we don't want too many people to know about it. It's an interrogation room of sorts."
"So a torture room."
"Alice and I prefer the term interrogation." She shot a knowing glance at Alice, who returned the smile.

Weaver

"We shoulder the burden, Kara and I. We're the only ones who have agreed to do this if the time ever came." She brushed a hand through her long, red hair, flipping it out of her eyes. "And we want to find out what compelled him to attack us." As we neared the infirmary, the wide glass windows cast a dark reflection, indicative of evacuation. "I can't believe so many had to leave." I shook my head in disbelief. "They'll come back once we're finished. We still have around two dozen to help us fight. We'll make it." Val's words did little to satisfy the feeling of loss as we stepped inside. It was silent as we moved through the halls, unlit and empty.

"It's through here." Alice opened a door marked for custodial purposes, but was revealed to be a nearly empty room, the only inhabiting objects being a single chair and table. No cliché two-way mirror or security camera gave hints to frequent use. The walls were lined with a black, pyramid-patterned foam, assumedly for soundproofing. Kara sat the slumped figure into the chair without restraints or precautionary measures.

"Hey, Jalix." Alice winked at me and walked to the corner of the room. The radiant heat from her body lingered for a moment before fizzling away. "You get to watch Kara and I work today."

She walked over in front of him and stood for a moment. She didn't show any signs of being nervous, standing stoically. Val closed the door after Tony and Krystal stepped inside, both eerily silent. Krystal's figure was hunched slightly, still in obvious pain.

"Hey!" Alice barked, startling me. The man made no sudden movements, but groaned and leaned to the side, jerking up as he almost fell off the chair. He looked around rapidly, discerning his situation.

"Kill me now." He said in a flurry. "I can't tell you anything. Just kill me and get it over with." Alice giggled, approaching the table and standing next to Kara.

"Sweetie. You can tell me anything. It'll be our secret." The man looked at us, Val shrugging in reply.
"Yeah, man, I'll keep quiet."
"Baby, hush." The man turned back to Alice as she spoke, asking him a question. "What's your name?"
"Smith." He said confidently, as if he was defying someone.
"Your real name."
"Smith. John Smith." Alice leaned into the table aggressively, inches from his face.
"Your...real...name." She growled. He raised both of his hands slowly before reaching a trembling hand into his pocket. He pulled out a brown leather wallet and placed it onto the table carefully, resuming his neutral stance. Alice opened the wallet and pulled out a driver's license.
"Oh. John Smith. Hmm." She frowned, placing the wallet on the table. "For such an interesting person, you have a boring name." He sat in silence, utterly confused.
"You see, John...when my boyfriend and I brought you out of that hospital, we knew your name already. And it was Nathan. So...why John?" He furrowed his brow in obvious confusion, appearing to be legitimately puzzled. After a moment, he seemed to get angry, yelling at Alice.
"It won't work! You can mess with my head all you want, but I know my damn name!" Kara gently pushed Alice to the side and knelt down in front of the table.
"Who are *we*, John?" She asked quietly. He looked at each of us in succession.
"You're Sorrow. The leader of the...terrorists. Whatever you want to call yourselves."
"And why do you think we're terrorists? What have we done?"
"You're trying to bring down the heroes. They're going to *save* us. All of us. They're going to make the world a better place."

"Who is going to save us?" He shook his head violently, grabbing at his hair viciously. He looked like he was losing his mind.
"The bird. The black…bird. The…crow."
"The raven." Kara breathed. My breathing grew heavy as I realized what he was saying.
"I won't tell you anything! She'll kill me!" He screamed, slamming his fists into the table.
"Who will kill you?" I barked, stepping forward. Alice and Kara looked up at me speechlessly.
"Her. The raven."
"Kara. Did you know about this?" She stood up and approached me apologetically.
"I knew it was a possibility, but this is the first time we've heard for sure that-"
"Don't act like you didn't know!" John screamed. "You killed my sister!"
"Wait." Alice said quietly. "The other woman? She's your wife."
"She's my sister!" He cried angrily. Alice pointed to his hand.
"Then whose wedding ring is that?" He looked at his hand, stunned.
"I…I don't know. It's mine. But…" His voice trailed off.
"Kara, something isn't right here." Alice whispered. Without warning, John fell from his chair, hitting the ground and shaking violently. His eyes were fluttering, alternating between wide-open and clenched shut. "He's having a seizure." She concluded, kneeling next to him. In a matter of moments, it stopped, and his eyes remained open. Two of Alice's fingers lightly touched his neck before she shook her head.
"He's dead."
"Okay…what the hell just happened here?" Krystal groaned, sounding significantly better than she did the last time she spoke. No one answered immediately.
"So Raven is behind this." I said aloud, hoping to spark an elaboration from Kara.

"That would explain how Shift Company is so well-funded. And equipped. They're a part of Raven Biopharmaceutical."

"And who the hell is that?" Val asked.

"They're a prominent medical company. They engineer vaccines for new viruses, cures for diseases, create mass-produced forms of expensive medicine. They're cutting edge. And Kara's right. They're *very* well funded. Which...may sort of be my own fault."

"It's not." Kara interjected. "Raven puts up a good cover of providing services to humanity. No one knew about this until now."

"So what can we do about it?" Alice's question hung heavily in the air.

"I'm going home." Krystal said suddenly, inspiring a sharp look from each of us. "Screw this. It's not worth dying over." She opened the door to leave and was stopped by a white-hot door handle. She jerked her hand back with a seething hiss, glaring at Alice's extended hand.

"You're not going anywhere. We need you."

"Bullshit. Kara proved about twenty minutes ago that no one here needs my help." She glared at me for a split second. "Except new blood. He's still got his training wheels on."

"So what, you're going to sulk in your manor?" Kara replied.

"Pretty much, princess. See you when the war's over." Her hand hovered over the handle for a moment before smashing it to frozen pieces. No one bothered to protest further as she opened the door and walked out of the room.

"Hey babe?" Val asked.

"Yeah?"

"Your sister is a bona fide, tier one bitch."

"Yeah, I know. Thanks." She turned to Kara. "Hey, why don't you go do some planning? Jalix and I have some things we need to talk about." I remained quiet, despite the fact that I had no idea what she was talking about.

"Yeah. That's a good idea. Jalix, I'll be in our room if you need anything." She kissed me on the cheek as she left, leaving Val, Alice, Tony, and I behind.

"I'll take care of the body. You guys go." Tony's voice came quietly from the corner, surprising the three of us.

"Thanks. I'll get the next one." Val patted him on the shoulder before motioning for Alice and me to leave with him. The hallway outside the interrogation room was noticeably cooler, sending a shiver down my spine.

"Alright, Jalix." Alice started, looking me in the eyes. "Do you want to marry Kara?"

"What?"

"It's a simple question. Yes or no?"

"Of course." I answered without hesitation, but felt uneasy as to why she asked.

"Good. When Eric took your measurements earlier, he was also doing it to fit you for a tux. Val and I have been trying to arrange it so you guys can get married as soon as the day after tomorrow."

"Alice, Jesus." I took a step back, overwhelmed once again by the absurdness of the situation. "You guys just evacuated most of the city, found out that a massive corporation is behind the faction set out to kill you all, and you're talking about us getting married?"

"What happens when you die?" Her question alarmed me.

"What do you mean?"

"What happens if you die in this fight? Or from another infiltration? Don't you want to have memories of your wedding? To give her the chance of having happiness before it's taken away? There's no better time to do this, Jalix. It will bring you two closer together, and give you both one more thing to fight for."

"Then...I guess. Yeah, that makes sense." She smiled.

"Good. Val wanted to take you out to drink beforehand. Why don't you two go kill some time down at Archangel while Kara is doing her work?"

"Don't say no yet, Jalix." Val said, grinning from ear to ear. "Think about it. What else are you going to do? Sleep? Nope, brain's too busy. Help Kara? She's got her own thing going on. See the city? You've seen it. You...need...a drink."

"You know what? Screw it. Seriously, I'm done thinking for a few hours. You guys haven't led me wrong, and I really don't think a bottle of rum is going to, either. I cannot keep going with the madness of your day-to-day." Val chuckled and threw an arm over my shoulders.

"If it makes you feel any better, it's usually not this exciting." I smirked as the walls of the infirmary disappeared.

"Actually, somehow it does."

Weaver

Sorrow

Breach
Kara

In all my nightmares, it's neither pain nor death that instills fear; it's a loss of control. Maybe it's something I shouldn't even bear, but a part of who I am is defined by having a compulsive need to control the things around me. To manipulate, some would say. Using powerful, natural gifts like charisma and intelligence would have led me down the wrong path long ago if I had used them the wrong way. But I didn't. It's how I became the powerful person I am. It's how I saved so many lives. How can control in such a degree, this manipulation of human minds and souls, possibly be used for something so good and pure? Is there something I'm not seeing? Am I truly doing the right thing, or is it some narcissistic delusion that I believe to be true? I can't escape the need to be a leader, to utilize that control. I'm good at it; it's a gift borne from years of the necessity to survive. But now I'm more than that. I'm past having to survive, and starting to realize that I have things to live for. Things to experience. For hundreds of years, I was hoping that death was around every corner. I was praying that something would come along and show me my mortality. But no ill omen ever did. No dark symbol or paragon of darkness ever came to show me that I was vulnerable. Instead, I survived. Why? Was it to finally meet Jalix? Was it to experience the inexplicable drive to make his life as happy as I could? Do I have something further in my future?

Weaver

I told Jalix that I wanted to be more than the sum of my actions. When I'm remembered, I want it to be for all the things I was, not the things that I did. I want people to know who I became. Anyone in the right place at the right time can become a leader. Anyone can fight a losing battle. But even when history isn't written by the victor, the people in those wars are forgotten. They're numbers, statistics, facts, pictures. Who do we become when we lose what we do? If we strip the parts of us that we've tried to be rid of, what's left? Jalix understands something I don't. I'm not sure what that is, but he knows something about life that I'm not aware of yet. There's something in his eyes when he's angry. Something in his voice when he's happy. He knows how to live. He knows how to create an image of himself. People see him for who he truly is, and I fear the same can't be said for myself.

I've brought a great many gifts onto this world, but none as great as the one Jalix has given me. The way he looks into my eyes, as though I'm his goddess. The way his body meets mine in the dark of night. There's some component of his everything that I can't find in myself. He's warm, almost, and I'm cold. His life is full of light, despite all the darkness he's had to overcome. I want my last thoughts to be of his life. When I finally die, I want the last image in my mind to be of the smile he gives me when I kiss him. I want to see his arms wrapped around me when I have a bad day. I want to feel him next to me on a winter day. I'm still not sure who I am yet, but Jalix is going to help me figure it out. He has become a part of who I am. And no matter what happens, he will always be a part of me.

***

Alice entered the room quietly, attempting not to distract me from my work. It failed, although I appreciated her effort. Most others would have been unaware of her presence, the only subtle giveaway being her hushed breathing.

"You can come in, hon. I stopped working a few minutes ago anyway. Got...distracted in my own thoughts." She took another step, cautious. "I don't mean to bother you. But you should talk a bit. I know you're just about as overwhelmed as Jalix."

"No, I'm not. He's going through far more than I am. I have no doubts about that." I ran a hand through my hair, letting the tangled strands slip through the cracks in my fingers. "And I do need to talk. I have...the faintest shadow of an idea. But I need help finishing it."

"Go for it." She sat in my chair, propping her feet on the coffee table.

"Alright. So we know Raven Bio is behind Shift Company, and Jalix's corporation helps finance them. So I'm thinking we can use Jalix as leverage to get close to Raven and her father. If they control the company, taking them out will cut the head off the snake. I know her father, Schillinger, he's calling himself now, is the mastermind."

"We both knew that." She sighed quietly. "We have for years."

"I just didn't know he had involved his own corporation. I had assumed he was smart enough to avoid merging the two. So it's an extremely vulnerable operation. We find Raven, find Schillinger, and kill them, and their entire scheme falls apart."

"What about Kilkovf?"

"He's a thug. He doesn't have the brainpower to take over for those two. He's in charge of the muscle, the Pyrate brutes. He's not coordinating anything, just taking orders."

"Alright, so how do we get those two close to each other? And how can we get near him? He knows who you are."

"But that's *all* he knows. Jalix could get close to him. He's not sure if Jalix is one of us yet or not. And if Jalix maintains a low profile, continuing to work for the company, he can get close."

"Do you really want to put him in that position, especially so soon?"

"Of course not." I said defensively. "But I think it's hiding in plain sight. They won't expect him to be on board so soon." Alice stood up, tilting her head.

"So soon? When did you plan on doing this?"
"As soon as Jalix finished converting. We'll keep a close eye on him, and when he gets his first craving, we'll take care of it and start to fill him in on the details."
"Kara, that could be tomorrow for all we know. And *take care of it?* It's not that simple. We've had people die because of their first craving."
"We'll take care of it. I'll keep him safe."
"Kara, you can't stay with him all the time. You have a city to protect. You have planning to do. You're our most brilliant tactician. You need the time we give you to develop ideas."
"I can handle it, Alice."
"You need more help."
"What are you getting at, Alice?" I hissed, rapidly approaching her. She recoiled, fearful. "Say it. I want to hear you say the words."
"You need Krystal." She whispered. "You and I both know it. You want someone dead? She's the perfect weapon to do it. Send her."
"She's unstable!" I roared, pointing into the hall. "Did you not see her an hour ago? She's hungry for power, she's out of her mind, and she's looking for a fight!"
"Then give her one." She said softly.
"If I rely on her...If I tell her that I *do* need her..."
"She loves you, Kara. You need to accept that. But she also needs to understand you're with Jalix now. Go talk to her." I knew she was right, and wanted nothing to do with it.
"No. She chose to walk away."
"She chose to fight on her own. What do you think she's doing right now? Waiting for you to be attacked? She's doing the same thing you are. Planning. Go talk to her." I closed the journal on my desk, handing it to Alice.
"Fine. Here's what I have so far on our situation. It has some of Raven's research labs, with notes on each. Try and figure out where

Sorrow

they're going to be." I spun around and opened the closet to my left, searching it for a bag.

"I'm not trying to force you to go, Kara. But I think you already know that it's time for you two to stand together. At least for now." I pulled out a black backpack, stuffing my handgun, cell phone, and wallet inside.

"I know. We can't all blame each other. It's just...our nature." She grabbed my shoulder as I turned to leave, stopping me.

"Kara, you know that's not true. We're not killers. It might be in our blood, but not in our souls. Those are *your* words. It's everything you stand for. You have to be careful with her. She's so much like you that you can't see it. She's...what you could have become. What you almost became."

"Alice, don't. We're nothing alike." I felt very aware of her burning feelings of concern as I began walking away.

***

What am I going to say?

After tapping my fingernails on the steering wheel for a final time, I got out of the car and looked outside. The sun was setting behind the gloomy rooftop of the Victorian mansion. Red and orange waves of light washed over the countryside behind the building, bathing my vision with a soft glow. The door to the house opened and Krystal stepped out. Silently, she waited.

"Beautiful, isn't it? Right as the sun goes down..." We both stood for a moment, watching the colors of the evening sky. "Come in, we'll talk."

Debating the sanity of my decision, I walked to the door and looked into her eyes, a light cerulean blue tinting her irises. I followed her into the house and sat down on the brown leather sofa in her parlor. The fireplace next to me was alive, roaring with content. The amber waves of heat rippled over the white marble mantle and onto my skin. I looked around the living room for a moment, gazing through the open window.

"Ele`?" She asked, extending a wine glass.

"I think drinks would make this easier." I said truthfully. She picked a bottle of wine from an ornate cabinet next to the couch, filling the glass and handing it to me.

"The question of the day, Kara...what are you doing here? What do you want?" She spoke not with aggressiveness, but with legitimate curiosity. She filled her own glass and replaced the bottle, taking a small sip.

"I want to come to an understanding, Krystal. Whatever that takes."

"We have an understanding. You don't want me around."

"Don't be a child. This is about more than you and I. This is about the entire city."

"Yeah, big picture stuff. I get it. So what do you *want*? You came here for a reason, and that wasn't to give me a warm and fuzzy feeling." I took another long drink of wine.

"I want you to come back to the city. We could use you. We need soldiers, not just people willing to fight."

"I'm willing to fight, Kara. But do you want me to fight for *your* cause...or mine?" She sat on the couch next to me, looking intensely into my eyes.

"I don't care why, as long as our enemies are the same. And Jalix isn't your enemy. Focus on the real threat." She laughed, catching me off guard.

"The real threat? Kara, they've been kept at bay for years. It's about time they had a successful attack. If that's the best they can do, I'm okay with that. My *real* threat is anything that gets in my way."

"Jalix isn't in your way. You are. If you'd stop acting like such a child, I'd be around a lot more often."

"Please. Your entire life changed once Jalix came into it. You would leave the city for a week and never call, expecting us to handle everything. Not that we can't, my point is that you stopped caring about us and started caring about Jalix."

"I *never* stopped caring about the city, Krystal. I trusted Alice enough to run things in my absence. And you know what? God forbid I try to have a normal life. I'm so sorry that I tried to be something more than the head bitch in charge. *Some people* want a life outside of that."

"And you think I don't?" She screamed, slamming her wine glass into the table. It shattered into frozen pieces, chunks of solid wine falling on and around the couch. "You think I don't dream *every day* about having a life with you? The image, the *dream* of being around you in any meaningful capacity is the only thing I can think about on a daily basis. The only physical contact I can have with you is when we fight! If you think for a goddamn *second* that I wouldn't rather be here, or in the city, with you, you're more deluded than you think I am!" She stood up, her lips quivering with the precursor of tears.

"Krystal, we've discussed this a thousand times. What you want from me *cannot* happen. I'm sorry. I've told you this a thousand times. I just don't understand how you have to make everyone around you miserable because you can't live the exact life that you want." The fireplace crackled, embers rolling down the side of the stone masonry.

"I don't make everyone miserable, Kara. I make people see the truth. For example, I know you're better in the ring than I am. But I managed to hurt you. I needed Jalix to see that you're not indestructible."

"And why is that, Krystal? Why can't he have something to believe in?" She didn't respond, leaning into the marble mantle of the fireplace. "What makes it so wrong for him to see me the way you do?"

"He doesn't." Her voice began to break down. "No one sees you the way I do, Kara. No one. I have loved you longer than most humans are alive. My friendship with you has lasted longer than any other in history. And yet it means nothing to you."

"It doesn't mean *nothing*, Krystal. I'm flattered, and it makes me feel horrible that I don't feel the same way. But I'd be living a lie if I told you I loved you too." I paused. "Actually, I wouldn't. I do love you. Just not in the same way."

"I know. I'm like family, right?" She scoffed, sniffling.

"No. I do love you. I don't just see what you are. I see the things you can become. And that's what I love. Your talent, feeding into your potential. It's amazing. But I'm not romantically involved with you, Krystal. It would be…dangerous. We're too volatile. It just doesn't work."

"How do you know if you've never given it a chance?" She hissed, spinning around. Her emotions got the best of her, the fire dimming with an expulsion of cold energy from her body. It roared back to life a moment later, illuminating her eyes in a bright yellow light. Her pupils, clear to see against the snow-white of her irises, were severely dilated.

"Krystal! You told me you were clean!" I stood up and set down the wine glass on the coffee table. She didn't move her head, or react at all.

"I know…" She said slowly, looking up at me. "I am…sorry. I shouldn't have lied to you. But…painkillers…are not going to hurt me." I threw my hands in the air and ran them through my hair.

"It's…hurting *me*. Krystal. Seeing you like this. I like who *you* are, not who this is." She smiled and laughed.

"So…you *do* care." I sighed.

"You're really far gone, aren't you? You know, I thought…" I sighed and closed my eyes. "I thought I could trust you. Why do you keep going back to this? What…are you hiding from?" She laughed hysterically and flopped back onto the sofa.

Sorrow

"Hiding? All my secrets are out. I've got nothing left. You're engaged. The city's going to shit. So all I have left is this empty castle. I'm the queen of nothingness here." She shook her head. "Kara. I'm in love with you. So much. What...what the hell do you see in Jalix that you don't see in me? I'm smart. I'm funny. I'm-"
"An addict?" I said harshly. She cringed. "I'm sorry..." I immediately apologized, but she didn't move.
"Just go away, Kara. I can't...I can't even bear to see you anymore. You're not the same person I knew." She sighed, her chest trembling, and I saw a tear fall down her face in the reflection of the fire.
"Krystal I-"
"Just go! Please...I can't even be near you anymore." I stood for a moment, listening to her pitifully sob. It tore me apart to see her so emotionally bared. "I hate you. I hate you! Why do you do this to me? Go! Leave me alone!" She screamed.
"If you want me to leave, I will. But don't expect me to come back for you." I whispered, the same emotional tears Krystal fought finally making their way into my eyes. I turned around and threw the door open, running to my car. A mixture of anger and grief gripped my throat, closing it off from speech. The door to my car squeaked angrily as I heaved it open, then slammed it shut.
"Damn it, Krystal. I'm so sorry." I whispered, setting my head on the steering wheel. "I'm so...sorry..." Out of the corner of my eye, I saw Krystal's door open again, her body leaning into the frame. She stood for a moment before walking toward me, sobbing. I got out of the car again and stood to confront her.
"Kara, please don't leave me. I'll do anything." She fell into me, wrapping her arms around my chest and leaning into my shoulder. "I can't live without you. I...I don't know how I can..." Her speech was almost incomprehensible, choked sobs forcing their way out involuntarily. I stroked her hair for a moment before pushing her by the shoulders to look into her eyes.

"Krystal. I care about you. I need you to know that. It…it tears me apart to see you like this. I hate it. I hate myself for it. I hate you for making me say the things I do…but I don't want to leave you, either. You're a friend to me. We've fought together. We've cried together. Laughed. We've got so much to lose. That's…that's why I need your help in this fight. *That's* what I'm fighting for, Krystal." I wiped the tears from my eyes, my voice returning. "I'm fighting to keep this friendship. Our families. Our friends. The love we all have for each other. And I think you're fighting for that, too. Whether you realize it or not." She nodded, making every effort to stop crying.

"I'm so sorry, Kara. I love you so much." She hugged me again. "The thought of losing you…It drives me insane." I chuckled.

"Sweetie, I don't think you need me for that. You're already halfway there." She giggled, interrupted by several sniffles. "And you're not going to lose me. So long as you're there to watch my back." She nodded, her face still buried in my shoulder. I heard a buzzing noise, originating from inside my car. I gently moved her away, climbing into my front seat and grabbing my backpack. Opening it, I found my cell phone, ringing from Jalix's call.

"It's Jalix." I explained, answering the phone. "Jalix. Can I call you back?"

"Hey…babe." He immediately burped, loudly and directly into the phone. "Oh, I'm so sorry. I'm sorry. That was rude." Val distantly cackled and yelled something to Jalix. "No! No more! No…alright, one more." Jalix answered Val's mystery question.

"Jalix?" I asked slowly.

"I'm sorry. Hi. Listen. I love you…so much. And Val's with me and we're having a great time. But I just wanted to let you know, I tried to quit my job."

"You what?" I was unsure of how to feel about his statement, extremely disadvantageous to my plan to stop Raven.

"Yeah, I tried to quit. But he was all 'No, Jalix, Raven is doing this whole big thing soon.' So I'm gonna have to go tomorrow to see one of their labs."

"You what?" I repeated, completely bewildered by his statements. I put him on speakerphone, beckoning Krystal to listen.

"Yeah, they're going to try and...Val, not now, man. Anyway. He wants me to stay in the company. So he's going to try to show me this new thing Raven is working on. He says it'll make me want to stay."

"Jalix, that's great. Just...don't call anyone else tonight. How much have you had to drink?" He roared in laughter, and the sound of crashing glass forced me to turn down the volume on the phone.

"Val says 'all of it.' But I think he's still got a bottle left. I think he's messing with me." Val interrupted, talking loudly into the phone.

"Kara. Hey! What's up? So listen...Jalix needed to relax. And the...virus hit his liver. So he can drink as much as we can. We're...we're on our third bottle of rum." My jaw dropped and Krystal cackled from behind me. A smirk found its way onto my face as he continued. "I'll take care of him, I promise. Is...is Krystal there?"

"Hi, Val." She answered, smiling.

"You two...you two should kiss." Jalix chuckled in the background, and a loud chant began.

"Kiss! Kiss! Kiss!"

"Val, how many people are you with?" Jalix answered after a long pause.

"All of the guys that were left...decided to throw me my bachelor party. So there's like...thirty of us." A raucous chorus of cheers echoed on the other end. "And seriously, if you two kiss, take pictures." He finished, laughing.

"Alright, Jalix. The best part of this situation is that you're going to remember *all* of this tomorrow. I have to go. Be safe."

"I love you!" He yelled. The crowd taunted him in the background, making fun of his words of affection.

"I love you, too." I ended the call. "Dumbass."
"I feel like Val and Jalix get along nicely." Krystal smirked, chuckling.
"Yeah. I have a feeling they're going to be thick as thieves. If our stock in liquor can handle it."
"The club has a lot of-" She stopped suddenly, looking away. "Stock." She looked back at me. "I know how we can get close to Raven. Follow me."

  Her hair flared around her neck as she spun around and headed toward the door to her house. Placing the phone in my pocket, I followed closely behind, curious as to her train of thought. She began voicing her thoughts aloud as she closed the door behind us, slowly making her way up the mahogany staircase.
"Jalix is going to be in with Raven tomorrow, right? And we know they're behind Shift Company. As soon as he said that, I started thinking about ways we can use that to our advantage."
"Krystal, no. I'm not putting him at risk-"
"Exactly my point. He's at risk no matter what." She flashed a knowing smile over her shoulder before finishing her statement. "Unless we go with him." Reaching the top of the stairs, she turned the corner into a dimly lit hall, throwing open one of the many doors and strolling inside. Rounding the corner, I realized it was her office, an open space illuminated by the dying light falling through the lone window. "Have a seat." She finished, sitting at the desk. I sat in the chair across from her as she opened her laptop.
"Krystal, we can't go with him without drawing attention to ourselves."
"And that's where you're wrong. That single word, 'stock', gave me an idea. At the press conference you two just attended, the news also covered the financial stability of their organization. The owner's daughter, Raven, is a massive shareholder of the company. In fact, she owns more than her father does, making her the deciding factor in any large decisions. She's obsessed with the money, presumably

because she's laundering it and stowing it into smaller divisions for research into our virus." As she spoke, her fingers nimbly danced across her keyboard. "If a few rich investors decided to suddenly take a vested interest in their stock options, we could tag along under the guise of shareholders. Our names will be on the paper officially, and we get a free tour of the bad guys' house."
"Yeah, and a buy-in to any significant share of the company is going to cost a fortune. Where are you going to get-" She looked at me derisively.
"I didn't get this house for free, love. Steel and oil. They run the world."
"Right. I forgot you're disgustingly rich."
"I wouldn't phrase it like that. I just have...a vast array of assets."
"And three imported racing cars, a Victorian mansion, two beach houses-"
"Three, dear. You forget the one in Maui. And by the way, Alice and Val now hold five percent of Raven Biopharmaceutical's public shares."
"Each?"
"No, jointly. Each would have been a little pricey. Might've had to sell a beach house." She chuckled, closing her laptop. "Now all that's left is for *you* to tell them the plan and tag along tomorrow."
"I noticed you didn't buy it under your own name. Why are you refusing to go?"
"Refusing?" She said incredulously. "Who do you think is going to keep everyone safe while you're gone? Didn't you come here to ask me to come back to the city? Didn't you need my help to keep it safe?"
"Yes, I did." I interrupted her before she could continue, growing irritated at her sudden burst of self-appreciation. "But I asked. Nothing more. I fully expected you to tell me no." She scoffed.
"Because you know me so well, right?"

"Damn it, Krystal! Why can't you just help without expecting something in return? Why do you have to seek this... gratitude? I've saved your life, a dozen times over. I don't throw it in your face or expect things in return."

"No, your reward is getting to do whatever you please with no repercussion." I stammered for a minute, my infuriation so great that my ability to speak was hindered by a dozen insults and petty remarks I had to hold back.

"I get to do whatever I want?" I stood up, knocking over the chair in the process. "I have to live with the fear that any time someone in that city is harmed, it's my fault. It's my responsibility to keep hundreds of lives safe, every day. I just had to tell them to go find somewhere else to live because I couldn't guarantee their safety anymore! Entire families need to find houses! People are uprooting their lives because, even though I spend every second of the day running the place, I couldn't keep our enemies from coming in and trying to kill them!" She stood up to meet my rage, challenging me.

"It's hard to do things by yourself, isn't it, Kara? Imagine living your *entire life* that way, when you know the person you love doesn't love you back!"

"I *was* alone!" In an outburst of fury, my hand went to reach for her neck, but I found myself able to control the emotion in time. "For hundreds of years, I was alone! For hundreds of years, I managed to stay sane! And you? Dragging me down every step of the way? Contorting my emotions and wrenching my heart the entire time? If you don't think I debated whether you were right for me or not, you're dead wrong, Krystal! I spent *years* confused about you. I didn't know if I loved you or hated you! And now, you have the *audacity* to look me in the eyes and tell me you're alone? After all I did for you!"

"You've done nothing for me! The only thing you've ever done is cause me pain!" My hand struck the side of her face sooner than expected, catching even myself by surprise. The force of the impact was so strong that she stumbled a moment before recovering herself and looking at me in shock. My face was firm, but my heart was racing, fully aware I had done the wrong thing.

"You...don't know...pain, Krystal. And the worst part? I hope that you never have to go through what I have. Because no matter how much you spit in my face and scream at me...I would never wish that agony on you. You think you *feel* sadness? That you *feel* heartache?" My voice dropped to a low growl as I descended on her, backing her fearfully into a corner. "There is a very good reason my name is Sorrow. I...am...pain."

"Then maybe that's why I love you." She whispered. My next vicious remark was cut off by my phone ringing once again. I took a step away from Krystal and answered the call sharply.

"Jalix, not now."

"Kara? It's Alice. You need to get back here *now*. Jalix is in rough shape." Krystal's eyes widened. She reached over to the desk, grabbing her handbag and running out of the room. I followed behind her, continuing the conversation with Alice. "What happened? Is he okay?"

"He'll be fine. His body's reacting to the virus. He had his first craving and nearly killed someone. We gave him the injection to calm it down, but he's still in pretty rough shape." Krystal held the door open for me as I ran to my car, turning it on in a frenzy. She slid into the passenger seat next to me.

"I'll be there shortly, Alice. Thanks for letting me know. Do what you can to keep him out of pain." I ended the call as the engine roared to life under the pressure of my foot.

"Kara?" Krystal said quietly as we turned onto the highway.

"What, Krystal?" I replied tersely, not wanting to continue our argument. She hesitated for a moment, thinking about how to phrase what she wanted to say.

"When this is all over...when we don't have to worry about being hunted, exposed...killed...are you still going to be there for me? Or are you going to disappear with Jalix?"

"I'll always be there for you, Krystal. I have a lot going on. But when you need me? I promise you that I'll be there. Even when you don't want me to, like today, I'm there. You need to open your eyes a little. I am here. I'm not going anywhere. I promise." She nodded silently, staring out of the window.

***

    I pushed the door open to the infirmary harder than what was likely necessary, the frame creaking unhappily. Val stood just inside the door, alone.

"I told everyone else to go home. They didn't need to be here for this. Alice is in there taking care of him."

"How bad is he?" I asked immediately, my lack of information highly disconcerting.

"Now? Not so bad. Some pain, but mostly confusion. He's lucky I was there to hold him back. I haven't dealt with many people as strong as he is. He'd give Jared a run for his money."

"But he didn't hurt anyone?"

"Not seriously. One guy ended up with a broken arm, but he's fine."

Val stopped talking as Alice came out of one of the care rooms.

"You guys can come in." She immediately disappeared back into the room, Val and I following shortly after. Jalix was curled up uneasily on a bed, shaking and shivering violently. His skin was a sickly pale color, sweat beaded in various points on his body. His shuddering eyes made their way to meet mine, flaring open in positive recognition.

"Hey...babe." He grunted, his head falling into the mattress. "How...are you?"

"Jalix...are you okay? God...you're a mess." He leaned over and vomited profusely into a trashcan, spitting several times before returning to his fetal position.

"I'm...great. Val and I...had fun...just kind of...hung over, I suppose." He gagged again, leaning into the trashcan. There was a long pause before he continued, unmoving from his precautionary position. "Alice says that this...happens to everyone...so I'm not too worried. Small price to pay...to be a superhero." He sped up his last words so he could continue retching into the can. Alice sighed and shook her head.

"And it doesn't help that he was drunk as hell when it happened. His body is rejecting everything he drank tonight, trying to purify the liquor in his bloodstream, and crave blood at the same time."

"Yeah, speaking of which..." He croaked, trying to hold back his heaving. "How does...all this work again? Do I need a...cold shower and a coffee...or another one of those...amazing shots?"

"First of all, I gave you three shots of morphine and a shot of what we all take to keep our cravings at bay, which is why you're not begging to die right now." Alice chipped in. "And no, there's nothing we can do at the moment. Luckily, this is the easy part. If Val wasn't there to hold you back, you would have gone into a frenzy attacking people."

"Val?" Jalix croaked. "I love you, man. Thanks for...not letting me kill...people." Val smiled broadly, his outgoing demeanor shining through.

"Anytime, man. You're a great guy to party with. I've never seen so many body shots in one..." He stopped talking as I glared disdainfully. "You're a great guy to party with."

"Thanks...You should see me...when I'm not dying..." He was breathing heavily now, but placed the can next to the bed and rolled onto his back, stretching his body. Alice looked at me and handed me a clipboard with some scribbled notes on it.

"This is just a timeframe of events from tonight. I expect him to be ready and willing to talk in about an hour. Speaking of ready to talk, can we step out of the room for a second?" I nodded, following her around the corner. She lowered her voice, presumably so Val couldn't hear.

"How'd it go with Krystal?" I rolled my eyes.

"Exactly how I expected it to go. We fought for half an hour, then Jalix called, drunk. She got an idea that I'll fill you in on, and then we fought some more before coming over here. She's been stealing morphine from here again." She sighed.

"I was hoping it wasn't her, but I had noticed the theft. I'll have a talk with her. Is she alright?"

"She's fine. She went to go check on everyone else while I came here. She's still…clingy. She wants a lot of my attention, and I can't give that to her right now."

"She gets like that. These next few days will keep her busy, though. She'll be a lot of help. And speaking of which, you said she had an idea?"

My introduction to Krystal's plan was interrupted by a clatter in the next room, followed by the sounds of Val and Jalix struggling with each other. We rounded the corner in a flash, confronted by the sight of Jalix and Val locked in, what appeared to be, a very fake fight. Jalix had Val in a headlock, and Val was trying as best he could to fend him off.

"You tried to get me to sleep with a stripper! You can lie, but your stupid smile can't!"

"Did not!" He grunted, laughing as his face slowly turned red from lack of circulation.

"Hey!" Alice barked, immediately separating the two. Most of the color had returned to Jalix's face, alight with happiness. His eyes met mine and the smile disappeared, replaced with a look of reverence.

Sorrow

He walked toward me slowly, putting one hand on the side of my face and roaming his eyes over my body.
"You are so beautiful..." He breathed, awestruck. I blushed, smiling.
"Jalix, you've seen me hundreds of times. It's just the morphine."
"Never like this." He whispered, his eyes locked with mine. "I can see...everything. Every little scar...every...small detail. It's like I've been looking through glass my whole life. And now everything looks...clear." He stroked my hair, his hands grazing the tips of my ears. "I can feel every strand. Is this what life is like as one of you?" My eyes stung with tears, overwhelmed with the fact that he seemed happy with the transformation.
"Yeah, Jalix. It is. Listen...all the sounds outside." He closed his eyes for a moment, his smile slowly growing wider.
"I can...hear people talking down the hall. I can hear your heartbeat. It's quiet. But it's there." He gently placed a hand on my chest, the fluttering heartbeat it contained pounding against his palm.
"Welcome to life as a Vampyre, Jalix. And you couldn't have picked a better time to join us." Val said, patting him on the back. Jalix smirked, looking into my eyes again.
"Kara, if this is what you're fighting for..." He picked up my hand and held it delicately, sensing a change in his strength. "I'll do anything for you."
"Just don't die for me." I whispered, pulling him in to embrace him tightly. Hot tears rolled down my cheeks, disappearing into his shirt. *He's finally safe.*
"Jalix..." Alice said quietly, trying not to interrupt the tender moment. "You really shouldn't be up and around already. Are you sure you feel okay?" I felt him chuckle against me.
"I feel great, Alice. Not sure how, but I do." He pulled away from me to look at her. "It was really sudden, like someone threw a blanket on me. I got warm again and stopped being nauseous. Then I

remembered things from the bachelor party and...decided to retaliate."

"Yeah, and by the way, dude? Neck still hurts."

"That's what you get for making me do body shots off of Maria."

"She *really* liked you."

"She really likes everybody, Val. She has some...fatherhood issues she needs to deal with." He laughed and shook his head before glancing over to see me with my hand on one hip, tapping my foot.

"Oh, really?" I asked playfully. "What else was involved in the whole two hours I was gone?"

"*Well*, Jalix-"

"Shut the hell up, Val." Jalix said with a smile, effectively stopping a spillage of secrets. "Um...Wow, I can actually remember it all really clearly. Val and I started with a game of beer pong, which quickly turned into a round of shots for a few people that walked in. They called their friends...who called *their* friends...who called the dancers...yeah. Wow. It got crazy pretty quickly. I remember when Val and I opened our...fourth bottle, I think. I told him I would call Gregory and quit. I told Val I wanted to stay... and I didn't want my old life getting in the way of things. And then...the rest you know."

"Really? You collapsed *right* after you hung up?"

"Yes." He replied way too quickly, and Val cackled.

"I don't think there was a woman in there that *didn't* give Jalix a lap dance."

"Val, shut the hell up." He said through gritted teeth. "I was also insanely drunk. Seriously, we almost ran out of booze. Completely." He looked at me apologetically, and I tried as best as I could to keep from smirking.

"Just lap dances?" I asked.

"Just lap dances."

"Alright. I can let that slide."

"I think."

"Wait, what?"

"I'm kidding!" He chuckled, putting his hands on my hips. "I just told you, I remember everything. And I would never risk losing you for something so stupid. Although, Val was apparently telling one of the dancers that I was going to run away with her. That's why I tried to kill him a second ago."

"And again, still hurts." Alice interrupted the banter, not as amused as the rest of us.

"Can we focus on something more important here? Kara and Krystal came up with a good plan, and I have yet to hear it."

"Plan?" Jalix asked. "Plan for what?"

"To end this." Krystal's voice called from the entrance of the infirmary. She had changed her clothes, now donning a black skirt and a dark blue, tightly fitted blouse. Her black combat boots tapped the tile floor as she moved towards us, carrying several sheets of paper. "Kara and I came up with an idea to get a better picture of what we're dealing with." She handed a sheet of paper to Alice, Val, and myself before leaning against the wall and explaining herself. "Alice and Val now hold a decent share in the company, courtesy of me and my wallet. Jalix, you had planned on going tomorrow anyway. You can call back and let them know you're bringing investors. I'm sure they won't mind with the kind of money they just put out, not to mention that they want to do everything they can to keep you happy right now. The four of you will go in and map the place out, memorizing every last crevice of the place. They'll probably take you through a tour, or at least to whatever big thing they're working on. You find out if there's any link leading to Shift Company, see if Raven's father is involved, and leave. We can always go back. This is reconnaissance only. Got it?" Her gaze diverted directly to Jalix as she spoke. "I'm talking to *you*, new blood. Don't do anything stupid. They don't know you're one of us, yet. They don't even know if you're involved with us. For all they know, you're in the dark and Kara hasn't told you anything yet. Got it?" He nodded, unhappy at her attitude. "Good. I'll be here, listening for phone calls, pictures, anything you guys can give me. And if you need anything, information or otherwise, I'll do what I can."

"So what do they do at...wherever we're going?" Val asked. Jalix spoke up.

"They wanted me to go to one of their research facilities. They do a lot of testing at this one, and less paperwork. It's where the action takes place, and they only have two. So we're lucky that we get to see this one. We need to make it count."

"What do you expect us to find?" I asked quietly. He shook his head, grimacing.

"I don't know, to be honest. He said they were working on a massive project that would change my mind about leaving. But that was it."

"Think it has anything to do with Shift Company?" Krystal echoed almost the exact question I asked, changing the tone to sound more accusatory.

"Yes, Krystal, I think they have a bunch of you guys down there in cages, testing shampoo all day long." He retorted, turning away. In an instant, Krystal had taken advantage of Jalix's distractedness, grabbing him by the neck and slamming him into the wall. Alice lunged forward, but I grabbed her arm, shaking my head.

"I have friends that have died to those bastards." Krystal seethed, an inch from Jalix's face. Jalix looked perfectly calm. "Don't you dare take that lightly." Jalix nodded thoughtfully before placing his hands on her chest and shoving her backwards. She flew several feet across the width of the hall, smashing into the concrete and falling to her knees.

"You didn't care about them enough to stay in the city. Kara had to come collect you like a runaway pet." Jalix moved toward her, crouching to her level. "And me? I'm in the game now. I gave up everything to help you with your cause."

"You're here because of Kara!" She yelled, swinging at him and missing by several inches.

"Then we're at an understanding, aren't we?" He smirked, peering down at her like she was a slave. "I don't have time for you, Krystal. I don't need to be soft on you like Kara is. You get in our way? You risk any of us getting hurt for your own personal gain? You'll regret it."

"We'll finish this later, Jalix. You're not as strong as you think you are." Krystal stood up slowly, walking past Jalix and leaving the medical wing entirely. He shook his head as I let Alice's arm go. Without hesitation, she walked behind Jalix, inspecting the back of his head for injuries.

"I'm fine, Alice." He said dismissively. She smacked him abruptly in the back of the head, prompting a yelp from Jalix and a chuckle from Val.

"Don't instigate her." She concluded, crossing her arms. "She's enough trouble as it is."

"I'm not worried about her. I'm focusing on tomorrow's events. Does anyone *not* want to do this? It's a lot of risk."

"And a lot of reward." Val said, pondering the idea. "We get to look at whatever they're working on, create a plan, see their level of involvement. I like the idea."

"I like the idea, too. But in practicality, it's dangerous. They could know everything we're doing right now. They could easily rope us into a trap and kill the four of us." Alice voiced her thoughts before a smile slowly grew on Jalix's face.

"The five of us." He smirked, turning to me.

"Absolutely not. We're not taking Krystal. And that doesn't help the-"

"Not Krystal. My boss. He's the one that invited me, remember? They won't hurt the man supplying them with millions in funding."

"I...forgot about your boss. They wouldn't have even invited him if they planned on pulling something. Right?" The four of us stood in silence for several moments.

"I can think so much clearer as a...well, as one of you. You know how there's usually a thousand smaller thoughts buzzing around your head normally? They're gone. It's so quiet."

"And that's another thing, Jalix. Are you sure you're going to be okay to go with us? It's not an easy change, getting used to all the new capabilities. You can't be walking around staring at light bulbs tomorrow just because you can see some infrared."

"That's a thing?"

"That's a thing."

"Trust me, I can keep it together. I want to take some time and discover all the things I can do now, but we don't have that kind of time. If they're getting confident enough to attack us, they're not going to stop at one move. Everything is in motion now, and we're not waiting on anything anymore." He shot a glance at the doorway to the hospital. "Or anyone." Val leaned against the wall, taking in a deep breath.

"I guess this is it, isn't it?" We all paused, looking at him in his rare moment of solemnity. "Our last moment of peace. Once we commit to this...there's no going back. We push until we win...or die trying. Everything from this moment on is war-focused. We're not going to be able to sit back and wait on things. We won't have time to fight about our differences. It's going to be like things were...before your time, Jalix." He looked at me with concern, my eyes darkening as I understood his meaning. "And it's not going to be a pleasant experience."

"We follow you, Kara. You know that." Alice looked at me with a sense of veneration, reminding me of days I thought were long buried in my past.

"At no time do I expect any of you to follow through with this." I said quietly, prompting looks of confusion from the group. "You all have lives outside of this place. What none of you seems to understand is that this is *my* home. This is the place *I* created. You are all here as guests. You have no duty, no obligation to defend it. If, at any time, you want to leave...do so. I'm not going to stop you. But if you're all going to follow me, I expect you all to take every word I say as the truth. Every command is law. Every single thing that comes out of my mouth is to be executed without hesitation. If you can all do that...if you can all do what you do best and help me keep our haven safe...we can get through this."

"Understood...Sorrow." Alice put an arm on Jalix's shoulder briefly before walking away.

"I'll meet you in the training room tomorrow morning, guys." Val said, turning to follow her.

Jalix and I stood alone in the room, uncomfortably staring in opposite directions. I kept quiet, waiting for him to say something, but the moment never came. I looked at his face, into his eyes so different than they were before. I could see a new light in them, a new flame for something I was unaware of. His typical concentrating gaze was changed, an enlightened look of understanding spread across a hidden smile.

"I'm jealous of you, you know." I started quietly. He smirked and looked at me confusedly.

"How so?"

"This was given to you as a gift. You accepted it and appreciated it for what it could be. You had friends here when you changed. I'm...glad you didn't have to go through what I did."

"What about the others? Did they go through...whatever you did?"

"No. It was me. I changed them, when they were ready. Val was always younger than I was. When I stopped aging, I realized Val was getting older. I got scared. He asked me to do it. I had to infect Alice and Krystal to save them. They were going to die otherwise. And there were...others. Only one other person had to undergo a...forced change...but she's not around anymore." I swallowed hard in an effort to push out the familiar pained sensation in my throat.

Weaver

"I'm so sorry, Kara-"
"Aside from you." I whispered, fearing that he would come to his senses and start to hate me at some point.
"Hey." He said quietly, cupping my face in his hands. "I want this. I need you to know that. I need this. To be in your life fully, to understand what you are...I need this. I have another life to live now. And I have forever to live it." I wrapped my arms around him gently, trying to convey how I felt without speaking.
"We should get some sleep. I feel...drained." He said quietly, his hands gently pushing my shoulders back to look me in the eyes.
"Yeah. I don't think that's a bad idea." I agreed, taking his hand in mine and walking down the hall to the infirmary's exit. The main hall was open and empty, long abandoned for sleep or other late-night activities by the few citizens that still inhabited the city.
"Forever isn't that long, Jalix. It goes quickly after the first few years. And sometimes I think forever isn't long enough for all the things I want us to do." I turned the corner to a short hallway, walking until we reached the door to my room. I held the door open, allowing him to enter the room first. "But I'm not unhappy in any way, Jalix. I love you with all my heart. And I'm blissfully happy with you. I'll just be happier when I know we're safe for good. Safe from all this. The war. The fighting."
"Well...I understand. I feel the same way, I suppose. But for now, I want to enjoy the time we have." He closed the door and smiled at me, placing his hands on my hips.
"I think we can arrange that." I smirked, grabbing his face and pulling him close to kiss me.
"You know you don't have to be gentle anymore, right?" He mumbled. He wrapped his arms around mine and kissed me, our breaths hot and shallow. I threw my hands around his waist and pushed him onto the bed powerfully, conveying that I wouldn't be gentle anymore. The frame bent several inches outward as I followed suit, jumping and

Sorrow

landing on top of him. He pulled back to reach down and playfully bite my shoulder. His fangs sunk in, and I began bleeding immediately. It felt odd. It wasn't painful, but it put a chill in my throat, like a carefully controlled blizzard. The sensation washed over me, sending a chill down my spine.

"Kara, I'm so sorry. I didn't know-" I interrupted his apology to pin him down and bit back, clenching my jaws on his neck with just enough control not to kill him. The same feeling overcame him and he quickly understood why I didn't mind his aggression. I let go and looked at him.

"It heals quick, don't worry." I smiled and pulled on his shoulders, rocking us off the bed entirely. We hit the floor simultaneously, rolling onto the rug. I sat up, wrapping my legs around his waist, driving my lips against his. Our fangs locked for a moment and I growled teasingly, stroking each one slowly with my tongue.

"Your fangs are nicely formed," I panted, grinning. "It's just a Vampyre thing, by the way. You're not actually hungry right now." He shook his head and stood up quickly, shoving us both against the wall.

"On the contrary. I'm *very* hungry." I grabbed the front of his shirt, ripping it into two pieces of warm, damp fabric.

"You're...breaking things..." He sighed, trying not to complain. I nodded.

"If you're not careful, the next thing...might be you." I panted. He grabbed my waist and swung me around, throwing me against the kitchen counter. The stone top cracked and fell into pieces, giving in to the impact of my hips.

"Try me." He grabbed a handful of my hair and pulled on it, allowing him access to my neck again. He bit down carefully, shudders traveling down my entire body. My fingers dug into his back like claws, certainly leaving marks on his skin. His muscular arms were pressing my hands against the remnants of the counter, attempting to hold me in place.

"You can't hold me back." I whispered, breaking free and shoving him back to the bed. I leapt from the counter and pounced like a cat, landing gracefully with my hands and feet restraining his to the mattress. The wooden bedframe snapped under the pressure and collapsed, dropping the mattress onto the floor. We both bounced, and immediately got lost in a mess of strewn sheets. I giggled and picked up a pillow, smacking him with it gently, unable to find another object of choice. He smiled and looked into my eyes, sparkling and alight with joy.

"I love you." He whispered, beaming. His fangs stood out among his other beautiful white teeth.

"I love you, too. So much." I said, dropping the pillow. He grabbed my hand and kissed my engagement ring.

"I wouldn't be the same person without you." I smiled gently. He leaned in without touching me, almost no distance between our lips. "I'm in the middle of a war, and I can confess that my life is perfect. I've been waiting for this moment my entire life. I'm so glad you're here." I whispered, my lips brushing against his with each syllable.

"Me, too. Without you...I'd be so lost." I kissed him gently and ran my fingers over his neck where I had bitten. It was healed completely, as if nothing had happened.

"I chose this life the moment I said yes to you. And I'm glad I did. You're my girl, no matter what species you are. And the last I'll ever love." I chuckled, running my fingertips over his bare chest.

"Hey, Jalix?" I said quietly, burying myself under the sheets.

"Yeah?"

"We broke the bed."

"I know."

"And the countertop."

"I know."

Sorrow

"You've only been a Vampyre for an hour."
"Go to sleep, Kara."

Weaver

Sorrow

Emissary
Jalix

As I did a thousand times before, I tugged the deep black sleeve of my favorite suit over my shoulder, conforming the beautifully stitched fabric over my arm. I gently smoothed my hands over the faint wrinkles between the seams, perfecting and completing my professional appeal.

"You look great, Jalix." Kara said quietly, slipping on one of her stiletto heels.

"I know..." I returned gazing in the mirror. It wasn't cockiness that prompted the uncharacteristic response, but rather a noticeable difference in my complexion and muscle tone. I looked significantly healthier somehow. Faint blemishes on my brow and uneven eye color were corrected to a flawless complexion and sharp blue irises.

"Do you think they'll notice?"

"It's not as noticeable as you'd think. Your vision is picking up things that you wouldn't have normally seen before. You'll...we'll...be fine." I watched her approach me in the mirror, her arms outstretched to wrap around my shoulders. She had an odd look of content, and one I rarely saw. She was nervous, but keeping it at bay. It was something at which she was clearly skilled.

Footsteps echoed down the short hallway outside our room, and I immediately began analyzing them subconsciously. One set was

heavy, slow and deliberate in gait. The other was alongside and slightly behind the first, much lighter and slightly faster in pace.
"Alice and Val are here." I said, turning around. A brief moment passed before the couple came strolling through the door, Val donned in a navy blue suit and Alice in a fire-red dress.
"Holy crap."
"Oh, lord." Their comments were overlapped and matched in surprise when they looked around the apartment, pieces of crumbled granite and splintered wood littering the floor. I fought against a smirk that desperately wanted to sprawl across my face. Val's ear-to-ear grin didn't help my cause.
"That-a-boy." Val jeered, extending his arm for a high five.
"Thanks, Val." I reluctantly returned the gesture, much to Alice's disapproval.
"Typical men. Kara, sweetie, did you sleep okay? The last few days have been rough and you haven't had much time to yourself."
"I slept just fine, Alice. It was nice to cuddle again, once he stopped freaking out and worrying I was going to kill him." She smiled at me innocently, clearly not intending any disrespect or offense.
"Well, the day's not over yet. And speaking of which. We should get going before we're late to our own party." Val awkwardly attempted to fix his shirt by tugging on different areas of the jacket as he spoke.
"Let me help." I stepped forward and sharply pulled upward on his collar, removing the wrinkles I assumed were on his chest.
"Wow. Thanks. I'm assuming this is your day-to-day attire?"
"Yeah. I don't mind, unlike some people. It looks good on me."
"Kara looks better, out of the two of you, if we're being honest." A porcelain complexion and blue mess of hair poked its way into the doorframe, the majority of Krystal's body still outside the room.
"What do you need, hon?" Alice asked, trying not to give the impression that she wanted Krystal gone.

Sorrow

"Honestly? I thought you guys were gone. I came to check out the mess they made last night. But since I'm here, just wanted to say good luck. Check in once you get back." Her eyes met with Val's briefly before she vanished again from the doorway.

"She's got to be light on her feet." I began, tilting my head. "I can't even hear her footsteps right outside the room."

"That's Krystal for you. But she's right, we should be going." Kara led the way out of the room, stepping over a large chunk of broken countertop on her way to the door.

"Hey, so...odd question. Where's the...door?" The group stopped and turned slowly, confusedly looking at each other. "As in, how are we going to leave? Is there an elevator, a big door...a...hatch? I was kind of drugged when I got here, and I haven't left yet."

"Oh." Alice's expression lightened when she realized the intent of my question. "There's an exit next to the training room. We'll show you."

"It's not a dumb question." Kara reassured as we continued on our way. "I'm surprised you haven't asked me sooner."

"You seem surprised at everything I say and do up until this point. What's the usual reaction for someone that you choose to...convert?" Alice replied instead of Kara.

"There's usually a pretty broad adjustment period. More than the two days you've had so far. Typically, Kara and I tell them what's going on and why they were chosen. Most people have a pretty severe reaction. It's difficult for a human mind to learn that everything it thought was a fairy tale is suddenly true. We keep them contained here, isolated from others until the virus finishes its transformation. After that, it's easier for them to grasp. Their minds work quicker and more logically, so it's easier for them to understand the gravity and reality of their situation. Sometimes it takes weeks."

"What about those who choose not to stay?" The answer to my question jumped again to Val.

"Everyone wants to stay. Whether they realize it or not at first, they all choose, at the very least, to keep our secret. Some do choose to go back to their families under the guise of medical cures, miracles, stuff like that. But they all know what would happen if the word got out that there was...something more than humans making the world what it is."
"So you guys are really *that* good at hiding what you are?"
"We have to be." His quiet reply was disheartening, but nonetheless an answer. Meandering through the main hall, we approached the training room. Conversation echoed from inside, the telltale traces of Krystal's voice coalescing with that of another young woman's.
"Who's in there with Krystal?" I almost began to grow annoyed at the rate at which I was asking questions.
"Her name is Violet. She's a wonderful girl; I'll make sure you two get some time to talk when we get back." The infamous cage fell into view as we entered the room, the sight of Krystal and the young girl confirming our assumptions. Neither of them turned to look at us; they were both carefully balanced in striking poses as Krystal talked through the mechanics of some martial art.
"The door is right through here." Kara said, motioning to an open closet filled with boxing gloves, sports equipment, and piles of open boxes. Stepping inside the dark closet, there was another closed door immediately to the right. I reached over and opened it slowly, exposing an unlit concrete hallway. It was far smaller than other structures within the city, lesser in proportion in both height and width. At best, two people could have walked side-by-side. Kara moved in front of me and I followed closely behind, listening to her as we walked.
"This was a very early part of the city. Hence its difference from the rest of the architecture. And we really can't do much to improve it because the entrance is so close to the surface."

"Although..." Val closed the door behind us, dim strips of light illuminating the long hall. "A renovation would be convenient for those of us that aren't three inches wide." I turned around to see him occupying a good portion of the hall, ducking to avoid the low ceiling. Kara smirked before continuing.

"And now you know where the door is, Jalix."

"Indeed I do." I said quietly, allowing my far improved vision to adjust to the light.

"Not to diminish the importance of Jalix's understanding of Aerael's infrastructure, but we should probably discuss a bit of detail for our pending meeting. Are we really just going to waltz in, take a tour, and leave?"

"No, we're not." I said firmly, interrupting the short breath Kara drew in to respond. "We're going to hunt for every piece of information we can find. We're not going to take whatever they hand us. We're going to ask for details, insight; we'll look in their computers if we get the opportunity. I don't know how yet, but I plan to learn everything I can about what they're doing to you guys. Well...us." The hall began to enter a long curve, sweeping upwards and to the left, maintaining its apparent endlessness.

"And how do you plan on doing that?" Val's deep voice echoed quietly through the hall.

"I'm not sure yet-"

"We're going to use this." Kara reached into a pocket on her dress I wasn't aware existed and withdrew a small black device, a short cable attached on the side.

"And that is...?"

"It's a storage drive. It's got a neat little program on it that copies as much information as it can hold. When it's full, it erases all evidence that it was ever plugged in."

"Oh. Well, yeah, we're going to use that." Kara chuckled quietly at my sarcasm before replacing the device in her hidden pocket and resumed speaking.

"Alright, Jalix. Welcome back to the surface." The hallway's long curve ended in a plain door, with no telltale signs of light creeping from its seams. She pushed it open and continued walking, strolling into a musty basement. Smells of old dust, mold, rotting cardboard, and insecticide struck my senses harder than I would have expected. It wasn't that the odors were strong, but they were firmly distinct, with a strong discernment between them. Without being able to see well, I could tell that it was the sub-level of a structure. The faintest creaking from wood beams over my head coupled with fine rays of light shooting from between the floorboards gave a strong indication that this was indeed a cellar.

"My nose is going nuts." I remarked to Kara as she moved toward an obstructed staircase. She moved aside an old wooden crate and climbed the first few steps.

"Mine too. You learn to ignore it over time." I followed closely behind her, with Alice and Val trailing in the rear of the group.

"Aside from...not down there...where exactly are we? That tunnel was close to a quarter mile long."

"We're underneath a framing shop. You know the one on Oak Street?"

"Wait, that place that no one ever..." I smiled, understanding the purpose behind the store. "Goes in. Yep. That one. What's more boring and unobtrusive than a place that frames photos and paintings?" Her smirk echoed in her voice as she pushed open the door at the top of the staircase, welcomed by bright natural light from the glass storefront.

"Hey, guys." A voice called from the store. I stepped into the shop and moved aside so Val and Alice could enter, as well. Looking around, the studio was exactly how I expected. Empty frames with small price stickers were hung with care on the wall, none too flashy or

Sorrow

expensive. A few large photographs of the Massachusetts countryside speckled the blank spaces, covering the walls in insignificant décor. A man sat on a barstool alone behind the front counter, his feet propped up next to the cash register as he occupied himself with a tablet.

"Hey, James. This is Jalix." Kara introduced me with little effect. He looked at me briefly, acknowledging my existence with a brief wave before returning to his device. "We rotate shifts for who occupies the shop that day. It's pretty dull. You sit and make sure no one goes into the basement. For obvious reasons."

"Not that they ever do." Alice chuckled. "We get three people in here a day, if we're lucky."

"Hate getting stuck up here." Val grumbled. Kara turned to him with a smirk, relishing his pouty look.

"It's a necessary crime, Val. I only stick you up here when you irritate me." She shook her head amusedly, the tips of her ebony hair bobbing over her hips before continuing to the front of the store. "And Jalix, we do have a large parking lot in the back that you can use, if you'd like to bring your SUV here after the meeting."

"Oh good, you guys validate?" My somewhat sardonic response was ignored by Kara, instead choosing to hold the door open for the three of us. I stepped out of the door and onto the sidewalk, beckoning Val to lead the way. Aside from having the aesthetic of models, the four of us stood out from the citizens of the city by our attire, clearly dressed for a more important event than the otherwise menial tasks to which they were attending. Traffic seemed to move slower than I had noticed before, each small rotation of the tires appearing more deliberate. Looking to my right, I saw Val's frame turn the corner into an unkempt alleyway, clearly underused by the nearby populace.

"Come on. We have a meeting to get to. You can gawk at all the shiny things later." Kara took my hand and allowed the glass door to close, leading me into the same alleyway around the corner. Poorly maintained asphalt provided a rugged base for the thin road leading into the parking lot behind the building.

"Shotgun." Val called, opening the door to a black sedan and throwing Alice the keys.

"Looks like we're sitting in the back." Kara sighed.

"That's probably best. It would be tough for me to focus on driving right now."

"Who said I didn't want to drive?" She winked at me, smiling, before moving to the car and sliding into the backseat. I sat down next to her, closing the door behind me and taking a deep breath.

"This is going to be a hell of a meeting."

"If anyone can do it, you can, Jalix." Alice said reassuringly.

"Well, it'll be a group effort." Kara and Val both looked at me as I spoke.

"Not…really. We have no idea what's going on." Val's quiet words forced my heart into my stomach.

"What do you mean?" Alice gently pulled out of the lot and turned onto the alley's short strip of road.

"I mean…like, you've done all this before. Meetings and conferences and all that crap. But aside from their website and social media, we don't know anything about the company. So you and Kara are going to be doing most of the talking. Alice and I are there as eyes and ears under the pretense of being investors. Just investors. We're rich and wanted to make more money in the stock market, that's all we have to our story right now."

"What? You guys couldn't come up with anything? A backstory on why you invested? That the…child you almost lost years ago is now all grown up thanks to their technology and you decided to repay the favor by investing? Nothing?" Val and Kara stared at me, open-mouthed as I realized I formed a solution to the problem in a matter of seconds.

Sorrow

"I mean...that works." Val returned to leaning against the window quietly.

"See, Jalix? You're quicker on your feet now. You'll do just fine." Kara put a hand on my shoulder, leaning into me and instilling the familiar sense of comfort her presence had on me. "I love you." She added.

"I love you too. But I'll be damned if I don't have a heart attack in the next three hours."

***

It was almost unfamiliar to pull up to one of the massively imposing buildings and not have a crowd waiting for me. I wasn't vain enough to look forward to seeing them, but I was also thrown into discomfort by realizing that fewer eyes meant less accountability. Nonetheless, it was unusual.

"We're here..." Alice said in a halfhearted singsong voice.

"Alright. We'll play it cool. Unless we see something we like, mouths shut, eyes open, and let me do the talking." My choice of wording triggered an amused response from Alice and Val, and a dazed look from Kara.

"Yes, sir, mister boss man." Val opened the door and crawled his way out of the car as Alice shut off the engine.

"So...I'm keeping my mouth shut, am I?" Kara said slowly, attempting to hide a patronizing smile.

"Well, not you. I didn't mean you. You can talk all you want."

"Oh, thanks for the permission, dear. I'm so glad I'm allowed to do that."

"What? That's not-"

"And what do you mean, we'll play it cool? Are you saying I'm going to freak out in there? You don't trust me?" My shocked reaction began to fade as she condescendingly dropped her eyes to meet mine, indicating that she was being sarcastic.

"Oh...you're kidding."

"Yes, dumbass. If we go in there and we're arguing a little bit, it might give us an excuse to split up later if we have to. I can...go use the restroom or something."

"Wouldn't you be able to do that any other time, too?"

"Or I could throw a punch and get ejected from the building if you're looking for a more significant response."

"Nope, bathroom sounds great."

"That's what I thought. Now...play it cool in there. Mouth shut, eyes open, and let me do the talking." She grinned as she mocked me, prompting a sharp pull on her chin followed by a kiss.

"Let's go meet the bad guys." I opened the door and stood up, looking at the face of the building. It was a plain, unadorned concrete building with few windows and no significant structural obtrusions. Essentially, it was a big gray box. My boss stood with Robert Schillinger in front of the main door, chatting idly and occasionally looking over at us. Their demeanor was professional, yet positive.

"Greg! Robert!" I called, smiling. I walked around the car and trotted up the cement stairs to shake their hands.

"Jalix. How'd my prodigy enjoy his vacation? Or honeymoon. Whatever you kids decided it was."

"It was...eventful. Got attacked in a casino and decided to lay low for a bit after that." Schillinger decided to interject.

"Yes, we saw that, unfortunately. How are you after that? Not too traumatized, I would hope?"

"No, thankfully. I've moved past it." It was a stunning realization that I had forgotten about someone holding a gun to my head only days ago.

"Good." He continued, looking at me oddly. "We were starting to think that it was what made you call to quit your position. It was...rather unexpected."

Sorrow

"Yes, it was. Unexpected, that is. But the truth of the matter is that Kara and I are very happy together and are planning on moving. It would be rather difficult to conduct business from the west coast."

"West coast?" My boss asked incredulously. "Why the distance?"

"She has family in California. I've saved enough from the military and from this job that we can afford to buy a nice house out there." There was a brief moment of silence as they reflected on my answer, and I couldn't help but to feel immense pride at the speed and intensity of the story I managed to fabricate.

"Gentlemen. It's wonderful to see you. Thank you so much for graciously allowing us to take a tour of your facilities." Kara emerged behind me, with Alice and Val standing by her side.

"Ah, yes. Karalynn. How have you been?" My boss extended a gentle hand while Schillinger stared idly in silence.

"Well, aside from my wonderful fiancé deciding to quit and our honeymoon being interrupted by a man with a gun, it's been wonderful." Her voice intentionally ran bitter, the theatricality of the situation dripping with tension. "Mr. Schillinger, these are two of my close friends, Allison and Valterius. I spoke with them briefly in regards to the success of your company, and they decided to make a considerable investment. I hope you don't mind if they accompany us."

"I'm sure they'd have minded less if you'd given them any warning." I muttered just loud enough for the two men to hear. Val stepped forward to shake Schillinger's hand when the door behind him opened and Raven stepped out. Instantly, I felt cold, as if the already chill air had suddenly turned to ice. My vision narrowed as I focused on her, but the detail of her features remained crystal clear. I could see every line in the wrinkles of her cocky smirk, supplemented by sharp, glaring eyes already accusing me of things I hadn't done. She was disgusting to see, despite the fact that there was absolutely no reason to see what I did.

Weaver

"Jalix...I missed you while you were gone." Her lips curled into a shark-like smile, gazing directly at Kara as if to insult her directly. I cleared my throat and coldly extended my arm to shake her hand. "Wonderful to see you, too, Raven. I would assume-" She bypassed my arm and embraced me, pressing her body against mine in an extraordinarily inappropriate fashion. I felt my muscles harden with the tenseness of an attack. Some mystery rage filled my blood with an overwhelming desire to throw her away from me.

"I was worried when I saw the news. But I have to admit...you look good, despite almost dying. How'd you get away? I heard you fought him with your bare hands." She released her grip from my back, and I instantly took a step back, distancing myself as much as I could.

"I got lucky, I guess."

"Seems like you get lucky a lot, Jalix." My boss remarked, unnerved at Raven's behavior. Schillinger stood, unmoving, as if the events unfolding in front of his eyes were pieces of a chess game that he played no part in. Almost bored, he allowed Raven to behave the way she did with no change in his reaction.

"Well hello, miss. Am I to assume you're the company's namesake?" Val hid his usual humor in exchange for metered respect and courtesy, stepping between us to talk. He briefly glanced at me, his look inviting me to take my place once again beside Kara. While they spoke, I stepped next to her and wrapped an arm around her waist, wondering if they all saw in Raven what I did.

"Yes, and you must be the new investors. I want to thank the two of you for helping the company so...generously. And I have to say..." She slowly rotated her eyes to look at me once again. "Your timing was nothing short of perfect. We have a lot to show you."

"Yes, and I have to admit, it's getting a bit crowded out here, wouldn't you say? Let's step inside and see what this is all about." My boss said directly to Schillinger. For the first time, his expression changed into

Sorrow

a positive, jubilant smile while moving to the front door and holding it open for us.

"Absolutely. I think you will all be thoroughly excited by the things we have to show you. Aside from the scientists inside, you'll be some of the first individuals to see the technology shaping the future of humanity." I drew in a short breath, paranoid at his choice of words, but just as quickly released it as I realized that it was a simple statement. My boss was the first to enter the building, followed closely by Raven and Val. Alice decided to bring up the rear of the group as Kara and I stepped into the building's warmth, a corporate-style front desk awaiting us. Schillinger turned to the group, now gathered in a small circle.

"I suggest that we take two groups in order to move a bit quicker through the labs. They're not built for large groups. Raven, dear, would you mind taking a few of them through the new project? I'll take the rest with me to see our supplementary labs."

"Of course. Jalix, Mr. Hartman. And I'm sorry, I didn't catch your name." Raven looked at Alice inquisitively, invoking an immediate response.

"Oh, I'm Allison. I'm sorry, I thought we were introduced."

"Oh, that's right. I forgot already." She chuckled while Alice fought off a look of irritation. "You three can follow me."

"I guess I'll see you later." Kara and I were both clearly unsettled by being separated, although I should have expected nothing less from Raven. She kissed me quickly on the cheek, attempting to maintain the appearance of being upset by our bickering.

"Now, Miss Raven, what can you tell us about this new project?" My boss looked at me while he spoke, continuing his train of thought.

"From what your father has told me, it's absolutely riveting. Something I'm sure that would encourage Jalix to stay as a liaison between our companies." She sneered quietly as she walked, rounding a corner and taking the three of us out of sight from the group.

"This project, Project Catalyst, as we're calling it for now, is actually a twofold program." As we walked, we passed by several glass walls that illuminated a view of large laboratories, spacious in size, yet distinctly lacking in an abundance of personnel. "The first step we took was the reason we needed your company's investment; the research we conducted bankrupted us. We hired top scientists, engineers, neurosurgeons from around the world in order to fulfill our demands." She paused, turning to look at us directly. "We managed to successfully duplicate the human mind." My boss spoke out without a moment's hesitation.

"Successfully regenerating human brain tissue? Incredible!"

"No, actually, we took a shortcut." She paused in front of a large glass window, now several hundred feet from where we first began our tour. "We didn't regrow the flesh. Instead, we took the electricity inside the human mind, recorded it, and stored the readings digitally. Which, in itself, is relatively easy." She beckoned to a large, awkward-looking device in the middle of the room. Most of it looked archaic, with colorful wires protruding from every opening and scattered haphazardly along the floor. The center of the device was a table, enclosed by a curved ceiling, and only stood about five feet tall. "But *our* goal was to put those readings back." Alice and I looked at each other hurriedly, then at Raven.

"How is that even possible?" Alice asked, almost pressing her face into the glass.

"The human body is simply chemistry. We're all made of matter and energy. Both...can be manipulated. Our first trials were messy. We were using primitive electro stimulation designed to shock the brain repeatedly, but it was far too inaccurate. Messy. So we designed this machine. It works like an MRI, emitting pulses of targeted magnetic energy, focused into a tight beam, and re-stimulating the synapses of

the brain. Instead of trying to change the *matter*, we changed the *energy*, carving new pathways into the mind. There are only two in existence; one in this facility, and another...more refined version in our other research lab." Her pride was overwhelming as she spoke.
"Human technology is...years away from something like this." Alice whispered.
"Human...what an interesting concept." Raven's head turned slowly to look at Alice. "And that's what Project Catalyst is about, Allison. Making us...a little bit more than human. Imagine being able to learn all the knowledge in the world...in a matter of hours."
"The mind can't handle that. It's not made to process so much information." I responded, looking at the machine.
"True. But even diluting the span down to years is incredible." Gregory looked dumfounded, grinning ear to ear and gazing into the glass. "Truly amazing work, Raven."
"Don't forget, Mr. Hartman. This is only the first part of the project. If you're impressed with this..." She smiled before turning and walking down the open hallway again. I dropped back to maintain a steady pace with Alice as we made our way to Raven's destination.
"How does this tie in?" I mouthed, barely breathing so Raven wouldn't overhear. Alice remained silent, shaking her head with a firm grimace. Looking forward, the hall turned into a narrow corridor, the style of the walls fading from glass and wood to concrete and industrial metal. Corner upon corner, we made our way deeper into the facility, moving hundreds of feet further inside. Closed doors with biometric locks sealed the hall into a narrow width, not meant for several people.
"All of these are separate labs. Some dedicated to medicine, others to machinery. The one we're heading toward is the most secured. As my father said, this is a very privileged project." We came to a massive steel door, closed by several large locking mechanisms and guarded by two military-style security staff. Each wore black body armor and

carried a loaded rifle. My eyes narrowed inadvertently to the small steel engraving on the weapons. I could read the manufacturer, serial number, and caliber from a dozen feet away. "And before we go any further, I'm unfortunately going to have to ask you both to sign a nondisclosure agreement. This is just to protect the company from any of you leaking the information to other research firms, think tanks, and the like. It's just a formality, I assure you." As she spoke, her voice grew further and further excited, reaching a point of giddiness. One of the security guards opened a bag at his side, pulling out a few sheets of paper and pens.

"A trivial price to pay for such incredible insight, wouldn't you say, Jalix?" Gregory looked at me excitedly, passing along two of the sheets of paper. I feigned a smile and handed one of the papers to Alice, along with a pen.

"My curiosity is piqued, boss. I'll see what's in store for the company. But I'm not making any promises." I quickly scanned over the paper, ignoring a majority of the legal phrasing, and signed it, handing both items back to Raven.

"And another brief point, although I shouldn't need to warn any of you." The three of us looked at Raven. "Each vial of chemical, each piece of equipment, and every scientist in that room is tagged with a slightly radioactive card. If any of them are removed from this room without express permission, documentation of the system, and deactivation of the collar, the room is rigged with thermite, designed to destroy all evidence of our research, in order to preserve the integrity of our work."

"What? That's outrageous! Who would agree to work there?" Alice responded with ardent apprehension, voicing the same thoughts in my own mind.

"This is the door leading to the machine you saw earlier, as well as some of the most advanced biochemical, viral, and genetic experimentation that any country has ever dared to produce. I

Sorrow

promise you that every scientist, researcher, and assistant in that lab has agreed to work under those conditions. I can assure you that setting off those alarms would have to be intentional, and a built-in timer is also integrated so there can be no accidents. Personnel have two full minutes to enter their security code and return either the item or themselves to the lab. If the security code is approved by my father, the alarm shuts off. If the item is returned, the alarm shuts off. I can promise you, none of you are in any danger." She smiled at us, the sickening pseudo-warmth she exuded making me physically sick to my stomach.

"Well, we all signed." My boss laughed, clearly eager to explore the secrets inside the door. "I'm ready if they are."

"We're fine, Raven. My colleague was simply worried about the stability of your systems. She isn't as familiar with your corporate integrity as I am." I explained, covering for Alice's clearly irregular behavior. Raven smiled and nodded to the security guards, who typed in long numeric codes on the keypads against the wall. The door let out a pneumatic hiss, releasing the locking mechanism and swinging open silently. Large detectors stood on either side of the door, on both the near and far side.

"Those are the alarms, I assume?" My boss asked, gesturing to the large plastic columns covered in sensors that extended to the ceiling. She stepped through and twirled briefly, signifying that there was no danger.

"Yes, Mr. Hartman. Those are the sensors. I can assure you, that unless you have some radioactive isotope in your pocket, they are extraordinarily safe." I immediately strolled through the door, leading the way for the rest of the group. I saw a faint flickering of light from the sensors as I stepped through, an odd red-green color with which I was unfamiliar.

"I can assume they also use infrared for motion-detection?" I asked. Raven looked surprised.

"Yes, they do. Impressive. How could you tell?"
"I was just guessing. I'm sure you don't want anything that *isn't* tagged to go through these doors, either." My lies again came all too quickly and naturally.
Kara was right, I can see infrared.
"If any of you have questions, please feel free to interrupt me, but I'll explain the research as we walk. If you don't mind, the first thing I'll ask each of you to do is don the proper protective equipment for the lab environment. I only require that you wear a protective lab coat and face shield to avoid the spread of contaminants. I'll be doing the same." She beckoned directly inside the door, where a locker-room style area displayed several unused lab coats and plastic face shields. Extending an arm to welcome us inside, we followed Gregory into the room, grabbing the lab coats closest to our size and placing them over our business attire.
"So, Raven, I have to ask, what is the other group doing while we're here?" Raven responded with a mild look of disgust as she pulled on a lab coat over her red cocktail dress.
"Your girlfriend is just fine, Jalix. And so is your other friend. We didn't think it was necessary to show all of you this lab. As I said before, this is very well kept information, and we want to restrict it to as few people as possible. If you'll excuse me for a moment, I'm going to inform the researchers that they have guests. Their doors need to be closed so you're not at risk for picking up any…unwanted microbes." She smiled as if what she was saying was a joke before walking away. I immediately looked at Alice, picking a plastic mask off the wall as I spoke.
"This is pretty deep in the heart of the building. Starting to get a little claustrophobic in here. I hope we aren't here too long." Alice picked up on my connotation and responded with matching casualness.

Sorrow

"I know what you mean. But so far, everything has gone pretty well, and I don't foresee things going any differently from here on out. I'm sure we'll be out of here in no time."

"I should hope not!" Gregory exclaimed, running a hand over his white goatee. "This is amazing. I can't imagine the wonders of medicine that we're going to witness." I nodded, agreeing to sound less concerned.

"I agree. I'm positive that this is...advanced. Whatever it might be." I almost felt apologetic to him, the wrinkles of his age enhanced by a constant smile that extended into his eyes.

He doesn't have any idea what's really going on.

Alice saw the pity in my face and nodded subtly. Looking around the room, I noticed multiple cameras, as well as a lack of personal artifacts on the lockers. Raven emerged from the far side of the room a moment later, motioning for us to go with her.

"You can follow me again. I'm very excited to show you this project."

"I can tell. It looks like you have a very vested interest in your work." I was trying to be subtle with my phrasing, but it came out more direct than I had intended.

"Of course. I plan to inherit the company one day, and I also have a large monetary foundation in these projects. It's part of my duty to oversee the research."

Alice smiled at me as she stepped through, knowing what was going on in my head. Raven took several slow steps forward, pointing to the walls as she spoke. They were in much the same style as the windows in the front of the building, providing a good view of small, well-lit laboratories. The hall we were in, however, was not lit at all, the only indication of where we were stepping being the remaining fluorescent light trickling in through the windows.

"These are micro-labs, as we call them. Each one carries a single researcher and a single assistant, minimizing the need for intensive accountability and shared research. Each lab has its own specialization, isolated from the rest of the project. They all know what their individual goal is, but no idea as to how it all ties in together."

"That's smart. A little controlling, but smart." I wanted to physically bite my tongue as I voiced my thoughts.

"It is, Jalix, absolutely. But it's also the safest way to conduct the research we're doing."

"Which is what, exactly? You still haven't mentioned what the second part of the project is." She grinned, continuing to walk down the narrow corridor. Each window she gazed into seemed like a jail cell with two captives, each one under her control. I could nearly feel her sense of supremacy as she passed several cubicle-sized areas.

"Well...I suppose it *is* time." She stopped in front of one of the larger windows, rapping her knuckles against the glass. The researcher inside was suited in a white plastic garment that covered their entire body, sealing them in from whatever the room contained. They jumped uneasily, turning around to look at her and nodding before returning to a small panel on the wall. The researcher pressed a few buttons, illuminating a screen on the wall in front of them. There was nothing on it, a white rectangle of light hovering on the wall above their head.

    Fidgeting with a series of plastic containers and medical tools, they placed a pink object directly in front of them, visually echoed on the screen above them. It appeared to be organic, some unknown organ or piece of flesh clean from any contaminants or fluids.

"What is that?" Alice asked quietly.

"That, Allison, is a piece of ocular tissue. It's a bit of flesh from a human eye, the sclera to be more specific." As she spoke, the scientist took a scalpel, and with a shaking hand, drew a thin incision into the organic material. I winced, the cut certainly having been painful if it were still attached to a person.

"And this...my friends...is Project Catalyst." Theatrically, she took a step back, the incision slowly healing itself before our eyes. Thin, almost microscopic bands of tissue covered the wound like natural stitching, creeping over the cut and pulling the flesh back together. The entire process was slow, taking about two minutes from start to finish, but was nonetheless fascinating in the most horrifying of ways.
"How..." Gregory started, shaking his head but refusing to look away. The researcher took the piece of tissue and sealed it in a new plastic dish, immediately picking up a notepad and scribbling text onto its surface.
"Viral engineering." Raven concluded. A shock ripped through my body, as I understood the context of the experiment as a whole. My knees started to feel weaker, despite the strength I knew they were now capable of. My first reaction was dismay, followed immediately by anger. I wanted to kill Raven in the hall, tearing her body to pieces with my bare hands. She continued talking, and I leaned against the glass in order to stay upright. My stomach churned with emotion, trying not to think of the implications that accompanied a woman like herself having control over the Vampyres' virus. "We found this virus years ago, and since its discovery we have been manipulating it and rewriting its code. Chemical manipulation has proven to be nearly impossible. You see, this specific virus changes with its environment. It adapts to almost anything we throw at it. It's almost impossible to kill, remarkably resilient, and changed the organic matter it inhabits."
"Where did you find this?" I croaked.
"That's unfortunately classified. But I can tell you, we're not done with it yet. We're actively seeking out more samples."
"More samples?" Alice asked. "Forgive my bluntness, but I'm a doctor. I studied neuroscience and virology at Harvard. Why would you not be able to replicate the samples you have? Let it...breed, so to speak?"
"We've tried, it does reproduce remarkably. But the most interesting thing is that each virion, a single piece of the virus, rewrites its DNA

in order to fulfill its goal. They manipulate themselves based on their local environment; so for example, they would have a different job in your brain than they would your eyes. However, some parts of the virus's DNA actually require a different *host* DNA in order to rewrite itself. And, like humans, it almost has its own...lineage. We're trying to find a source very far removed from this one. One that was allowed to evolve for a long period of time, creating a genetic diversity between the two strains."

"Why don't you use different organic samples to cause that?" Alice rebutted.

"Excellent question, and we have. However, basic biology tells us that all viruses need a cell to live off of, to leech from, so to speak. They don't produce their own energy in enough significance. So dead flesh doesn't work well enough to allow the virus to rewrite its own DNA."

"Have you tried it on rats, or other living creatures?"

"We have, with limited success. You see, the virus does its job well enough on its own. As you saw, it regenerates destroyed tissue, enhances cellular function, but the one things it doesn't do is create its own energy. It's not enough to survive outside the host. The strain of the virus we have is old, very old. We need a fresh sample, one that's had time to evolve on its own separate from our own strain."

"This is all very technical." My boss added quietly, staring into the small lab.

"It is." Alice added, turning back to Raven. "And it's remarkable that you're so familiar with all of this. Do you have formal medical education?"

"No, I don't, but the experts we have certainly shared a great deal of insight with me."

"What's your goal?" I asked, standing up and turning around. It was nearly impossible to avoid shaking, wondering how easy it would be for her to tailor the virus to kill us, or worse.

"We are trying to make the virus self-sustainable, at least for enough time that it can revitalize dead cells."

"What?" Alice exclaimed. "That's...insane. It would have to feed on some form of energy...unless it's producing its own...but it would have to..." She stammered, shaking her head and closing her eyes. "My god...what you're saying is actually possible."

"What's keeping you from finding these...new samples?" My boss asked, the three of us now focusing on Raven's explanations.

"Think of it like this, in simpler terms. This part of the project is a puzzle. We have most of the pieces, and we know what the image is. But nonetheless, if we don't have those final pieces, we can't finish the puzzle. Once we find a variant strain of this virus...we'll be able to bring back the dead. And much more."

"So how does the first part of the project relate to this one?" Alice had notes of dismay in her voice, but only enough to be picked up by enhanced hearing like my own.

"Well, if we can bring someone back from the dead..." Raven looked directly at me. "Like fallen soldiers, for example, their brain tissue would be damaged with the lack of oxygen. Especially if they've been dead for days. But if we can restore their memories-"

"You'd have to record them first, you can't just-"

"I'm well aware that we can't pull a person's memories out of thin air, Allison, but if we have them stored, we can retrieve them. And then implant them."

"You're talking about bringing back the dead." My boss said incredulously, laughing. "This... this is amazing. Absolutely incredible. Jalix, what are your thoughts? You've been quiet." I shook my head, trying to remain as neutral looking as possible.

"I'm just in shock. This is something I never saw coming. I figured maybe you had discovered a cure for cancer or something."

"Oh, we did, dear." Raven smiled and began walking back the way we came. "The virus has a goal, somehow. Hard-wired into its own DNA is a purpose. Much like our own human instincts tell us to eat…breathe…reproduce…the virus wants to stay alive. And in doing so, needs its host to stay alive."

"That must require an enormous amount of energy." Alice retorted again, trying to squeeze every drop of information out of her.

"It does. The virus loves to feed on blood, particularly two chemicals: hemoglobin and albumin. The first one, hemoglobin, is what carries oxygen through your body. Naturally, it doesn't use enough to kill the host, but can become problematic if more isn't created or introduced to the host periodically. The animals we tested ended up eating each other after a few days; they had these…intense cravings to replace the chemicals." She laughed as if the matter was funny, then continued. "The second, albumin, is a protein in your blood plasma. Fairly abundant, and easy to regenerate. It's plentiful in most mammals, which is why the virus evolved to use it with such prevalence. The body burns a lot of energy to reproduce these cells, and in doing so, usually results in a…violent…first infection."

We reached the entry to the labs once again, confronted by the towering pillars of sensors on either side. Raven unlocked the door and stepped through, again conducting a half-twirl to indicate that there was no danger. I stepped through, my knees discreetly shaking, followed closely by Alice and Gregory.

"See? No harm done. You can remove your protective attire and place it in the bin over there." Quickly, I unbuttoned the lab coat and threw both coat and face mask into the large red bin. "You seem like you're in a hurry to get out of here, Jalix. I hope you're not unnerved by our research." She stood warily, watching me with intense eyes.

"No, of course not. I'm blown away by the good you're doing here. I'm just claustrophobic." I dismissed her sense of caution, instead replacing it with an all-too-familiar look of patronization.

"Not to worry, Jalix, we'll be out of here in no time. And the entire lab system has its own ventilation that circulates clean, fresh oxygen throughout the entire building." She opened the door again to leave the security guards outside the door standing in the same spots they were before we entered.

"I have to admit, dear, this is all a lot to take in. And not to call you a liar, but I would certainly want to see more from this project before we make another investment-" She interrupted him, waving a hand dismissively.

"This wasn't a sell, Mr. Hartman. I don't want your money just yet. I want your support. All I need to know is that if Raven Biopharmaceutical needs you, that you'll be here to support us." We crossed the threshold back into the main part of the building, the massive steel vault door closing automatically behind us.

"Allison, did you have any other questions before we return to our daily business?" Raven asked, a condescending smile looming in Alice's eyes.

"I mean...thousands...but I'm sure the answer to all of them is that it's classified."

"Well hopefully what you saw was enough to sate your appetite. Keep your investment safe. It's bound to grow astronomically." Silently, we walked through the series of concrete halls once again. My mind was reeling with outcomes of the situation.

That virus could be modified to kill us. They could let it loose on society. They-

"Well, Jalix, it was good to see you again." Raven said as we rounded the corner into the main part of the building once again. "Don't be a stranger so often. Most of the time, I'm holed up in our corporate building downtown, but the drive isn't too far if I end up here."

"No offense, Raven, but I don't see any reason to come back. It's not like I can contribute anything to your research here. I'm a finance guy, not a scientist." We passed the long glass windows once again to expose the metal machine built to read people's minds.

Weaver

"Well, yes, but if you're staying with the company, then you'll want to see our progress on certain things."
"Yeah...except I'm not." The group stopped in its tracks, just around the corner to the lobby. I cringed as Raven looked at me with scorn, and my boss with disappointment.
"Are you serious, Jalix?" She hissed, pointing down the hall. "We're bringing technology to this world the likes of which hasn't been seen in human history, and you're turning your back on it?" My boss cut in, defending my decision.
"No one is happy to see him leave, Miss Schillinger, but it *is* his decision. And that decision is that he wants to start a family." He looked at me, a forlorn smile on his face. "Jalix, when I was your age, I threw away my opportunity. I had a beautiful wife and two smiling daughters, but I chose to take the position I was offered in Europe. And after a few years, when I came back to the States, they were gone." He sighed, clearly distressed. "She left me the house, the car, the money. But I didn't want any of it. It's not what life is about, kid." He extended a hand with tears forming, the redness in his eyes apparent. "It was great while it lasted. But go start a family." It was strange seeing him so emotional, when he normally kept an air of humor, not unlike Val's. I shook his hand and brought him in for a brief hug, clapping him on the back.
"Thanks for the opportunity, Greg. I definitely wouldn't be here today if it wasn't for you." He nodded, smiling and wiping the tears from his eyes.
"Ah, look at me. I'm a damn mess." The three of us chuckled, while Raven remained with a hand on her hip and a look of disgust smeared across her lips. "I'm gonna go home and get cleaned up a bit. I'll email you your benefits information so you won't need to come into the office. Might as well make it easy for us both. You ever wanna come back, you tell me." He smiled and put a hand on my shoulder as he walked away. "Never forget something, Jalix." He turned back to

look at me. "You became a damn hero. Nearly dying for your country in the army? Working out deals with this place? With those vaccines for Egypt and Iran? Quitting or not, that's going to follow you." I nodded as he let go, leaving through the main doors of the lobby. A grim silence befell Alice and me, hoping that my decision was for the best.

"Jalix, listen." Raven started, advancing on me as if I was prey. Rebuking her, I stood straight and looked directly into her eyes, not intimidated by whatever it was she had to say. It clearly had the right effect, as she sighed and took a step back. "Look. We don't want to lose you. You're a negotiating genius. You could make this project global once it's finished and people would pay us...billions. Trillions over enough time. Come work for us."

"Raven, no. I'm moving on. It's time for me to lead a normal life." She scoffed contemptuously.

"A normal life? You? Jalix, this is who you are. You're made for bigger and better things than...what, being a dad to some little brat with your trophy of a girlfriend?" I felt a heat wave roll off Alice as she took a step back, allowing me full access to Raven's throat. Ever so gently, so as not to kill her, I pushed her against the wall, just out of sight of the lobby. Our eyes darted in the direction of the entrance as Kara and Val's voices grew near.

"Look at me, Raven." I hissed, invoking fear in her eyes. "I'm walking away. But if you ever say anything like that again, you're going to pay for it. You have your money. You can keep my stock. You can keep *her* stock. But I don't ever want to see you as long as I live. You understand me?" I growled, struggling not to press my fingers straight through her throat. "You disgust me." I finished, letting her fall and slouch into a ball on the ground. Casually, I smoothed the lines in my suit and rounded the corner to the front of the building.

"Hey, hon. How'd your tour go?" Kara asked, smiling genuinely.

"Eventful." My words were curt; I wanted to leave as soon as possible. "You?" Val spoke up, his booming voice alight with discontent. "Boring. Like, mind-blowingly boring. Man, I expected like cyborg arms and lasers and shit. They're just making like…vaccines and pills and crap like that. Yawn!" Schillinger stood behind the two of them, shaking his head with his hand burying his face. Despite Val's characteristic attitude and nonchalance, I could make out the faint edges of a wrinkle between his eyebrows, a clear sign of stress or anger. I ignored it, choosing to focus on the problems at hand.
"Well, I apologize that your tour of our facilities was…unsatisfying. I hope that your investment remains intact." Schillinger continued.
"Well, no shit, dude. I'm gonna make so much money off this place." Val shook his head and made his way to the door. "Come on, guys. Nothing to see here. Let's go drink." Kara turned to Schillinger to apologize.
"I'm so sorry about his…eccentricity. He's always been a bit…slow."
"Not to worry, Karalynn. He isn't the one I expect to support Raven in its endeavors." He shifted his abstract gaze to me, looking curiously into my eyes, as if to look through me.
"Have you made your decision then?"
"Yes, father, he has." Raven came storming into the room, stalking behind him, as if to use him as a shield. "He's decided that we're not worth his time."
"That's not what I said at all." I explained, beginning to reiterate what I had previously said to my boss.
"I'm sure, Mr. Kane. My daughter can get a little…emotional when thinking about the future of our legacy. I doubt she truly understands how well we can suffice on our own." His voice was odd, an unusual tempo rolling through his pattern of speech. "Raven, dear, go into my office, I'll be in shortly." After shooting a look of rage at me, she turned away from us and stormed into the large room adjacent to the

lobby. "Now, then. I assume our business is concluded?" He extended a hand, and I took it warmly, conveying my gratitude.

"It is. Thank you for allowing us to gain insight into all the wonderful things you hope to do someday." He frowned.

"*Will*...do someday, I can assure you of that, Mr. Kane. Safe travels on your way to...California, was it?" Kara and I nodded. "Yes." He nodded, turning around and leaving. Val remained at the door, holding it open for us. Alice silently followed me through, each of us trying to maintain a casual rate of speed on our way to the car. None of us spoke, the complexity of the situation overwhelming. At the very least, to Alice and I. We moved to our respective doors on the vehicle and opened them, almost simultaneously closing them behind us.

"Holy shit, we're so...oh, my god." I let out, exhaling a massive breath. Val and Kara turned to me confusedly, looking back and forth at Alice and me.

"Wait..." Kara began. "What happened? Our tour was actually insanely boring. We got nothing." My eyes shot open as Alice turned out of the parking lot and onto the highway. The openness of the surrounding environment was a dark contrast to the interior of the building, the lack of other structures nearby a sharp distinction between the narrow, winding halls of the labs. I took a deep breath and recanted, as best and as quickly as I could, the frailty of our situation.

"Alright. Raven has our virus. The one that makes us Vampyres. She's experimenting with it and trying to bring dead people back to life. It's working, but she needs a fresh sample of the virus to get it back on track, a strain from something old. Far removed from what they already have. Until then, they can only use it to heal damage, like the cut on your head the other day. They also have this mind-machine-thing. It takes a copy of your memories and stores it somehow, on a computer or something. And they can implant those memories back into a person. They want to be able to bring soldiers back to life with all the memories they had before. They're either trying to make humans immortal...or trying to make them inhuman." A deafening silence ominously loomed over the vehicle, the only sign I had said anything being Alice's head bobbing up and down slowly.

"Wait, you're kidding. Jalix, that ain't funny, man." Val said desperately, trying to cope with the explanation. "No..." He continued. "They don't. No way."

"Jalix, how much did she tell you?" Kara spoke out, realizing she had to quickly gather information.

"The information they have is super-restricted. Only the top scientists, Raven, and her father know the details behind it, although she said that the mind-copy machine had a twin at another facility. So there must be another facility just like this out there. She also can't get it to work fully. She *needs* another virus sample. As in, from someone else."

"Has she done anything significant with this stuff yet, or is it all just research?" Val inquired, slinking into his seat.

"I don't know. From what it sounds like, they've been stuck for a while. She said they found the virus decades ago...but only now have gotten it to where they're ready for the next step."

"It has to be Raven, then. She's the one heading the research on the virus. Schillinger must have turned her into a Vampyre within the last few weeks." I sat, stunned for a moment as Kara visibly winced and bit her lip briefly.

"What." I said, more of a statement than a question.

"Jalix, we couldn't tell you, man. Trust us; it was for your own good." Val defended.

"What the hell are you talking about, Val?" I screamed, staring into the back of Alice's head as she calmly drove. "You. Did you know about this?" Alice said nothing for several moments, but remained visibly upset.

Sorrow

"We've always known about Schillinger. How do you think they got the virus sample? It was from him. And with Raven...you didn't see it, Jalix?" She asked quietly. "When you saw the infrared light on those sensors, she noticed. She looked surprised. She was lying when she said that the scientists taught her about medicine, she rushed her words too much. Little speech patterns. And when we were putting on our lab coats, she left. When she came back, she had a faint mark on her arm. She had to take something to keep the cravings at bay."
"Why the hell didn't you say anything?" I demanded. My anger levels were soaring, nearly to the point of making me nauseous. I wanted nothing more than to leave the car and punch something repeatedly.
"Jalix, we couldn't." Kara spoke up again. She sighed loudly, then turned to me and put her hands on mine. "Look, when we heard about Schillinger inviting you, we knew what we had the opportunity to do. Remember when I said we had some guesses on who the leader of Shift Company was? That was a lie. We know who it is, and it's Schillinger. The reason Val, Alice, and I went with you...was to confront him. We wanted to either bargain for the lives of everyone in Aerael, or kill him. But since there was so much security, and the place was rigged to blow-"
"Wait, that was just the labs." I said quietly, disheartened by Kara shaking her head.
"No, the entire building. Two minutes after the alarm goes off, that facility is rubble. They won't risk their research spreading across the globe, they're at least that smart. And since we knew that, we couldn't kill him. We had to see if Raven was a Vampyre, and how much she knew."
"So what, I was bait?" I yelled incredulously.
"No! Absolutely not. You were a vital piece of our efforts, Jalix. They wouldn't hurt you or your boss in a place like that. They wouldn't have been able to hide the fact that they had killed you both. They would never do it on their property, if they can help it. This whole

war is a secret, and the same way that we have to stay hidden, *they* have to stay hidden. Do you really think anything they do is legal?" She paused for a moment. "If they're discovered, they'll shut everything down, and Schillinger will have to start all over again building up to fight us. It's been a cold war until now, when they sent those people in to attack us."

"My god..." I breathed, my eyes widening. "That couple. The one that tried to kill us. Remember how they used to be husband and wife, but he clearly said that it was his sister? He couldn't remember his name or why he had a wedding ring?"

"Oh, shit." She said quietly. "That device."

"That machine." I confirmed. "They're using it to...brainwash people. Trick them into thinking that they're a part of the cause."

"That must be why they're working with the Pyrates. The Pyrates, and Kilkovf, are under the complete control of Shift Company...and therefore, Raven. In fact, the more I think about it, the more I realize that Shift Company doesn't exist. It's their whole operation."

"The plot thickens." Val muttered sarcastically.

"Shut up, Val." Kara reprimanded sharply.

"Don't tell me to shut up. I'm thinking. But it's hard to do with all the yelling going on."

"Jesus, Val, I'm sorry that some of us have had a couple hundred years to think about this and I've been here a week. My bad. I'll try to keep it down." My vicious sarcasm evoked an odd reply from Alice.

"I got here a hundred years after they did. So..." Her sentence trailed off, assumedly because her attempt at humor didn't help the situation. Kara sighed.

"Look, we need to get this information back to Aerael. Krystal and a few others can help me come up with a good plan."

"Can we stop by my apartment first? I'd like to pack my things so I can move down to the city completely." I sounded aggravated, but Kara seemed pleased at the request.

Sorrow

"Yeah, of course. Alice?" Alice nodded, turning onto a different road to go to the apartment I planned on leaving behind.
"Sorry. I just...need a few minutes to process this."
"It's fine, Jalix. I completely understand. We'll drop you off, head back to the city, and I'll send someone to pick you up in a few hours. Alright?"
"No, I'll bring the SUV over to the frame store and come down there myself. But thank you." I looked over at Kara, a faint appearance of disappointment haunting her beautiful complexion. "Hey…" I whispered. She looked up at me. "It's not you. It's this whole…thing. Alright? I dealt with becoming one of you, and I seem to be handling that correctly. I just needed time. Same with this. I just need to think it over for a few minutes. Who knows, maybe I'll get a good idea or two." We both chuckled, knowing that I wouldn't be able to formulate a plan on my own.
"Jalix." Val turned around in his seat again to look at me. "No more secrets. Alright? That was all we had. We didn't tell most people what we just told you. You are now just as informed…hell, more so than I am. You got into that lab. We didn't. You're one of us now, a hundred percent." He paused as I nodded. "I mean, not saying it's going to be easy, or that there won't be more surprises, but they won't come from us, if we can help it." He clapped me lightly on the shoulder before returning to his seat. "You okay?" He asked Alice, putting a hand on her thigh. She sighed and nodded silently. "You know I love you, right?" Alice bit her lip, the preemptive redness of tears forming. "I love you, too." She removed a hand from the steering wheel and put it atop his. The image was sweet, and not something I expected to see from Val. Kara smiled gently and leaned into me, realizing we were on the road leading to my apartment.
"Be safe on your way back, okay? Driving is going to feel a little different."

"You know I will. I always am." I kissed her forehead as the car slowed to a stop outside the apartment building. I didn't wait at all, instead choosing to open the door immediately and leave the car without looking hurried.

"I definitely need some time to myself." I whispered as the vehicle drove away. Climbing the steps in front of me, I was trying hard not to repeatedly go over the images in my head from the lab. Over and over again, I saw in my mind the careful regeneration of the eye, Raven's crooked smile, my hand pinning her throat to the wall, the massive steel doors of the vault.

Sighing, I took the key ring from my suit pocket and opened the door to my apartment, immediately smelling Kara's rosy perfume. It was more fragrant than before, the subtle notes of lavender and simple sugar reminding me of our first dates. It immediately calmed me, helping to improve my focus on the task at hand. I set my keys on the table and closed the door behind me, heading straight for the bedroom. Opening the closet, I saw the suitcases we had packed for the honeymoon, empty and clean.

"How did she..." I didn't finish the sentence, instead choosing to shake my head and assume that Kara was simply that talented. I started removing clothes from the hangars in my closet, throwing them in the largest of suitcases and muttering to myself. "Manages to drag me a couple hundred miles, into an underground city filled with superhumans *and* manages to bring the luggage. Good pick, Jalix. You lucky bastard." The last of my shirts were thrown into the suitcase unenthusiastically, and the bag was zippered shut. The closet still held my tuxedo, as well as its accompanying accessories, since I assumed I wouldn't need them any time soon. I stepped into the bathroom, pausing to look at Kara's piano.

"I never thought I'd end up here. With the man I love."

Sorrow

Her words played through my mind, granting me a soft smile as I gathered my razor and shaving cream, placing them into a travel bag and moving back to the bedroom.

"I guess this is it, apartment." I sighed, looking around. Small pictures of the two of us littered our nightstands and dressers, reminding me of far simpler times. I heaved the suitcase onto the floor and rolled it into the living room. Looking back at the apartment, I briefly pondered whether or not I should take anything else before opening the door and setting my suitcases outside.

"I'm going to have to pay my rent..." I muttered to myself as I locked the door. "Even though I won't be living here." The wheels on the suitcase noisily rolled down each cement step as I made my way back to the parking lot. I pressed the button on my SUV's remote, unlocking it and prompting a quiet chirp. The door to the back seats flew open when I grabbed the handle, nearly jerking it off its hinges. "Right. Super strength. Gotta work on that." I hefted the suitcase into my backseat, closing the door gently and moving to the driver's seat. The engine started up easily, despite being left sitting for several days. Testing Kara's theory of driving being different, I gently shifted into drive and touched my foot to the pedal. The vehicle moved forward a few inches and I automatically saw what she meant. Rather than my eyes focusing on where the car should be going, my vision picked up everything around me, all moving at the same speed and clearly visible. My peripheral vision was almost flawless.

"Okay. Drive slow, then." Very carefully, I pressed harder on the gas and eased the vehicle onto the road. Driving wasn't more difficult, but it felt slower and more deliberate. I felt each small movement of the wheel as I turned the corner and pulled up to a stop sign. The buildings to my left were detailed in my vision, despite the fact that I was looking straight ahead. The scene to my right was a bit harder to see, the distance between my head and the window creating a barrier for my eyesight. It was almost over-stimulating to my eyes.

Weaver

Looking to my right just to be sure there wasn't an oncoming vehicle, I passed through the intersection and moved two blocks ahead, stopping at another sign.
"Damn, I *do* need my tuxedo. I'm getting married." I lightly tapped the steering wheel in frustration, not wanting to break it. Sighing, I looked behind me to see if I could turn around.
"Looks like I'm going ba-" I had a split second of thought when I was thrown into the frame of the car, hitting my head violently.
Goddamn it, not again.

Tourniquet
    Kara

The city was unusually empty, catching me off-guard as I left the training room and entered he main hall. A few men stood outside Archangel chatting idly and staring at a television, but the hall was otherwise vacant.

"Yeah, we just got back." Alice continued. She put a hand on her hip, holding the phone to her ear and listening to Krystal halfheartedly. "Okay, fine. But hurry up and get over here. This is important." She hung up and replaced the phone in her pocket, shaking her head.

"She'll be out in a minute."

"Do I want to know?" I asked, knowing the answer. She shook her head.

"Do *I* want to know?" Val asked.

"She's in the shower."

"Doing what?"

"Showering!"

"Oh."

"Pig." Alice muttered, gently pushing an elbow into his ribcage.

"Well, if she's just showering, why wouldn't Kara want to know?" He defended.

"Because she doesn't *care*. We have bigger things to worry about than what Krystal is doing at the moment."

"Which, just to clarify, is soaping herself up." A much harder elbow was thrown into the same spot on his side. He groaned and took a step away from her, hunching over.

"Yeah, I deserved that."

"Damn right, you did. It's gross. That's my sister."

"Your hot sister." He flinched as soon as the words came out of his mouth, taking several steps away as the tips of Alice's hair began to smoke and smolder. "Alright! I'm kidding. I mean, I'm not, but I'm just messing with you." Alice took a deep breath, closing her eyes and slowly containing the waves of heat rolling off her body.

"Val...one of these days, she's going to kill you. And I'm going to watch." I said, smiling.

"Yeah, thanks, big sis. I appreciate the sentiment." Val looked up as one of the men broke away from the nightly news to walk toward us. After a moment, I realized it was Jared. "Hey, man!" Val called, standing up a bit straighter. He waved a massive hand at us as he approached, looking around.

"Where is everybody? Did Jalix decide not to stay?" He asked, his massive frame towering over my own.

"He's getting his stuff from the apartment, bringing it down. He's moving in."

"Great! And Alice, where's your hot sister?"

"See!" Val exclaimed, pointing at him. "It's not just me!"

"She's currently showering."

"She's currently not." Krystal's voice echoed from across the hall. She emerged from the living areas, holding a small towel and vigorously drying her hair as she approached. "Sup, guys? How'd the little pow-wow end up? Is he dead yet?"

"I'm going to pray you mean Schillinger, and no. I was waiting for you so I could explain the entire situation." Alice walked up to Krystal and placed her hands on the mess of wet blue hair. Closing her eyes, waves of steam emerged from between her fingers, and after a moment, Krystal's hair was dry.

"Hey. Thanks." She tossed her wet towel to Jared, who caught it and looked at it confusedly.

"The hell you want me to do with this?"

"I have no idea. Cry into it later when I emasculate you in the ring. Anyway, Kara. Update me."

I turned to Alice as our resident expert, who spoke up after a moment.

"Raven is a Vampyre. Schillinger must have converted her. They both are experimenting with the virus. They've had some success, but they need a sample of a different strain to complete their research. Their big project is bringing back the dead. They want to engineer the virus to revitalize dead flesh instead of just regenerate damaged tissue. They also, apparently, have a device that can copy the signals in your brain and store your memories, experiences, and knowledge. That way, whatever they're waking up isn't brain-dead." Krystal sat in stunned silence for a moment, cocking an eyebrow.

"Is that all?" She asked quietly, running her hand through the newly dried mess of chin-length hair. "Damn, girl. Way to give me split ends. Anyway..." She sighed, looking at the ceiling. "It kinda figures. Their mission statement is basically to spread the virus to the human race. Is it contagious yet? Airborne?"

"No, not from what we can tell. They don't want it spreading before it's ready." Without warning, Krystal furrowed her brow and looked behind me, then at the rest of the group.

"Where's the boy toy?"

"Fiancé...Krystal. And he's at our apartment gathering his things."

"He's actually staying. Hmm." She smirked, as if something was amusing to her.

"So let me get this straight." Jared started. "The bad guys are now as badass as we are?"

"No. They're still operating very low profile. They don't want to be noticed yet. Everything is privileged, secret, classified, whatever. They're the same as before...right?" Alice looked at me near the end of her sentence, unaware of what happened between Val, Schillinger, and myself.
"We met with him. We knew it was...almost a neutral ground. If they killed us, they would have had to kill Jalix, and he's still the focus of the media right now. There would be too many questions. We figured it was a safe bet, so we took the chance. He hasn't changed. He wants us gone or on his side. But either way, he's going to stop at nothing until we're no longer a threat."
"So what, you guys just talked about the weather? What did he say, exactly?" Krystal inquired, now genuinely interested. My teeth clenched inadvertently, the memories still to fresh to ignore.

***

"I guess I'll see you later." His voice was nervous, and I could tell by his facial expression that he didn't want to leave me. For the sake of keeping up appearances in front of Raven, I kissed him on the cheek quickly and turned back to Val.
"Off they go, I guess." I said quietly, the other group now busied in conversation across the room.
"Shall we?" Schillinger said, extending an arm towards his office. I nodded, taking the lead in front of Val. We took several steps before he opened the door, exposing a very large, posh office space.
"Your money's been kind to you." I said coldly, taking a few steps toward his desk. His computer sat on the floor, the back exposed under his desk. Discreetly, I ran a hand over the storage drive in my hidden pocket.
"Yes, well, when you help so many people, karma is often kind." He closed the door to his office and turned to us, speaking directly at me.

"Helping people? In the short term, I can see it. In the long term? You want to force these people to be your slaves."

"Slaves?" He said incredulously. "No, I do not, Miss Sorrow. I want to unite this world. I want our race to stand as one."

"Don't call me that." I hissed, gritting my teeth. Val stood protectively by my side, flinching every time Schillinger or I spoke.

"Calm down, Valterius, this is a business meeting. There will be no confrontation here. And we all know it." He paused, taking a seat in his luxurious leather office chair and uncapping a crystal decanter of alcohol. "Don't we?"

Val reluctantly took a step away from me, gazing out of one of the only two windows in the room. We were silent for a moment, playing a game of psychological chess. He was right, there would be no confrontation. It would be too matched of a fight between the three of us, and I was sure he had an alarm system to alert his guards. Leaving the situation immediately would imply that we were too weak to make a stand against him. Asking him to change his mind would have been as futile as asking the same of a brick wall. So, for a moment, we were at a standstill. He knew what I was going to say, and I knew his response.

"Mr. Kane doesn't know about me yet, now does he?" He asked, catching me by surprise. Despite my attempt to hide the reaction, he was far too wary to let it slip past his vision. "Ah, so he doesn't. Perfect. And no doubt he has no idea about my daughter."

"Raven?" Val asked, looking back at me.

"Yes, I decided that if she were to truly join my side, she would need to understand what we are. Not to worry, I have specifically instructed her on what to show them, what to tell them, and that they will not be harmed in the slightest. Under fear of death."

"You're that much of a coward that you would kill your own daughter if she took a kill from you? Or would you have your thug puppet, Kilkovf do your dirty work? You're sick." I took a step toward him, standing directly in front of his desk.

Weaver

"I am sick, miss Sorrow." He stood up and turned around, facing the other window in the room. Rapidly, I withdrew the device and silently pushed the cable into the computer, standing back up in one fluid motion. "I'm sick of watching the world...die."

"How characteristic. Facing the window and telling us about how you're not that bad, you're just misunderstood. Right?" Val sneered, mocking his theatricality.

"I should not be misunderstood, Valterius. My motives are clear, and I stand behind the actions I have taken to accomplish my task."

"Like trying to kill my people?" I hissed.

"I gave you an offer long ago, Sorrow. I told you: if your people wish, they may join the new iteration of this world. Free from hiding, free from prosecution. And free from being hunted. It is, quite undoubtedly, the most generous offer I could possibly make you. You, instead, choose to keep your...dysfunctional family...pitted against me."

"Because you're not giving the humans any choice! You're going to force them to change into us!"

"They are...one of us, Sorrow. Don't you understand?" He turned to face me, taking a drink from the glass in his hand. "We...are...human. We're just sick."

"Tell them that once they can't come back from this...disease." He smiled, turning back toward the window.

"They won't want to come back. They're not being forced, they just don't know that they want it, yet. You act like I'm going to kill them. In fact, I'm going to keep them from dying. Once they're all...a bit smarter...less emotional...racism, religious prosecution, borders...they're going to disappear. And our world will be united."

"And what then? What happens when everyone lives forever? Our planet dies. We live miserably. Doomed to an eternal existence, we slowly decay into machines with no will to live."

"I plan to fix all of that." He returned curtly.

"How? How can you fix that? It hasn't even been half a millennia and I've tried to kill myself countless times." I cringed at the thought, but successfully maintained my composure.

"When we have control over the virus, we can...thin the herd, so to speak, at will. Every few centuries or so, we replenish the world."

"Oh, so people live forever until you decide it's time for them to die? You're talking about the genocide of billions of people to avoid the deaths of billions of people. It's literally madness."

"It's life." He returned. "Don't you understand? It's systematic. No more chaos. No more infighting. The world will live at peace and die in peace. Would you rather they live in fear of their own mortality until it finally grips them?"

"You don't understand." I said quietly, trying to help him for the first time in my life. "You don't live with them. You don't see what I see. We really are just like humans. Just because we're smarter doesn't mean we live without emotion. It doesn't mean we don't have our own selfish wants and needs."

"Your...subclass of our race is a failed experiment. Our race wasn't meant to have emotions. That's a human element, and one I'm sure to eliminate."

"So you want us to live in peace, but not happiness?" He sighed heavily, swirling the glass in his hand and draining the majority of its contents into his sneering mouth. He remained facing the window, granting me an unforeseen opportunity. I quickly swept the device up from the back of his computer, hoping it had time to download the information I needed.

"This discussion is likening the explanation of atheism to a religious practitioner. You are deluded in your beliefs, and I am in mine, with neither of us knowing which is correct. But as always, we will war and the victor will be proven right or wrong in time."

"If you're comparing us to a human facet of existence, then why do you think this conflict will end in any less hostility?" Val returned. His statement took both of us by surprise, capturing our undivided attention. "If you think that this will end with one of us being wrong, then don't you think we can let the humans decide? We can present our race as an option to them. A choice."

"And they will abuse it as they've always done!" He spat, throwing his hands in the air. "Do you not see what I've done with the industry I created? I built an experiment. A worldwide experiment. I would provide a gift upon humanity. A medicine, a vaccine, something of the like. And I would give it to them freely. I would share it with the other medical institutions around the world. What have they done with it? They've sold it for their own greed. They make their own hospitals pay for medicine they need. They profit off the sick and weak."

"And Jalix is standing against that. He is proof that there are good humans out there. He convinced you to donate millions of dollars of vaccines to third world countries." He smiled broadly.

"And he's not human anymore, is he? In fact, I'm sure he told you that he's glad that you changed him. And why? Because he knows our race is the one made to rule this earth."

"No, he accepted it because he loves me." I argued.

"It's true." Val vouched. "I can tell he wouldn't have accepted it otherwise."

"And what has love ever done for humans? When reciprocated, it only lasts until death. When it doesn't, they kill themselves over it. Don't you see? You're proving everything I pursue to be correct."

"No. That's not true." I growled, looking into his watchful eyes. "You don't know because you've never felt it before. Love never dies. It doesn't vanish at the end of your life. It dies with you. If love is the last thing I ever feel, then I will have died happy. But if I had never felt it before...and died without ever being in its presence? Then I wouldn't say it was ever worth living."

"Then our game ends in a stalemate, my dear Sorrow. Logic can never win when pitted against emotion, because they're juxtaposed. But we will fight this war, my dear. I can assure you, we will fight heavily. And like I have always done, I will show you what your emotions can do for you. What little worth they have."

"Jalix will not die as long as I draw breath."

"You said the same in regards to your dear Sonya. How is she, by the way?"

"Her name is Samantha now...and she's recovering. She's back in the fight."

"And yet, she's a different person. As strong as our beloved affliction is, brain damage that strong is hard to overcome."

"But she did."

"Her body did." He rebutted, holding up a single finger. "But her mind did not. I know enough that, upon waking, she had no memory of you."

"You have no right!" I screamed, clenching my fist. The glass in his hand shattered, shards of glass cutting into his skin. He grinned, flexing his hand and holding it up for me to see.

"My beloved Sorrow. This is the metaphor of our conflict. My hand...heals. Because of what I am. And yet...your tears...remain. Because of who you are." The cuts on his hand vanished quickly, tiny sparkles of glass falling out of his wounds and onto his lap. I wiped the tears from my eyes and turned my back to him, hearing Jalix's low voice in the hall adjacent to the lobby.

"You and Raven are all that hold your legacy together. And you're both going to die."

"And you and Jalix are all that stands of your own cause. And I can assure you, you will see the end soon enough." My eyes widened, the tears in my eyes vanishing.

"And what about Jalix?"

"Jalix?" He laughed, standing and brushing the glass away from his suit. "I'm not going to bring death to your beloved. I'm going to show him what your cause stands for." He smirked, his eyes darkening, lowering to meet my own. "I am going to break him."

Weaver

***

"Nothing new. He tried explaining his cause again, trying to get us to empathize with him."
"Yeah, world domination usually gathers a pretty big following."
"You know what I mean, Krystal. He tried offering us a...twisted way out. Like he always has."
Val nodded thoughtfully, staring at the ground.
"It's almost worth taking up sometimes. You know? It's not right, but sometimes I wonder why *we* have to be the ones standing up for humans. Why they can't fend for themselves. Why we should have to sacrifice our lives and our happiness for them."
"Because we can, Val." Alice said, putting a hand on his arm. "We're the only ones actually capable of standing up for them. If we wait until Raven and Schillinger have the power they want, they're not going to give the world a choice. You can't exactly start a militia to fight a virus. And it would take humans...hell, it would take anybody decades to find a cure. Humans? Way longer. And by then, it wouldn't matter. We need to fight for them because they don't know the war exists."
"It's all a load of shit, Val." Krystal asserted, provoking glares from the rest of the group. "The truth is she feels bad it exists in the first place. It's basically survivor's guilt. I'm just along for the ride."
"Do you really believe that, Krystal?" I turned on her, growing angry.
"Hell yeah, I do. I fight for you, not a bunch of weak, whiny humans. They start rioting because of name-calling. Humans are the infant species of the world. Everything else has its shit together. You don't see tigers setting cars on fire because someone called it a leopard. Monkeys didn't start a war with mice because they believed in a different god. To be honest, I couldn't care less what happens to the

Sorrow

human race. If I have sex, drugs, and hard rock, I'm good to go. And I usually prefer if you're involved in any of the three with me."

"You think this is just a big joke, don't you?" The group took a step back as I confronted her, once again growing infuriated beyond the limits of my self-control. "I'm fighting to keep everyone here alive, and that includes you. So if you don't care about my cause, my fight, then you don't give a damn about me."

"Are you serious, Kara? I don't *care* about you? How many times do I have to throw myself at you for you to realize that I love you?"

"You *want* me, Krystal, that doesn't mean you love me. Once I told you I was yours, you'd get bored of me and throw me aside. I know you."

"You don't even know love! How dare you!" She screamed, her palm striking the side of my face. My pulse instantly lowered, preparing my body for a fight. I felt adrenaline course through my veins, tensing every muscle and sharpening my visual acuity to a razor-sharp deadliness. Knowing what was coming, I calmly turned around and started walking away.

"I'm not doing this, Krystal." I murmured, taking a step into the empty hall. My hands shook with rage, trembling uncontrollably. The back of my head bucked after being hit with a ball of snow and ice.

"Krystal, no." Alice stepped forward, but at the flick of my wrist was forcefully placed back in her position next to Val.

"Kara, please-" I pushed my hand in Jared's direction, sending him tumbling backwards as I descended on Krystal. Her eyes were fixed on mine, alight with a mixture of anger and adrenaline.

"Come on, Kara. You know you want it." She taunted, a grin smeared across her perfect pink lips. She cocked her arm back to swing at me, a move taking mere fractions of a second to occur. Before she could shift further, the sole of my boot was pressed into her ribcage, crunching the bones it contained into tiny, fractured pieces of nothingness. I pushed with everything I had, unleashing the full potential of my abilities, watching her limp body soar effortlessly into the concrete fortification behind her. Her back impacted first, sending her upper and lower halves crashing into the wall with a somewhat lessened force. Like shattered glass, pieces of the wall cracked and fell loose, tumbling with her body as she fell to the ground. I closed my eyes, trying to compel myself to stop. I knew she was broken, and I knew she wasn't getting back up, but everything in my body told me to end her.

"Krystal!" Alice screamed, sobbing. Val and Jared moved quickly alongside her in order to assess her condition. Alice's crying lifted me from my vengeance-fueled turmoil, and I immediately regretted what I had done. Sobbing hysterically, Alice put her fingers on Krystal's neck, searching for a pulse. Finding one, she began gingerly touching areas of Krystal's body, judging the extent of the damage I had done. "V-Val...help me c-carry her..." Val wrapped his arms around Krystal's frame with the utmost of care, lifting simultaneously with Alice. I stood, horrified, as her limp body contorted in ways it shouldn't have. Making their way down the hall, Jared ran in front of them in order to make sure no one got in the way. As if in a trance, I followed them, the revulsion and shock of my actions haunting every step I took toward the infirmary.

Jared pushed open the massive glass doors, creating an opening large enough for Alice and Val to move through. He let the door close and ran in behind them, vanishing into a care room. I followed slowly behind, unwelcome in my own mind. I turned the corner to the room and leaned against the doorframe, nauseous and cringing at Alice's panicked yelling.

"Val, h-hand me the IV b-bag!" Alice quickly retrieved a needle from the nearby drawer and slid it into Krystal's arm, opening the small refrigerator seconds later. She retrieved several bags of blood, neatly contained in clearly marked bags. She closed her eyes and clutched them to her chest for a moment, crying and warming them to meet

Sorrow

Krystal's body temperature. Val moved a pole to Krystal's side and hung the IV with care, trying his best to help.

"What can I do?" He asked, kneeling down to her level.

"I n-need my tools." He nodded and sprinted out of the room, taking care not to touch me on the way out. Alice connected another needle to Krystal's arm and attached one of the bags of blood, hanging it on the pole. Retching, I turned around and leaned over, seeing the shadow of Val's frame whirl past me again. Alice stammered, issuing instructions to Val and Jared while I fought back the same sobs Alice suffered from. I bit my lip and rounded the corner, watching Alice remove Krystal's shirt. Her ribcage was crumpled like a piece of foil, caved in at the center and grotesquely mutilated. Alice struggled to maintain a modicum of composure, sliding a scalpel along Krystal's bare chest. Val hid his discomfort to the best of his ability, but cringed as Alice pulled back her skin and revealed the damage underneath. Taking a deep breath, Val handed her a pair of long tweezers, watching Alice work.

Each piece Alice touched invoked a quiet groan or a sob, adjusting each shard back into its place. She worked quickly, taking only a few seconds per rib, watching as they slowly began to fuse together. Her breastbone was pushed deep into her chest, and Alice worked delicately to avoid the pieces surrounding her heart. I looked closely, trying to ensure that none had punctured anything critical. She was breathing raggedly and unevenly, her unconscious body scarcely holding onto life.

"How...Kara?" Jared asked simply, unable to find any other words. I shook my head, tears streaming down my face.

He turned back to watch Alice work, retrieving pieces of bone that were embedded in the flesh of her chest. A shuddering sigh marked her completion, gently placing the folds of skin against her frame and letting the virus seal them together. She again reached to Krystal's neck, checking for any sign of life. Her head bowed and she let out a massive sigh, shuddering with sobs. I could faintly see the artery in Krystal's neck pulsate with the indications of life.

"Alice." Val gestured, pointing to Krystal's head. The back of her skull was dripping with blood at a steady rate, running off the table and pooling on the floor.

"I h-have to wait until h-her ribcage is healed. I c-can't turn her over to work on it."

"Is she stable enough that we can hold her upright? Jared and I?"

"Y-Yeah. Yeah, let's do that." She sniffled and stood up, pulling a massive syringe from the same drawer that she retrieved her other needles. "Once I...put the pieces back into place, I n-need to give her this. It'll ease the p-pain if she wakes up."

"Can't you sedate her?" I whispered, hardly able to speak. My face was wet with tears, cold and unwelcome as I spoke.

"I can, but m-my solutions are in the other room."

"I'll go get them." I turned the corner without hesitation, running to the cabinet at the end of the hall. Not bothering to unlock it, I threw the doors open and looked over its contents. A single shelf clearly held a series of sedative, so I grabbed an armful and ran back into the room. Gently, I placed them on the counter and stood back. Val and Jared were holding Krystal's body upright, her top half uncovered, attempting to keep her as still as possible. Alice's hand was on the back of Krystal's head.

"Okay." She whispered, taking several deep, rapid breaths in succession. Groaning, she shifted her hand and a large chunk of bone moved into place with an audible crunch. I turned away to avoid vomiting, but found myself thrown back against the doorframe when Krystal emitted an unearthly scream. I had never heard anyone scream with as much pain as she felt in that moment, completely agonized and fully awake. Her eyes flew open, instantly flooded with tears. Her earsplitting screams echoed in the hall, unchecked by other noise. In a matter of moments, Alice had one of the large syringes

Sorrow

embedded in Krystal's neck, pressing the plunger with all the strength she had. Krystal's screams slowly turned into agonized weeping, then finally falling into silence. Val and Jared lowered her body slowly onto the table, each of them sliding onto the floor. Alice picked up another syringe and more softly pushed it into Krystal's arm, slowly allowing the medicine to flood her veins. She tossed the needle into the sink and leaned against Val, clutching her knees to her chest and crying quietly. Val shook his head slowly, refusing to say anything.
"I'm sorry." I whispered. "I'm so sorry."
"You know, maybe Schillinger was right, Kara. Look what your emotions do to people." Val condemned, stroking Alice's hair. I turned around, crying and running back into the main hall. I managed to make it a few feet outside the glass doors before I finally collapsed, curling into a ball next to the infirmary's entrance.
"Miss Sorrow, are you okay?" I heard a familiar voice call to me from my left, but I chose to ignore it, unsure of how to respond. I took a few breaths and tried to regain my composure, failing miserably.
"Miss?" The voice was close now, and identifiably Eric's. I saw his knee touch the ground as he knelt next to me, watching as if I was volatile.
"I'm fine, Eric. Please leave me for now."
"Forgive me, miss, but you're not fine." I sat up, wiping away my tears and looking into his eyes. He was genuinely concerned for my sake.
"I hurt Krystal. Badly. I almost killed her. I reacted...disproportionately to something she said." He nodded silently, absorbing the information.
"Krystal is a strong woman. I'm sure she'll recover in no time at all. And I'm also sure that you were not the one to provoke the conflict." I shook my head, keeping him from rationalizing my actions.
"It's not an excuse. I'm supposed to take care of you guys. Not break you. Not hurt you."

"Everyone has their weak moment, miss. We have things we love, and when those are threatened....well, I shouldn't have to tell you. You're leading a war because you love us. You, of all people, know how far some of us are willing to go for the ones we care about." He extended a hand to help me to my feet, and I reluctantly accepted it. "Things will work out just fine. How did the meeting with Raven go?"

"Oh. Here." I had forgotten about the data I had stolen from Schillinger's computer, retrieving the storage device from my pocket and handing it to him. "This is everything I could get." He smiled, taking the drive from my hand graciously.

"I'll get to work on this right away, ma'am."

"Eric, please, for the love of God, call me Kara." He turned away smiling, heading to his room.

"Yes, ma'am." I shook my head, unable to smile, and leaned against the wall heavily, sniffling and wiping away the remaining tears from my eyes. His words echoed in my mind, reassuring me of my doubts. *Krystal is a strong woman. I'm sure she'll recover in no time at all.*

"She's going to live." Alice's voice said quietly from several feet behind me. I spun around to look at her, standing alone in the doorway. "Val and Jared are going to watch over her for now. She's going to take days to wake up, and weeks to heal completely, but she'll recover fully in time."

"Alice, I'm so sorry-" A flood of apologies spewed from my mouth, but she turned her head and held up a single finger, indicating that she didn't want me speaking. I obliged and fell silent.

"You have some issues you need to work out, Kara. That response? Not normal. Not even close."

"I know, Alice. I'll talk to her as soon as she wakes up. I swear-"

"No, I didn't say *you two* have issues, I said *you* have issues. You need to...talk to me. You need to let out whatever you're feeling before it kills someone. Ever since you met Jalix, you've been sensitive. You're reacting too harshly to Krystal's normal behavior, and she doesn't deserve what you've been giving her. Why?" I shook my head, not knowing the answer.

"I don't know, Alice. I just feel...I feel like the stakes are higher now. Before, I was a soldier. I was just fighting for my cause. Now, I feel more like a person. I have my own reasons to win. And I haven't felt this way before."

"You're afraid because you're becoming more human. You're letting people get close to you, and that makes everything more complicated. But if you want to keep those people close, you have to deal with everything about them. Not just the good parts."

"I know."

"You're afraid because Krystal loves you." I looked up, confused.

"I'm not afraid, I'm...angry. I'm confused. I'm in despair because I can't give her what she wants."

"That's called being afraid, Kara. You're allowed to have fear. It's what separates us from people like Schillinger. You're losing sight of what divides the two of us."

"I'm never going to be like him."

"Kara, if all you're fighting for is your cause, and not the people behind it, you already have." I balled up my fist in anger, not at her, but at myself for realizing that she was right.

"I do love you. All of you. So much. It's just...I feel like Jalix does right now. I'm adapting to these new experiences. It's complicating my life, and I'm trying to untangle everything."

"I know. And that's why I forgive you for what you did to Krystal." Her words instilled a sense of euphoria, thankful I hadn't lost a friend. "And I know she will, too, in time. You just need to get a grip on things, reassess your situation, and move on. Lead us. We'll still fight for you. But we need to know that you're doing this for the right reason."

"Of course I am." I whispered, taking a step toward her and locking her in a tight embrace. She reciprocated the action, her warm body comforting against my cold skin.

"Kara!" A man called from down the hall, forcing me to pull away from Alice.

"Yes?" I called back, realizing it was one of the men from Archangel. His tone sounded anxious.

"You need to see this. Now." I looked at Alice, concern of equal magnitude haunting both our faces. We ran through the hall, stopping just in front of the small group as they pointed to the television. A large red banner indicated that this wasn't typical news, and I held my breath as the announcer spoke. A picture of Jalix's boss framed the right half of the screen, a male newscaster explaining the situation on the right.

"Motives for the attack were unclear, but police are investigating a recent visit to a Raven Biopharmaceutical lab, where sources say he was visiting to discuss the possibility of investment in some of their new projects." The screen disappeared, replaced by Schillinger surrounded by microphones and cameras. He spoke with calmness, a seemingly rehearsed story echoing in my ears.

"We are deeply sorry for the loss of Mr. Hartman, and will provide full cooperation in the police investigation of his death. Mr. Hartman was an invaluable asset to our company, and I considered him a close personal friend. A subdivision of my company will be conducting round-the-clock surveillance and additional security will be on all Raven premises. We fear that this attack may stem from competing companies searching for information on our new projects, and we expect to gain their full cooperation upon investigation into this matter. Thank you." Dozens of reporters began speaking at once, yelling questions as he retreated into the building. One of the questions was timed perfectly, resonating in a brief moment of quiet.

"What about the attack on Mr. Kane?" My heart missed a beat, the familiar nausea of the last few minutes creeping into my stomach once again. Schillinger turned around, a staged look of confusion on his face.

"Mr. Kane? I wasn't aware of any incidents regarding him." A different reporter spoke up, immediately following through with the questions.

"Sources say his vehicle was found along the road in an accident, and Jalix Kane is now missing. What do you have to say to that?" Schillinger paused, pretending to contemplate the scenario.

"As I said, I had no idea that our beloved Jalix was involved in any accident. We, of course, will provide as much information as we can in regards to these cases, and we hope that, in time, our company will be cleared of any accusations. We would never hurt our own." He disappeared into the building, the news flashing back to the anchor.

"As previously stated, federal police are now pursuing the death of CEO Gregory Hartman and the simultaneous missing person's case of executive Jalix Kane. Police say that there appears to be no correlation between the events, including the method of attack, but many are wondering if escaped convict Kilkovf Strevieg is behind Jalix Kane's disappearance. For those of you watching that aren't aware, he was recently arrested for attempting to *murder* Mr. Kane in cold blood at a casino in Pennsylvania. Only minutes after his arrest, he escaped custody, and an ongoing investigation is underway. For more information, be sure to log into our website and tune in at eleven...tonight."

"Jesus...Kara." Alice turned to me, placing an arm on my shoulder and looking between myself and the group of men standing in front of Archangel.

"Let's go get him." One of the men said, hitting another on the arm. I looked up, drained of emotion, staring at them confusedly. The three of them looked at me and nodded, the first man speaking up once

again. "It's gotta be Raven, right, ma'am? I say we go in and kick their asses. Take Jalix back."
"Hell yeah. It's about time we get to kill some of these bastards."
"No." I said softly, looking into Alice's bright green eyes. "I'm going alone." I turned around and started running to Eric's room. I knew he could help me get in.
"Kara, wait." Alice called, following closely behind me.
"I don't have time to wait, Alice! This just happened, and if I don't act now, then he's going to be…" I didn't finish the sentence, turning into the narrow hall by the living quarters and barging into Eric's open room.
"Hack, what have you got so far?"
"I saw what happened, ma'am, and I'm already on it. Raven took him, definitely." He pulled up some blurry images on the computer screen in front of him, too fuzzy to make any sense.
"These are bad quality, but they're pictures of the same van. They're marked as an industrial cleaning company, but the plate is registered to a vehicle in Pennsylvania. It was easy to keep track of. It ended up going straight to Raven. They kidnapped him." He sighed and opened a new window on the computer, playing a short video clip from a security camera. A massive white van barreled into Jalix's SUV, throwing his head and shoulders out of the driver's side window. Someone got out of the van, threw open his door, and dragged Jalix's limp body into the back of their vehicle, driving away in a matter of seconds.
"What can we do?" Alice asked, turning around as Tony walked into the room carrying a black bag.
"Alice, you're not going with me. You need to take care of Krystal, and I need to do this on my own."
"Sorry, ma'am, but I brought too many guns for one person." Tony's quiet, low voice mirrored his actions as he dumped half a dozen

silenced pistols, holsters, and accompanying magazines onto Eric's desk.

"Jeez, dude, trying to work here." Eric muttered, opening yet another picture on his screen. "Kara, this is what I came up with so far. That van is marked for a cleaning company that Raven hires round-the-clock. Since their labs are so sensitive, they have the areas that the cleaners aren't allowed to touch marked on a floor plan. It's not very detailed, and won't help you, but I was able to run an image search and found the same floor plan, made by the company's construction firm."

"Jesus, Hack. I only gave you that data a few seconds ago."

"None of this was from the data you gave me, miss. I tried to focus on Jalix's disappearance. Anyway, the plans aren't complete. There's this massive blank space in the heart of the building that they left out, probably to be constructed by a different company, in order to prevent exactly what we're trying to do now: find a way in that isn't the front door. I pulled up a satellite image of the building and compared it to the floor plan." He looked up at me from the computer. "They don't match up."

"And how does that help us?" I asked, picking up two of the weapons and accompanying holsters.

"Because the electricity for the building has another line. It's not uncommon for a lab to have two different electrical inputs into the building. One of them...runs behind the building, disappearing into the ground behind it."

"A back door." Alice said, picking up two of the same handguns that I did. "Raven said that if anyone left the lab without permission, the thing would blow up. They had these massive towers filled with sensors guarding the entrance to the lab. If a company is conducting illegal work, they want to sneak in their research, but they still have to make sure it's regulated. Those sensors have to be part of what that electrical line is powering. It's guarding their back door."

Weaver

"How do I get in?" I asked, leaning into the computer. I was beyond distress at this point, focusing on the fact that Jalix's rescue was entirely possible.

"I don't know. I can't even see a door. All I know is that their security was just tripled. I can use the data you gave me to try and mess with their alarms, delay them for a bit, but I can't do much else. You *will* be seen on the security cameras, and you *will* set off the alarm at some point. When that happens...there's nothing I can do." I turned to move away, but he grabbed my arm and looked into my eyes. "Kara, I won't tell you not to go. In fact, I think you should. But you need to understand that once you do this...there's no going back. This is going to throw us into an all-out war."

"I'm going to kill Schillinger, his little bitch daughter, Kilkovf, and anything else that gets in my goddamn way." I pushed off of Eric's chair, running for the door, but ran into Valterius on the way out. My head hit his chest with a considerable thump, knocking the both of us back several feet. Before I could say anything, he spoke up.

"I saw what happened, and I'm coming. Explain your plan on the way."

"Val, I don't have time to-" He looked over my head, catching two guns thrown to him by Alice and looking down into my eyes. "You're right, you don't. Let's go."

***

The light was fortunately to our advantage, the shadows of dusk masking everything but our silhouettes as we lay in the forest. The building was several hundred feet in front of us, with no clear indication of our objective. The only telltale sign indicating we were even close was the lone, large wooden pole marking the backup electrical line.

Sorrow

"How many people are outside?" Val asked, referring to my slightly superior eyesight. I could see a few shadows near the corner of the building, huddled together for warmth and noise concealment.

"I can only see three. In that group over there. Wait, there's one on the roof, too." I whispered, pointing to a shadow moving slowly across the top of the structure. "So four." Alice sighed, her breath creating rolling waves of mist that vanished into the dark night. I could faintly hear the guards talking, consumed in their idle conversation and unsuspecting of anything going wrong for them.

"What's our plan? There's no door on the back of the building. Where's our entrance?" Alice looked at me, knowing I didn't have the answer to her question yet.

"I say we go through the wall. I can take out the concrete." I asserted quietly.

"Yeah, and those alarms are going to go off instantly. I know you want to get him back, sis, but we need to be patient. If they wanted him dead, he wouldn't have been kidnapped." Val's words were an attempt at reassurance, but only managed to distress me further.

"Fine. What if we distract those three, then scale the wall and go in through the top of the building?" Alice shook her head, but didn't respond aloud.

"Goddamn tree roots digging into my side." Val grumbled, moving over several inches. "Things are massive." I shook my head and stared out at the open stretch of land between our tree line and the building. It was a well-kept field, with no cover whatsoever and only knee-high grass to hide behind.

"Wait. Val, the tree roots." I said, motioning for him to move aside. He looked at me as if I was crazy, complying with my request nonetheless. I wrapped my hand around the rough, dirty surface, feeling every inch of its belowground tendril. I slowly pulled with my mind, seeing in my head the path that the root took through the earth as the tendril quietly broke through the ground with a muffled crunch several feet in front of us. I watched as it erupted through the dirt in a fairly straight line for several yards before sharply veering to the right. I let go, a faint headache stemming in the back of my head. "It's underground." I whispered. "The door is a trapdoor, going straight down." Alice smirked, apparently amused by my brief ingenuity. "Think you can make a distraction?" She nodded, extending her hand toward an empty spot in the parking lot, remaining still for several seconds. After a moment, a small fire started in the distance, dancing and sparking its way between several cars. The security guards on the ground shouted and ran toward it while the one on the roof made his way to the front side of the building.

"Go." I whispered. The three of us stood, hunched over, and sprinted to where the tree root veered off to the side. Sure enough, an empty spot in the grass marked a steel door closed by an electronic keypad and heavy locking mechanism.

"Aw, hell. Now what?" Val groaning, laying in the grass on his stomach to avoid being seen. Alice grunted, the lock suddenly glowing a bright yellow hue. I looked at its shape and imagined my hands gripping the cool steel bar of the lock. Under my control, the soft metal gave way and tumbled into the hole below, hitting the ground underneath with a surprisingly quiet thud. Val jumped in first, grabbing the metal rungs of the ladder and sliding his way down. Alice followed him as I looked up, watching the guards search for the cause of the fire in the parking lot. Without warning, a massive explosion resonated from directly in front of the group, throwing them aside in a fiery burst of violence. Gingerly avoiding the hot metal, I climbed into the hole and made my way down, quickly descending the ladder. My feet met hard ground, and I looked at Alice.

"What the hell was that explosion?" I asked, prompting a shrug from both of them.

"That fire must have been underneath someone's gas tank." Alice offered. We looked around, the only feature of the tunnel in front of us being two large sensor towers, similar to the ones Alice described. "Hopefully Hack is doing his job." Val whispered, creeping toward them slowly. The hall was lit by red strips of faint light, only enough to highlight the walls with an ominous glow. I couldn't make out the typical red-green hue of infrared light emitting from either tower.
"I'm pretty sure they're off." I added, doing little to ease the tension.
"Well. Then unless you have some radioactive isotope in your pocket..." Alice whispered, strolling past Val and walking between the pillars. I cringed, waiting for a sound or alarm that never came. She gave a halfhearted twirl, her red hair swirling around her shoulders. Val sighed and moped his way over to her, clearly emasculated by her bold action. Smirking, I followed them through the hall, grabbing Alice's shoulder gently and prompting her to stop.
"What do you remember from this place?"
"I don't know anything about this part. Raven never showed us the full length of the hallway that the labs were in. I'm going to assume that we're right behind it, but until we get there, I have no way of knowing for sure." With yet another unhelpful response, she peered around the corner, sighing and turning back to us. "I think I'm right. There's a camera in the corner, but I can take care of it. And there's another door. Bigger than the one we came though." I nodded, glancing over at Val.
"Ready?"
"Hell yeah. Let's go kick-"
"Ah, not yet. Until we're discovered, we're silent. Got it, Val?" He disappointedly nodded. A quiet snap of Alice's fingers preceded the three of us rounding the corner and confronting the massive steel door she mentioned. A soft pile of melted plastic hung from a tangled mass of wires on the ceiling.
"Told you I'd take care of the camera."

"Yeah, great, now let's focus on the door. And be careful. We have no idea where Jalix is, and I don't want to end up catching him on fire."
"I'm not my sister. I have a little bit more self-control."
"Tell that to the car you blew up." Alice rolled her eyes at Val and pressed her hands against the hinges of the door. Slowly, they glowed with a dim orange heat, rippling waves of warm air quickly heating the small tunnel we were in. Val and I grabbed the steel bars on the door, heaving with all of our strength and tearing it from its hinges. Gently, we lowered the massive construct onto the ground and stood back up, brushing the small pieces of concrete off our clothes. Alice stared into the hall in front of her, eyes wide and mouth agape.
"What is…" I looked to where her gaze indicated to find a scientist standing in a plastic garment, alarmed by our presence.
"Shh." I held up a single finger to my lips, slowly approaching the individual. "We're not going to hurt you if you cooperate. I'm just looking for my fiancé."
"He's on the other side of the building, down the hall, through the next door, and in the machine lab." The voice was muffled and quiet, but clear in its answer. The three of us stood in shock for a moment, stunned in disbelief.
"What?" Val asked.
"You're trying to save him, right? He's a good guy. They never should have brought him here."
"Wait, why are you helping us?" I interjected, looking around for a trap.
"You have to help us. Please. Let us leave with you. I don't know how you got in, but you can get us out."
"Wait, you don't want to be here?" Alice inquired, stepping forward. The scientist gingerly lifted the plastic seal around their neck, exposing a thin rubber collar marked with a red dot.

"We're trapped. We're not allowed to leave the labs. And if we don't meet our demands, they threaten to use us for their project. That's where we get most of our organic samples."

"Oh, my god..." Alice whispered, inspecting the collar. The name Tammy was written in poorly scrawled pen, along with a lengthy number. I had nothing to say, stunned and silent.

"Get back in your lab." Val mumbled.

"What? Val, we can't leave them here-"

"And we won't. But if they try to make a run for it, and they manage to set off the alarms, we won't have time to save Jalix." He turned to the scientist again. "Go back into your lab. Seal the door, and wait for us. We won't be long." She bowed her head, nodding slowly and walked over to one of the doors, closing it and sealing the lock. She didn't move, staring at us through the glass window. Val turned to the open hallway and kept walking, leaving Alice and I behind. I caught up to him quickly, touching his arm to get his attention.

"Are we really coming back for them?"

"Well, we have to come back this way. We'll get shot if we try to run *around* the building back to the car. So, yeah. We can grab them on our way out. Until then, they stay put." As we walked by the remaining labs, the researchers were occupied in their own studies, facing the tables away from the windows.

"This is the second door." Alice whispered, moving around a stack of wall lockers and bins filled with lab coats. "There should be two guards outside, and two more sensors." I nodded, inspecting the exit for exploitable weaknesses. "I've got this one. Just be ready to move."

"Wait, what?" Val hissed as Alice punched a long number into the keypad on the door. The lock beeped twice, and a pneumatic hiss emanated from the hinges, but the door didn't open.

"What's your name?" A husky voice called from the far side of the door.

"It's Tammy." Alice said weakly. "I have something that they need to see. A breakthrough."
"What are the codes on your research items?" The voice demanded. Alice shook her head, looking at us confusedly. I shrugged, along with Val. "I just have my notebook." She offered quietly.
"Oh, alright. Make it quick, I'm setting the door to close in five minutes, and you know what happens if you're not inside." The voices outside all chuckled, and it certainly sounded like more than two. I glared briefly at Alice, informing her that I wasn't happy with the confrontation so early. Another hiss radiated from the door, spinning the locking mechanism and beginning to open. I moved to the left side of Val, closest to the opening of the door. I didn't plan to leave anyone alive for them to take care of. Light crept in from the other side of the door, illuminating the silhouette of two men with their backs facing me. I didn't hesitate, lunging through the door and snapping the first one's neck. Instinctively, I threw my foot outward, catching the guard to my right directly in the stomach. His body armor was apparently soft, and crumpled along with most of his organs. My pulse pounded once in my ears, telling me too much time had already passed. One of them started to shout something, interrupted by his friend's body impacting him with the force of a freight train and slamming them both unconsciously into the wall. The remaining guard unclipped a radio from his vest, attempting to call for help. Before he could make a sound, I had him by the throat and pinned against the wall. Alice's familiar blaze of heat rounded the corner and sighed, standing behind me and looking down the long hall to our front.
"Dammit, Kara, leave one for us."
"Jalix. Where is he? I demanded, tightening the grip I had around the sides of his neck, causing him pain, but allowing enough air in his lungs to tell me the information I needed.

Sorrow

"The machine lab...down the hall." My hand tightened again, and looking away from his eyes, I kept the breath he struggled to gain from entering his lungs. Very little time passed before he fell limp, the weight of his body resting against my wrist. I let him fall, sliding down the wall quietly and onto the floor.

"I know where that is." Alice whispered, maintaining a view of both directions of the hall. "It's about halfway between here and the front of the building. I can guarantee they have mountains of guys in the lobby, but probably not too many between us and Jalix."

"That's great, but we need to move." Val hissed, grabbing both of us by the arm and moving down the hallway. "Didn't you hear that guard? That door we just came through closes in five minutes."

"And it'll probably set off the alarm if it's still open by then." I concluded, maintaining a steady pace alongside him. We passed row upon row of sealed doors, none with windows or markings indicating what was occurring within. "Can't we cut through any of these labs? Take a shortcut?" I asked Alice, shaking her head.

"No. Raven said each of these rooms is sealed off independently. They even have their own air supply. They're isolated." Gritting my teeth at the answer, I stopped at a corner and peered around the wall, taking extreme care to expose as little of my body as possible.

"It's empty." I whispered, seeing the walls fade from concrete to finished wood. "We must be close."

"It shouldn't be like this, Kara. Hack said they tripled their security."

"And you said yourself they're probably all gathered in the lobby. Or investigating the explosion in the parking lot, for that matter. Who cares? He's close, and once we take him, we can leave." They were both clearly unsettled by my haste, likely believing that I was sacrificing my sense of situational awareness.

He's close. Just keep moving.

I rounded the corner and ducked underneath the first window, carefully peering inside. The lab was empty and the lights off,

assumedly because the researchers in that particular lab were allowed to go home. Alice and Val stood at the corner, watching for danger. I shook my head at them, indicating that it wasn't the right one. Val caught up to me, leaving Alice behind on her own.
"I told her to stay and watch our backs." He whispered. "I'll take the lead. As soon as I see the lab, I'll let you know. The second you break in, I'll keep the guards off of you while you drag Jalix back to the car."
"Val, no. If you get trapped-"
"We don't have time to argue. It's already been close to two minutes, and we need to make it through that door if we want Jalix back alive. Just follow my lead." He looked down the hall, judging the distance to the next large window. "You doubt me too much, sis." He said with a smile, sprinting to the next lab and crouching to avoid being seen.

In the same way I did, he craned his neck to view the contents of the room, shaking his head before moving on. My heart pounded, my eyes transfixed on the end of the hallway, waiting for a patrol of armed guards to round the corner. I looked back at Alice, visibly distressed by Val's massive lead in front of me. The hundred feet between us felt like miles. Leaning slowly, he looked through the subsequent window in front of him, quickly sitting back down and sighing. He nodded at me. Despite the excellent self-control I maintained over my own body, I couldn't keep my heart from racing, viciously beating against my skin and threatening to break loose. I tore through the corridor, sliding into place alongside him and taking several breaths.
"He's in there, breathing and alive. He's inside the machine, but it doesn't look like he's connected to it or anything. He's just lying there, asleep or something. But there's wires hooked up to the window. It's going to set off the alarm." I nodded, refusing to say anything for a moment.
"Two minutes." I said, the adrenaline surging into the muscles in my legs.

Sorrow

"Two minutes." He smiled, leaping up and jamming his fist into the masonry of the wall. He tore away a massive chunk of stone, nearly as large as my body, and heaved it through the glass, much thicker than I had initially anticipated. I pounced, tumbling through the pieces of broken window and crashing into the machine ungracefully. Instantly, the alarm sounded with a blaring resonance. I leapt up and looked at the machine, the only exposed part of Jalix being his legs. I grabbed him carefully and pulled, dragging his body out of the plastic tunnel that surrounded him. He was either unconscious or drugged, his eyes fluttering and his breathing slow. I gingerly slapped him on the face repeatedly, yelling at him to wake up.
"Jalix! Jalix, you need to wake up, now!" My efforts were to no avail, disheartening me even further as gunshots rang out in the hall. I put my hands on the piece of concrete, throwing it into the hall and holding it steady with my mind. Several loud crunches and cracks were the result of a barrage of bullets impacting its surface.
"Thanks!" Val called lightheartedly. I hoisted Jalix onto my shoulders, one hand between his legs and the other holding his arm.
"Val, is it safe to come out?" I called, screaming over the sound of gunfire.
"Depends on your definition of safe!" He yelled back.
"Val!"
"Yes, go!" I jumped over the short divider between the rooms, taking care not to trip over the remaining pieces of glass stuck in the window frame. Val had the piece of concrete in his hands like a shield, huddling behind it for safety.
"Val, hurry up!" I called over my shoulder as he began to fall behind. He groaned loudly, indicating that he was doing the best he could. Alice moved from around the corner, searing hot orbs of flame in her hands. I moved to the side, allowing her to throw them on either side of Val, catching two of the guards in their legs. They screamed, falling behind as Val picked up his pace.

"Let's go!" Alice shouted, leading the front of the group. The walls again transformed into concrete, the familiar doors of the labs passing us by. Val was still fifty yards behind me, struggling to remain a barrier between the guards and ourselves.

"Val, come on!" I looked over my shoulder as the massive steel door came into view, hanging open to reveal the locker room. Alice sprinted inside, once again preparing a blazing flame for her attack. I stopped at the corner between the hallway and the locker room, watching Val slowly creep toward us, his back moving to us inches at a time.

Without warning, several of the guards screamed and the gunfire stopped, creating a tense silence unlike any I had ever experienced. Val looked back at us slowly, the block of concrete he held dropping a few inches. I saw past his head, watching Schillinger step over the bodies of his men and advance toward him.

"Val!" I screamed, pointing. He looked back as the chunk of concrete in his hands exploded, knocking him off his feet.

"Alice, take Jalix!" I yelled, offering his limp body to my friend. She stepped back quickly, holding up her hands.

"I can't, I'm too hot! I'd kill him!" A deafening hiss erupted from the door, the massive steel structure beginning to close behind me.

"No..." I whispered, looking back at Val. His eyes met mine, Schillinger now only a short distance from him.

"Go! I can take him! Get out of here!" He waved a hand at me and leapt up, striking Schillinger in the face.

"Val!" Alice screamed, stepping toward the door. I pushed myself through the narrow opening, sealing the three of us into the locker room. "No!" She screamed at me, pounding against the door with her fists.

"Alice, we have to go! He can get out, but if we go back for him, we're all dead!" She sobbed once, punching the door a final time and sprinting down the hall we came from. The windows that lined the hall were filled with the faces of researchers, begging us to let them out. I let go of Jalix long enough to search for a handle on one of the doors, my pursuit revealing no such thing.

"They're locked..." I whispered, looking at Alice. "They're sealed in. You have to melt the door."

"I don't have time, this place is going to collapse in seconds!" She looked through the windows in horror before sprinting away once again. Knowing there was nothing I could do, I followed closely behind her. Their panicked, desperate screams echoed down the hall, muffled by the doors that separated us. As we passed, some of them were silent, calmly watching us leave without them.

"I'll go up first." Alice said, stepping onto the ladder. A muffled blast echoed down the hall, accompanied by a wave of heat and low rumbling. "Val!" She screamed, releasing her grip on the ladder. I pushed her back onto it, forcing her to move upwards.

"He got out!" I yelled, not knowing if it was the truth. "Now it's our turn!" She climbed the ladder in seconds, extending a hand to reach for Jalix. I lifted him above my head, releasing him to Alice's strong hands. Looking back, I placed my foot on the bottom rung of the ladder, listening to a deafening rumble spit dust and debris into my face. I climbed without thinking, the heat beginning to sear my skin and singe my hair. My face breaching the gap into open air, I gulped in a huge breath. Alice had Jalix's body slung over her shoulder, sprinting with all her might to the car parked in the forest. I pulled myself through the hole, running into the tree line. I paused, looking back to watch the building crumple awkwardly, one side of the structure caving in more than the other, and all of it sinking into the ground.

"Kara, come on!" She yelled, reaching the vehicle. She threw open the door and stuffed Jalix into the backseat, sitting him upright and fastening his seatbelt. I walked backwards, searching for any sign of life leaving the building.

Weaver

Alice joined me by my side, watching as the rubble went still, creating another deafening silence that hung in the air like a low cloud. My eyes roamed over the parking lot, the adjacent road, and the surrounding field, and saw no movement other than settling dust. It was impossible to tell whether or not Alice tried to speak; her hand was over her mouth and hoarse sobs echoed from her throat.

"No, Alice. He's not…He can make it…" The pounding in my chest refused to cease. I stood completely still, inspecting every inch of fallen timber, every block of fallen stone, waiting for the moment I would see him crawl his way out. Sirens echoed in the distance, clearly in reaction to the triggered alarm.

"Val!" Alice screamed, her voice reverberating through the chill air. I watched for a response that never came. Slowly, my throat began to close up, impairment in my eyes and in my own head beginning to overtake me.

"Alice…" I croaked, pushing her forcibly into the passenger seat. "We have to go. We can't let the police find us. But they can find him." Tears trickled across my cheeks freely. "And when they do, we'll just rescue him, okay? And we'll bring him back." As if I was speaking to the pile of rubble that sprawled in front of us, I received no response. Her face was buried into the dashboard, her incomprehensible crying smothering every attempt she made to speak. I shook my head, fighting against the will to lie on the ground and wait for my brother. My body moved itself to the driver's seat, my fingers moving familiarly to the steering column and starting the engine.

"Please don't leave him." She whispered, leaning her head into my shoulder.

"I'm coming back for him." I ran a hand through her hair, turning off my headlights as the police swarmed into the scene, sirens and lights exploding in a shower of sensory bombardment.

Sorrow

Within

Jalix

The heat was something I had grown accustomed to over the last few years, blistering waves of up to a hundred and twenty degrees rolling through the summers of Afghanistan. Thankfully, today was one of the few cooler days, and even at noon, decided to linger at eighty degrees.
"I'm almost cold." Warren said, taking a long drink from his bottle of water and setting his pack down on the russet-colored dirt. "I'm half-inclined to cuddle, sir."
"I wouldn't recommend that." I chuckled, opening my own bottle. "I don't smell like roses right now. I smell like...gun oil and...ass." He laughed, replacing the bottle in his bag.
"Sir!" My weapons sergeant, Hawes, called me from his spot on a nearby bank.
"What, man? I'm taking a break."
"I know, sir. It's up to you, but you should probably come see this." I looked back at Warren, his medical bag hanging idly off his shoulder.
"Alright. I'm coming." I groaned as I sat up, the carrier for my armor plates digging into my side as I leaned forward. Ambling by his side, I laid on my stomach as he handed me a pair of binoculars. "What am I looking for, brother?" I sighed and looked through the lenses, watching a group of white-robed locals shout at each other.
"Two of the local tribes. They're not exactly getting along."

Weaver

"Dude, if this area of the world got along with itself, we wouldn't be here." I handed him the set of binoculars and sighed.

"ODA! Rally up!" I called, invoking the group of 11 other men to pick up from their positions and gather in a circle around me.

"What's up, boss?" Hawes asked, chewing on a protein bar.

"Those two tribes decided to start name-calling. I know we're supposed to bypass them, but...we're not really sure which of these villages has the building we're looking for anyway. You guys feel alright checking it out?"

"If it'll give me a chance to warm up." Warren joked, invoking chuckles from the group.

"What do you think the odds are it's hostile?" Benson asked, picking at a piece of dirt smudged across the front of his weapon.

"I'd say minimal. But with that being said...you guys know how shit is right now." They nodded quietly. "So we're good? Alright. We roll in two." They picked up their packs and checked their weapons, ensuring they were still on safe and loaded correctly. I unclipped the radio from my vest and turned it on.

"Basilisk, this is Spartan six, SITREP to follow, over." The radio operator from our headquarters picked up immediately.

"Go ahead, Spartan."

"Basilisk, we're picking up and moving a kilometer east, there's some neighboring villages that don't look happy. Break." I paused. "And they might have what we're looking for. Over."

"Roger, you're cleared green by Basilisk one. Reminder, check your ROE if you receive contact, how copy?"

"Copy, Basilisk. Six out." I placed the radio in its pouch and looked over my shoulder. "Green light, time to move. Put your makeup away, Benson." The group taunted him as we stepped off, making our way down the hill into the nearby village. Faintly, I could see bodies turning toward us and either running indoors or shouting things in Arabic. The downhill slope made the journey quick, arriving in the heart of the village much quicker than I had expected to. One of the village elders approached me.

"Happy afternoon. We come with no harm." I said in mediocre Arabic, smiling through my rough beard. The man scowled and pointed a finger at me.

"Americans kill. We want you gone. You cannot give us good things, only bad." He returned.

"We search for Hajir Al-Saban. We know he kills your people. We want to kill him. Help us." He stepped back for a moment, looking at our group. I glanced over my shoulder, watching them shift into their respective positions. To anyone but myself or the other men of the detachment, it would have appeared as though we were simply fanning out to look at the village. Rather, we were preparing for a counterattack if engaged.

"Go now. Americans must go now." He sounded frightened when he spoke, despite the effort to sound aggressive. He wasn't the one in charge here. I shot a glance over my sunglasses, looking into the houses inconspicuously. There weren't enough women and children to make a typical settlement. Most of its inhabitants were young men or boys, all angry, and all lying in wait.

"Well, boys, let's pack it up. It's all rainbows here." For those few in the village that spoke broken English, they wouldn't have picked up the code word used to indicate an imminent attack. It was something I had developed with them personally over the years, one of the many that were specific to this group.

"All rainbows, huh?" Benson noisily chewed on a piece of gum, watching for signs of danger.

   It was silent as we skirted along the edge of the village, taking care not to get too close to any of the buildings. Rather than going back the way we came, we had two options: to go left or right. Behind the village was a mountain ridge, with no purpose in us climbing it. And right would have taken us toward the village we knew was hostile. All logic dictated that this was the way to go.

"You know, Kane..." Hawes started. "We need a better code word. I'm thinking something like...balloons. You know, something that isn't too obvious." I looked over my shoulder, passing the last building and watching for indications of the inhabitants leaving their dwellings. They did not.

"It's not over yet, Hawes. Stay frosty. Something's...wrong." I didn't often convey harsh truths to the group unless it was something I truly believed in, so when they heard me say that something was wrong, the idle chatter was instantly shut down.

"What are we looking for?" Benson asked quietly, watching the mountainside. I shook my head, trying to figure out what I was missing. Hiding indoors. Sending a false leader. Women and children gone. No direct attack when we approached.

"Hold up." The group stopped at my command and took a knee. I picked the radio up once more. "Basilisk, this is Spartan six." The other end responded with haste again.

"Go ahead, six."

"We spotted some odd activity in the village. No women or children, and the leader was frightened. Please advise. Over."

"Sir...?" Benson's voice rung out as alarming, the never-afraid young sergeant suddenly fraught with distress. I looked up to see him holding a piece of copper wire leading into the ground. He tugged on it gently, and it lifted from the dirt and ran past my leg toward the village. The radio crackled with words I wasn't heeding, trying to determine the best, most immediate course of action.

"Get back to the village." I stood up and turned around to face the settlement, when the leader I had spoken to emerged from a hut. He held a small device, a faint, familiar copper wire trailing from the end. "Now!" I yelled, prompting them to sprint without hesitation toward the village. I took two steps before a deafening explosion occurred,

Sorrow

what felt like inches behind me, throwing me off my feet and face-first into the sandy dirt. Gunfire echoed over my shoulder, faint from the damage to my eardrums. I saw Hawes crouch over me, grabbing me by the arm and helping me up. I stumbled forward, but quickly regained my senses and followed the group. Benson and Hawes took up the right side behind a hut, while the rest spread out and took the left side of the village. I slid behind the hut on the right, unclipping my radio and immediately calling for assistance.

"Basilisk, this is Spartan six requesting immediate close air support on my location. How copy?" I set the radio down long enough to fire my rifle at the largest house, where collectively, the most fire was coming from. It exploded shortly in a shower of debris after a well-placed grenade by Hawes. The radio hissed, indicating it was either broken or jammed. Either way, we were in trouble.

"Kane, you're hit." Hawes pointed to my knee, a slow trickle of blood dripping down the leg of my pants.

"Just shrapnel. I'm good."

"Sir, the mountain!" Joyce yelled from across the street, pointing to a series of distant muzzle flashes. A bullet snapped by my ear, so I ducked down and tried the radio again.

"Basilisk, we need support!" I threw it to the side as it fell completely silent, void of static. "Hawes, Benson! Get across to the other side!" I fired into the mountain, targeting the dense groups of flashes as the soldiers across the street started preparing a rocket.

"Kane!" Benson screamed, halfway across. I looked up to see the vapor trail of a rocket fly over my head, hissing violently, and explode a hundred feet behind me. He turned around and kept running, diving into place to help the rest. Hawes followed shortly after him, joining Warren in a barrage of gunfire against the mountain. I took a deep breath, preparing to cross the road. With no precursor or warning, a stabbing pain erupted in my shoulder, knocking me to the ground. I

Weaver

quickly put my hand to it and pulled it away, a good amount of blood covering my palm.
"Warren!" I called. He turned around briefly, keeping up his rate of fire.
"My radio's down! I'm hit! Call for hogs!" He repeatedly looked over his shoulder as I hurriedly yanked a pressure bandage from the first aid kit on my side. Understanding my message, he unclipped the radio from his vest and began to call headquarters. Another loud hiss gathered my attention as I cinched the bandage shut. Too late, I saw the vapor trail of a rocket descending from the mountain. I kicked off from my hunched position into a sprint, moving just a moment too late. The rocket hit the building I was using for cover and knocked me out.

    Hours must have gone by. Days, even. It was dark. I was thirsty and couldn't move. It was hard to breathe. Dirt filled my nose and covered my mouth. There was pressure on my chest. Darkness turned to light.

"Kane!" I heard them calling, but I felt dead. I had been lying for too long, buried already. Dead already.
"He was using that building for cover."
"He got out of there too fast."
"No, he was behind it." Too many voices were speaking to make sense. I didn't want to call for help, even if I could have. They shouldn't have been there. They shouldn't have come back.
"Sarn't! I think I found him!" Gloved hands removed pieces of dirt, wood, rock, and so much else. I was uncovered, facing the light of day once more. A young, wide-eyed man stood crouched in front of me, yelling for a medic.
"We're gonna get you outta here, sir." He said, following it up with several more yells. A slow shadow blocked out the sun, a familiar figure sauntering toward me.

Sorrow

"Kane. Quit nappin'." The voice was familiar, but even more recognizable was the noisy chewing of bubblegum, mouth agape in humor.

"Benson..." I coughed, my voice rough and hoarse from dehydration.

"We're all here, Cap. Wouldn't let you hang out all by yourself." I smiled, despite the immense pain in my lips from them cracking and splitting open. A woman appeared behind him, crouching down and tending to my wounds. She removed her helmet, letting her work with her vision unhindered. She was beautiful. Wide, silver eyes were framed by thick, jet-black hair and completed by full lips telling me that I'd be okay.

"I know I'm okay." I whispered, setting my head down on the ground.

"Captain Kane?" She whispered, removing the bandage on my shoulder. The pain from the wound instantly became more intense, like it was fresh. I screamed, my throat ripping apart on the inside. "Kane, you have to get up." She demanded, the pain in my shoulder growing unbearable. The light from the sun behind her was blinding, searing my eyes with its light.

"I am!" I groaned, trying to lift myself up. She grabbed me by the arm, pulling me to my feet and smiling. Unlike the other soldiers, she wasn't wearing a combat uniform. She was wearing a black dress, trimmed in a deep scarlet red. She put a hand on me gently, cradling the back of my head. I smiled, reveling in her beauty. It was intoxicating, just breathing in her presence. Despite her smile, a single tear rolled down her cheek.

"You have to get up. I need you." She whispered, still smiling. "I need you." I took her arm, pulling her in close to hug her.

***

"Oh, thank god." She whispered, wrapping her arms around me. Like a car starting up for the first time, my brain went into overdrive, trying to comprehend how I went from the unforgiving desert of Afghanistan to an air-conditioned medical room.

Weaver

"Where am I?" I demanded, trying to blink enough that my blurred vision would repair itself.
"You're safe. You're in the city with me."
"With you. Kara." I said blankly, the shadows of closer objects beginning to fade into view. My eyes fixed on her face, wiping away the haze of nightmare that lingered over my mind.
"Jesus. I swear I was just back in Afghanistan. Just now, seconds ago. Like, I know it happened years ago, but I...I don't know. Like I relived it somehow. Then I...woke up? Wait..." I rubbed my temples in an effort to clear my mind. "I remember...being in the car accident on my way back to the city. Then..." I sighed, bearing no recollection of anything past that point. "Then I guess you pulled me out of my SUV and brought me here." I chuckled and looked up at her, my vision returning to normal. There were sad tears in her eyes, a thing I only saw rarely. She shook her head slowly, and I let her speak.
"You're okay. I promise. But...they took you. They kidnapped you and took you back to the lab. I think I got to you before they did anything." I looked around to ensure we weren't in a Raven lab, confirmed by Kara's vigorous head shaking. "I brought you back to the city." Stunned silence overcame me for a moment, baffling and disconcerting.
"Raven labs...what did they want with me?" She shrugged, sniffling. "I don't know. We found you in that...machine. The one that takes your memories." I sighed.
"That explains the vivid recollection of some...not-so-fond experiences." I assessed myself, flexing my joints and bringing recent memories to the front of my mind. Nothing seemed to be out of place, mentally or physically. "How long was I out?"
"Twelve hours."
"Are you okay?" I asked, wondering why she didn't appear to be as happy as she normally would have after seeing my recovery. Without

thinking, my eyes roamed over various points on her body to search for clues in her body language.

She won't look me in the eyes, indicative of shame. No discussion on my rescue. She didn't invite others to be here with her. She feels isolated. And ashamed.

"Did someone get hurt?" I asked, placing a careful hand on her shoulder. She bit her lip and bowed her head, knowing that she wanted to talk about it. I waited patiently, knowing that the answer was painful to her.

"When...we came to get you out, we set off the alarms. And we knew we would. But Schillinger came after us, and...Val stayed behind to give us time to get you out. We don't know if he made it out or not."

"He did." I concluded quickly, using pseudo-logic to make her feel better. "He had to make it. Schillinger is too vain to let himself, or his daughter, die. And if he made it out, Val would have followed them."

"It's not that easy, Jalix. That building came down on top of everyone. It...killed everyone! Don't you understand? All of those people down there died!" Her voice was soft, but she was angry with herself, fighting hard against an impending breakdown.

"I don't understand, Kara. But you can help me do so. I wasn't there. Tell me what happened." She took a deep, shuddering breath and looked at me, still avoiding eye contact.

"The lab had a back door, so we managed to sneak in. Alice and Val went with me. We made it to where you were, and all hell broke loose. Val kept the guards off our backs while Alice and I went back the way we came. It was our only option. The main steel door to the lab was timed, and Val was too far away to make it through. Alice and I went through the labs, trying to rescue the scientists, but...we couldn't. We barely made it out. And we waited for Val, but...we didn't see him leave."

"Did you see Schillinger leave?" She shook her head.

"No. Alice and I were the only ones we know that left the building."

"Then don't assume you lost him. He's a tough guy. And contrary to popular belief...he's pretty smart. He'll be okay." I moved to sit beside her. "What do you mean you tried to rescue the scientists, though?"
"They weren't guests. They were prisoners." I sighed, my hatred for our enemy growing even more. "Dammit, Jalix. I keep hurting people. Everyone I care about is suffering because of me. I got you kidnapped, Val's...missing. Krystal almost died."
"Wait, what happened to Krystal?" I turned to look at her as she stood up and pointed to the room across the hall.
"Go see for yourself." Warily, I stared at her for a few moments before leaving the room and walking the short distance into the next room. Jared stood quietly by Krystal's side, her body subtly convulsing with slight tremors. She wore a loose men's tank top, clearly not put on by herself, and likely one from Jared's wardrobe. I could make out a fading scar running from the base of her neck to the center of her breastbone, as well as a purple hue covering what was visible of her torso. Jared looked up at me briefly, meeting my eyes, before watching Krystal continue her rapid, shallow breathing.
"What happened?" I breathed, looking at the dried pool of blood under her head. Her hair was matted with sweat, beads trickling down her neck despite her shivering.
"She wanted to fight Kara again. She said the wrong thing, and..." He put his massive palm on her forehead, checking her temperature. "I don't know what's wrong with her, man. But you need to talk it out with her. Before she kills somebody." He looked at me honestly, both afraid of insulting her and genuinely concerned for us all. I backed out into the hall, bumping into Kara.
"What the hell, Kara?"
"I'm sorry, Jalix. I swear, I didn't-"
"Didn't what? Didn't mean it? I watched you fight her last time. You know exactly how strong you are. You knew you already hurt her chest. This was *not* an accident."

"It was!" She asserted. "I didn't mean to hurt her so badly. She was talking about us, and how I couldn't love you."

"She says that because she knows it's a weak spot of yours. Clearly, you're sensitive about it. Why?"

"What do you mean, why? I have to protect you. All of you." I gritted my teeth, taking her hand briefly and guiding her into the main hall. Walking toward the training room, I continued our discussion.

"You say that like we can't fend for ourselves. You're not our shield, Kara. You're another sword in our fight."

"No, Jalix, I'm not. And if they could fend for themselves, they wouldn't need me."

"Have you ever stopped to think that the reason they respect you is because of *who* you are? Not *what* you are?" I turned to her, trying to make her see the error in her thoughts. "That little speech you gave the city before you told them all to leave? They listened to you because they know you want them safe. They know your intentions. And those that stayed behind? They want to protect *you*. Otherwise, don't you think they'd have let you fight alone?" She opened her mouth to speak, but I continued. "You're not perfect, Kara. And I understand that now. I used to see you that way, but now that I'm here? Now that I've seen you in action? I know it's a lie. It doesn't make me love you any less, but I know for a fact that you can't act as a shield anymore."

"I have to!"

"You don't! You can't! The more you try to do that, the further away you're going to push them! They don't know whether or not you see them as people. They think you see them as objects. Things that need locked away and kept safe. If you let them..." I sighed, trying to think of a way to phrase my words properly.

"Kara!" A woman's voice screeched from the other side of the hall. We both spun around so see a young girl running toward us, a bag slung

over her shoulder and her face streaked with tears. "What did you do?" She sobbed, pointing to the infirmary. "Why did you hurt her?"
"Violet, I-"
"You almost killed her! Look at what you did!" Violet screamed pointing to the wall next to the training room. Crushed pieces of cement lay scattered on the ground, spots of blood staining the ground from where Krystal assumedly fell. Kara started to break, her eyes alight with a mixture of anger and sadness.
"I didn't mean to do it, Violet! I was angry! Okay? She wanted to fight me again, and I couldn't! I didn't want to hurt her anymore."
"Well...you did." Violet hissed, wiping the tears from her eyes. "When you came to save me, you told me that everyone here got along. I believed you. But how can you say that when you hate her so much?"
"I don't hate Krystal...I swear. She makes me...so mad sometimes. But she's a beautiful person. She's a good friend that does bad things sometimes."
"Kara, you're the closest thing I've ever had to a mom. But...I'm afraid, now." She gritted her teeth to avoid crying harder. "What if *I* say the wrong thing? What if *I* make you angry?" With no indication that she was going to do so, Kara lunged forward and grabbed Violet, embracing her tightly against her body. They both stood quietly for a moment, Kara softly stroking Violet's hair.
"I would never hurt you, Vi. And I promise I'm going to make this better. Jalix is going to help me. He already has, so much." I smiled softly, glad that Kara saw my advice as assistance. Violet groaned loudly, doubling over in Kara's arms.
"I need to go take my shot." She said suddenly, throwing the bag off her shoulder and hastily digging through it. "Give this to Krystal, please, for when she wakes up. It's the last page in the book." She withdrew a notepad and handed it to Kara, picking up her bag and walking away quickly, hunched over in pain. Kara opened the notepad and showed it to me, an immaculate drawing of Krystal's

likeness illustrated on the first page. Flipping through its pages, she found the last page and stopped, holding it in front of her. Krystal's face was looking down at Violet, both of their images almost photorealistic. Violet's face seemed happy in the picture, smiling at Krystal with open, green eyes framed by hair as black as Kara's.
"What shot did she have to take?" I asked, looking back at the room Violet disappeared into.
"Remember how our virus feeds on our blood? It's the one I told you about that keeps it nourished. It can be painful when it wears off." She looked back at the notebook, smiling.
"She's so talented. Those two get along so well...I feel like it's the closest that Krystal's ever gotten to someone other than myself." She chuckled softly and closed the pad, tucking it under her arm. "They're thick as thieves, too. One time, they snuck in while I was asleep and took apart all my furniture."
"Why?"
"I beat them both at chess." She giggled, remembering the moment fondly. "But the next game, I beat Krystal and let Violet win. Since then, they've been arguing over who's better." She sighed, the smile slowly vanishing from her face. "I know what you've been saying, Jalix. Sometimes I really *do* forget that they live their own lives. All I see is their role in the conflict because...that's all I really saw in myself. Until I met you."
"And that's why they still call you Sorrow. They know that you're their leader...but as an army? Or as a people?" She sighed, taking a step toward me and kissing me gently. Her lips weren't quivering anymore, which meant she was finally calm. I returned the gesture, moving my hands to her hips and holding her for a long moment. I touched my forehead to hers and looked into her vivid, silver eyes.
"I *will* help you through all of this, Kara. But you need to understand something. Love...isn't a feeling. It's not an emotion or...something that just happens. It's something you do. It's a gift that you have to

give someone." She draped her arms over my shoulders, resting her head against my neck.

"After so long it was all I knew. Killing, fighting, training. Love is new to me. It's going to take some getting used to, you know? But help me work on it." She pulled away from me, rubbing the back of her neck. "Alice wanted to see you when you woke up. And I need to go get a shower. She's in Archangel." I turned my head to see the doors to the club closed, devoid of music or any indications of life inside.

"Alright. I'll come back to the room in a bit. I love you." I kissed her on the cheek and strolled the few feet to the massive wooden doors, listening for people inside.

    The quiet clinking of glass indicated that there was, in fact someone in the club, but no crowd. I pulled on the brass handle, revealing the dark interior of the room. Alice sat alone at the bar, a bottle of liquor and tall glass keeping her company.

"Hey." She whispered without looking up. I closed the door behind me and approached the bar, taking a seat next to her. The tips of her red hair sat idly on the bar, motionless and still, as I waited for her to say something. Alice's features were indistinguishable in the dim light of distant purple neon.

"I know the answer. But how are you feeling?" I spoke softly, treading lightly around her emotions.

"Well...we got you back." A faint smile met her lips, dying slowly. "But we lost Val."

"Hey...you don't know that yet."

"I do, Jalix." Her eyes moved to meet mine, the familiar green of her irises surrounded by swollen redness. "It's not that I'm being pessimistic or morbid...just realistic. I watched the building come down with both Schillinger and Val inside it. And I know that Val wouldn't have let him escape. He'd rather die a hero than let our worst nightmare get released back into the world." She sighed heavily, clearly exhausted from emotion. "I know him well enough to

see the truth. And I've met my peace with it."
"I don't think Kara feels the same way."
"No...she doesn't. She's in denial. There's no way that she would believe she could lose someone again."
"Again?" Alice took a long drink from her glass and exhaled, the pungent smell of strong alcohol washing over my face.
"Before...all of this...before Vampyres, before this city, Kara was a girl. Just a normal girl. A lot of things happened and it led to her being one of the first of us ever to exist. Kara and another girl. Her friend, Sonya. Val was with them, but he was lucky enough to avoid being infected. Kara and Sonya were inseparable. They fought wars together. They *won* wars together. They were best friends, and going up against the two of them? No one would be able to handle it. She was a nice girl, too. Sweet. Pretty." She refilled her glass, taking another sip. "Right before she met you, they were posing as security contractors in the Middle East, in Afghanistan. But they were chasing after Schillinger. He was selling cheap weapons to terrorists to fund his research, and they thought, they *knew* they had him. They tracked him down and he saw them coming, so the two of them were attacked. There was an explosive device hidden in the road, and Sonya's vehicle hit it. Kara went...berserk. No one had ever seen destruction like that before. And Kara rescued her. Brought her back here to the city. And she nursed the poor thing back to health. When she woke up? She didn't have any memories of Kara." She grimaced, watching my reaction. "She didn't have much of any memories, actually. Brain damage is too hard to heal. It takes a long time, and it's touchy, even for us. Kara lost her mind. She was alone now. Even though she had all of us, it was Sonya that shared all of her experiences, all of her pain. Sonya was even the one to give her the name Sorrow. And now...she was gone. So Kara left. We took care of Sonya, gave her a new name, introduced her to the world, and Kara stayed away from the city for months. She only came back because

she saw what Raven Biopar...bi...whatever. I'm...drunk. She saw what that company was doing and that it was led by Schillinger. In the meantime, she had met you. And slowly...we could see her start to heal. To gain some humanity, finally. She saw something in you, Jalix."
"But why me? Because I was close to Schillinger?"
"She had no idea about that until months into your relationship. No, she knew...you saw things in people. You were strong...but caring. You were smart, but you listened. As a human? You were perfect. And that's what she needed. A human element."
"But...she could have chosen anybody."
"And that's why Krystal is jealous. That's why everyone respects you. She could have." She smiled at me, playfully kissing me on the cheek and walking to the other side of the bar. "But she didn't." She poured me a drink and slid it to me, pouring one for herself and raising the glass. "To Val." I raised the glass and took the shot, an unfamiliar taste catching me by surprise.
"What is that?"
"It was Val's favorite whiskey...I figured now would be a reasonable time to finally open it." I nodded in agreement, as she poured another drink. A flood of light emerged from the door and several men entered the room, chatting to themselves.
"I guess I'll see myself out." I said to Alice, turning to leave. One of the men put his hand on my chest and stood in front of me.
"Actually, we came to talk to you, Jalix." Jared stood behind the group, calmly waiting for my response.
"I'm listening." He sat down next to me and smiled, shaking his head.
"We want to finish the fight, Jalix. And we want you to be a part of it." I raised my eyebrows, having expected a confrontation rather than an invitation. Hack pushed his way from the back of the group, holding a laptop and placing it on the bar. Words spilled from his mouth in a rush, barely comprehensible.
"Remember the data drive Kara gave me? Well it had a lot of

Sorrow

information on it, and quite frankly, very little I could use. However, I noticed one thing in particular. Although all three of Raven's research labs are funded equally, and I mean to the dollar, the amount of correspondence coming from one is much greater than the other. I mean detailed accounts of research activities, security requests-"

"Hack, slow down. And shorten it."

"We know where Schillinger is going to be. And we want to go kill him." The group of men behind me showed their own signs of agreement, smiling, chuckling, or stepping forward.

"How do you know this information for sure? Schillinger is probably dead."

"Except he isn't. He had a press conference a few hours ago on television, declaring that the lab incident was a result of an attack by a different company." My eyes widened, but I continued to listen. "He doesn't care about the company, but his goal? The research? He cares about greatly. He's got four buildings to the company: one headquarters downtown for business, and three research labs. One, we just blew up, the Salem branch. Another is in Pennsylvania, and the third is in Boston. Now, the one in Boston is the one that has the other machine. The...mind-reading one. I can tell from their emailed reports. Everything is phrased all...shady. But the one in Pennsylvania is the one that the public face sees the most. It produces vaccines. Medicine-"

"I said the short version."

"Right, sorry. This lab, the one in Pennsylvania, he's going to visit, so he doesn't draw attention to the other one. He'll give the Boston lab enough time to hide their research in case they're investigated."

"Wait, why would they be investigated?" I asked, looking back at Jared. He looked up for a moment, as if the answer was written on the ceiling, before frowning and answering my question.

"Your kidnapping wasn't really a secret. It was all over the news. And they also...killed your old boss." I looked around, waiting for someone to reveal the joke.

"What? Hartman? Why?"

"To cover their tracks. He knew too much, and with you leaving? They wouldn't risk it. The media was led to believe Kilkovf was in charge of your first assassination attempt, the one in the casino. After your boss was killed, they let everyone assume that he's the one after you. The whole visit was a trap."

"Jesus..." I whispered, running a hand through my hair. I looked at Alice, wiping out the glass with a rag and setting it on the bar, leaning against it.

"I want to go." She said, looking up at us. "If I can get a shot at the man who killed Val, count me in."

"Alice, if Schillinger escaped, Val could have-"

"If Val got out, he would have come back to us by now. I can accept...no matter how hard it is, that he's dead. He saved us. But what I can't accept is that the man who killed him is going to live. So I'm going." She crossed her arms conclusively.

"Alright, well...what's the plan?" I looked at Eric, who closed the laptop and grinned, moving back to the rest of the group.

"We already have everything laid out in the conference room. Come with us." Jared pushed open the heavy doors to the club, the crowd following behind him. Alice and I lingered for a few moments, allowing us to fall out of earshot.

"Hartman's really dead?" I asked quietly, not doubting the truth of the story. We meandered behind the group, watching them walk through the empty hall while they chatted amongst themselves. "This war is real."

"You didn't think it was?"

"It's not that I didn't believe it...It's just hard to see fighting a battle that only we know about. The...humans, I can't believe I'm using that term, see something else. They see a dispute between companies or

Sorrow

something, something less than what this really is. But now...people are dying. It's real."

"People have been dying for a long time, Jalix. This fight was never intended to go quiet. It just happened that way. We got lucky. We all forgot about what it was like to live in fear. And I think that's why Kara is taking this so hard. She's not ready for things to go back to the way they were before."

"They won't." I gently grabbed her shoulder, looking into her eyes. In the improved light of the open hall, I could more clearly see the exhausted redness from crying. Her face was gaunt and paler than usual, undoubtedly breaking under the stress. "Kara and I...all of us, we're going to put an end to all of this. We're going to kill Schillinger. We're going to kill Raven. And we're going to dismantle their company. I mean, without them, Shift Company won't exist. It'll just be serving the purpose it was always meant to. Helping people." She sighed and resumed walking as the group vanished around a corner leading into a smaller hallway.

"We needed someone like you, Jalix. I think it's getting too personal for a lot of us. Myself, Kara, Krystal, too many of us. *You* have the bigger picture in mind. And we need that." We rounded the corner, confronted by a single door, held ajar by Jared. His massive, dark figure was almost too ready to move, tense with anticipation.

"So this is the conference room." I muttered, stepping inside the open room. A large table occupied a majority of the space, several seemingly miscellaneous items strewn about its surface. Stacks of documents and photographs littered the tabletop, with some items standing out among the rest.

"I don't like where this is going." I murmured, running my hand over a packed parachute, neatly compressed into a backpack-style sack.

"Jalix, listen. We can do this. It's going to be a big risk, but we can shut this thing down."

"Parachutes? Seriously? I cannot *wait* to hear how you plan on making this work." Alice took a seat at the table and inhaled deeply, a shuddering sigh echoing in the otherwise quiet room. Eric stepped forward and spoke timidly, the rest of the group watching.
"There's been a lot of talking and planning. It's a lot to handle, even for us. But we know that if we just wing it, we're not going to get the results that we want. So...since Kara assigned me to plan stuff like this...I did. And I doubt any of you are going to like it."
"Nice, man. Way to pump us up." Jared said quietly.
"I know Krystal isn't awake right now, but we don't have time to ask nicely. I'm sure that she would be okay with us using her resources. As I'm sure we all know, she's fairly well endowed." Even I couldn't help but to stifle a laugh as the group chuckled, despite our precarious situation.
"Wait, no. Not what I meant. I mean she's rich. Damn, guys. Stay focused. Anyway...her private jet has its perks, but just the same, it's heavily tracked by the government. The same as any other aircraft. We can't just fly it somewhere and land it conveniently."
"Wait, I have a few questions." I started. "First of all, seriously? She has her own *jet*? And secondly, why can't we just drive there?"
"I'm getting to that, Jalix. Yes, she has her own jet. She's filthy rich. And we can't drive there because pulling up to their front door sort of ruins the element of surprise, doesn't it?"
"Well, yeah, but-"
"Do you have a better idea?" He barked, taking all of us by surprise. I shook my head, leaning back and listening to what he had to say. "I'm sorry. It's been stressful. And I'm asking a lot of all of you. But before you all start chiming in, I need to at least lay the foundation for the plan. Val...god rest him, was our pilot. He could fly pretty much anything. And he was licensed, which was very helpful in keeping everything legal, and therefore quiet. As we all know...he's not with us anymore. But we can work around it. Krystal...is also licensed."

Sorrow

"Krystal is in a coma." Alice interjected, cocking her head to the side. "Not to mention extremely fragile, emotionally unstable, and has no goddamn clue what's going on right now."

"Well...we need to fix that." Eric said quietly, crossing his arms. "Look, there's no other way around it. I've looked at the Pennsylvania facility. It's way up in the mountains and guarded at every road. By the time we got there by vehicle, they'd be too ready, and Schillinger would be gone. And we don't have time to walk. So, again, unless *anyone* here has a better idea, we're going to get in Krystal's jet, fly over the facility, and parachute onto the facility's grounds." A stunned silence captured the voices of the group, trying desperately to figure out another way.

"What if they look up? They'll shoot us out of the sky, and warn Schillinger." Alice asked.

"We're only going to be out of the plane for about a minute. We'll be too small to see until we're already on top of them. And don't worry about Schillinger escaping. I already thought of that." As he spoke, he pulled a photograph from a large envelope and held it up to show us its contents. Satellite images showed a helicopter pad, a single aircraft parked in its space. "This is a helicopter the company owns. They use it for flying corpses, organs, and other biological matter to and from their facility that they are allowed to experiment with. But...just like every other aircraft, it has to get clearance to fly. He won't get that in time before you all reach him. The only shot he has is fleeing into the mountains, and I doubt he'd be able to escape all four of you.

"Wait, what?"

"Four of us?"

"What do you mean four of us?" A chorus of voices exploded in the room, inducing a cringe from Eric.

"Alright, shut up! I was getting there. Look, if the only way in without being noticed is by air, the only way out is the same technique. The roads will be guarded, the facility is more than likely going to explode again, and *none* of you want to be there when the police show up. It's the fastest way. The only problem is…their helicopter only seats four. Two passengers, a space for a body bag, and a pilot."

"Okay, so first off in a *long* list of questions, what happens when we get out of there? We have to land the helicopter at some point."

"You can all get dropped off at Krystal's mansion, there's enough empty space to land in the field, and then we dismantle it. It's not our problem if the helicopter goes missing because it's not in our name. The jet, however, is definitely our problem."

"Why?"

"Because who's going to pilot the helicopter if Krystal is in the jet?" It grew quiet again for a moment. "Krystal is going to have to parachute down into the mountain with you and let the jet crash."

"Are you insane, Eric?" Alice stood up, the table thrown forward several inches. "No, seriously, are you honestly *insane*? Krystal can't even stay awake on her own right now, let alone *parachute* into a combat zone, then fly back again. I don't know when she'll be able to *walk* again!" A quiet rapping gathered our attention from outside the glass entrance, garnering a look from the assembly. Krystal's petite figure stood, smirking sarcastically, outside the door to the conference room.

"Krystal!" Alice cried, throwing open the door and standing in front of her. Alice's eyes combed over every square inch of her body, baffled at how she was recovered. "You need to be in bed, immediately. You're going to hurt yourself."

"The bones are fused, Alice. Not healed, but they'll hold together unless I get kicked again. My skull is still…" She reached a hand to the back of her head, lifting up the bloodstained hair and gingerly running her fingers over the injury. "Kind of a mess. But again, as long as I stay out of trouble, I'll be able to fly."

"Wait you heard all of that?" Alice exclaimed, putting a hand on her hip.

"Yeah, I've been standing there for, like, five minutes. I eavesdrop. It happens."

"How...are you even able to move? You should be in excruciating pain."

"I stole some morphine. A lot, actually. I'm high as a kite right now. But I'm good enough to fly." I scoffed, prompting a sharp glare from everyone.

"Okay, so let me reiterate our plan..." I cleared my throat and simplified the situation into its core components. "We're going to take a private jet over an armed facility. Then, the four of us, including our drug-laced, injured pilot, are going to skydive into the mountainside, then proceed to kill a superhuman criminal warlord. After that, we're going to steal his helicopter, fly it back to aforementioned pilot's mansion, and take it apart with our bare hands."

"Well, not our bare hands, Tony has a degree in mechanical eng-"

"Alright, so I'll let that one slide. Fine. We'll use power tools. But regardless...*this* is our plan?" My words grew fainter and my vision more obscured as I realized that everyone was okay with this horrible amalgamation of ideas. Sitting back down, I sighed and buried my face in my hands, trying to wonder whether or not I had done anything half as crazy in my life. "Who would even go? Who's the four of us?" I asked, my voice muffled by my palms.

"Well...Krystal has to go." Eric said, pressuring Alice into an immediate response.

"And I have to monitor her condition."

"Well, that's two."

"I'm going." I said, sighing. "There's obviously a reason that you all asked me to go, and I'm guessing it's to give Kara support."

Weaver

Everyone's heads turned away from me, either looking at each other, or at an inconspicuous spot on the table. "Wait, Kara's going, right?" "Jalix..." Jared started. "We thought she should sit this one out. She's too close to it. I'm not saying she'd ever purposefully put us in harm's way...but maybe she needs to get some distance from the situation. She can help go after Raven when we're done with Schillinger. I'm gonna go in her place."
"Kara's your best fighter, and her abilities would come in handy. You're really sure leaving her behind is the best idea? And she'd never let me go by myself."
"Wow. You're really going to let her tell you what to do?" Krystal asked, her face unfamiliarly not stained with sarcasm. "I'm being honest, here, Jalix. If you wait for her permission for every move you make, it's not going to end well. For either of you. You're strong. And independent. You're one of us. She's our leader, not our dictator. If you want to go...you should." Everyone's eyes were pinned on Krystal, shooting her looks of suspicion. "Shut up, okay? All of you. Look, am I pissed at Kara for what she did? Yeah, more than you know. But do I forgive her? Yeah, because...I love her." Her eyes locked with mine as I heard the words from her mouth for the first time. I should have felt jealousy, or anger, but I didn't. I was sorry for her. I knew she was suffering emotionally. "I respect her for who she is. But she's not perfect. We all know that. And I think it's time we let her sit this one out."
"That's why she's not here, Jalix." Eric said quietly. "We knew if she found out, she'd never quit until we let her go. I'm going to talk to her when she gets back and help her with taking down Raven. We'll have a solid plan by the time you all get back."
"Alright, so Jared, Krystal, Alice, and myself." I stated, standing up again. "When she's out of the shower, I'll let her know." Hack took a step toward me.

Sorrow

"Wait, shower? She told me that she was going to get your tuxedo that you left behind." I opened my mouth to express that she could do both tasks before Alice turned to us with fear in her eyes.

"She told me that she was going to look over the data that she gave Eric."

I pushed my chair back and sprinted out of the conference room, followed closely by Alice and Jared. Tearing through the hall, I made my way past the training area and hospital, both of my followers yelling for me to wait. I rounded the corner, charging into the living space we shared and yelling her name.

"Kara? Kara!" I looked around, the room cleaned of the debris we had created. The bed was somewhat fixed, with a small scrap of paper lying on her pillow.

"Jalix, wait, she could be-" Alice's voice stopped when I picked up the piece of paper and read its contents.

"Jalix, I want you to know how much I love you. I'm not leaving forever, but something you said made me think about Val. You told me that love isn't something you feel, but something you do. I have to find him. Please don't follow me. If I don't find what I'm looking for, I'll be back in a day. I promise I won't leave you behind to deal with my mess. Wait for me. With all the love left in my heart, Sorrow."

Angrily, the ball of paper was crumpled in my fast and held tightly.

"Jalix...she'll be alright. She's good at staying hidden, and she's not chasing down Schillinger."

"But that doesn't mean she has the right to leave without telling me first!"

"You're going to do the same thing, Jalix." I gritted my teeth, trying to formulate an argument for her retort.

"Jalix, she's going to be fine. We need to focus on *our* mission. She can take care of herself, I promise." Eric's reassurance meant little to my racing mind.

I know she'll be fine.

Weaver

Sighing, I dropped the paper onto our bed and sat down, looking up at Krystal as she walked through the doorway. Her face was unusually neutral, realizing that I had no problem confronting her if she caused problems.

"She left, huh?" She asked quietly, leaning against the doorframe.

"Well...I have to go grab my things and call the airport to let them know we're coming. I need to request a take-off time and get flight approval."

"I'll take care of that, Krystal." Eric gently placed a hand on her shoulder. "You sit with Jalix for a few minutes. We're two rooms over if you need us." He motioned for Alice to follow him as they both left the room. She stood silently, gazing into the kitchen with no intention of moving.

"I'm sorry for what Kara did, Krystal." She scoffed and shook her head slowly as my muscles tensed, awaiting a sarcastic, inappropriate response.

"Don't be. It was my fault. I know she's dealing with more than even I could handle, and yet...I keep trying to make her angry."

"You really do have brain trauma, don't you? When have you ever been as nice as you're being right now?"

"No, Jalix, I don't have *brain trauma*, I just know when I'm wrong. Sometimes. And this is one of those times. Look...I can't keep getting in the way of you two. I'm going to end up getting killed. And I also want to see Kara happy. So if this is what makes her happy...I'm all for it. I'm done playing games. I heard what happened to Val. I'm not going to risk the same thing happening to Kara." She smiled at me gently, expressing genuine emotion for the first time since I had seen her. "I care about her too much."

"Then why do you do it?" I asked honestly. "Why do you push her so close to the edge? Look at what she did to you. Why would you...want that?"

Sorrow

"Because *she* wants it, Jalix. Until she met you, I was her only emotional outlet. And yeah, those emotions were anger and sadness, but it was something. I made her *feel*. And she loved it. It...deepened our bond. The talks we'd have after every fight, the honesty we had with each other. I'm a person, too, Jalix. I have wants and needs. I like to cuddle, believe it or not." I chuckled, unable to hold myself back from imagining Krystal as an affectionate girlfriend. She joined me, giggling and wincing in pain. "But I'm serious, Jalix. I really do want these things. I'm just...not ready to put Kara in harm's way for them. I'm not a serious person, and I hate feelings. If I didn't have them, I wouldn't be in as much pain as I am. So most of the time, I'm able to shut them out. I don't *want* emotions in my life. I'm at peace with being...a machine. But Kara? Kara needs them. So don't get angry that she's leaving. Be glad that she loves her brother enough to do so." I nodded quietly, appreciative of her honesty.

"You'd take care of her, right?" I asked, invoking a curious expression from Krystal. "If anything happened to me, you'd take care of Kara, right? You'd help her?" Krystal looked away briefly before responding.

"Jalix, if she lost you...there would *be* no helping her. You're all that's holding her together. The...hope...that she can be something more than Sorrow. You embody that. So in all honesty, despite my threats about *hurting* you, which are entirely valid, I would never take you from her. She wouldn't be Kara anymore. She'd just be..."

"Sorrow. Yeah. I think I'm beginning to understand why Sonya gave her that nickname."

"Wait, you know about her? How?"

"Alice told me the story." Krystal nodded slowly, frowning.

"She was such a sweet girl. I liked her. A lot. She was funny, a great singer, loved whiskey. Her personality was... brilliant. If Kara hadn't found you a few days later, she'd have lost herself completely. And I'm glad she did." I smirked, standing up and walking over to Krystal.

Her eyes were a deep, sapphire blue as opposed to their normal pale azure.

"Thanks, Krystal. I'm glad to know there's a person in there."

"Yeah...there is. And she's a bitch. And she wants to go kill some bad guys, so how about we go see my sister?" I grinned, glad that her personality wasn't altered.

"You mean your hot sister?"

"She wishes." We chuckled, walking across the hall into Alice's room. She stood up from her chair and furrowed her brow, glancing at the two of us intermittently.

"Are you two...getting along? Like, as friends?"

"Alright, Alice, let's not push it. We had a moment, it's over. Now...how do we go kill some bad guys?" Eric grimaced, holding out a parachute bag to Krystal.

"Put this on. I want to see how well your ribcage and spine are holding up." Grunting, she managed to pull the pack onto her shoulders by herself, breathing heavily and sweating from obvious pain. "It's going to jerk you back and pull on your shoulders. You're gonna go from really fast to really slow in about three seconds. Think you can handle it?"

"I'm not really sure. You know that I'm not one to shy away from injury, but getting ripped in half internally as I'm falling? Not on my bucket list. Alice, is there anything you can do?"

"I'm not a miracle worker, I can only repair what's broken. After that, it's up to your body. The best I can do is to make sure you have painkillers for the flight. But we're not going to be in the air for long."

"Yeah, it'll be about forty-five minutes from take-off to letting my poor plane crash itself. I think I'll be okay by then." Alice shook her head violently.

"There's no way your body is going to be healed by then."

Sorrow

"No...but I'll have more drugs in my system. And adrenaline? A hell of an anesthetic." She hiked the bag onto her shoulders and cinched the strap shut, bouncing up and down to test its effect on her body.
"I think I'll make it. But I'll need some time after I hit the ground. I'm definitely not going to be in any condition to fight."
"I didn't plan on you fighting, Krystal." I spoke up. "You can steer yourself toward the trees and hide there until we're done."
"*You* didn't plan on her fighting, Jalix?" Alice asked, coking her head in the way she normally did when she had a rhetorical question.
"Yes, Alice. Me. *I* didn't plan on her fighting. Since Kara isn't here, and you're too emotionally attached to killing this guy, I'm taking the lead on this one. I've had a bit of practice getting in and out of bad situations, and it would do you some good to let me have this."
Pulling her hair into a ponytail, she sighed and agreed.
"Yeah...that's probably a good idea. Krystal...you're positive you can make it? You're the key piece to this plan. Without you, it falls apart. I don't want to force you-"
"You're not. We need to kill Schillinger. It's for all of us. Even if we die, which I don't plan on, everybody will be able to move back to the city. It'll be safe, finally." Eric nodded, a grim appearance overshadowing his usual self. "Do I have flight clearance?"
"You'll obviously need to check in at the airport, present all your documents, go through pre-flight checks, everything of that sort. But your pre-flight clearance and airspace has been approved. Your destination is Harrisburg International Airport in Pennsylvania. Obviously, the plane won't make it, but for paperwork reasons, you're flying there on business." Krystal looked at me and shook my hand awkwardly.
"Well, thanks for flying ice bitch airlines. We hope your flight doesn't end in crashing and dying." I rolled my eyes and looked at my watch, checking the time.

"It's late. We should leave now to avoid running into a crowd at the airport in Boston." Krystal nodded once and pulled her cell phone out of her pocket. Dialing a number, she waited for a few seconds before speaking.

"Jared? Yeah, we're leaving for the airport." She grew quiet for a moment before her mouth dropped open. A massive grin washed over her face before she responded to the voice on the other end of the line. "*How* afraid of flying?"

***

I knew my circumstance, and despite my best attempt at conveying that point to my doctor, he gave up with a sigh and placed my x-rays on the table before leaving.
"Nurse!" I called into the hallway, prompting a young girl in a lab coat to run into the room.
"I'm sorry, sir, is everything okay?"
"No, it's not. Disconnect these things. They're just fluids, I don't need them anymore."
"Sir, I think it's best-"
"I don't remember asking you what you thought was best. I can drink on my own. I don't need a needle jammed into my arm all hours of the night. I need sleep, not water." She sighed and reluctantly removed the needle from my arm, wrapping it in a cohesive bandage.
"Thank you. Sorry for being rude. Just tired, is all." I attempted to appear mild-mannered, prompting a soft smile and a pat on the head before she left.
"Thank god." I muttered, throwing the pile of blankets off me. The chair held my duffel bag lazily and squeaked as I picked it up, rifling to find my clothes. "Stupid...gown." I hastily removed the medical gown and looked at the scars on my chest, the majority of them covered by a large bandage. Throwing on my jeans and shirt, I grabbed the leather jacket

from the coat rack and called the first number on my contacts list. He answered almost immediately.

"Captain Kane? Holy shit, you made it."

"Yeah, I made it, alright. Did you guys make sure to bring my car over, too?"

"Yeah, dude. It's in the lot, all the way in the back. Section C. Wait, you're not leaving alre-"

"Thanks for the help, Warren. I owe you a beer when you get back stateside." I ended the call and turned off my phone, rounding the corner into the hospital's hallway. My throat was sore from speaking, despite the few words I had said. It matched the faint pain in my shoulder and knee.

"And I don't give a damn, I said you're letting her out. Now!" I stopped in my tracks as a female's voice rang out from a room I had passed. "I have another doctor ready, she's going into private care!" I took a step back and leaned against the wall, eavesdropping for no reason.

"Kara, you need to-"

"Don't tell me what I need to do, Alice. I need to get her the hell out of here." I heard another nurse talking in a much quieter voice, reassuring the women that their friend would be taken care of.

"Alice, call me when you move her. I doubt they'll have the paperwork together before tomorrow. I need a drink." I realized my mistake as soon as she rounded the corner, a mess of tangled black hair slamming into me and re-awakening the massive pain sleeping in my shoulder.

"Ow. Watch where you're going..." I looked into her eyes, the bright silver reflection of her anger staring straight back. "Please." I finished quietly. Her clothes were stained and dirty, a tight-fitting tactical shirt covering her chest and loose pair of camouflage cargo pants hugging her waist. She was, in a word, flawless. And somehow, she was familiar. She stared back at me for a moment, presumably thinking the same thing I was.

"You...look familiar. You're not...a patient here, are you?" She asked in

her perfect, melodious voice.
"What, me? No, I'm...visiting a friend. Joe. Smith. He's a friend of mine."
"Yeah, genius, you mentioned that. But...since there's blood dripping from your arm, I'm going to say that you suck at lying." I looked down frantically at my sleeve, wondering which one of my bandages broke. "Busted." She said quietly, smirking at me with her tongue pressed against her perfect cheek. I frowned, taking a step toward her. Despite my having several inches in advantage to my height and easily fifty pounds, she didn't back away or cower. She maintained her cocky posture and raised her eyebrows, maintaining her smug grin.
"You never saw me." I asserted, walking toward the nearest exit to the hospital. Reaching into my jacket pocket, I pulled out a pair of sunglasses and donned them as the metal doors opened automatically, the frigid autumn air of Maryland whirling around my face. I stared out at the parking lot for a moment, a mixture of relief and anxiousness washing over my racing mind.
"You're fine. You need...fast food? Strip club?" The girl's words echoed in my head several times before they made the distinction to become an active thought. "A drink. You need a drink." I whispered, walking through the massive parking lot. I found my car and slid into the driver's seat excitedly, happy to be home after a long absence. Opening the center console, I grabbed my keys and started the engine, backing out of the busy hospital's lot and turning onto the main road.
"Thanks, Warren. Now to find a bar..." I drove for several minutes until I saw an old, half-decrepit tavern slung awkwardly into the corner of a busy street. "Perfect." I hastily parked in the lot and locked my car, feeling sorry for the poor thing after only driving it for a short period of time.

 The atmosphere inside was warm, and unsurprisingly calm, being a weekday afternoon. The bartender looked up at me, clearly recognizing my clean-cut hair and strong build.
"Another soldier free from the hospital, huh?"

Sorrow

"Yeah, I'm assuming you get a lot of stops here?"
"A dozen or so every week. The first beer is on me, but only if it's American."
"Wouldn't have it any other way." I smiled and took a seat, looking up at the quiet television. The scene was heartening; I no longer had to peer into every corner or check every room as soon as I entered the building. I knew I was safe, and I knew I was home.
"Here you go, sir. Cheers. You the type to share the story, or prefer to have a quiet visit?" He seemed like a nice guy, scraggly red hair and a bushy mustache adorning his face.
"No story to tell, really. Got into an unlucky spot and lived to tell the tale. I just feel bad for my friends. They have another month to go, and I was lucky enough to come home early."
   A strong gust of cold wind permeated the serene environment, accompanied by a brief wave of bright light. I took a long draught from my glass, the alcohol bracing against the cold. Turning around slowly, I immediately recognized the woman standing behind me.
"You." I said abruptly, turning around again to face my drink.
"What are you doing here?" She asked in a rather accusatory tone. I finished the glass in front of me, tapping it lightly so the bartender would refill it.
"I'm having a drink. I'm pretty sure that's legal here." She scoffed and took a seat several feet away from me. "Why would you follow me?"
"Gin and tonic, please." She said politely before turning to me with a scowl on her face.
"I wanted a drink, asshole. I'm pretty sure that's legal here." Her mocking tone aggravated me, but I was in too good of a mood to allow her to ruin it.
"It is. And it's also legal for me to buy it for you." I handed the bartender my credit card as he set the drink down in front of her, a surprised look on both of their faces.
"I'm not interested. Not in the slightest."

"Good, that saves me the trouble of wasting my time. Regardless, it's on me." She sighed heavily and moved to the seat next to me, retaining her demanding demeanor.
"Why?"
"Because you need a drink."
"Why did you pay for it? I haven't done a thing for…" Her eyes widened as she realized who I was. "You…were that officer everyone was looking for. The one I helped find."
"Good job, detective. I'm assuming you were crying into my body the entire way back to the states? Wondering how such a perfect man would be taken from you?" In a single gulp, she swallowed her drink and rapped her glass rudely on the counter.
"Believe it or not, no. One of my friends was almost killed. But you know, if it's gonna be about you…"
"Look, lady. You're a contractor. You're not military, despite what you might think. You're outlaws with guns hired to sit in the heat for six months. Forgive me if I don't see a broken ankle as almost being killed."
"Excuse me?" I appeared to have stuck a nerve. "A broken ankle? She was in a vehicle hit with a fifty-pound explosive device. She has nearly no brain activity. Want to keep talking?"
"If that's the case, then I apologize. For real. That shit's rough. I lost one of my own guys a few months ago." Her face softened, trying to hold back her emotions. She sat more comfortably in her seat, sipping on her new drink.
"What were you, infantry?"
"Special forces." She almost choked, holding a hand over her mouth to keep the drink from exploding all over the bar. I grinned and finished the second beer, beckoning to the bartender for another. "Yeah. Thanks. Massive boost of self-confidence there, lady." As she cleared her throat, red-faced and humiliated, I couldn't help but repeatedly think to myself about how beautiful she was. Despite the ragged attire, her skin was flawless, a pale shade of unmarred ivory. Her long, black hair flowed

down to her perfectly curved waist in long waves of onyx black. I couldn't look away.

"Wow. So you...actually have a right to be here. I was with your ODA, your team. We were helping them find you. The way they talked about you, I figured you for some kind of god."

"And what, I'm not?" I retorted, swiveling to face her. She smirked, genuinely amused. When she smiled, her eyes grew brighter as they fixed on me, captivating my attention. "Enough about me. What's your story?"

"Army for three years. Marine Corps for five. Got tired of rules and found a job as a contractor. My partner and I were chasing a...terrorist leader of sorts across the desert when I found your group looking for you." It was my turn to nearly choke, partially in disbelief at her words.

"So you're telling me, you happened to run into me overseas, happened to be three hospital rooms away, and just so happened to come to the same bar? I think someone has a crush." She chuckled and buried her tongue into her cheek.

"You're...interesting, Captain."

"Jalix. Just call me Jalix." She arched an eyebrow.

"Jalix? The hell kind of a name is that?"

"Mom wanted Jasper, dad wanted Alex. They sucked at negotiating." I took another long gulp and dared to ask her for her name.

"And yours?"

"I told you I wasn't interested."

"Good. And yours?" She grinned, finding our repartee amusing.

"Kara. Kara Marie Valencia. It's Dutch."

"I don't think I asked for any details, miss Not Interested." The bartended leaned over, sliding us both drinks and grinning.

"I don't know who's going home with who, but this is on the house." I chuckled, shaking my head.

"She says she's not interested, barkeep." I turned my head slowly to look at her with a sense of irony. *"And yet, here she is, carrying on our*

conversation." Somehow, I managed to find a shade of blush in her cheeks as she looked down, shaking her head.
"Maybe I'm a little interested. But don't get full of yourself. It's just for the free drinks."
"Well, of course. I wouldn't expect to be buying you dinner or something. Just drinks." She smiled and finished her drink, standing up and moving to the door.
"Maybe dinner could work. I'll have to check my schedule." She called over her shoulder. Her eyes met mine once again, invoking something I had no way of describing. My heart seemed to slow down and speed up at the same time, wrenching my chest into an awkward pounding.
"I should probably get your number, just in case." I called as she pushed the door open. She paused for a moment.
"If I'm still interested...I'll find you." The door shut and the cold breeze piercing the tavern ceased.
"I'll find you?" The bartender echoed in disbelief. "Brother, she sounds certifiably insane."
"She sounds...like my future wife."

***

   I jolted awake as the jet started to accumulate turbulence, bouncing me lightly in my seat. Rubbing the haziness from my eyes, I looked over at Jared, staring nervously out of the window.
"Hey. We're fine."
"I know, man. But...shit, I hate heights. And flying. Shit that takes you off the ground, you know? We ain't made to fly. You see wings on my back? No." I smirked, looking into the cockpit at Alice and Krystal, occupied with the controls.
"How long?" I asked quietly, my voice carrying easily through the muted aircraft.
"Five minutes." Came Krystal's reply through the PA system. She was

Sorrow

short in her words, not out of anger or fear, but the same unsettledness that the four of us shared. Alice stood up from her seat and walked back to us, leaning against the frame.

"Krystal's getting ready. You guys prepared to die?"

"Thanks, Alice. That's really reassuring." I sighed, shaking my head.

"Not what I meant. We're all passengers on this plane, both on paper and in actuality. When it crashes in about six minutes, no one's going to know we jumped. We're all going to be legally dead. Or missing, if that's what they decide to go with."

"Hey, can this wait until we're not in the air?" Jared asked quietly, sinking his colossal frame into the leather seat.

"No, I get what you're saying, Alice. But I quit my job and I have no family left except you guys. I really don't think it matters that everyone's going to think I'm dead. I mean, it's a little late to back out now, anyway. We're almost there."

"One minute." Krystal called.

"That...was not four minutes." Jared croaked, picking his parachute off the ground and slinging it onto his shoulders. I did the same with my own as Alice talked us through the process once more.

"Alright. She's going to cut the engine right after we jump. She'll follow behind us and stay away from the chaos. As soon as we land, we hide if they haven't seen us or fight if they do. And we move quickly. Stick together, kill everyone, and find Schillinger."

"Easier said than done." I grunted, forgetting how heavy parachutes were. Alice moved her hands to the door of the plane, running her palms over the hinges.

"You know, it's been like eight years since I went through my airborne training for the army."

"Well, let's hope you remember." She smiled as the hinges started to glow like oven elements, glazed over with a red-orange glow. "And in case you're wondering, there's something like two thousand pounds of pressure on this door, so I can't just open it."

"Oh, good. So it's going to break off into the air. Instead of just opening."

"Jared, man, come on. You volunteered for this."

"Not really, no one else agreed to go through with all this."

"Wait, what?"

"Ladies and gentleman, we are experiencing some issues with the aircraft at this time, and it is advised to jump out like morons into the mountainside. Thanks for flying!" Krystal's voice legitimately sounded happy as she made the announcement, throwing off her headset and grasping a red lever on the roof of the cockpit. Alice grabbed the hinges and pulled, stretching the hot metal like dough before they broke off, releasing the door and overwhelming the interior of the plane with massive gusts of wind. My breath struggled to stay in my lungs.

Alice gave me a wordless thumbs-up and jumped out of the door, finally causing a full-blown panic. I grabbed Jared, knowing that he would need assistance exiting the plane. He didn't struggle, but it was difficult for him to stand in the doorway, staring down at the trees. "Father, holiest of-" Knowing that we were losing time, I shoved the back of his pack, causing him to tumble into the open air below. Despite the unreal level of noise, I could almost faintly hear him swearing at me as he fell. I took a deep breath and followed suit, leaping into the empty space that awaited me. I immediately grabbed the metal pull-ring on the bag, getting ready to deploy it when it was time. I flipped over and watched as the plane suddenly veered to the right, falling at a steady pace to the ground. A small, dark spot in the sky indicated that Krystal jumped with us. I exhaled slowly as the wind rushed around my face, deafening my ears. The trees looked distant, even the ones atop the mountains, giving me a false sense of the time I had before I hit the ground. I struggled with pulling the ring, knowing that if it were too early, we would be seen. Several hundred feet below, Alice's chute flared out above her, catching in the

Sorrow

wind and expanding to several times its original size. I could see a grey roof below me, accompanied by a helicopter's landing pad. As if there was a chance that we were in the wrong spot, I felt relieved to know we were in the right area.

Jared's parachute flared next, catching him awkwardly in the wind. His legs were kicking ferociously, an obvious sign that he was struggling with his phobia. They grew nearer, my pack not yet deployed. Looking up for a final time, I saw Krystal's parachute open early, a sign that she was worried about its effects on her body, had she been falling any faster. I gritted my teeth and fell past Alice and Jared, far too eager to start the fight. I was freezing now, the cold air made worse by the altitude and rate at which I was tumbling through the air. I was only a few hundred feet away now, perhaps a thousand, and decided that it was almost too late. I ripped the metal ring out of its secure fastener, my body jerking back quickly. The evergreen-covered mountainside maintained its green blur as I fell, heading straight toward the roof of the building. It was close now; I could see black-garbed security personnel pacing in front of the building, their gaze fixed on meaningless points in front of them.
None on the roof, two by the front gate by the road, two by the helicopter pad.

I analyzed the situation quickly, falling closer and closer to the roof. The mountains towered over me now, several hundred feet above my head and waiting for Krystal to land within its safe blanket of foliage. Taking a deep breath, my feet hit the roof and I rolled, avoiding the parachute's entangling embrace. It deflated by my side, flattening itself onto the concrete as I laid silently, staying out of view. I ripped the bag from my shoulders and flipped over, watching Jared and Alice descend into the same point, rolling the same way I did and laying perfectly still. I watched as Alice threw off her pack quietly and gave me a thumbs-up, inquiring as to how I was doing. I returned the gesture and we both looked at Jared, buried under a hill of fabric and support ropes. She crawled to his wreckage slowly, staring off the roof and toward the road to ensure we weren't seen. She ripped back the fabric to see him roll out quickly, shoving the material away from him.

"You good?" I whispered, moving between the two of them. He nodded, shaking subtly. We rested beside each other for a moment, catching our breath.

"What's the plan?" I asked, looking at Alice. She was staring into the sky, watching Krystal's parachute float through the canopy of trees not far from our location.

"I don't know. I expected them to see us, to be honest."

"Well, it's not like they're looking for us. They're watching the road. *Normal* people drive to where they need to go, not jump out of a perfectly good airplane." Jared's agitation was mildly amusing, but provided a valid point. We still had stealth on our side.

"Can we sneak in?" I asked Alice, knowing she had more experience than I did with breaking into these facilities. She shook her head.

"We had Kara with us last time. No offense, but we can't get in without her here and Eric keeping the alarms off."

"Do we have any options? Other than, you know, fighting our way inside and letting everyone know we're here."

"We're only here for Schillinger." Alice said quietly. "But I have no idea how we would be able to pinpoint him and isolate him enough to make a direct move."

"Do we need to? I mean, how many of these guys could there be? A dozen? Security is expensive."

"Yeah, and thanks to you, they can afford it now." She instantly apologized. "I didn't mean that. I'm sorry."

"The longer we wait here, the higher our chances are of being seen. We need to make a decision now."

"Jalix, we can't just-"

"Fine. Then don't." The growing anticipation of the ensuing fight was

starting to grip me, the adrenaline in my body hardening my muscles and honing my thoughts to a fine point. "What weapons do we have?"
"Jared has a pistol and I have a couple of knives. That's it. We couldn't smuggle anything else through the airport."
"Give me the knives." She reached into her waistline and withdrew several short knives, simple pieces of solid metal just under eight inches long. I tucked one into my boot and grasped the other two, getting a feel for their weight and balance. Slowly, I crawled my way to the edge of the roof and looked over the short lip extending toward the ground. I could barely make out an empty lobby through the glossy reflections of the glass.
"Jalix, you need to slow-"
"No. You need to catch up." I vaulted myself over the edge of the roof, bracing my legs against the impact from the ground. My boots crunched into the dry dirt, drawing the attention of the two guards by the front gate. Recovering from the fall, I managed to pull myself upright long enough to align my shoulders with my intended target. Without a chance to test my skill, I hurled the knives outward at the same time, my vision able to somehow focus on both men at once. As if an extension of my own body, they flew forward at an inconceivable speed and sunk themselves in the skulls of the lookouts before they fell to the ground with dull thumps. Whirling around, I confirmed that the front lobby was empty and moved to the side of the doors, out of view from wandering eyes.

Alice's ruby hair fluttered in the faint breeze, her bright green eyes glaring down into mine from the rooftop above. I motioned for them both to come down, returning my gaze to the foyer of the building. Jared landed a few feet behind me, catching Alice's graceful physique as she fell and lowering her to the ground.
"Now what?" She hissed, unhappy with my course of action.
"Now we go find him. That's what we're here for. We're wasting time by trying to come up with some elaborate plan. And he'll be expecting

that. We need to terrorize our way in and not give him a chance to run."

"We don't-"

"Have time to argue. And *you* don't have time to fabricate a strategy. I need you to get ready to burn anything that comes down the hallway, from either side. I'm going to check his office around the corner while you guys keep an eye out." Without waiting for her reply, I pushed open the massive glass door and stepped inside, skirting along the wall nearest to me. The facility's lobby looked exactly like the last, with only minor changes in décor and style. The structure remained unchanged, much to our advantage. Jared and Alice stepped inside, crouching behind the front desk and peering around the corner to stay out of sight. I moved slowly, wary of the hastiness of our actions. *Why are there no alarms? Why is no one here? What happened to the guards?*

Obvious questions rung out in my head as I approached Schillinger's office, exposing as little of my body as possible in order to see through his office window. Forest-green carpet, mahogany desk, and an empty chair; he was missing. As I looked back at Alice, shaking my head, I realized that she was beckoning to me. I looked down the hall to ensure it was safe before sprinting to her and crouching to her eyes level.

"Notice the silence?" She whispered, looking around. "And the lack of people? Something is up. Last time, there were half a dozen hired guns in this room."

"No shit, something's up. But *what*? And where is he if he's not in his office?"

"Probably the labs." Jared whispered. "It's the only reason these places exist. If he's anywhere, he's there."

"Which lab? There are dozens." They both shrugged, giving me the reaction I should have expected.

"Alright. We're not getting into the vaulted ones. They're too secure.

Sorrow

But what about the one you found me in? They have two of those machines, right? One got blown up, and the other is in the Boston facility. What's in *that* lab if the machine isn't there?" She raised her eyebrows, thinking for a moment.
"I don't know. But it's worth looking for."
"It's worth a shot." Jared stood and rounded the corner, pistol drawn to aim down the long hall of glass windows. He motioned with his head that we were safe to move to him. Alice led the way, staying low to avoid being seen. The windows to our right were black, as if they were shut down or empty. Even the blinking lights that indicated computers or machinery were hidden by the obscuring darkness. The silence was deafening, even the muffled breathing between the three of us hardly making a scratch in the empty void of the building. *Something isn't right here.*
"Jalix!" Alice hissed as a loud buzzing resonated from my pocket. My phone droned angrily, creating a racket unlike any other, forcing my hand to silence it hastily. "Why...is your phone on?" She growled deeply, anger and anxiety alight in her eyes. I shook my head and slunk lower, scanning the room behind the wall as if I would be able to make out any movement. Rarely had I seen anything so dark, so impossibly invisible as the space behind that glass. Jared looked back to us with wide eyes as muffled chuckling reverberated in that empty, dark space, indicative of someone's presence.
"Jalix, no need to let it go to voicemail." The voice was distorted, hushed by the layer of thick glass between us. Instantly, the room was illuminated by a bath of iridescent white light, the clear image of Schillinger flipping a master electric switch burning its way into the back of my eyes. The three of us jumped up immediately, backing against the wall and preparing for a fight. Alice's hands were already alight with blazing yellow heat, billowing fire dancing around her fingertips. Jared's pistol was drawn and aimed squarely at Schillinger, waiting for the opportune moment to fire. I was unfortunately

without a weapon, and stood silently as his eyes met mine, matched in hate and tension. A second figure moved from behind him, exposing himself to the small group of us and increasing my rage by tenfold.

"Mr. Kane." His thick Russian accent taunted my emotions, invoking a level of violence I had rarely felt toward another living being.

"Kilkovf. It's about time you and I had a fair fight." My entire body was alight with the same electric sensation of being in combat. A single twitch was all that stood between myself and the now-thin-seeming layer of glass. He chuckled, shaking his head and striding to the window. His arm was out of sight, hidden behind a wall for several seconds before the pan of glass slid sharply upwards and retracted into the wall. Realizing we had lost any hope of retreating, we stood firmly, starting to pace out courses of action in our minds.

"We want to talk." Schillinger said coolly, his voice saturated with hues of arrogance and condescension.

"About what?" I hissed, beyond any hope of calming down.

"Whatever you want." His reply was highly unexpected and prompted confusion.

"What, you're going to play therapist? Let's see...I've been having these really bad dreams. I think they stem from issues with my mother-"

"No, Jalix. I do not want to investigate your meaningless problems." My humor was apparently lost on him. "I want you to know me. You and I have never spoken in regards to our separate endeavors. You don't know my purpose, and I don't know yours. Rather than resort to meaningless...and I truly mean that, for three of you are no match for the two of us...violence, I would like us to come to an agreement. Something that has proven impossible between your companion and I. Speaking of our dear Karalynn...where might she be? Hiding?"

"She decided not to come with us." Alice responded sharply, looking to me for guidance. I remained neutral, hoping to gain more time.

Sorrow

Schillinger and Kilkovf exchanged a smile.

"I can hear the lies in your voice, my dear. But I sense fear. Not confidence. And so, regardless of where she is, I am sure she's not here."

"My friend can smell your lies from a mile away." Kilkovf chimed in.

"Why don't we remain polite? Both sides will tell the truth." The shock I felt must have been obvious on my face; it was hard to imagine us being an enemy to someone so...apparently civilized.

"I won't lie, Schillinger. After I found out what you stand for, I imagined you as more animal than man."

"Mister Kane...I can assure you, I am no animal. No longer. Those days are long past, and rest assured, I did not wait for you today for our meeting to end in bloodshed." He walked toward us, moving around laboratory tables and equipment to stand next to Kilkovf, only the empty barrier of the former window between us.

"What do you mean you waited for us?"

"Your kind acts as though they are unpredictable. Your...methods may be unorthodox, but you always end up with the same result. Here. With me. It's one of the reasons I believe so strongly that we should not be separated in our ideals. We will continue to meet, we will continue to coexist, as we have for many years now. But rather than holding each other back, someday we will move forward together."

"Not going to happen." Alice declared. "You want to infect humans without giving them a choice. We don't want you to do that. It's a pretty simple fact that opposing ideals don't make a foundation for good friendships."

"Ah, miss Allison. A question. Those that you deem worthy to join your world...do you tell them exactly what is going to happen to them? Or do you offer them a mysterious way out of their pain? Because it seems that one of us isn't going to keep what we're doing a secret...and the other is betraying the humans' trust in order to build

their ranks."
"They would die otherwise!" She screamed, emotional and angry.
"They would. But many have already made their peace. Now, instead of fulfilling their own destiny, they will linger while their families die." She shook her head violently, dismissing his words. "But, Miss Allison, I'm not here to speak with you. Nor am I here to speak with Karalynn. I am here…to know Jalix." His head once again swiveled to meet mine, a matching, smug grin spread across Kilkovf's face.
"What do you want from me?" I demanded.
"I want to know…do you agree with them because you have no other choice?"
"Of course not. I agree with them because I believe in what they stand for." I answered quickly with, what I believed, was the right answer. I felt odd though, as if what he was saying had any sort of merit. "And I haven't forgotten that you've tried to kill me twice now."
"Three times." Alice corrected.
"Four times." Jared corrected once again.
"Jalix, if I had tried to kill you, you'd be dead." Kilkovf said, chuckling. "The casino? That was to scare your wife. I could have pulled the trigger as soon as the gun was drawn. I'm very good at what I do. The car accident? Me, as well. I fled instead of snapping your neck and making it look like an accident. Your kidnapping? Those intruders in your city? Mister Kane, we were sending you a message. Life with *their* kind…is too dangerous. Living with Karalynn…it's deadly."
"It nearly was for Sonya. And it was for Valterius." I argued, trying to force the point back on them. "If you're so agreeable, why'd *they* have to suffer?"
"Sonya destroyed nearly everything we stood for. She was as powerful as Karalynn, but emotionally vulnerable. We had no choice. And Valterius was an…unintended side effect. While I don't wish he was still alive to help you…we did not aim to kill him."
"I'm done talking. To both of you. You're ruthless. You're evil. And

Sorrow

you try to play it off like you're heroes. You want your vision to become true, and nothing will get in the way of that. Whether it's for a good cause or not...it doesn't matter. You shouldn't be prepared to sacrifice those you care about for anything."

"Mark my words, Jalix." Schillinger's voice instantly grew enraged, alight with anger at the fact that he had lost any hope of control over me. "No one is prepared to sacrifice those that we love. But sacrifice will come to you. Loss will take you. And I promise you...I will be the one to cause it." As he leaned in, his head was exposed to a perfect angle, taken advantage of by Jared. His massive fingers pulled the trigger on the gun, catching Schillinger by surprise. I was able to faintly see the bullet whizz through the air for a short distance before exploding inches in front of Schillinger's face. Tiny shards of lead and copper sprayed his face, but inflicted very little injury.

"I am very hard to kill, Jalix. Your wife could not. Valterius could not. And you? You are going to witness my immortality." The gun in Jared's hand shattered into fragments of hot metal, spewing into the empty hall and clattering to the floor. Jared winced and withdrew his hands, sticky with blood. Alice looked at me with fear in her eyes, realizing the impossibility of the situation.

"You know, Schillinger..." I started calmly. "You're making a mistake, and it's one that I saw Kara make, too. You think you're a shield, something impermeable and invincible defending your cause. But you're not. You're another sword in this fight. And there's a reason wars aren't fought with swords anymore." I lunged forward, the might of every muscle in my body straining to keep pace with the boiling retaliation that burned in my brain. My hand gripped his neck, my fingers digging into the flesh and creating a perfect grip on his body. "They dull over time."

Weaver

Sorrow

Ice
Kara

It was surprising that the sound of reporters outweighed the sound of the thousand law enforcement voices, as well as the accompanying responses over their radios. They barked angrily at anyone that walked by, demanding that their craving for information be satisfied. National Guardsmen roamed the thin line between civilians and police, holding back the rush of curious journalists from overtaking the mound of rubble.

"So he's yelling for other people to come over, and I'm arguing with him, right? Acting like I don't want anyone to know I'm here. And he *listens*. He acts like he's going to be this big hero for digging a poor trapped guy out of this collapsed building. He's *telling* me all of this, talking about how he's going to be regarded as this big hero, that my family will thank him. It's frickin' hilarious. As soon as my arm's free, I knock him out and pull him into my little hole-" A group of three police officers jogged past us, and Val grew silent, pretending to talk on the radio clipped to his uniform until they passed. "So I pull him down, make sure he's still breathing, and I steal his uniform. I swear to god, sis, *no one* has asked me who the hell I am. It's perfect."

"I wouldn't call giving me a damn heart attack *perfect*, Val. We thought you died."

"I'm too damn stubborn to die. Anyway...we need to get you out of here before someone recognizes you." He turned to look at me, running his eyes over the mess of hair hastily stuffed into the baseball cap on my head. "Your shitty disguise only gets you so far."

"I thought it was decent. I was just surprised I was able to find a vest like this sitting in one of their trucks." I pulled at the bright orange reflective vest on my chest, embossed with the logo of the local utility company. "Now, what's my story? We need to get out of here without drawing attention."

"You were...digging through the wreckage and twisted your ankle. I'm taking you to the hospital to make sure it's not broken." He paused. "And by the way, utility workers don't wear skinny jeans when they're working a site."

"I was off-duty when they called."

"Off-duty? What are you, a cop?" I chuckled at his familiar sense of humor, part of me just thankful I could hear his voice. A small recession in the crowd marked a perfect exit point for the two of us, slipping past the uniformed soldiers and throng of ear-piercing correspondents.

"...in what some experts say was a planned bombing-"

"...signs of any life within the rubble-"

"...coinciding with simultaneous attacks against former employees-"

I tried my best to ignore their monologues, fully aware that I needed to be as hasty as possible. We fought our way to the back of the crowd, which opened up to a parking lot packed with vehicles, yet oddly devoid of people. My car sat idly, the engine still running, blocked in by a news van that decided to impede me from pulling away.

"Dammit." I sighed, looking behind me to check for watching eyes. I hastily pulled the hat from my head and tore off the orange vest, looking into the windows of the van. "No one's inside. Help me move it." Val walked to the far side of the van, out of sight from the crowd, and pushed against the frame, slowly inching the vehicle away from my car. I pressed my palm against the side, the entire structure of the vehicle outlining itself in my head like a blueprint. I pulled gently, moving my hand toward me and mentally grasping the vehicle. It shifted outward quickly, and bounced slightly as Val and I both released our grip.

"You're lucky you're so damn strong, Val. If you hadn't dug yourself out, I wouldn't have been able to get to you."

"Eh, I work out." He shrugged my compliment away in his usual manner before clambering into the passenger seat of my car. I sat in the driver's seat and pulled the car away from the lot slowly, inching my way through the multitude of police cruisers, military vehicles, and news vans, finally turning onto the highway and breathing a massive sigh of relief.

"Thank you." Val said quietly, staring out of the window. I furrowed my brow.

"For what?"

"Rescuing me."

"You kind of rescued yourself there, genius."

"But you came back." His voice was soft as he turned his head toward me, honesty in his face.

"Val...you're my brother. I love you. Why wouldn't I come back?"

"No one said I'd be alive in there. And I almost wasn't. I got lucky. But you...believed in me."

"Do I really seem that cold, Val? That I would leave you behind without at least...making sure?"

"No, of course not. But you didn't send someone else. You didn't bring anyone with you. So you probably left without telling anyone. And you never do things alone anymore."

"Is that a bad thing?"

"No, it's a good thing. Look..." He sighed and turned his whole body so he was facing me. "You used to do *everything* alone. Because you didn't trust anyone. Then when you lost Sonya, you couldn't trust yourself. So we always went *with* you. Now...I think you're starting to

trust yourself again. And I'll bet Jalix had something to do with that. Speaking of which, how is he?"
"Probably worried sick. Oh, about the...right. He's fine. We think they copied his memories, but that's it. He woke up and was remembering things he hasn't done in ten years. Other than that, he seemed fine."
We sat in silence for a moment as I drove, focusing on the road rather than let any emotion present itself as the more dominant.
"Then why don't you sound happier?" I shook my head, trying to understand, myself.
"Krystal is still hurt. Jalix probably doesn't trust me now. I almost got you killed-"
"Whoa. Stop right there. I *forced* you to take me. I didn't give you any choice, and I knew you were emotionally vulnerable. You didn't have the time or energy to argue. So don't you dare put what happened on your conscience."
"I have to, Val. It's my job to keep you safe. All of you."
"By taking away our choices? Our free will?" I almost responded immediately, explaining that if I was the one making the calls, I would be able to take responsibility. Before I could speak, I remembered what Jalix said. Sighing, I looked at him for a moment.
"No. Of course not. That's why I fight, for us to have a free life. But it doesn't mean I don't feel guilty for letting these things happen to you."
"Good." He said, smiling.
"Good?"
"Good. It means you're more human than you'd like to believe." I smiled, finally letting one emotion peek through my mask of neutrality.
"Now, fill me in on exactly what happened. The last I saw, you clocked Schillinger in the face, and Alice and I were locked behind a vault door."

Sorrow

"Right. Well, you know the labs between the open ones and the closed ones?" I looked at him confusedly, dumbfounded as to what he meant. "The ones in that long hall? Not the ones with big-ass windows and not the ones behind that big-ass door. The ones in the middle. I was *right* outside them when you guys left?"

"Oh, those. Yeah, what about them?"

"Apparently, they're self-contained. They're individualized. Schillinger ran right after you guys got locked in, probably because he assumed you'd be trapped. He used his...exploding...ability, which I'm pretty confused about, and pretty much obliterated the path behind him as he left. I just dove into one of those labs and right before everything got all fiery, it sunk."

"It...sunk."

"Yeah. It dropped like, eight feet. There wasn't even anything in the lab. It was like a...control room or something. All these big electrical panels and crap. But I guess it was protected. It dropped into the floor and everything collapsed on top of it. I had to punch a hole in the roof until I could start tearing pieces of the concrete away, and everything kind of filled the room. It made a chasm in the rubble, and I was able to climb out."

"You're lucky you're strong."

"Not just strong. I still have handsome going for me. And charming. I could lose a trait or two and still be awesome." I chuckled, shaking my head.

"I'm going to call Jalix and let him know I'm on my way back. I feel like he could use some good news."

"Sounds good. After you hang up with him, fill me in on what I missed. And tell them to get a shot of our magic blood-cocktail ready. I'm not feeling good. At all." I reached into the glove compartment immediately and withdrew a small fabric case, handing it to him. "Here. They're the last two I have outside the city. I need one, too. I feel like shit." I couldn't suppress the distant, dull pain in my abdomen anymore, succumbing to one of my few physical needs. He pulled out the matching syringes and buried one of the needles in his arm, sighing a breath of relief.

"Thank you. I'll do yours, just hold your arm still." I maintained my posture as I drove, the tiny pinch of the needle followed by a sensation of brief euphoria accompanied with unparalleled energy.

"Thanks. Just put them back for now. I'll throw them out later." I pulled my phone from my pocket and dialed Jalix's number, cocking my head to hold the phone in position between my ear and my shoulder. It rang for several moments before forcibly disconnecting. I pulled the phone away, looking at it quizzically before redialing. It immediately disconnected, not ringing at all.

"I think he turned his phone off after I called him." I sounded hurt, my petty relationship problems deciding to overthrow the normal confidence of my voice.

"He'll be fine. He's just irritated. I'm shocked he's still doing so well."

"I'm going to call Alice." I asserted, hoping that I still had a friend left. After dialing, the phone disconnected in the same manner, failing to ring on the other end. My heart sank, knowing that something was wrong. Hastily, I tried one more call, praying that it would go through.

"Yes, miss? What can I do for you?" Hack's meek voice was a boon as he agitated me once again.

"Eric, I told you to call me Kara. Can you tell Jalix to call me, please? I'm on my way back." He waited, taking his time with a response and fueling my uneasiness.

"He's not here right now. He...needed some time."

"Fine. Put Alice on." Silence once again forced my heart lower into my chest. "Eric."

"Ma'am...we need to talk once you get back." I ended the call and pressed my foot into the gas, racing through the busy highway.

"What is it?" Val asked.

"I should have brought them with me." I whispered. "I should have brought them."

***

The urge to forcibly wring his neck with my hands was an actual struggle to fend off as he recoiled, almost tripping over the mass of wires trailing across his floor.

"Miss, they had a plan, and I know they're going to be okay."

"They're not going to be *okay*! You're telling me they're on their way to go kill someone I haven't managed to even scratch after three hundred years, but *they* can do it? Jalix has what, six people helping him?" I shot him a mixed look of disbelief and horror as he slunk back once again without speaking. "Damn it, Eric! How many people left with them?"

"Alice, Jalix, Jared, and...Krystal." I scoffed, my mouth somehow open in a mocking smile. "Oh. Oh, good. Krystal is with them. Let me guess. Barely conscious. Ribcage still shattered. Skull still healing. And yet, they're *skydiving* into the goddamn *mountains* to fight off the warlord wreaking havoc on our way of life. And this...was *your idea*?" He was backed into the wall at this point, my figure towering over him as I descended like a hungry wolf on easy prey. Val's hand gently grasped my shoulder, pulling me back ever so slightly.

"Kara." He stepped past me, looking into Eric's eyes with kindness. "Why didn't you tell her, Eric? She would have helped."

"We..." He sighed. "Look, I'm wrong now. And I realize that. But a lot of us thought you were too...emotional...to go after Schillinger. We didn't want you getting hurt."

"And I don't want *them* getting hurt!" I yelled, standing my ground.

"Someone is going to get hurt, Miss." He said quietly. "That's why they left. We agreed that this can't go on any longer. We thought we lost Val. We lost two of our own that used to live here. We lost Sonya.

Weaver

People were falling apart left and right. Krystal is hurt. It was a damn miracle Jalix made it back alive. And most of everyone else is gone. We need to put an end to this. First Schillinger. Then Kilkovf. Then Raven. And then it's over."

"Unless they *die* because they're waging a war of their own. Eric, when we went to recover Jalix, we couldn't stop him."

"You were held back. You weren't *there* for Schillinger. You were there for Jalix. Kara, I know you."

He used my name.

"You might not think of me as a close friend, but I know you. I know the way you look at Jalix. You see that he has your strength. Alice has your intelligence. Krystal has your passion. Jared has your willpower. Everyone here needs you as much as you need them. They can do this. We just need to let them. And you don't have a choice." He crossed his arms and furrowed his brow, staring blankly at his computer screen. "There's no way we would be able to get there in time to make any difference."

"Eric is right, Kara. We need to focus on what's next. Plan for them to arrive back here safe and sound. It's pointless to imagine anything else. We'd drive ourselves crazy. So let's think. What happens when they get back?"

"Val, it's not that easy-"

"What...happens...when they get back?" He grasped me lightly by the shoulders, looking into my eyes. "When. Not if." I smirked lightly, the stinging precursor of tears closing off my eyes and throat.

"Yeah. When." I took a deep breath and opened my eyes, placing my hands on the top of my head. "I think the next step is Raven. Kilkovf is strong, and he's definitely Schillinger's watchdog, but without Raven, everything falls apart. I say we go after her."

"Alright. Now we're talking." Val smiled, cracking his knuckles. "So what do you think? Classic assassination? Poison her? Fake a break-in?"

"I don't know yet. Eric, do you have any information on her?" He nodded, running a hand through his brown shaggy hair.

"Yeah, actually. But it's all public knowledge. Schillinger doesn't trust her by herself. So he has her living in their corporate building downtown. She basically lives in an office on the top floor. There's constant security there, but it's more for show than anything. Their labs are where the magic happens. This place is just for paper-pushers."

"Alright, how can we use that to our advantage?" He smirked.

"Every year, they hold an annual charity ball. Get this. It's called the Raven's Nest." I rolled my eyes.

"How theatrical. What's the goal?"

"Not much. Rich people gather to drink expensive booze, rub elbows, and donate money. It's exactly what it sounds like. It's two days from now, and it's a black-tie only event. Very tight guest list."

"Can you get me on it?"

"Get you on it?" He looked genuinely surprised when I asked him. "They're going to notice if a random name appears on their list. Raven hand picks the guests. I *can* put you on the list, but it's going to raise some questions."

"Don't worry about it, then. I want to keep this low profile. I'll think of something." I gasped, clutching my stomach as an intense pang of pain erupted, right in the center of my abdomen.

"Kara?" Eric asked, placing a hand on my back and looking me in the eyes.

"Blood." I groaned, doubled over. He rushed to his desk drawer and pulled out a syringe, driving it into my shoulder and pressing down. I felt relief instantly, the pain subsiding from an intense spasm to a mild cramp.

"Kara, you just had a shot…not even an hour ago. Are you okay?"

"Yeah…you forget, I've been using my abilities quite a bit. That thing with the tree root yesterday, that chunk of concrete, the news van today...they took a toll, I guess." I straightened my back, sucking in a deep breath. "Anyway..." I continued, the remnant pain subsiding slowly. "I'll get Jalix to call Raven and tell her that he changed his mind. That he's staying with the company. I'm sure that will prompt an invitation."

"Yeah, except...on paper, Jalix is probably going to be dead. And by probably, I mean definitely. Remember how they took Krystal's private jet? And...how they're going to let it crash?"

"Dammit." I hissed. "His name is on the paperwork as a passenger. He has to stay out of the public from now on." Eric nodded, looking over my shoulder at Val. He stood in the doorway several feet away, out of earshot and on the phone with someone.

"What is it, Val?" I asked. He held up a single finger, indicating that I needed to wait until he was done.

"Yeah. I just think it's time." He waited for several long moments while the person on the other end spoke. "Thank you. We'll see you soon."

"Who was that?" I asked cautiously, approaching him.

"Look, Kara-" Val was interrupted by a small, female figure appearing in the doorway behind him. Her eyes widened as she realized who she was standing behind.

"Val!" She exclaimed, wrapping her arms around his shoulders and leaping up, wrapping her legs around his midsection and holding on. He laughed, reaching behind him to tousle Violet's hair.

"Hey, kiddo. How are you?"

"Better now. Are you okay? Everyone thought-"

"Ah, no one has any faith in me. They forget that I'm kind of a badass. I crawled my way out of the rubble, disguised myself as a cop, and walked myself right out of there." He grinned, smiling at me.

"Although I might have had a little bit of help." Violet released her elated grip on his shoulders and ran up to me, embracing me tightly.

Sorrow

"Thank you, Kara. I love you." My hands were frozen for a moment, trying to embrace her, but failing at returning the gesture of her words. Slowly, they made their way to her back and pulled her closer to me.

"I love you, too, Violet. I'm so sorry again. For everything."

"Don't be." She pulled away, wiping away the tears in her eyes. Her eyeliner streaked slightly, fixed by a gentle smudge from my thumb. "I know you had your reasons. I'm sorry I doubted you." I smiled softly and ran a hand through her deep black hair, the solitary streak of purple floating next to the outline of her face. "I want to help." She said earnestly, looking at me with pleading eyes. "There has to be something I can do." I shook my head and answered her honestly. "Violet, there really isn't anything you can do. Not because I don't want you to be involved, but because there's nothing *to* do. Even the three of us are just...waiting for Jalix and his group to get back."

"We're not going after Raven?" She looked up at Val, who shook his head.

"No. We do things together from here on out. No more splitting up." She nodded.

"Speaking of which." Eric said quietly. "Our plan involved us meeting back at Krystal's mansion. My brother is already there with a few guys. They're setting up workbenches to dismantle the helicopter they're bringing back. It looked like he was well prepared. Acetylene torches, chop saws, the whole nine yards. And he took two trucks. He'll have to hide the cut-up pieces down here somewhere, so he's planning on bringing them back."

"You guys really thought of everything, didn't you?" I smirked, lauding his scheming abilities.

Jalix is in danger at this very moment. Maybe even dead.

"Oh, Val. Who were you on the phone with? Anything I need to know about?" I turned to him as I asked the question, watching his expression fall into a mix of fear and sadness.

Weaver

"Kara…" He started. "You have to understand. We need help. We're running out of soldiers."
"Val…who was on the phone?"
It's her.
"Kara, I'm so sorry. It's time for her to come back. Okay?"
"Valterius…please…"
"She's already here. She called me when she pulled up to the frame shop. I was texting her on our way back from the wreckage." I balled up my fist tightly, unprepared for the emotional roller coaster that was about to unfold in front of me.
"You should've asked me. You should have said *something*." I shook my head, a disturbing turmoil overtaking my active thoughts. "I can't go back to that place, Val!" I screamed, approaching him. "I spent long enough trying to get myself away from the past! And then…you go and do *this*? How could you?" I pushed him to the side and stalked out of the room, heading toward the main hall.
She's gone. She's not here. She'd dead. Let her go.
The massive cavern opened up in front of me as I passed through the exit of the living quarters, staring emptily at the training room. A tall blonde woman stood idly by the entrance to our city, looking around at the destroyed pieces of concrete that littered the ground. I clenched my eyes shut, taking a step back and leaning against the wall. My breathing was heavy, a facet of my physical distress that I couldn't control.
She's alive.
Val rounded the corner down the hall, stopping in his tracks and waiting, unwilling to be the first person to see her.
"You can do this." He whispered to me. "I know you can." I shook my head, the wisps of my dark hair whirling into a frenzy around my shoulders.

 I forced myself to lean forward, pushing off of the wall and meandering into the main hall. She stood silently, her hands timidly

shoved into the pockets of her jeans. She shifted her weight from one leg to another, accommodating a heavy backpack.
"Samantha?" I called cautiously as she looked up at me before smiling.
"Kara. It's really good to see you." I approached her, my heart telling me to lunge forward and my brain telling me to run away. She took a step forward and hugged me lightly, looking around.
"This place has seen better days. Last time I was here, it was...crowded. And less..." She looked down at the broken, bloodstained concrete.
"Yeah, I'm sorry about that. It's been a rough few months."
"Well, listen. I have a few things to say, if you don't mind." I swallowed hard to clear the swelling from my throat, to no avail.
"Alice has been sending me a lot of correspondence. Journals from our days together, emails filled with old stories. I've gotten a lot better. I mean, it's not all back yet, but...slowly. You know? Things feel more familiar now."
"Good. I'm really glad. How are the headaches?"
"Better. A few cups of coffee in the morning and they're gone for the day. Honestly, my biggest headache is the name change. All the journals and emails say *Sonya* or *Spirit*, but my new identification says *Samantha*. It's...hard to keep track of, oddly enough."
"Well...it's whatever you prefer. Just like everyone else."
"I'm Sonya. It's who I am. Nothing will change that." I forced a smile, nodding.
"Well, Sonya. I'm glad we have you back. And to be honest, it wasn't my choice I'm so sorry we pulled you away from your life-"
"Up there? Sweetie, I work in retail. I'll take kicking ass and taking names over *that* any day. Now where's Valterius so I can thank him for calling?" I spun around to call for him, but Val was already around the corner and walking toward us.
"Hey." He called quietly, approaching her slowly.

Weaver

"Hi. Thanks for giving me a chance to come back. I know you guys don't trust that I'm up to speed, but Alice has kept me very well informed. And my physical condition also isn't an issue. I've been meeting with a few others on the surface to get me back into fighting shape."

"Did you expect to come back? Sounds like you've been preparing." Val asked courteously.

"Sort of. The more information I've gotten, the more I've wanted to come back. And since I'm feeling well...there's not a better time, I suppose."

"Agreed." He shook her hand warmly before taking a step back and beckoning me to get her up to speed.

"Well, we have a lot to talk about, Sonya. Before you do much of anything, I want Alice to check you out...when she gets back."

"Back? Back from what?" I sighed, hating that I had to say the words aloud.

"Four of us are out right now. We cornered Schillinger. They're going to try and...they're going to kill him." She paused for a moment, taking in the information.

"Wow. Well, if they succeed, they'll have done what we never could."

"I have faith in them. My fiancé is among them. And he's...one of the best. An incredible soldier. And a great person. I can't wait for you to meet him."

"Jalix, right?" She asked, wandering further into the hall. "Alice spoke very highly of him." As we walked, I began to feel more comfortable in her presence. Her personality was returning, the curious, mild-mannered girl I once knew shining through the fog of her lost memories. "Tell me about him."

"I really don't know where to begin." I knew exactly where to begin, but memories of her injuries were still raw. "We met at a bar and he just...captivated me. He was witty, but grounded. Confident. He just seemed...perfect."

"He sounds like it. Handsome?"
"Very."
"Well, I'm proud of you. I'm glad you've opened up a little. Let someone in." She paused. "So what made you decide to introduce him to our world?" I grimaced.
"Well...he was attacked. Twice. I wanted to keep him safe, and I felt like he was ready. Plus...he proposed, and I said yes. I wanted him to see who I really was before we got married."
"Well...that makes sense. Has he handled everything okay?" Val spewed his feeling towards Jalix as we walked.
"The guy's a hero. Drinks like a fish, fights like a lion, and he's holding it together like glue. We couldn't have asked for anyone better to join our cause at a time like this. I mean...present company excluded." Sonya laughed, shaking her head.
"No, trust me, I won't be much help. I can fight, don't get me wrong, but I'm a little behind on information." Val continued to be uncharacteristically helpful.
"I'll summarize it. Shift Company is co-run by Schillinger and his daughter, Raven. Both Vampyres. They have our virus and they're trying to perfect it to do a couple things. One of them being to bring back the dead. Once they can do that, they'll use this machine they have to replace the dead person's memory. Now, the machine is finished, but they're still messing with the virus. They need a really old strain that didn't originate from Schillinger, so from someone like you, Kara, myself, pretty much anyone that isn't new. Once they finish the virus, they're going to infect humans, make them immortal, and force them to see the world under a unified perspective, changing the course of human history and creating a cohesive new world order. Did I get it right?" Val looked at me, grinning from ear to ear as he managed to take a five hundred year old problem and narrow it down to a short paragraph.

"Yeah. Pretty much. Things are going back to the way they used to be. Humans are going to find out about us at some point during this war. It's public, the humans just don't know it yet. They killed Jalix's boss, kidnapped Jalix, and blew up one of their facilities."
"Probably two if Jalix and his crew gets the job done."
"Yeah. Thanks, Val. Anyway, Sonya, it's very complicated. We're going to handle this thing one piece at a time. Our next step is going after Raven. Hopefully, it won't be too hard. Then, we can take out Kilkovf, and everything will...be okay." The words felt foreign coming out of my mouth. It was impossible for me to see a future in which Vampyres weren't hunted, but nevertheless, my mind attempted to visualize it.
"Will it?" She asked quietly. The three of us stopped, Val and I turning toward her confusedly.
"What do you mean?"
"Well...if we *are* discovered, which we will be someday, don't you think someone else is going to take Schillinger's place? Evil doesn't die. It just sleeps."
"We can't afford to think like that. If something else ever happens, we'll be ready. But for now, we can take care of this and have many years of peace ahead of us. And besides...I trust the humans. We were all one at some point." I smirked and patted her shoulder before continuing to walk down the long hall.
"Aren't we still?" Val asked quietly. I stopped, my shoulders sagging with the weight of his question. I turned around slowly, looking into his eyes.
"Of course we are, Val. We're just a different kind of human."
"You really *have* changed, Kara. But in a good way." Sonya smiled, looking around at the emptiness that surrounded us. "So what happened? Why is everyone gone?"

"The city wasn't safe. It's a long story. There were a few of us that stayed. Eric is in his room. Jalix, Krystal, Jared, and Alice are all out right now. And Tony took everyone else over to Krystal's mansion."
"Why?"
"To dismember a helicopter." Val said cheerily. "I'll explain later." He waved his hand dismissively as the smile disappeared.
"Val, why don't we let Sonya get settled in? You and I can do some plotting against Raven."
"Ooh. Plotting. I love that stuff."
"Thank you for the opportunity to help." Sonya added, hiking the backpack up on her shoulders. "It's not a problem. I'm glad that you're here." I smiled, watching her walk down the hallway to her living quarters.
"Are you, really?" Val asked quietly, turning to me.
"Yeah. I am. I know I have issues to figure out, but...I think she's going to help me with them. Seeing her here...it reminds me of good times, actually. Not bad ones." I sighed. "Now I just have to wait for Jalix to call me back."

***

The campfire crackled and spit, deep red embers scattering around the ring of rocks on the forest floor. I took a long drink of water from my canteen, brushing Sonya's long, blonde hair out of the way as I replaced it on the ground. Stroking her hair gently, her head nestled in my lap, I watched the waves of orange dance upwards, trying to break free and float into the night sky.
"I love fire." She whispered, her fingers mocking the way it spiraled and twirled through the chill air. "I love how free it is. Dancing, bending...and the whole time, it helps us stay warm."
"Yeah. It really is pretty." We sat in silence again, the slow rise and fall of her chest the only movement in the light of the fire.

Weaver

"Do you ever wonder what life would be like without the stars?" She asked quietly, gazing at the faint orbs of light embossed in the dark sky. I shook my head, waiting for her thoughts. "It's not just how they look from here...sure, I'd miss the beauty of it all. It's the only thing besides the moon that has any light after the sun goes down, but...I'd miss the hope."
"The hope?"
"Yeah. Looking up, I wonder how many other planets there are like ours. In this infinite galaxy within an infinite universe...what else is looking up, wondering about its place in the sky?" She grew quiet again, a quiet smile fading over her perfect lips. "It's hope. If they were gone, there wouldn't be any wondering. No mystery."
"Wouldn't it be easier just to...know? To really know that we're the only ones?"
"Who would it be easier for?" She smiled at me, knowing that it was typical of me to be the logical thinker out of the two of us. "I like wondering. I like thinking that, maybe, a long time from now, we'll be a part of something bigger. We'll get to see it, you know? Being immortal and all. We'll get to see who we share the sky with." I laughed quietly.
"Maybe. Someday."
"You think I'm crazy, don't you?" She looked up at me, closing her eyes and rolling onto her side.
"No. I think you're creative. I wish I had your sense of curiosity. It's...like fire. It's unpredictable. And dangerous..." I chuckled again. "But pretty. And fun to watch at work."
"Thanks, Kara. I think you're pretty, too." I smirked, shaking my head gently. Her breathing slowly lessened in pace, her face slowly growing more peaceful.
"Hey, Kara?" She murmured, almost asleep.
"Yeah?"
"I love you. I can't compare it to a sibling, because...I've never had one. I can't compare it to a spouse for the same reason. But as a friend?" She

Sorrow

sighed softly, snuggling into the mess of hair that became her pillow for the night. "You're the best friend I've ever had." I stroked her hair gently, allowing her to fall asleep against me.
"I love you too, Sonya. You'll always be my friend." I looked into the fire, its crackling subsided to a quiet roar of heat. "Always."

Weaver

Dominate
Jalix

The smell of burning flesh wasn't what I had expected it to be. I was surprised that it wasn't the smoky, musky scent of charred steak coupled with a coppery, metallic odor. It was instead a rancid, sour-milk stench infused with spent matches. The consuming reek of Alice's searing hands burning their way into Kilkovf's skull was as horrifying as the sight itself. I grunted, throwing my weight against Schillinger as Kilkovf's screams echoed through the empty building. Caught in a war of strength, which I was quickly losing, I saw out of the corner of my eye Kilkovf's foot drive into Alice's stomach, doubling her over in pain. Kilkovf mashed his hand blindly against a panel on the wall before stumbling out of the room.

"I've got him!" Jared yelled, releasing his hold on Schillinger and sprinting after Kilkovf. All of the weight Jared was holding back was sent directly into my shoulders, giving Schillinger the advantage. I ducked my head and squirmed my way out of his inconceivable grip, landing a quick punch to his eye before taking a step back to gain distance. He recovered quickly, seeing me stand between him and Alice's crumpled body. I heard her groan behind me, standing up and facing our mutual enemy.

"Don't make me kill you, Jalix." He snarled, taking a step toward me. He hesitated as a deafening blare rung out in the empty labs. "Kilkovf, you coward!" He screamed, looking around as the lab's alarms rung out. Alice took advantage of his distraction and pushed me aside, a gout of flame gushing from the palm of her hand and setting Schillinger's body alight. Motionlessly, he stood, as if waiting for her to be finished. She dropped her arm after a brief moment of intense heat, exhausted, as his flesh seared and fizzled, repairing the damaged sections and healing before our eyes. His suit was fused to his skin, an amorphous mass of synthetic fabric melted to his body. I took a step back, feeling the sharp metallic pinch of the blade in my boot. He chuckled, his voice hoarse and raspy from the blistering damage to his throat.

"You can't kill me. I spawned your existence!" He lunged forward and picked me up by the throat, slamming me into the wall to my left. "I allowed your kind to exist!" Seared pieces of his lips and tongue were spat on my face as he hissed, burning my own skin. His hand was reduced to a bony mass of exposed muscle.

"Alice!" I gurgled, trying to invoke her to take action. She took a step forward and buckled into the ground, unmoving. His eyes, highlighted orbs of white against bloody skin, turned back towards me, illuminated with the light of his success. Fire raged behind him as several pieces of furniture succumbed to the heat.

"Tell me...Jalix...." He loosened his grip so as not to decapitate me before he was finished speaking. "What do you want me to tell Karalynn before I kill her?" He tilted his hairless head to the side, pressing his scorching forehead against my own. My hand fumbled below me, trying desperately to grasp the knife hidden away in my boot.

"Tell...her..." I croaked, finding a firm hold on the knife. "That she really screwed up...if she's in hell with you." With every ounce of strength in my arm, I heaved the blade upward, sinking it into his neck and opening a massive wound through his arteries. His other hand quickly caught the side of my head as he released his grip, the bones of his knuckles nearly knocking me unconscious.

Sorrow

I fell to the ground, dizzy and surrounded by the flames of the lab. I watched through swimming vision as he withdrew the knife, holding it over the flame for several moments. Now a dull red glow, the side of the knife landed on his neck, searing the wound shut as he screeched in pain. I groped my way backwards, finding myself in a corner with Schillinger's grotesque body descending upon me. Taking no time to enjoy the theatricality, he hoisted me from the ground once more and pressed the blade to my neck.
"I told you...you can't kill me." He grinned, a macabre mass of teeth exposed to my eyes. It disappeared quickly, replaced by a gaping, blank stare. I blinked hard, trying to reduce the blur in my vision. My eyes made out a faint object protruding from between his eyes, a translucent object hissing its way through his brain. His hold on my throat failed completely, Schillinger's limp body falling to the ground with Krystal standing behind it.
"Maybe I can." She spat, whirling around to extinguish the flames. She rushed to Alice's body, helping her to her feet. "We have to go!" She cried, taking my hand and shaking my shoulders. "Jalix! We have to go, now!" I nodded, empty-headed. She wrapped one of my arms over her shoulders and rushed forward, nearly dragging my body out of the lab. "Alice, come on!" I heard her cry over her shoulder. The entrance to the building whirled by my eyes in a rush of color and light as we broke the barrier into fresh air. I closed my eyes, now useless for anything other than educated guesses of what lay in front of me. Clearly concussed, it took everything I had to stay awake.
"Did you get him?" Alice's voice was worried.
"No, you?" Jared responded hastily, taking my other arm and increasing our speed.
"Yes. We did. But we have to leave, now!" My legs buckled as they hit the edge of a hard, solid object. "Push him in!" She continued, the deafening roar of aircraft rotors affirming that we had reached the

helicopter. My body fell against the floor of the aircraft, the doors closing around me as everyone entered and took their seats.
"Krystal, how long-"
"Not long. I got this thing ready before I went inside."
"Guards?"
"Not anymore." I smirked as Krystal's tone resumed her normal, over-confident quality. A thunderous rumble reverberated through the air, coinciding with an intense jostling, the helicopter leaving the ground and lurching forward. I felt Alice's warm hands on my head, assessing my condition.
"Jalix, are you conscious?"
"Barely." I grumbled.
"Good. It's better than nothing. How do you feel?"
"Drunk." I croaked honestly. I heard the three of them snicker for a moment as I smiled, my eyes remaining closed. I couldn't move beyond that, but I felt much better as we hurtled through the air towards home.
"Jalix, I'm going to help you sit up. I want you to try to keep your eyes open. You should heal pretty quickly, but only if you stay awake." I attempted to nod, but only managed to move my head in one direction before Jared's colossal arms were braced underneath my body, propping me against the seat. I opened my eyes slowly, the same blurry vision I had before retaining its obscurity.
"Still...can't really see." I groaned, struggling to make out shapes beyond blobs of color. "Is that a...first aid kit?" I pointed, lifting my hand lazily and motioning toward a red, cross-resembling blur.
"Yeah. Actually, Jared, hand that to me." Alice answered confidently. After a brief moment, she grunted happily, grabbing my lower jaw and opening my mouth. "Swallow these." She forced a small handful of pills in my mouth, restraining me from making a crude joke. I swallowed hard, the mass of pills slowly making their way down my throat sluggishly. My mouth was forcibly opened again, cold water

making the transit of the medicine far easier. "And now a slight pinch." A syringe was jammed into my arm with unnecessary force as Alice depleted its contents and tossed it aside.

"What...the hell, Alice?" I rolled my head to look at her, the only discernable feature being her rose-red hair.

"Ibuprofen to reduce the swelling in your brain from the concussion and atropine to open up your pupils. They're constricted, which isn't helping things. You're going to feel funny for a bit, but it should help. Probably."

"Thanks, doc. *Probably* is great." I sighed, leaning against the seat and voicing my few thoughts.

"We did it." I started. "I wasn't sure if we were going to, but we did it."

"Kilkovf got away." Jared interjected. "Thanks to me. He disappeared into the forest and I lost him." Krystal's voice came over the speakers, adding to our conversation.

"We have about a two hour flight. Blaming yourself is going to make that a hell of a lot longer." Alice nodded, indicated by a bounce of her hair.

"She's right. The bastard is known for being slippery. That's why Schillinger hired him. But besides, we didn't come for him. We came for Schillinger and we killed him."

"Well, I did." Krystal's crackled voice jeered. "I mean, I had help, but I drove an icicle into his brain. So. One point for me." I chuckled, the edges of my seat beginning to grow more defined.

"I need to call Kara. I think she's the one that called me earlier." I reached down to my pocket to realize that it was gone, burned away by the fire at the lab. "Or not. Krystal?" I called.

"If you're interested in the safety features of your aircraft, please direct your questions to the hot, pole-dancing stewardess I wish was here right now."

"Nice. Can I borrow your phone?"

"Five bucks."

Weaver

"I don't have-...damn it, please?" After a brief silence, her phone was tossed over her shoulder and landed skillfully in my lap. "Thank you." I turned on her phone and was prompted with a screen to enter her password. "What's your password?" I called.

"Kiss my ass!" She yelled back. I sighed, running a hand through my sweaty hair.

"Krystal!"

"That's my password, numbskull! Kiss my ass. No spaces, no caps."

"Are you..." I began to ask the question, which I knew the answer to, when her phone unlocked and displayed a sweet picture of Kara and Krystal on her background. I smiled, knowing that she was fully aware I would see it. I opened her phone application and dialed Kara's number, listening to it ring several times.

"Krystal?" Kara's voice asked, clearly distressed. "Where are you? Are you all okay?"

"We're fine, Kara." I said, my smile growing wider after hearing her voice.

"Jalix? Why are you calling from Krystal's phone? Is she okay?"

"She's fine. I kind of lost mine. Kara...we did it. We killed him." She hesitated, sounding extraordinarily excited when she finally responded.

"It's over?"

"It's over. I love you. So much." She sighed on the other end, sniffling quietly.

"I love you, too. I'm so glad you're okay. I don't even care that he's dead, I just...I want you home. I need you here with me." Her voice turned emotional, attempting to hold back tears.

"I will be. Krystal says it's a two-hour flight. Probably an hour and a half by now. Did Hack tell you the plan? With the helicopter?"

"Yeah, he did. Val and I are on it." My heart leapt into my throat at her response.

"Wait...did you just say..."

Sorrow

"He's alive, Jalix. I found him. He's okay." I breathed a sigh of relief as Jared and Alice looked at me with curiosity. I held out the phone to Alice, who took it with hesitation.

"Kara? Hey. We got him. We-" She stopped suddenly. "Hello?" She waited for several moments before reacting. Her hand moved slowly to cover her mouth, her eyes flooded with falling tears. "Val? Baby? Is that you?" She cried through her smile, making several tries to respond to him. "Yeah. I'm...I'm fine. I can't wait to see you. I missed you so much. I love you." She shook her head and handed the phone to me, sobbing joyfully into her hands.

"Val? Hey, buddy."

"Jalix! Did you kick ass and save the day again?" I chuckled, watching Jared hug Alice warmly.

"*We* did. And suffice it to say, none of us could be home soon enough." He laughed, lowering his voice.

"Speaking of which. I was thinking, man. Why don't you talk to Jared on the flight back? See if he'd be alright with getting you guys married once you get here?"

"Wait, right now?"

"Yeah, why not? We're celebrating. We'll have a big party afterwards. And not to mention, there's not really a better time to do it. We're already figuring stuff out to attack Raven, but it can wait for a night. She'll be scrambling to figure out what happened with Schillinger and it'll give us some time. What do you say?" I smiled, my eyesight finally clear enough to make out everything I could before.

"Yeah. I'll talk to him. Let's do it."

"Sounds great, man. I'll set everything up." There was a brief pause as Kara's muffled voice echoed from the other end of the line. "No, he's gotta go." Val asserted, evidently arguing with her. "Yeah, he knows. Jalix! Tell Kara you love her!"

"I love you!" I called into the phone as they apparently fought for control over the device. I hung up and leaned back, grinning from ear to ear.
"What's up, Jalix?" Jared asked.
"You...are going to marry Kara and me when we get back." I said quietly.
"That depends."
"On what?"
"You gonna kick me out of a plane again?"
"Oh, you're still upset about that...sorry."

***

The helicopter rocked back and forth slightly as it lowered to the ground, kissing the grass with ease and winding down to a halt. The door was thrown open, Tony staring awkwardly into the cockpit.
"You guys are done with this, right? No more adventures today?" Krystal removed her headset and shook her head gently, untangling her hair.
"Nope. She's all yours. We need it bite-sized in a few hours, so I hope you brought your tools." Tony smirked as I climbed out of the aircraft.
"Oh, I did." I turned, looking at the design of its body. It was jet black, the massive white outline of a bird with its wings spread stretched over the fuselage.
"She really likes her branding, doesn't she?" I muttered, extending my hands to help Jared and Alice to the ground. Immediately, a crew of several men poured out of the back door of Krystal's mansion, carrying massive tools, gas tanks, and equipment.
"I swear, if here is a single scratch on that hardwood-"
"Tony, did you bring a car?" I asked, wondering how we were going to get back to the city on our own.

Sorrow

"I brought Kara's; the keys are yours. We brought a van and a truck with us, so we'll get back on our own. And by the way, I patched up your SUV. Mostly body work, no serious damage. It's waiting in the parking lot outside the frame shop. We'll meet you guys back in the city later tonight after we load up the scrap." He looked up at the looming task, sighing exasperatedly. "However quickly we can get it done."

"Wow. Thank you. Well, if you guys can make it, I'm getting married. Party at Archangel later?" He nodded, extending a hand.

"Congrats. We probably won't make the wedding. But you can count on us for that party. We'll bring beer."

"No light beer."

"Deal." I chuckled, breaking away from the group and catching up with Krystal as we moved through her massive home. "By the way, this is okay with you guys, right?" Everyone stopped in their tracks, turning to me with looks of bewilderment.

"Is what okay?" Alice asked, looking to her friends for help.

"That I'm marrying Kara. I mean, I'm not going to call it off, but..." I looked at Krystal, her eyes more sad than angry, for a change. "I don't want anyone to think I'm taking her away from you guys."

"Jalix..." Alice put her hands on my shoulders and took a step toward me. "You guys have been together what, three months? If this were anyone else, I'd be begging you to call it off. But you guys...you have something the likes of which this world has never seen. And clearly it's powerful. Her love, her gift to you brought us an end to someone we thought would terrorize us forever. And your gift to her? Your love for her? It made her...human again. I wouldn't have it any other way, Jalix." She smiled softly, continuing to walk toward the front door.

"I'm with her. You guys are two of a kind. You can handle her craziness and she...she makes you happy." Jared gave his brief blessing before trotting away to catch up with Alice. Krystal and I stood for a long moment, engrossed in the tension between us.

"I want to see her happy again." She said quietly. I nodded, assuming that it was all I'd get from her. "And that means that she needs to be with you. To be honest, it doesn't matter if you're married or not. No one cares. It's a stupid formality. But what you two have..." She drew in a deep, trembling breath. "Jalix, I wish every day that I could have what you two share. You know that. I love her. But loving someone means knowing what makes them happy. I'll never be able to let go of the devotion I have for her. My heart...belongs with her. I'd be lost if I didn't have the obsession. I'd be a different person." She scratched her head gingerly, avoiding the gash on the back of her skull. "Maybe that's what love is. Seeing yourself as incomplete without them. Knowing that when they leave with that piece of you...you'll never be the same again. But what you need to realize is that Kara doesn't have much to give. So when she trusts you with that tiny sliver of her soul? You hold onto that. And don't you ever let it go." Her eyes pled honesty, transfixed on mine with no alternate meaning or ulterior motive. Her words were filled with ardent passion as she spoke, her human side finally coming to full revelation.

"Krystal, when I first met you...I didn't know what to expect. I really thought this thing with Kara was just a...crush. Or some other crazy, hormone-driven lust that didn't mean anything. I'm glad to see I was wrong. It means you care. And it means she has someone that cares." I put my hand on her arm, lightly pulling her closer by a few inches. "Someone I can trust." Being several inches taller than her, I was looking down at the top of her head until that point, her eyes fixed on an arbitrary point on the ground in front of her. The instant the word *trust* escaped my lips, her eyes shot upward, locking with mine in a gaze I had never seen before.

"You trust me?" She whispered emptily, as if the words were foreign to her. I stroked her cheek gently, nodding.

"You're one of a very few people that I can say I trust completely. That doesn't mean you're...*predictable*. But I know that you'll act on your feelings. Whatever those might be. So as long as you're honest with me in how you feel, I'll always be able to trust you." She lifted her arms slowly, wrapping her forearms around my neck and resting her head on my chest.
"Thank you, Jalix."
"You're welcome, Krystal. Now why don't we leave before you make me late to my own wedding?" She giggled, pulling herself away and nodding, a genuine smile on her lips.
"I'm a little more excited for the after-party. If I'm not dancing on tables after an hour, I'm going to be *very* disappointed in you, Jalix." I chuckled, holding open her front door so she could pass through.
"Let's go, man! You got a future wife waiting for you." Jared called, leaning out the window of Kara's car. I picked up my walking pace and opened the car door, sliding into the back seat alongside Krystal.
"What took you guys so long?" Alice teased, pulling out of the driveway.
"Jalix decided to confess his undying love for me, called off the wedding, and now the two of us are going to elope to Vegas."
"You wish." I playfully elbowed her in the side, prompting an immediate and severe reaction.
"Dammit, dammit, dammit, dammit!" She hissed, leaning into the car door.
"Krystal, I'm so sorry. I completely forgot." I genuinely felt bad, having forgotten about her injuries.
"It's alright...I deserved that one." She sucked in a breath and held it for a moment, exhaling slowly.
"So...how's it healing?" I offered, turning toward her with a smirk.
"Until then? Just fine. I can actually lean backwards a bit and bend over without feeling like a pack of firecrackers went off in my chest."

"Does that mean you're ready to help take out Raven?" Alice asked, shifting the topic of conversation rather suddenly.
"Hell, yeah. We need to take her down."
"Easy, tiger. I poked you and you almost died." I taunted. "Maybe stay out of the fight until it's time to go after Kilkovf. I think Kara and I can handle Raven."
"Jalix, man, I don't know. I mean, sure you can *handle* it. But you're supposed to be dead. Remember? We all are. Kara might have to go at it by herself. Or she'll have to take one of us." Jared countered.
"Right. Dead. That's going to take some getting used to."
"It's no big deal. Gets boring after a while. I've been dead a few times. It's no fun." Krystal added indifferently. The car grew quiet for a moment as we turned onto the downtown exit. "Well, until you get arrested. *Then* they have all kinds of questions."
"You know, Krystal...it sounds like you have some very unique stories."
"Get me drunk tonight and I'll tell you plenty."
"Deal."
"Can we talk business for just another minute or two?" Alice asked gingerly. "I know we're having a good time, and I don't want to ruin that, but the charity event is in two days. Day after tomorrow. We should probably come up with a plan before we leave for the event. Whoever...*we*...is."
"Yeah. You're right." I said thoughtfully. "Here are my thoughts on it. Security notwithstanding, Kara can get into the event. The press would go crazy if the widow of Jalix Kane got turned down for a charity ball. Raven might not like it, but if Kara calls and says she's going, there's really no stopping it. Alice, she can take you as a partner. Then, one of you gets her alone, disposes of her quietly, and gets out before anyone is the wiser." The plan's sheer simplicity provoked a long, thoughtful quietness from the group. "It's going to be a busy event. And she's a...celebrity, basically. No one's going to

care if it looks like she left for a few hours. Or hell, if she left for the night. Until they find her body, or a couple days go by, no one is going to care about her."
"It's a little too easy, Jalix." Krystal returned. "How are we supposed to get her by herself?"
"Tell her we blew up the third research lab." Once again, silence. "She'll either want to talk to Kara alone or she'll have to go check to see if that's true."
"Or she'll call our bluff and wait for one of her employees to confirm that. It won't work." I snapped my fingers as yet another idea sprung forward.
"Those buildings are rigged with thermite, right? Those labs? Thermite destroys literally everything. Its melting point is something like two and a half thousand degrees. Schillinger's remains are nonexistent. We can fake his kidnapping. We tell her that we have him captive."
"Yeah, and then she demands to speak with him on the phone. Again, too easy."
"She will! My point. But she won't do it in public. She'll want to go somewhere private. Like maybe…her office bedroom on the restricted top floor?"
"Jalix, that's…genius." Krystal marveled.
"I agree. That's amazing. I'll update Kara tomorrow." Alice said, pulling the car into the alleyway next to the frame shop. We slowed to a halt and climbed out of the car, an overall pleasant sensation of hope and victory overtaking our expressions.
"Now if you all don't mind…Jared, what do I need to do for the wedding? What do I say and stuff. This is kind of my first time, and it's not like I've been practicing." He chuckled.
"My weddings are easy. I say some stuff, then ask you a question. You say I do. I lead you into your vows, you do your vows. Then I say some more stuff and you guys go get hammered." The four of us

laughed, making our way through the small shop and into the basement.

"Jared, how the hell are you a pastor?"

"Me and God...we have a special relationship." He opened the door to the tunnel and allowed the three of us to go in front of him. "You see, the people I kill...he didn't make. That was all the Devil's doing. The sins I commit? I like to believe that the whole no-sinning thing was made for people that only have to make it sixty, seventy years without *coveting thy neighbor*. You know? When you're alive for a couple hundred years...you're gonna mess up. And I think he gets it."

"You think God...*gets it*?" I laughed incredulously, inspired by his optimism.

"Hey, if he didn't want me here, he'd have done something about it by now. I'm doing something right. And we both know it. He doesn't damn my eternal soul to Hell for all eternity, and I teach life lessons on most Sundays when I'm not hung over. It's a fair trade." I shook my head, pushing open the door to the city and striding through. It was empty, aside from a well-dressed Valterius standing several feet in front of me.

"It's about time you guys get here. Didn't you say that flight would be, like, an hour and a half? Try three." I grinned, clasping Val's hand and clapping a hand on his back.

"Good to see you, man."

"You, too." I stepped back to allow a frantic Alice her moment of joy, leaping into Val and nearly knocking him over.

"Don't you ever leave me again." She moaned, muffled by his shoulder. He stroked her hair gently, smiling.

"I won't. You know I'd never leave you." He set her on the ground and looked into her eyes, kissing her hand.

"Gross." Krystal teased, slapping Val on the rear as she walked into the open hall. "I'll be getting ready if anyone needs me!" She called over her shoulder. Alice sighed.

Sorrow

"I should go help her. No one likes a Goth at a wedding, and I don't think she knows anything else." She kissed Val on the cheek before following her sister.

"Hey, Val. We need to catch up later." Jared shook Val's hand, patting him on the back briefly before walking away. "But for now, I've got a wedding to plan."

"I guess it's just you and me." I sighed, hoping that he had a plan.

"Yep. Come on, I have your tux ready." He motioned for me to follow him as the other three figures disappeared into the hallway around the corner. "You'll have to get changed in *our* room. Sonya and Kara are taking up yours."

"Whoa. Sonya?"

"Yeah. Long story. You first. How the hell did you manage to take that bastard down? Looks like you got a good cut from the fight." He pointed to my forehead, the wound already forgotten in all the haste.

"Yeah. I got hit pretty hard. Um...where to begin?" I sighed heavily as we rounded the corner to the hallway, the doors to the apartments closed and lining the length of the hall. "Well, getting in was easy. No one saw us as we fell out of the sky. We pretty much sat on their roof for a full minute trying to decide what to do."

"Wait, you didn't have a plan?"

"Our plan kind of hinged on getting caught. We expected to be loud, not stealthy. I got a little...impatient and started the fight."

"How so?"

"I impaled two security guards and went in the front door." He paused for a moment as he pushed open the door to his apartment, bewildered.

"A *little* impatient?"

"A little. Once we got inside, the building was practically empty. But Schillinger and Kilkovf were waiting in one of the labs." I threw off my shirt, a mangled mess of burnt cotton and sweat, allowing it to drape haphazardly over a chair. A tuxedo and accompanying

Weaver

accessories sat on Val's bed, laid out in perfect order. "You mind if I get a shower quick?" I asked, beckoning to my singed chest and ash-covered shoulders.

"Yeah, bathroom's through that door. Don't use my loofah. How were they waiting for you? Did someone tell them you were coming?"

"No, they just...knew." I turned the water on the highest setting, allowing the cold water to cleanse my skin of impurities. "And why do you specifically want me not to use your loofah?"

"I guess they always know that sort of thing. He's been lucky, trying to stay ahead of us. And because, man. It's my loofah." I shook my head, ignoring his ridiculousness and continuing the story.

"Anyway. They talked for a bit, trying to convince me that I was on the wrong side. Jared took a shot at him, but the bullet kind of...exploded...before it hit him. And then the gun blew apart in Jared's hands."

"That's his power. He breaks down molecular bonds, usually explosively. At least, according to Alice's best guess."

"Well, he doesn't anymore. Jared and I tackled him while Alice grappled with Kilkovf. Slippery bastard got away. He hit Alice pretty hard and tripped the lab's alarm on the way out. Coward. Jared ran after him and Alice and I killed Schillinger."

"Killed, how? Are you sure he's dead?" I lathered my face quickly and rinsed off my head, raking a hand through my now-clean hair.

"Well..." I turned off the water, blindly reaching for a towel on the nearby rack. "Alice slow-roasted him to extra-crispy, I slit his throat, and Krystal shoved an ice cream cone through his eye socket. Even if he lived through that, the building exploded and came down on top of him. I'm pretty sure he's dead. He got me good, though." I dried off my hair gingerly, avoiding the bruised lump on my brow. "Pretty sure I have a concussion."

"We won't notice a difference." He jeered as I exited the bathroom, my towel wrapped around my waist. "Well, thanks for the story. It'll be a big hit when I re-tell it to the ladies. Replacing you as the hero, of course." I chuckled.

"Whatever helps you sleep at night." I sighed, looking down at the formalwear. My pulse grew harsher for a moment, anxiety gripping me for a brief moment. "I can't believe I'm actually nervous. I just...*just* got back from jumping out of a plane, faking my own death, fighting off two partnered, superhuman kingpins, and committing about a dozen felonies. And I'm nervous about having to tell the woman I love that I want to be with her forever."

"Hey..." He put a hand on my bare shoulder as a gesture of sincerity, then quickly withdrew it and cleared his throat as he became aware of the awkwardness. "I don't know about a *dozen*. Two counts of destruction of private property, one count of murder in the first degree, two counts of murder in the second, one attempted murder, arson, conspiracy..." He ran out of fingers, shaking his head. "Yeah, not a dozen. It's like eight. No big deal." I laughed, shaking my head as I pulled on the dark black pants that seemed to fit perfectly.

"Yeah. Not a big deal. I'm sure. I'm lucky that I'm technically dead."

"Oh, and faking your own death. So, nine."

"Seriously, Val. I'm crazy about Kara. Why do I have any feelings other than...good ones?" He tossed me a white shirt, looking in the mirror to adjust his bow tie.

"Answer me this: can you keep up with her crazy endeavors, keep her from going crazy, continue to protect her, and love her no matter what?"

"Yeah. It's the other stuff I'm concerned about." I wrapped the jacket around my torso, straightening the fit as I spoke.

"Other stuff?"

"Yeah. Who's going to do the dishes? Whose turn is it to do the laundry? Why'd you get back late last night? That stuff."

Weaver

"Jalix...you're a soldier in this world's greatest and longest war. And you're worried about who's going to take the dog on a walk?" I turned around and looked at him, shrugging.
"Yeah. This fighting stuff is easy. Get close, kill the bad guy, make the next plan. If we die...we die knowing we were protecting each other. This is going to be the most intense period of our long lives. What if...what if we get bored? Neither of us knows how to live a normal life. We've never had it." Val chuckled, facing me and wrapping a black bow tie around my neck.
"Brother, that's what the fun is all about. You guys are going to have to figure it out by yourselves. Together. Taking care of a dog. A kid. Watering the plants. They're going to die a dozen times over before you get it right, but you will."
"Wait, the kid or the plants?"
"Jesus, dude, the plants." He shook his head, continuing. "It's going to take some figuring out, but you guys are going to shape the face of the world. You'll have plenty of time to figure it all out. For now, get through the vows and go drinking. You can ponder the meaning of life tomorrow." He grinned, clapping me on the back and turning me toward the mirror. "What do you think?" I inspected myself, looking over the clothes briefly before I settled on my steel-blue eyes. I was visibly nervous, by brow furrowed in a chaos of lines and discontent. "I think this is going to happen. So I'd better get to the chapel."
"Let me call Sonya first. I want to see if Kara's almost ready or not." He reached into his suit pocket, pulling out his phone and dialing a number. I stood quietly, listening to the conversation to distract myself. "Hey, you. Is she almost ready?" A long pause followed the question, Sonya's muffled voice spewing a long line of information with which Val was clearly disinterested in. He rolled his eyes and tilted his head back in a silent scream of agony, waiting for her to finish speaking. "Okay. So you're basically saying her hair's not done yet? Okay, why couldn't you just say that? All right...all right. Thanks.

See you soon. Oh, Jalix and I are heading down now." He looked over at me, pondering the answer to a question I couldn't hear. "Yeah, he looks alright. Okay. See you soon." He hung up and replaced the phone in his pocket, turning toward me. "Thanks. Ass." I rolled my eyes and smoothed my hands over the jacket to ensure I looked as suitable as I was able.

"Let's go, cowboy." He turned and exited the apartment, ambling slowly down the long hall. I followed behind him, completely engrossed in my own thoughts.

I only have one shot at this. I hope I look good enough for her. Is she going to change her mind?

"Jalix! You look great!" Jared called, standing in the entrance to the main hall. I smiled.

"Thanks. So do you." As opposed to his recent attire of black cargo pants and a plain white shirt, he was well groomed and donned in black vestments. "Now, go over this for me one more time. What exactly am I doing?"

"I'm going to stare at you and let you perform the ceremony by yourself. What do you think? I'm going to babble about how special you guys are and then tell you *exactly* what to do. Stop stressing about it. The only part that's on you is your vows."

"My *vows*." I repeated apprehensively, realizing that I had no time to prepare anything. "I have no idea what I'm going to do."

"Just say whatever is on your mind."

"Bad idea. Hey, Kara, I'm sweating bullets right now because the fate of humankind rests on our shoulders. Love you!" I rehearsed mockingly, stressing myself to the point of no return. Jared sighed, placing his palm over his face.

"Jesus Christ, you're a mess."

"Can you even *say* that?"

"Can you say your vows without fainting?"

Weaver

"Touché." I croaked, disliking the implication of his remark. We walked a few hundred feet in silence, approaching a set of heavy wooden doors, each adorned with a silver crucifix. Taking a deep breath, my hand met the door handle and I shoved, forcing the doors open and exposing the chapel's interior. Eric stood on a ladder, a dozen feet in front of me, placing a white satin streamer over the podium.

"Hey, guys!" He looked cheerful, eager to put the finishing touches on the already beautiful scene. Tall vases of white flowers hung from the ceiling, suspended by ivory ribbons and floating angelically over each pew. Alice and Krystal stood in the aisle, chatting idly amongst themselves. I walked up to them slowly, trying to avoid interrupting them.

"Hey, Jalix." Krystal said cheerily, combing her eyes over my body. "You clean up well." I gawked at her slender form, outlined in a sky blue gown. Her traditionally straight hair was curled into loose waves, the eyes that were fixed on me framed in deep black eyeliner. She was, in a word, striking.

"Wow. You, too. You look great. You both do." I turned to Alice, her longer hair fashioned in much the same way, complementing her dress in waves of multilayered shades of scarlet.

"Thanks. I had to give Krystal another dose of morphine and she wasn't able to do her makeup. So I'm glad you like my handiwork." She chuckled, patting Krystal on the back gently. Krystal's gown cut sharply into a plunge at her chest, and while not inappropriate, exposed a still-healing scar that traced the center of her ribcage.

"Stop staring. You're married." She teased, pulling me in for an unexpected hug. "How are you feeling?"

"Nervous. Concerned. Unprepared. Inadequate. Should I keep going?"

"You'll do just fine. Now hurry up and get this over with so I can go drink." Alice disputed her request, but was quickly interrupted.

"Mixing alcohol with opiates isn't a good-"

Sorrow

"Not my first rodeo, Alice. I'll do just fine. But thanks. Now go sit down before you catch the flowers on fire." Alice shook her head and took Krystal's shoulder's, gently guiding her toward a bench.

"We're going to have a seat, Jalix. Kara and Sonya are going to be out any minute. Why don't you go up front and sort of...mentally prepare."

"Thanks, Alice. I'm glad you guys could make it." I turned around, watching Eric neatly fold the ladder and set it on the ground, out of sight. He took a seat next to the sisters, staring at me awkwardly as I strolled to the front of the chapel.

"This is it, huh?" I said to Val quietly, moving up the shallow steps one foot at a time. He looked at Jared, occupied with flipping through the pages of his Bible.

"Nah. This is just the start. And thanks for letting me be your best man, by the way."

"Didn't have much of a choice, did I?" I muttered, watching the front doors intently, waiting for someone to walk through them.

Not just someone. My wife.

I tugged at my collar, the stress heating my body to a simmer. Hastily, the doors flew open and a tall, slender blonde woman rushed in, glancing over her shoulder with an ear-to-ear grin. She rushed to the front, struggling with her high heels, and took her place opposite of my position, next to the podium. The doors closed loudly and without further intrusion.

"Hi, Jalix! I'm Sonya. Kara's maid of honor. And...best friend of, like, a billion years." She whispered loudly, waving at me enthusiastically. Blowing a lock of golden hair out of her eyes with discontent, she looked at the miniscule crowd at our front and waved once again.

"Nice to meet you. I'll have to get to know you after-" The doors crept open slowly, a young woman inching her way through without revealing who was behind them. Violet stood for a moment, beaming with tears in her eyes and a small basket in her left hand. Slowly, she

took a step forward, reaching into the basket and scattering a small handful of pink flower petals on the ground behind her.
Here it comes.
I held my breath for a moment, making every effort to avoid hyperventilating.
I don't deserve her. She's too good for me. She's going to regret marrying me.
The solid oak entrance crept open once more, far too slowly for comfort. The rose-red carpet of the aisle stung my eyes and confused my vision against the snowy white of its surroundings, forcing me to blink harder than necessary. Kara's face faded into sight, slowly inching into the view of our small audience. Out of the corner of my eye, I saw Krystal, Alice, and Eric stand, turning to look at the beautiful woman walking toward me.

    I was awestruck, completely unable to comprehend the icon of magnificence making her way up the aisle. Kara's hair was curled into long waves of flawless ebony, draping around her shoulders and kissing her waistline. The ivory tones of her sweeping gown perfected and emphasized every faultless curve of her physique. As always, the singular object of her being that captivated my attention was the gleaming, teary silver of her eyes, transfixed on mine with a loving smile. There was no music to accompany Violet's careful laying of petals, no gentle symphony or tranquil noise to parallel her careful steps as she approached, yet I felt euphoric at the simple knowledge of her presence so close to my own.
This is love.
Sonya extended a dainty hand, taking Kara's and guiding her to my front. I expected Jared to speak, or for some incomprehensible event to decay the quality of the moment we shared, gazing deeply into each other's eyes. None came. I absorbed every inch of her face, committing every detail of her visage to memory, as if there was some chance it would someday be lost.

Sorrow

"I love you." She whispered, her full, red lips moving deliberately to tell me something I could never live without.
"I love you, too." I whispered, breathless. She looked away as she smiled, the faintest tinge of pink staining her cheekbones.
"Good morning, guys. We all know each other here, so I'm not going to make anything unnecessarily formal. We're here today to celebrate and unite Jalix Kane and Karalynn Valencia. I'm going to skip the part that asks if anyone objects." We all chuckled quietly as Jared continued. "In the eyes of God, there is no union more permanent, more binding, and more sacred than the bond of marriage. To represent this bond, it is tradition for the bride and groom to display rings, symbolizing their commitment. Eric?" I panicked for a brief moment, until he asked Eric to come forward, who stood from his seat and walked to the podium with a small wooden case in his hand. Like a tiny treasure chest, he delicately handed the container to Kara, who opened it with the contents facing me. Inside were two silver bands, polished to perfection and resting on cotton pads.
"I had Tony make these for us, since he's so good with metal." She removed one and took my hand, holding it close to my face before placing it on my finger. "The inside is inscribed. Mine says *moestitia*. It's Latin for sorrow. Yours..." The fit was perfect as she placed it at the base of my finger, lightly resting against my skin. "Says *vita*. Which is Latin for life. Because you took the sorrow out of mine...and I want you to remember that." I removed her ring and handed the empty box to Eric, who rushed to his seat afterward. The inscription on the inside of the band was an embossed script, crafted with incredible skill and precision.
"I'll always be here to do that for you." I placed the ring on her hand, resting it above her engagement ring.
"And now..." Jared looked at me pointedly, indicating that I was being queued for something. "I will ask that the bride say her vows."

"Oh, yeah. Sonya?" Kara looked over her shoulder as Sonya handed her a folded piece of paper.
"Oh, good. You...wrote yours down." I sighed dejectedly. She shook her head gently, her wavy hair swaying with her movement.
"It's not much. When you were playing poker in the casino, on our vacation, I went to the bar and wrote this on a napkin. I only managed to re-write them a few minutes ago." She cleared her throat briefly, scanning the page for a specific section. A long silence permeated the air before I said something.
"You okay?" She sighed, the smile fading from her face.
"Not really. These are...they're not..." I cradled my hand against the side of her face and pulled her towards me, crumpling the pieces of paper between our chests. My lips met hers with warmth, a tear from her eyes rolling onto my cheek. I held her for a moment, only letting her go far enough that I could look into her eyes.
"Kara, we've *killed* for each other. You chose me after hundreds of years of other choices, and I gave up my normal life for you. There is nothing that will be able to put into words how we feel. So...let's not." I gently removed the page from her hand and set it in my jacket pocket, replacing the smile on her face.
"Thanks, Jalix."
"Alright...since the vows are over...I guess..." Jared took a deep breath and looked Kara in the eyes. "Karalynn Marie Valencia. Do you take Jalix as your...kind of lawfully wedded husband, for better or worse, until death do you part?" She looked back at me and said the simple words that I was expecting.
"I do."
"Jalix Nicholas Kane, do you take Kara as your sort-of lawfully wedded wife, for better or worse, until death do you part?"
"What does sort-of lawfully mean?" I whispered hastily.
"I can't submit the certificate, dude, you're technically dead." He muttered back.

"Oh. Yes. I do."

"Since you've *already* kissed the bride, Jalix, I'm not sure what to tell you. But congratulations. Kiss your wife again." Kara giggled and wrapped her arms around me, holding me as tightly as she was able while we kissed.

"I love you, Jalix. So much." She whispered, tucking her face into my shoulder.

"I love you, too. More than the world." I kissed the top of her head as everyone broke out into raucous applause.

"Attaboy, Jalix!" Eric called.

"Congrats, guys!" Violet cheered, dumping the remaining flower petals over our heads. Kara took a step back and rolled her eyes, grinning as the pink veil washed over our faces.

"Thanks, Vi. That was definitely necessary. You're helping me pick them out of my hair later."

"Good job, man." Val took a step forward, speaking to me privately as Kara rushed into the combined arms of Alice, Krystal, Sonya, and Violet. "I told you that you'd be alright."

"Yeah. I shouldn't have doubted you."

"You know, people say that a lot around me. It's a pattern. You guys should put a little more faith in me." I nodded silently, watching the women laugh amongst themselves. "We're lucky to have this. I've never seen her this happy. Not in her whole life." He finished, crossing his arms.

"Yeah. We all needed this moment. Kara, especially, but...we all needed an excuse to celebrate. We're going to come back together. As a city...as a people. We'll make it happen." He looked away from the group, flashing me a knowing smile.

"Not tonight, we won't. Tonight, we're going to party." I laughed, looking up as the colossal doors to the chapel opened once more.

"Hey!" Tony called, holding up a case of beer in each hand. "We've been standing out here waiting for you guys to finish! Party at Archangel!"

"Oh, excuse me, guys." Jared pushed past us in a rush, removing the vestments as he ran and exposing a pair of loose-fitting jeans and a tight black shirt.

"He...is the worst pastor ever. He has to be." I concluded, making my way to the back of the room.

"Yeah, but I'm pretty sure he owes me a drink. And I'm excited to see Krystal dance again."

"Wait, she was serious? She mentioned it earlier, but-"

"Vodka is her weakness, Jalix. Give her enough of it and you're in for the best show of your life. Now, if you see her drinking whiskey...run away. That's *never* a good thing." We exited the chapel, entering the main hall and heading for the club. "Man, I wish that fast food place around the corner still had people working in it. I could go for some food. I haven't eaten in a while." I stopped walking for a moment, thinking about the last time I ate.

"Me neither. It's been a few days. It's weird that I haven't noticed."

"You don't notice it until you *smell* a freshly fried burger. Then you want to eat again. Just for the hell of it." The distant group of men propped open the doors with a case of beer, rushing inside. The group of women followed suit, still consumed in chatter.

"So...what can I expect from-" Thumping, heavy music erupted from inside the club, indicative that the celebrating had begun. "This party?" I finished.

"Well, Eric controls all the lights and sound. He's good at what he does. Alice is going to mix drinks, and everyone else is going to kick back and relax."

"I could really use that." I mumbled, walking into the lively heart of celebration the nightclub had already become. Violet handed syringes

Sorrow

to Val and I as we walked in the door, scuttling away to rejoin the group.
"What's this for?" I asked him, raising my voice over the music.
"It's the shot we all take. Feeds our blood. If you take one before you drink, you still get drunk, but you don't get sick." He uncapped the needle, holding out his arm to demonstrate how to properly inject it. Aligning the tip with one of his veins, he pushed the metal into his arm and emptied its contents into his bloodstream. I held my arm out hesitantly, uncapping the needle.
"It's fine, Jalix. You're due for one anyway." I sighed, pushing the device into my skin and allowing the drug to work. It felt cold at first, squirming its way up my shoulder and into my chest, where I instantly gained a tremendous boost of energy. Like waking up in the morning, I felt rejuvenated and focused. "Gimme." He held out his hand, taking the syringe from my palm and tossing it into a nearby garbage can. "Now, let's drink."

***

Alice lined up a row of shot glasses, uncapping a fresh bottle of some unknown liquor, dumping it in a perfect line and filling each glass to the brim without spilling a drop. Violet took one for herself and handed me mine, her face alight with happiness and content.
"To Jalix and Kara!" She shouted, raising her drink with the rest of the group.
"Hell, yeah!" Alice subsequently threw back one of her untold number of shots, grimacing at the harsh burn of the liquid. I choked mine down after raising it briefly, ready to take a long pause from drinking.
"What's the matter, Jalix? Ready to give up?" Violet leaned in, taunting me as she flashed her perfect teeth in a drunken smile.
"Not a chance." I lied, tussling her hair. "Just want a few minutes to enjoy the scenery." I swiveled on my barstool, spreading my arms at

the dancing platform. Krystal was partially removed of her clothing, twirling around the stage's brass pole wearing a midnight blue bra and black lace underwear. Kara, Jared, Sonya, and some of the men from Tony's group cheered loudly as she hoisted herself upward and removed her hands, keeping herself upright with only her legs.

"It's a hell of a sight, ain't it?" Val bumped my shoulder, beaming with excitement.

"Yeah. I can't tell if it's really *weird* or really *awesome* that my wife is enjoying this more than Jared." I cackled as Kara removed her wallet from the table she was sitting near, opening it and throwing a fistful of dollar bills at Krystal's inverted body.

"My vote is awesome." He raised his eyebrows and took a sip from the bottle of beer he was nursing.

"You alright, man? I figured you'd be over there enjoying the party. Or catching up with Sonya. Something." I asked, concerned that something was amiss.

"I'm good. Trying to keep my senses about me, I guess. Someone has to walk all of you home." I gave him a skeptical look as he sighed, realizing I could see right through his lies. He pulled out his phone and flipped through his pictures, stopping at a photograph of an intricate diamond ring.

"Wow." I said quietly, pushing the phone out of Alice's sight. "Tonight?"

"I was thinking about it, but...she seems happy already. She's having fun. I want her to be herself tonight."

"She'll be herself whether or not you propose. It's who she is."

"Yeah, but you and Kara literally *just* got married. Won't she see it as the...you know, heat of the moment?"

"Hey, if you have the ring already, that means you've been planning this. And she thought you *died*. It's not like she's going to have second thoughts right now. You should go for it." He nodded thoughtfully,

Sorrow

taking a final draught from the bottle before standing up and walking out of the club.

"Is he okay?" Alice called, moving closer to me. The music made it nearly impossible to hear her.

"He's fine. Needed air." I waved a hand dismissively, convincing her to return to her conversation with Tony. Sighing, I turned to Violet. "Life here is crazy. It's either miserable, and someone's trying to kill me, or I'm having the best time of my life. Is there any gray area?" She laughed and shook her head, nearly falling off her seat.

"Never! It's always this crazy! But we love it." She smiled and looked back at the stage. "This is what we work for." I nodded, watching Sonya yell and cheer from her seat. Despite the dim light and artificial haze of fog, I couldn't help but notice the pink flower petals entangled in the web of Kara's hair. "I'm just surprised that Krystal is having a good time." She finished, smirking.

"Why are you surprised?" She looked back at me, mouth agape.

"The love of her life just married another man. She's still...although it doesn't look like it, broken physically from what Kara did. She's holding on by a thread right now, probably by morphine and adrenaline."

"You guys are pretty close, aren't you?" I deduced, intrigued by her fascination with Krystal. The smirk faded from her face, replaced with a somber gaze.

"We're really all either of us have. Kara's like a mom to me, and Krystal...well. You know. So we both care about her and not much else. I have no family, very few friends. We just *get* each other. You know? She knows she can come to me when something happens. And she *does*."

"So what's your story? How'd you end up down here?" I changed the subject in an attempt to retain some lightheartedness in the conversation. She sighed, calling for Alice to pour two more drinks.

"Same as about half of the people that live down here. Parents gave me up when I was younger, but not young enough for anyone to want to adopt. Kara came along, offered me a new life. A way out. So I lived down here as a human until I was seventeen, and she converted me. That was...ten years ago, now."

"Wait, so you're technically twenty-seven? You look...hardly twenty-one. And that's being generous."

"Your wife was alive before America existed. And she doesn't look thirty. Same with Sonya. It's not a stretch. Tony and Eric were teens, too. A little older. Wait, maybe Tony was twenty. I don't remember. But their parents were killed in a car accident. Dad was driving drunk, mom was long gone. Both of them in the backseat ready to move out to college. Head-on collision with a guardrail. Dad died instantly, they were both paralyzed. Eric wasn't breathing on his own, and Tony wasn't supposed to walk again. But Kara saw the story on the news, saw their potential. Eric had a full scholarship for software engineering, and Tony was already working for some huge engineering company. Geniuses." She swallowed a shot as Alice handed her the glass, continuing her story. "Kara went to them in the middle of the night and asked them if they wanted a fresh start. She told them that...there would be a lot of pain at first. That they might die. But afterward, if they lived through it, they would live their own lives. Fully healed. Obviously, neither of them could turn it down. She did it that night. They've been young ever since."

"So why did Kara wait for you to get older? Didn't want you to be stuck as a little girl forever?"

"It doesn't work like that. Vampyre kids are just a handful. They age normally until a few years after puberty. You start to slow down after nineteen. But boy, do they go through a lot. Insatiable appetite, constant injections to keep them growing, and imagine having a kid that never has to sleep." She rolled her eyes at me, pointing to Kara. "Give it a few years, you'll find out."

Sorrow

Kara saw Violet pointing and stood up, gathering the group of people she sat with and moving to the bar. I quickly finished the drink in front of me, suppressing a gag and swiveling around to face them.

"How are you guys doing?" Kara kissed me on the cheek, her breath reminiscent of a winery.

"Just talking about all your abductions." Violet chimed, winking at Kara.

"Did you tell him about Jared's?" She asked, grinning in his direction.

"No! How could I have forgotten that one?" Several of the men standing behind Kara scrambled for chairs, pulling them around and taking seats for the evidently epic story. Violet took a deep breath and started to speak before being interrupted by Jared.

"Little girl, just remember I'm about six times your size."

"Yeah, and you're about half the man I am. Sit down and shut up, I'm telling a story." The group roared with laughter in response to Violet's retort. He rolled his eyes and heaved a massive sigh as she restarted. "Alright, so mister Big Shot over there was in some badass gang in Philadelphia before he got shot by another thug for turning his friends over to the cops. They were apparently involved in some bad stuff, and he didn't want them to get hurt. Great intentions, bad execution. So Kara visits him in the hospital, and blah blah blah. He comes down here and sees how super-strong he is, still thinking he's some tough thug."

"Now, Val didn't like him to begin with." Kara added. "He thought we shouldn't have trusted him."

"Yeah, Val *hated* Jared for the first week. So Jared decides that he's going to square up with Val and try to fight him." I looked at Jared amusedly, his face buried in his hands and trembling with suppressed laughter. "They get into the ring, and Jared never lands a punch. Not one. Val knocks him out cold in three seconds flat." I nearly fell off my chair laughing, listening to the guys around Jared mock him relentlessly.

"I didn't know that the bastard could lift a dump truck!" Jared cried, throwing his hands in the air. "All I know is this idiot walks around acting like he owns the place and..." He shook his head in disbelief.

"He didn't wake up for two days!" Violet shrieked, leaning against the bar for support. Kara shook her head slowly, smiling at me as I enjoyed the moment.

"What the hell, Jalix? You stole my audience?" Krystal appeared at my side without warning, catching me off guard. I turned my head, confronted with her nearly bare chest, and snapped it forward just as quickly. "Eyes forward. You're married." She chuckled, tousling my hair.

"Eric!" Alice yelled, waving her arms frantically at the booth he was exiled to, adjusting the controls for our music. He looked up and turned the volume down, reducing it far enough that we could hear each other more easily. She waved her arm, beckoning him to join the rest of us.

"While most of us are all in one spot, I want to have a special drink." Alice turned to each of us, serious in her expression. "Today's a special day. The city is a safer place, Kara got married, and Jalix has joined us once and for all...whether he likes it or not." We all chuckled quietly, finding the humor in an otherwise poignant moment. Eric meandered into the circle, shoving his hands deep into his pockets. "It's a big day. And our troubles aren't over yet. We have a lot of work to do. But nights like this are the reason we fight so hard. And I'd like to direct some attention to a few very important people." She poured another line of drinks from an intricate bottle, a sweet, honeyed smell wafting into my nose as she passed them around. "First of all, to Krystal." Krystal looked up in surprise, shooting a confused look at Alice. "Krystal has been in rough shape recently, and she still chose to do a lot of things. She sacrificed her private jet. She skydived into the

Sorrow

Appalachian Mountains. And she put the final stake in Schillinger's heart. She didn't have to do any of that. In fact, she shouldn't have, for the sake of her personal health. But she did." She smiled softly at Krystal, who blushed and returned the gesture. "Next is Eric." He retracted his hands and took a step back, equally as confused as Krystal was. "Without Eric, we wouldn't have been able to do a lot of things. He planned the assault on Schillinger. He helped Kara with Jalix's rescue. And he remained a good personal friend to all of us. I want to thank him for that." Alice's voice grew softer with each person, acknowledging their actions and displaying the utmost form of sincerity. "And finally to Jalix." It was my turn to look puzzled. "Jalix hasn't been with us for very long. And what he's already done is more than we could ever ask for. He single-handedly led the charge that killed Schillinger. He got us close enough to Raven that we were able to see their master plan. And most importantly, he stole the heart of our fearless leader. And for all of you…tonight is for you."

Alice raised her glass as the souls of the group erupted in ferocious cheer, lifting our drinks in remembrance of everything we had achieved. Before I could raise my glass, I looked at the doorway as a faint shadow crept into my peripheral vision. Turning, I saw Val standing in the front door with his hands outstretched as though he threw something. I followed his eyes, landing on Alice as something landed in her drink with no noise and very little visibility. Her eyes closed, she tilted the shot glass and poured its contents into her mouth.

"Alice, don't!" I yelled, reaching across the bar and grabbing her hand. Too late, she choked, leaning into the counter for support as she coughed profusely. The group stood simultaneously, crowding around her as she spit something onto the bar. Picking it up daintily with two fingers, she lifted the tiny ring and held it close to her face. Her head snapped toward the door as Val broke out in a massive grin.

"What do you say?" He asked quietly, watching her turn the ring over and inspect the shimmering diamonds mounted onto the band. Her mouth dropped open slowly, looking back and forth between Val and the ring. Smiles crept over everyone's faces slowly, appreciating Val's distinctive creativity.

"Yeah?" She said quietly, as if there was a question involved. After a long moment of staring at him, she leapt over the bar and rushed into Val's open arms, clutching him with all her might.

"Attaboy, Val!" I clapped, inciting applause from the crowd. He gave me thumbs-up and a wink behind Alice's back. Kara moved her way toward me, wrapping her arms around my shoulders and leaning into my side.

"Jared's going to have to start sobering up for tomorrow." She chuckled quietly.

"Tomorrow?"

"Who knows what we're going to stir up once we go after Raven? Tomorrow might be the best chance they have. Before we all get busy again." I raised my eyebrows, watching Alice and Val swaying in the doorway.

"I think busy might be an understatement." She nestled her head into my neck briefly before kissing my cheek.

"I'll leave the decision up to you, but if you'd like to get some sleep tonight...I would be very okay with that."

"Yeah, that would be great, actually. I'm having a great time, but...I'm drained. My brain needs a break. And I'd like to have some time alone..." I raised her hand and kissed it gently. "With my wife."

"Leaving already?" Krystal placed a frosty hand on my other shoulder, biting cold against the warmth of my skin.

"Yeah. It was fun, but..."

"Yeah, yeah. You want to get laid, I get it." I smirked, patting her hand gently. I stood up, looking back at the group as they immersed themselves in conversation. Eric was already back in his booth, turning up the music and dimming the lights. Taking my hand, Kara guided us to the front door, confronted by Alice and Val.

"I guess we'll see you guys in the morning?" Val asked, his arms wrapped around Alice.

"Yep. First thing. You guys gonna get married while the decorations are still up in the chapel? I have a feeling no one is going to bother taking them down between tonight and tomorrow." Val chuckled, nodding.

"Might as well. I'm going to have to keep a sharp eye on Jared, though. The last thing I want is him puking in the middle of our vows. I can see it already."

"Goodnight, Alice. Congratulations." Kara embraced Alice briefly, avoiding her clearly heated skin.

"You, too, sweetie." The air in the main hall was vastly different from that in the nightclub, cooling, refreshing, and crisp on my face. I looked around as we walked in silence, still in awe at the sight of the city's architecture.

"Why aren't they married already, by the way? How long have they been together?" Kara giggled, looking over her shoulder at the couple.

"Technically? About two years. Realistically, about twenty. They were both so nervous about telling the other how they felt, they avoided talking about it for...ever. I mean, *years*. Then one day Val went up to her, shoved her against the wall, kissed her like there was no tomorrow, and they've been together ever since."

"You know, for such a sarcastic, macho, indifferent guy...Val's kind of a romantic."

"Yeah. It's sweet."

"It's lame." She giggled again, gently pushing an elbow into my side as we rounded the corner to our apartment. The door was open, hair-styling instruments and articles of clothing scattered across the floors and tabletops. "Wow. You and Sonya made a mess."

Weaver

"Sorry. Hopefully you can ignore it for now. I'll clean it up tomorrow before we leave." I meandered my way around the chaos, standing in front of the bed and staring at the headboard. Four tiny holes marked the indent of Kara's infamous fork.

"I feel like I've been here for months. That little mark? Where you launched that fork at me? Feels like forever ago. I can't even fathom how I was feeling."

"First of all..." She began, stooping to remove one of her shoes. "I didn't *launch* it. It was more like a toss. And second of all, I know what you mean. I keep thinking back to how I felt when I brought you here. When I went back to the apartment, I unpacked our suitcases and I wondered if it would be the last adventure we would ever go on." She looked up, teary-eyed, yet smiling. "It wasn't. And I'm glad it wasn't."

"The memory that sticks out for me..." I sat on the bed, mirroring her as I took off my uncomfortable dress shoes. "Is the couple that attacked us. I keep thinking about that guy. When we were in the interrogation room. After Raven messed with his head, he couldn't...he couldn't even remember his previous life. When he tried to...he died." I shook my head, running a hand through my hair. "And then I think about when I woke up after you rescued me. I felt like...all the memories I had ever tried to push away re-surfaced. Like my brain was taken off the bookshelf and dusted off. I keep thinking...what if I end up like him?" She shook her head, sauntering her way to the bed and kneeling down.

"You won't. They didn't have time to mess with your brain. They probably just stole your memories. And to be honest, there's nothing they could have used. Your life as a human really doesn't mean anything to them. And besides, I was a badass and rescued you. Remember?" She stood up and turned around, craning her arm to reach the fastener of the dress. "You mind?" She whispered, turning her head. I stood slowly, placing one hand on her waist and the other on the fragile zipper. Her dress was cool to the touch, a sharp contrast from the radiating heat that rolled off her perfect, unmarred back.

"Remember the night before my car accident?" I whispered, sliding the zipper toward her hips with the utmost of care. The dimple of her spine grew further exposed as I pulled, culminating in an apex of ivory silk.

"It was one of the best nights of my life." She said quietly, shrugging the straps away from her shoulders.

"Do you remember what you said to me?" Twisting her waist, I spun her around quickly, her eyes meeting mine with surprise and anticipation.

"I told you...I would never be the same if you left me. That...I'd be here for you forever." The dress pulled away easily, sliding over her perfect skin and hitting the floor as I kissed her neck.

"When you said forever...I thought that meant until we die. Now? It really is forever." She shivered, wrapping her hands around my head and combing her fingers through my hair. Lifting her gently, I sat her on the bed and knelt down to look in her eyes again. To my surprise, her lips were curled into a snarl, wincing in pain. "Hey. Are you okay?" She whimpered quietly, clutching her stomach and doubling over. I saw, all too obvious, her perfect fangs stained against the dark flesh of her throat. "Do you have one of your shots in here? I'll get it for you." She nodded, wincing in pain and pointing to her nightstand. The drawer ripped free at my careless touch, exposing a small black case enclosed with a zipper. "Here." Tearing it open, two small syringes were exposed, each containing a straw-colored fluid. I took one and carefully uncapped the needle, sliding it into her arm, as the moaning grew further and further pained. Subsiding, her voice grew strong, taking in deep breaths.

"I'm sorry." She whimpered, shaking her head. "I didn't mean to ruin anything."

"What do you mean? Ruin what?"
"Our wedding night. It was going great, and then..." She looked away, tearful.
"Sweetie..." Kneeling down, I placed my hand under her calf, lifting it and kissing her thigh along the path of perfectly drawn roses. "I'm with you. Nothing could ever ruin this." She smiled, sniffling and kissing the top of my head.
"I'm still sorry."
"Didn't you take a shot before you started drinking?" Her hands combed through her hair, neatening the waves into a pile across her back.
"I did. But I drank a lot, and I've been using my powers too often recently. I haven't eaten, I haven't slept. I've been going through those shots like crazy." She spoke with a slight lisp, her fangs beginning to recede and transition into canines. Wiping away her tears, she sighed and pulled on my shoulders, collapsing into the bed with my body on top of hers. Idly, she traced her finger around my back, calming herself.
"Well...it's about time you get some sleep." I dragged our white silk sheets away from the pillows, allowing her to roll underneath them and clutch them to her chest. "It'll take me a minute to get undressed." I warned, standing up from the bed and beckoning to my layers of formalwear. Her hand gripped the tail of my jacket, refraining me from moving any further. "What's wrong?"
"Nothing." She replied quietly. "Just...don't take too long."
"Why's that?" She smirked, tilting her head slightly and opening her mouth. Her fangs were protruding once again; it would have been a menacing sight for anyone but myself.
"I'm assuming that's not because you're hungry." She shook her head gently.

Lament
Jalix

The glassy orbs of Krystal's cerulean eyes gazed up at me, full of hope at the single word I had uttered; trust. Is trust really so valued that even the sociopaths, the deranged, and the hopeless yearn for its acceptance? Why should we go so far, struggling and inflicting pain on ourselves to earn something that can be taken at a moment's notice? Trust in Kara, Val, and the rest were far easier than most when it had come to their actions. Despite all of Kara's secrets, her lies and deceptions, it had remained through the course of our trials that I bore neither uncertainty in her judgment, nor any loss of faith in her ability to be my friend. What is trust, that such small lies can shatter everything it builds to, yet through such direct and deliberate actions against my faith, I retained hope and conviction that her intentions were for my benefit? Torn away from my home, my life as I knew it, and presented with the most absurd of logical fallacies, disillusioned of everything I had believed to be true. And still, what she said rang true with every word, the implicit bond between us unbroken in the face of inconceivable odds.

A facet of trust is undoubtedly familiarity; awareness of the inner mechanisms of a person's mind. Krystal was unknown to me. Through countless engagements of violence, rage, and vengeance, she recurrently demonstrated blatant disregard of my ambitions: conforming to their society, to become familiar with its people, and to become acquainted with those I knew would become my allies. I witnessed, time after time, her endeavors to not only prove to herself that she was neither worthy of trust nor the bond of love, but the trials and tribulations that she inflicted to know her own pain. Kara resisted daily the compulsion to exile her, to destroy her, and to denounce her. But much akin to society, she realized that although there are penalties for the pain that we inflict on others, there is no punishment for the agony we inflict upon ourselves. And as such, I had become aware of Krystal's mind, as convoluted as it might have been. I became fully aware that she would take action according to the impulses of her emotions, damning the consequences and believing only in herself; placing trust in only herself. In that awareness, I began to realize that, while impulsive and volatile, I could trust in her to be herself. In that, I was sure.

Not unlike love and hate, war and peace, there's a fine line between trust and doubt. The difference is that people can hate others while gaining something of their own, whether that is attention or self-satisfaction. War can become a machine that engulfs a nation, wringing financial gain and the appearance of superiority. With doubt, there's no advantage. No tangible or emotional gain is gleaned from questioning the decisions of someone so near, so involved in our lives. But trust gives us something valued higher than all else: the precursor to our inner drive. Hope. Hope is what guides us through our sufferings, delivers us from our sorrow, and defends us from despair. That unimaginable prospect of optimism and courage, in spite of every sign and omen that dictates that we change, never falters. When we place our trust in those we love, we tell ourselves that we place our hope with them, for the future, for our goals, and for every action we take because of it. When we move forward with that same resolution, we find ourselves believing not in our principles, or in those intangible emotions, but in the ones we love. I trusted Kara. I had hope with Kara. And above all else, through every tribulation and deadlock with my *own destiny, I turned from all doubt and recalled every moment that led me to her side. Loving her, I could never be led astray.*

***

The empty void left by the absence of thought gave me the energy needed to finally roll out of bed, landing on the floor silently so as to avoid waking Kara. She lay quietly, curled onto her side with our sheets crumpled into her chest messily.

"No wonder I was so damn cold." I smiled in the darkness, shaking my head and tiptoeing my way to our closet. The door hung ajar, untidy hangars full of clean clothes strung onto the bar that spanned the width of the wardrobe. I turned my head as Kara groaned silently, waking slowly and stretching her body into satisfied contours.

"I already laid our clothes out…" She mumbled, propping her head lazily onto her elbow. Pointing, she gestured to a pile of fabric that sat idly on the kitchen table.

"Good morning. You look…well-rested."

"Shut up…not a morning person. You know that." Despite her dawn-inspired lethargy, she smiled at me, her perfect teeth capturing her happiness. "I just pulled out one of your suits. I hope that's okay."

"That's fine. If I know Val, he won't really care." I sorted through our clothing, separating her midnight blue dress from my suit articles.

"Dressing to match Krystal today?"

"Not intentionally." She yawned widely. "But most of my dresses are black, and it's a wedding."

The morning air seemed colder than it actually was, rushing me to get dressed as quickly as I was able. Kara's care in keeping my clothes clean and lint-free was apparent as I inspected my dress pants before pulling them on. I heard Kara's light footsteps as she wandered behind me, kissing me on the check before removing her dress from the table.

Weaver

"How do you think everyone is doing after last night?" She smirked, pulling the fabric over her hips.
"Well...I don't know what went down after we left, so who knows? Maybe they all went home, maybe they destroyed the club." I shrugged, simultaneously adjusting the jacket so it would sit properly on my shoulders. "You even got a tie out for me. You're the best." I kissed her quickly on the tip of her nose, turning to approach the wall mirror next to our bed.
"I try. And by the way...thanks for being patient with me last night. I know things weren't as...smooth as they could have been. I try to hide it whenever I feel like I mess things up, but you just...were there for me. So thank you."
"Well..." I chuckled. "You made it *well* worth my time last night. And besides, that's what a husband is supposed to do." I whirled around, zipping up the back of her dress as she began to reach for it. "Be there for you, no matter what." She blushed, shaking her head. "You look beautiful, Kara." I said, putting my hands on her hips. "You'll make a flawless bridesmaid." I kissed her gently and looked into her eyes. "Because you made a perfect bride."
"And aside from breaking all of my furniture, you make a great husband."
"The coffeemaker wasn't my fault." I defended, holding up a finger. "I know how to make coffee, and it was nothing I did."
"All I know is you said you were thirsty, you walked over to the coffeemaker, and the next thing I know, there's boiling water *everywhere*."
"Taught me a valuable lesson: never make coffee while naked."
"It taught me a lesson too. Keep *you* out of the kitchen."
"It's *your* job anyway. You're the wife."
"Excuse me?" She grinned, her mouth slightly open in shock.

"Nothing. Love you. You should call Val and make sure he's awake." She cocked her head, her tongue buried in her cheek before she reached for her cell phone.

"Nice change of topic. But I'm not going to forget that little comment." She shook her head, listening to the phone ring.

"Just saying." I muttered, straightening my tie. Her face fell into a confused frown as she hung up, immediately redialing.

"He didn't answer." She explained, putting her hand over the microphone.

"He's probably up to his elbows in...bourbon vomit." I suggested as be both waited for another long moment.

"Hello? Hey. Wait, Eric, why do you have Val's phone?" Her mouth dropped open, a look of panic striking her face. "He's *what*? All right, I'll be right there. I'm so sorry!" She turned the phone off and before I could ask, explained what happened. "Jalix, do you have any idea what time it is?"

"Um...like eight?"

"It's one. In the afternoon! We slept for twelve hours. They're already in the chapel and apparently waiting for us." She turned around, fleeing through our bedroom door.

"Kara?" I called, waiting for her to return.

"What? Jalix, we have to go! They're waiting for us."

"Neither of us have shoes on." I looked down, wiggling my bare toes.

"Shit. Well...hurry up." I shook my head, bending over to put my shoes on.

"Did you take sleeping pills or something last night? You passed out right after we...you know. I was laying there for like another four hours. I couldn't fall asleep."

"Vampyres don't fall asleep that quickly." She explained as she hastily threw on a pair of black heels. "And we don't sleep for that long, even on sleeping pills. When you were a human, I got five hours a night, at best, even when I took them."

~ 287 ~

"Wow. And you slept for twelve? That's...impressive."
"No, it's unhealthy. I'm going to check with Alice after the ceremony to make sure nothing's wrong." She stood up, ready to bolt out of the room again. I lightly placed my hands on her shoulders, forcing her to look at me.
"Nothing's wrong. You were exhausted. Two rescue missions, a wedding, a night of drunken debauchery, and that's just in the last forty-eight hours. It's not surprising."
"You're right." She sighed, embracing me in a brief hug. "But seriously, we should go." I nodded, turning to trot out of the room and leaving our apartment in a chaotic mess. We jogged into the main hall, hurrying the best we could. Closed stores and empty rooms passed us in a blur as we ran.
"Holy...shit..." Kara stopped, holding out an arm to slow me down. Her head was fixed on the massive oak entrance to Archangel, ripped from its hinges and sitting on the ground in a pile of splinters.
"You know, I was kidding when I said they probably destroyed the club."
"Do you have any idea how hard it's going to be to replace those doors?" She sighed, placing a hand on the brass handles of the chapel door. "Hopefully, they're all talking and we can sneak in unnoticed." She whispered, looking at me. I shrugged, hearing no noise from the interior. Opening the entrance slowly, an uncomfortable silence accompanied the watching faces of Alice and Val's wedding party. The couple stood at the altar, clearly exhausted and struggling to stay upright. Sonya was the most composed of them, standing by Kara's side with her hair entwined in a long braid that circled the crown of her head. My face grew red as we took a step inside, allowing the doors to close with a dull thud. Tony and his group of friends sat in one of the front rows, their bodies turned to watch us able our way into the aisle.

"Why do they have so many more people at their wedding?" Kara hissed, waving awkwardly to Alice.
"Because some of them were dismantling a helicopter."
"Well, it's a big difference. It's like twice as many people."
"That's still only twelve people." I whispered, giving Val an enthusiastic look and a thumbs-up. Pushing our way into one of the pews, we took a seat next to a fatigued Eric, reeking of whiskey.
"How late did you guys stop drinking?" I voiced my concern as he burped quietly, suppressing a heave.
"We didn't." He groaned, rolling his eyes. I grimaced, shooting a very patronizing look at Alice. She shook her head slowly, the attempt of curls in her hair bouncing sadly on her shoulders.
"Well..." Jared sighed heavily, looking around. "Now that we're all here..." Kara receded in her seat slowly, hoping to fall out of view. "We can begin." The couple stepped forward, giving each other soft, pained smiles. "We're gathered here today to-"
   The quiet impact of a body hitting the floor occurred as Tony fell from his seat, landing face down on the chapel floor and snoring loudly. I suppressed my laughter to the best of my ability, assisted with Kara's frantic slaps on my arm. Jared stared at me, clearly not in any mood for the humor. One of his friends looked down, nudging him with their foot and nodding as he groaned quietly.
"We are gathered here today...to officiate the marriage of Allison Nicole Vicente and Valterius Valencia." It felt odd hearing Kara's last name attached to Val, despite my awareness of their siblinghood.
"The bride and groom have elected not to exchange rings because they're...already wearing them. So...Allison. You may recite your vows."
"Where's Krystal?" I whispered to Eric, realizing that she should have been standing next to Alice.
"She went home last night. She wasn't doing well. Got real...depressed after a bit. Sat in the corner drinking whiskey after

you left. Took her and Violet back to the mansion and never made it back, I guess." I nodded slowly, eager to know whether or not she was okay.

"And now, Valterius, you can recite *your* vows." He pulled a piece of paper out of his tuxedo pocket, clearing his throat.

"Alice. When I first met you, you were amazing. And you still are. You're a doctor. You're a sister and a friend. And I'm excited that you're going to be my wife. I know I'm not always easy to be around, but I'm better than I used to be. You've made me a happier person. A better person. So...above all else..." he folded the paper and replaced it in his pocket, taking her hands in his own. "Thank you."

"Allison. Do you take Valterius as your wedded husband, for better or worse, until death do you part?"

"I do." She smiled genuinely, swept away with joy.

"Valterius, do you take Allison as your wedded wife, for better or worse, until death do you part?"

"I do."

"Val...you may kiss your bride." Wild applause erupted within the room as Val embraced Alice in his arms, jostling Tony out of his unconsciousness. Val lifted Alice's hand, throwing a fist in the air.

"Whoo!" Kara called, clapping loudly. She appeared to be extremely happy, overjoyed with her brother's happiness. The couple stepped down from the podium as the crowd stood, rushing to congratulate them.

"Where's Krystal? And Violet?" Kara whispered as we made our way toward the celebration.

"Back at her mansion. She wasn't feeling good, apparently."

"Physically or emotionally?"

"Probably both." Alice turned to us, hugging Kara tightly.

"Congratulations, Alice!" Kara squealed, rocking back and forth. "I'm so proud of you guys for going through with it finally. And especially today."

"Yeah..." Alice looked away for a moment, beaming. "Half of us...or more...are still drunk."

"You're not, right?"

"Not what?"

"Never mind." Val broke free from the group and rushed me, nearly knocking me over in the process.

"Dude, we're finally married."

"Don't say it like that. Gives out the wrong message when you're hugging me. But yeah, I'm really happy for you guys. How do you feel?" He pulled away and rubbed his forehead, grinning like an idiot.

"I feel great. I felt like hell this morning, but now I feel awesome." Unexpectedly, the sound of the chapel's closing doors echoed once more, the crowd turning to find the source. Alice was mid-sentence, stopping and slouching her shoulders.

"About time, Krystal. You missed my entire-" The two of us turned at the same time, equally as shocked by the sight that lay before our eyes. Alice put a hand over her mouth, taking several steps back. A middle-aged man walked toward us slowly, one foot in front of the other. His eyes were fearful, trembling with distress and panic as they darted between all of us. One arm had a cell phone outstretched, shaking violently as the other hand pressed a silver pistol into the side of his own head. In a flash, Kara knelt down, pulling her own handgun from an unidentified position and pointing it toward the man's face. Looking over, I saw Val reach into his jacket, removing an identical firearm.

"Why do you have your gun at a wedding?"

"Why do you have your gun at a wedding?" Alice and I voiced simultaneously. The man shook the cell phone, walking toward me and staring into my eyes.

"Mister Kane." He croaked, tears in his eyes. "I was told...to give this to you."

Weaver

"Who the hell are you?" Kara snarled, looking down the sights of her weapon. The man's finger twitched, indicating that he wouldn't hesitate to pull the trigger.

"Kara." I said quietly, pushing her weapon aside. His finger relaxed slightly, my hand reaching for the phone. She repositioned the gun, continuing to aim it at his head. I took the phone, inspecting it briefly before putting the call on speaker.

"Who is this?" I growled, expecting Raven's cocky voice to float through the air. A husky, Russian accent replaced it, obviously amused.

"Our dear Jalix. How are you?" I looked at Alice worriedly as she shook her head, unsure of what to say.

"I'm fine. How's your face?" He chuckled, a raspy laugh reverberating through the air.

"Healing. Your friend left me with some...scars. But nothing like what I'm going to leave on you."

"I have about a hundred pissed off people down here that beg to differ." I lied, trying to intimidate him. He roared with laughter, the phone growing more distant from his mouth. He took a deep breath, entertained, and continued speaking.

"Nice try, Jalix. I would estimate that there are...maybe fifteen of you. And everyone else abandoned the city." I stood in stunned silence, glancing at Kara.

"How does he know that?" She hissed, not breaking her glare away from the unidentified man.

"Karalynn. You'll find that I know a great many things. And your people...have been a wonderful help in making me aware of them. I'm glad you're here." His last statement forced a cold chill down my back, a rustling on the other end of the line occupying a few seconds of an otherwise silent interval.

"H-hello?" A young girl's voice echoed from the other end of the line, unfamiliar and clearly frightened.

"My name is Kara." Kara turned her head to speak, softening her tone.
"Who are you?"
"Maddie." The girl said, her voice breaking. Kara dropped the pistol, clattering to the floor as her eyes immediately welled up with tears.
"Kilkovf, you can't do this!" She cried hoarsely, her fists curled into masses of white knuckles. He picked up the phone and continued to talk, disturbing Kara further.
"Yes, Karalynn, I can. I have one of your precious families here. Out in the country...it's so peaceful. So quiet. And far enough away that no one is going to hear when I kill them all." The young girl began to openly cry after his statement, her voice disheartening our group and serving to infuriate Kara.
"What do you want?" Tears rolled down her cheeks as the helplessness of her situation gripped her.
"You, Karalynn. We've been waiting for you a long time. We want your body...your blood...we don't just want you dead. We want you to serve as the catalyst for all of humanity's change."
"My virus." She confirmed, turning away. "You want to *use* me so you can finally finish your disgusting work."
"My colleague's work, actually. Or, I should say, my *new* colleague."
"Hey, handsome." Raven's voice instantaneously converted my blood into a torrid frenzy of rapid pulses.
"You're there, too, Raven?" I probed.
"No, sweetie. Conference call. I'm at the Boston lab right now preparing a helicopter to come pick up your fiancé's body. You know, while it's still warm."
"You'll have to fight through a dozen of us to get to her."
"No. I won't, actually. You see, my Russian friend here is going to kill that family if you don't go to him. And I'd like to add, alone. You and Kara are the only ones allowed within ten miles of his location. And we have lookouts. We'll know."

"Then what?" I demanded, growing increasingly infuriated. "I just trust you to let them go?"

"We don't want *them*, Jalix." Kilkovf continued. "You and your fiancé share the oldest strain of the virus. Hers has had time to evolve...yours has not. This way, Miss Raven will have plenty of genetic material to experiment with."

"I still haven't worked out the kinks." Raven sighed. "So I'm not sure which one of you I need. This way...I get what I want."

"You're too used to getting what you want, Raven. It's just one family. I'm not going to sacrifice all of humanity for one family." I bluffed.

"Baby...we know where more families are. And he's not just going to *kill* them. But he's going to make them *wish* that they were mortal."

Kara snatched the phone from my hand, whirling around.

"Where are you?"

"Lynn Woods Reservation. It's about twenty minutes away, in a small cabin near the water. No vehicle access, it's by foot only. So I suggest..." He lowered his tone, growling into the speaker. "Coming alone." The phone went silent as he hung up, the deafening absence of noise in the room further increasing the ringing in my ears.

"What's the plan, here, Kara?" I asked as she picked up the pistol and lifted her dress, exposing a sewn-in holder on the inside seam.

"Who are you?" She ignored my question, looking at the man as he opened his mouth, shaking his head slowly.

"I'm...Maddie's father." The crowd recoiled synchronously as he pulled the trigger, ending his life with tears in his eyes. His head hit the hard wood of the pew as he fell, slumping to the floor.

"Jesus Christ." I breathed, turning to Alice. "Call Krystal. Tell her what's going on."

"Get her and Violet back to the city. Now." Kara commanded, looking at the group. "Val, lose the suit and go put on something dark. Jared, you too. You're both coming with us. Actually, Alice, lose the wedding dress. I need you, too. The rest of you..." She sighed, looking at Sonya

directly. "After we leave, seal up the entrance to the city. If we come back, we'll call first." She turned around, taking me by the arm to speak with me in private, but Sonya's gentle voice froze her in place.
"What do you mean...*if* you come back?" Kara sighed, turning her head.
"*When* we come back. We'll call first." She took my hand as the crowd scrambled to leave, not questioning Kara's decision.
"Jalix, I need you to trust me today."
"I always do."
"Good. We're not turning ourselves over, and we're not going to let them hurt that family...any more than they already have."
"What's the plan, then? He's not going to be alone, he'll have security, and Raven said they have lookouts on the road. How are we going to get away with smuggling in Jared and Val? They'll kill that family before we even get close."
"I know, Jalix! I'm thinking, okay? It's not just them, either. Raven said she'll be on her way, and I'm sure she'll have backup as well."
"The SUV I picked out is terrible." I said, mocking her words from a few days earlier. "But it makes up in storage space."
"How did I not see that? And tinted windows, so their lookouts won't be able to see how many people are in the vehicle. We'll tell them to wait in the back until we need them."
"Exactly. Now as far as the family goes..." My voice trailed off as Val entered the chapel again, garbed in a black turtleneck and carrying an impressive rifle in his arms.
"Don't worry about the family." Val grinned, propping the weapon on his shoulder. "Jared and I will take care of whoever's holding a gun to their head. You guys just need to get Kilkovf and get out."
"It's not going to be that easy, Val. He's tough. There's a reason Schillinger picked him as his number two. *And* I need to make sure he doesn't hurt that family. But come on, we're wasting time. We can talk on the way." Her pace was quick, the tail of her blue dress

thrashing against the force of her legs while we marched through the main hall. Jared and Alice rounded the corner together from the living areas and joined us, Alice calling to a group of men picking up Archangel's doors.

"Board it up! We're out of here." Alice had a folded shirt in her hand, the only clothing she managed to change into being a pair of jeans and a bra.

"Jared, you and Val are going to wait in the back of Jalix's SUV during the drive. His windows are tinted, so their scouts won't be able to see that we're not alone." We reached the training room, the exit to the city already swung open. "Jalix and I will go in on our own and you two will sneak around, trying to find a line of sight into the cabin. Then, Val, take out anyone threatening the family while Jalix and I take care of Kilkovf."

"What's the plan for me?" Jared asked, hunching over as we made our way through the tunnels.

"You're going to watch Val's back. If they do have guards set up around the cabin, he's going to need help with them."

"Understood."

"And what, I'm just supposed to stay behind, too?" Alice wondered, tugging the long, navy blue shirt over her torso.

"Kilkovf is going to know we're not coming alone. If it's just Jalix and I, he's going to know the other two are with us. We bring *you*, and it might be enough to trick him into thinking we're the only three."

"Kara, how are we going to deal with Kilkovf? I mean, we have no idea how many he's going to have with him, whether or not he's armed. One misplaced gunshot could kill that little girl."

"You don't think I know that, Jalix?" She shouted, shoving me into the wall of the tunnel. "Do you think this is the first time he's put someone in danger? You think this is the first time I've ever had to make a hard choice? I'm walking in there knowing full well that my husband could *die*!" I grabbed her shoulders, spinning her around and switching places against the wall. I leaned in and lowered my voice, calming her from her angered state.

"Kara. I know you're strong. I know we can do this. But you need to keep a clear head, here. If we go in hot-headed, we're going to get killed."

"He's right, Kara." Val added. "Remember what Schillinger said about your emotions? I'm not saying he was right, but we need to temper them. We're going to defend the people we care about, not kill the ones we hate." I released my light grip on her, turning to walk up the stairs to the frame shop.

"Hello?" I called through the open door. No return replied to the echo of my voice. Climbing slowly, we wandered our way through the basement and entered the shop. The corpse of a dead Vampyre lay behind the front desk, enveloped in a pool of his own blood. "He must have tried to stop the guy from coming down."

"George." Kara said quietly. "His name was George. He loved the peace and quiet up here...always volunteered to stay whenever we had a party so no one else would have to." The serene furnishings of countryside photographs surrounded us as she closed her eyes, restraining the temptations of her emotions.

"Come on. We have to go." I said quietly, taking her arm and guiding her through the glass door of the storefront. The streets were busy, hurried residents shuttling their way through the frigid air. Kara's phone rang unexpectedly, her fingers frantically answering the call. "Hello?" We continued to walk, hurrying to our mode of transportation. "It's Krystal." She explained, continuing her conversation. "Lynn Woods Reservation, one of the camper's cabins near the lake. You'll need to stay back, and out of sight. We can handle Kilkovf. Just stay behind in case we need backup...I don't know, listen for gunshots or something. And whatever you do, *do not* bring Violet." She hung up, thrusting her phone back into one of the hidden pockets of her dress.

"We can do this." Alice breathed quietly.
"We can. We take our time, wait for the right moments, and stick together. We'll be alright." Kara spoke softly, biting her tongue in fear of revealing her true beliefs. "We'll be fine." She repeated.

***

The gravel and dirt crunched quietly under the wheels of our vehicle as it rumbled through the backcountry road. Tony's work was evident, everything running as smoothly as it should have through the uneven terrain. Trees whirled by in bursts of green, evergreens and firs pressing their shadows against the fiery evening sky.
"You know Krystal is still twenty minutes away, right?" Alice suggested quietly, insinuating that Kara release her firm foot from its hold on the gas pedal. She didn't answer, clearly drowned in her own thoughts.
"You know, guys..." Val broke the silence, his voice low and somber.
"No." Kara replied. "Don't do that."
"I know. But just in case...I think we did a good job. Protecting humanity. Protecting our families...we did good."
"We're gonna keep doing good, man. We've got this." Jared smirked, nodding his head. "We just gotta do what we always do." A large concrete circle ended our path, the final parking lot before the hiking trails led into the forest. Kara turned the wheel gently, easing the vehicle to a slow stop, allowing the engine to idle for a moment before turning it off. Val and Jared instinctively slunk low in their seats, avoiding any watching eyes.
"There it is." Alice said, pointing. I followed her finger to a small cabin in the distance, masked by row on row of foliage. "It's not too far. I feel like, if we need to, we can make it back here to get away before they-"

Sorrow

"No." Kara repeated, her hands still on the wheel. "Either we walk away, or they do. Not both."

"It seems like when we went in to kill Schillinger, it was...less stressful." I implied a question, Kara terse in her reaction.

"It was. You all had the advantage. And he got cocky. He's not going to make the same mistake." Alice put her hand on the lock, opening the door slowly and taking a step onto the asphalt, followed quickly by Kara and myself. The rushing wind breezed through the forest, the only remarkable sound among us.

"Come on." Kara mumbled, lowering her head and striding onto the path that led to the lone cabin. I remained close as we walked, allowing Alice to remain slightly further back.

We can do this.

The wooden beams of the lodge grew nearer, its windows darkened by black shades and covered with dark shutters. The door shuddered as the wind blew, an indication that it was opened, albeit slightly. As if mounted on a swivel, Kara's eyes danced around our environment, searching for signs of activity, movement, or life. Finding none, she stopped in front of the oaken steps leading inside the cabin. I put my hand on her back gently, a show of support for her sake.

"Kilkovf." Kara's intonation was commanding, maintaining control over her composure. Her face was set in a hard, stoic expression, even more so once he finally replied.

"Karalynn. Come in." He called, no sign of his existence visible yet. She exhaled quietly and strode up the steps, shoving open the door with masterful force and entering the room dauntingly. I followed no more than the width of my body behind her, prepared for an immediate confrontation. The room was warm, a crackling fireplace throwing waves of orange over a beaten couch. Kilkovf sat at ease, a standing guard on either side. Each held a prisoner at gunpoint, a young girl and what appeared to be her mother. Despite the crackling fireplace, the air grew warmer still as Alice neared, maintaining her posture behind me.

If Kara can use her powers to throw the guards aside, she can sweep them up and run while Alice and I fight the three of them.

The guard's weapons clicked quietly as they switched off their safeties, displaying ardent hostility.

"We're here. What now?" Kara demanded, refusing to raise her voice above her normal speaking volume. Her tenor was metered, self-constraint far too obvious for comfort.

"I believe...I asked you to come alone." He smiled at us, widening his arms to gesture to Alice.

"Kilkovf, you're not that stupid. If we came alone, we'd be butchered. But we're here to negotiate, not to fight."

If Alice can melt the triggers on their weapons, they'd be powerless to hurt the family. I can move them to safety quick enough.

"Negotiate? My dear, you are in no position for negotiations. You have made a grave mistake in believing that any of you will leave here alive." The fireplace spit, cleaving a split log in half and throwing a grim shadow over the handprint-shaped scars on the sides of his face.

"We have no misconceptions about leaving. But you let them go first. Then, if you want us-"

"Kara, these aren't the only guards." I was alarmed as a shadow moved across one of the windows, throwing darkness into the doorway briefly before vanishing. "There's more." Kilkovf raised his eyebrows, impressed at my observation.

"Very good, mister Kane. We could use a soldier like you on our side. It's a pity you won't have the opportunity to serve us." He paused, placing his hands on the heads of his captives. "But again, you have made a grave mistake. You, see, I know of Allison's capabilities. She is...strong, both in will and in her abilities. But I am very unaware of those you held back...the ones skulking around near your vehicle."

Sorrow

My head snapped to Kara, her eyes open in fear and beginning to well with tears. Her mouth trembled, still set in a bitter frown.

"Please..." She begged quietly, her voice finally breaking. My hand moved to the doorknob, but was interrupted by Kilkovf's authoritative protest.

"I will kill them." He glowered, the guards pressing their rifles into the skulls of their victims further. The girl cried openly, collapsing in tears. I released my grip, the knob compressed into a knot of metal.

"Good." He finished, reaching over to one of the guard and plucking a radio from the webbing on his vest. "Kill them." The radio's static crackled for a brief moment, coinciding with Alice's despaired scream. She spun around, whirling out of the cabin in a blur of fire as gunshots rang out in the open air, crackling like fireworks behind us. Kara's eyes closed, clenched shut in fury as her hand met her mouth, collapsing onto the ground like a broken doll.

This isn't real. This isn't happening.

Alice's agonized screams pierced the evening sky, accompanied by the sound of rushing flames coupled with further gunfire. Growing silent, the room was dominated by Kara's suppressed sobs, muffled by the carpeted floor.

"What...do you want?" I growled, placing my hands slowly over my head to exhibit compliance. Slowly, Alice's cries turned to shrieking sobs, screaming at the body of her husband.

"Jalix...I am very sorry it came to this. You see-"

"Stop talking!" I barked, exhausted of his lectures. "Tell me how this ends. Now!"

"I'll tell him how this ends." Kara snarled, standing up and outstretching an arm to utilize her powers. An additional gunshot shattered the brief armistice, the limp corpse of the mother falling quickly to the floor.

"Stop!" Kara wailed, throwing her hands into the air and taking a step back. "Please!" She sobbed, shaking her head violently. The little girl

lunged to her mother, screaming in distress and shaking the lifeless carcass. "Not Maddie...please. I-I...I'll do anything. Please..."
This is a living nightmare.
Even I, through my years of experience watching heartless, cold-blooded murders by ruthless terrorists, fought back against a wall of tears for the little girl as she wept into her mother's body.
"You are no longer in control, Karalynn. Too often, you believe that your faith will guide you through to the light. Today...no longer. I...am not here to *kill* you, Karalynn. I am here to show you something. Miss Raven will have the pleasure of killing you and your husband."
"Please...please..." Kara echoed, a haunting tremble infecting her throat. "Not her. She's a little girl..." Kilkovf looked down at Maddie in silence, Alice's mournful sobbing forcing a hoarse choke into Kara's throat.
"You value your people so far over your own life that you would climb blindly into my trap, forsaking your friends' lives? Forsaking *their* lives? Had you given this any thought, Karalynn, you would have allowed them to die. Your...emotions...pulled you here. And for them...you will pay."

I clenched my eyes shut finally, a horrified sound emitting from my mouth as another trigger was pulled, ending the life of an innocent girl. My tears, hot and unchecked, fell down the lines of my cheekbones. I opened them, facing Kara as her face paled, lips curled into a ferocious, vengeful scowl. Her fangs exposed in a violent display of fury, they dug into her lip and dripped blood unforgivingly onto her chin. In my own share of killing, I had never felt the rage, the incomprehensible wrath that Kara's face so vividly articulated. Her movements slowed to a crawl as she shifted, my own shock forcing time to appear slower. She bellowed, ripping her arms outward. In an incredibly violent shockwave of bitter wind and deafening sound, the bodies of the guards were reduced to macabre shreds, collapsing into themselves as the walls of the cabin were annihilated into fine wood

Sorrow

splinters. The fireplace erupted into a chaotic blaze of torrid inferno, the likes of which would have terrified hell itself. Kilkovf's body, as well as those of the family, remained untouched, isolated in a small circle of tranquility: the epicenter of her destruction. Her arms fell slowly, dropping to her sides as the pieces of the cabin rained around us. Her animalistic breathing petrified him, a statuesque icon of fear amidst a source of unparalleled obliteration. She moved forward, her steps exploding in violent energy against the remnant pieces of the structure. Grounded by fear, I was unmoved on my own volition. He attempted to step back, pulled forward at her hands' bidding and landing in her grip by his scarred throat. Distorted by tears and red stains, her reflective irises looked into his eyes with some union of madness and lament not like any human emotion.

"There...is no Hell deep enough...no pain...great enough...to make you suffer for what you've done." Her hand enclosed instantly around his neck, severing through tendons, bone, and flesh, until her fingers were empty. His decapitated corpse dropped to the ground, the head falling to the side and rolling several feet. Kara turned to me, her fangs gleaming with the grisly splatters of blood from Kilkovf's spurting neck.

"I'm so sorry..." I whispered, frozen in place. Her face was streaked by an endless stream of tears forcing their way through the glassy orbs that gazed mournfully into my own.

"Me, too." She whispered, taking a step forward and falling to me. I caught her in a tight embrace, holding her body as she shook violently and shed tears without restraint. "Alice..." She whispered, her voice quivering into hoarse sighs. I looked over my shoulder, the biting view of Val's body tucked in Alice's comforting arms driving further tears through my eyes. The ground crunched under her feet as she moved to her friend.

"Kara..." Alice whimpered. "He can't be dead...he can't be..." Kara's hands roamed over Val's body as I grew near, tracing the pattern of

wounds across his chest and abdomen. Wordlessly, she wrapped her arms around Alice. The smell of searing skin permeated my nose as Alice sobbed, throwing off waves of radiant heat. Unmoving, Kara kept her hold.
"Jared?" I croaked, staring at Alice. She shook her head, unable to say the words aloud. I sunk to the ground slowly, finding no need to expend further energy on idle actions. Kara looked at me, a faint pink burn tracing a line on her cheekbone and forehead, cutting around her eye.
"Jalix...what do I do?" Their eyes both met mine as I shook my head slowly.
"Nothing...there's nothing we can do. They..." I inhaled sharply, the icy air shocking life into my lungs. "They died to protect us. They died giving us what we needed most...hope." I shook my head again, bowing it between my knees.
"Jalix!" Kara screamed, her voice wracked with pain. I shot upright, rushing to her side as she fell to the ground in violent convulsions.
"Kara? Kara, what's wrong?" She clutched her stomach, shrieking at bloodcurdling volume.
"She needs blood!" Alice replied, looking at the war-damaged wreckage of our vehicle. I threw open the door, ripping it from its hinges and tearing through the glove compartment. A black case with Tony's embossed name fell into my hands before I rushed back to Kara's side.
"Here. Hold still. It's okay." I tried my best to calm her as I pushed one of the two needles into her arm, disposing of it by throwing the empty casing into the woods. Her shaking slowed, breathing quieting to a slow rhythm before she screamed again, thrashing against the ground. Alice looked at me fearfully, uttering a single command.
"Give her the other one. Now." I thrust the needle into a different vein, slowly pushing its contents into her arm. Once more, she

Sorrow

calmed, taking in shallow breaths until her antagonized cries filled the air.

"Alice, what the hell? What's going on?" I demanded as she recoiled, lowering Val's body to the ground and staring at me solemnly.

"Jalix...she's pregnant." I stood far too quickly, falling on my side and shaking my head violently.

"No...no, she's not."

"Has she been taking a lot of shots recently?"

"Yes, but-"

"Has she been sleeping? Having violent mood swings? Insatiable sex drive?" Each question resounded with a fainter pulse in my ears, Alice's face evolving into a blackened blur of vision.

"Oh, my God..." I whispered, horrified. Kara rolled onto her back, arching her spine in agony.

"Jalix, you need to listen to me *right now*. Go in that wreckage. I need as many blankets as you can find and some kind of knife."

"What..." I breathed, stunned and watching as Kara's face poured tears into the ground.

"Jalix, now!" She bellowed, taking a position between Kara's feet and talking to her slowly. "It's going to be okay, Kara. Listen to me. I'm going to get you through this. You need to do *exactly* what I say, okay? Starting with breathing. I need you to take big breaths." I stumbled toward the cabin's remains, falling to my knees and digging haphazardly through the rubble. My hand met a snag of soft fabric and I tugged, freeing a large quilt. I rushed back to Alice, shaking the dirt and ash from its surface.

"Here." I whispered, handing it to her.

"I need a knife. Go...go check Val." Her voice lowered, remaining strong in the face of loss. "He usually has one in his left pocket." Combing my hands over his jeans, I grasped a pocketknife and pulled it away, taking a moment to mourn his unmoving body.

Weaver

"What now? What do I do?" I asked frantically, dropping the closed knife at her feet. Kara's face was pale now. Her skin turned into a paper-thin veil of grey flesh as she cried.
"There's nothing you can do, Jalix. This is happening right now."
"No…" Kara whimpered, attempting to sit up. Through the lines in her dress, I could visibly make out a moving shape in the increasing bulge of her stomach. "Not here." She whispered. With all the strength I had left, I clasped her hand in my own and moved to her head, kissing her on the cheek.
"You're going to be okay, Kara. Alice and I are going to get you through this. It's okay. I love you." I gritted my teeth and looked away, her shrill gasps tearing into my heart.
"I love you, too." She breathed, quickly sucking in large amounts of air. Alice moved between her legs, updating me on the progress.
"Another minute. Jalix…she needs more. Of the shots. A lot more."
"Where the hell am I going to get them, Alice?" I screeched, beckoning to the wilderness that surrounded us. As if an answer to my prayers, an expensive sports car barreled down the road at tremendous speed, the sky blue body of the vehicle screeching to a sudden stop less than ten feet away. "Krystal!" I bellowed, urging her to run to us. Violet followed behind her as their mouth opened in shock, looking down at the bodies of Val and Jared. Krystal's eyes met with Kara's body in an audible gasp.
"Kara…" She whispered, kneeling next to us.
"Krystal, she needs medicine. Now! As much as you have!" I yelled, looking up at Violet, as well. They both ran to the car, throwing open the doors and scrounging for a moment before returning. They each handed me a single syringe, which I took greedily and buried in the arm of my suffering wife. Each in rapid succession, they brightened the hue of her skin before fading back to the sickly pale color that sunk into her bones.

"No, Jalix..." Alice whispered, shaking her head. She croaked at her first attempt to speak, clearing her throat and forcing the words. "She needs more. A lot more. We won't find enough here..."
"What are you..." She bit her lip, shuddering and returning to Kara's midsection. "No..."
"Jalix." Kara whispered weakly, her screaming subsiding into wounded moans.
"Kara?" I smiled at her and ran a hand through her luscious hair, avoiding the sight of her increasingly gaunt cheeks. She licked her cracked lips and took my hand again.
"I was thinking...maybe...we're ready to have...a baby." I coughed, the tightness in my throat making a laugh impossible.
"Boy or girl?" I asked, feigning excitement as I ran a hand over her thinning arm.
"I think...it'll be a girl. How about...Amy? Amelia...Lynn..." There were no further sounds of her pain, a shallow, struggled breathing keeping life in her eyes.
"It's beautiful." I smiled at her, ignoring the river of tears falling down my face. "Alice, please..." I looked over at her, holding the knife over a tiny conjured stream of flame. "There has to be something we can do." Alice shook her head, refusing to look me in the eyes. "Alice!"
"Jalix...it's okay..." Kara whispered, a fading strength in her voice. "It's okay."
"I'm going to help you, Kara." I knew I was lying, and I hated myself for it.
"I know..." She looked at Violet and Krystal, sighing. "I love you all. So much." Krystal sobbed, whipping her hair violently around her head.
"You're going to be okay, Kara." She protested, taking Kara's other limp hand.
"Of course I will." She laughed, a raspy chuckle. "You guys showed me something...I'll never forget. You all...loved me. And I thought that was impossible..."

"Never." I argued, squeezing her hand. "We all love you so much."
"It's coming." Alice warned, struggling with something between Kara's legs.
"It's coming." I repeated, smiling through my tears. "We're going to be parents!" She nodded slowly, the muscles in her neck visible through her fading skin.
"Will you make me one last vow, Jalix?" She sighed, looking into my eyes. Despite every possible pain ripping through her body, her eyes were alight with happiness, the bright silver gleaming at me with all the hope she could bear.
"Anything, Kara." I whispered, shaking violently.
"Don't let Amy...become me. Show her how you lived. Give her...a good life." I sobbed, shaking my head.
"We're going to show her together, Kara. Just hold on. Please..." Violet knelt down, running a hand through Kara's hair as she cried. A shrill cry pierced the evening air.
"I've got her." Alice said confidently, the body of our child still hidden by the folds of Kara's dress. Kara smiled, rocking her head back and forth as one more tear rolled down her cheek.
"We did it..." She whispered, tightening her grip on my hand. Her knuckles strained against her skin, the bony digits digging into my fingers.
"Yeah. We did."
"I love you." She rolled her head over, watching as the last arc of sunlight faded from the dying sunset. "It's so...beautiful." She breathed, her chest falling still.
"Kara?" I shook her shoulder fragilely, struggling to remain upright. "Kara, please..." I sobbed, leaning into her body. "Please, no. I love you so much." Alice gripped the writhing child in her arms, clenching her mouth shut with all of the strength she had.
"Kara!" Krystal screamed, falling to her knees and placing her hands under Kara's chin. "Don't leave me!" She bawled, leaning into Violet

Sorrow

for support. A faint sound drew our attention, the distant speck of a helicopter appearing in the evening sky. I turned away, nauseous as Alice spoke.

"Jalix, we can't let them find her. We can't." I listened as the sound neared, the larger black dot splitting into three small ones. "And we can't put...Amy...at risk. We have to go."

"I can't leave her!" I lashed, allowing my sight to absorb the body so devoid of life. "I can't."

"She's gone, Jalix. We have to let her go. We need to leave, and get Amy out of here." I nodded, trying not to accept the reality of the situation.

This isn't a nightmare. This is Hell.

Alice handed Violet my child, swaddled in the blanket I gave her. "Jalix, grab her. Krystal, take Jared." She lifted up Val's body, cradling it against her own as she moved him to the wreckage of the cabin, smoldering with suppressed heat. I wrapped an arm under Kara's shoulders and hips, lifting and embracing her.

She's dead. Gone...

I placed her body next to Val's carefully, setting her head against a destroyed piece of couch cushioning. Krystal stooped, lowering Jared's body and wiping the tears from her eyes, refusing to accept the inevitable facts.

"Get to the car." Alice said quietly, spreading her arms. The helicopters were now clearly visible, less than a few miles away. I knelt down and placed a final kiss on Kara's forehead before stepping back. Krystal did the same, choking back a sob and refusing to get up. "Come on." I whispered, taking her arm and pulling her away.

"No. No! You can't make me leave! I'm staying with her!" I wrapped my arms around her, pinning hers to her sides and lifting, carrying her thrashing body toward the car. Violet reached into the driver's seat, turning the key and igniting the engine. "Please!" Krystal screamed, reaching toward the cabin. I looked over my shoulder, a vast gout of flame gathering between Alice's arms, growing in size and intensity. She lowered it, kissing it against the pile of tinder that ignited instantaneously, setting the bodies and the rubble ablaze with a searing heat. Krystal fell into the car, stumbling into the passenger seat as I made my way to the driver's side.

"How...?" Violet asked quietly, rocking my crying child in her arms. I shook my head as Alice climbed into the backseat, slamming her door shut and slumping forward.

"I'm so sorry..." I whispered once more, throwing the car into reverse and rocketing down the thin gravel trail.

Sorrow

Distortion
Raven

I stepped off the helicopter, gazing at the twisted, smoldering remains of the rubble that smoked angrily in front of me. My boots hissed at the ground, smothering the waves of heat given off by the blackened, scorched earth as I neared the body of the Vampyres. My scientists emerged from behind me and knelt down next to the remains, reduced to a perfect arrangement of bones by the searing warmth of their surroundings.

"We can harvest them. They're salvageable, but we only have two preservation caskets." My guard's voice was muffled by a respirator, but clear enough to understand. I nodded as two more of my subordinates removed a massive black box from my personal aircraft. The sarcophagus was opened slowly, the two mercenaries lifting the nearest corpses with care and placing them in their tombs.

"*This* one..." I stepped forward and traced a finger along the outside of the skull. Her mouth was agape in frozen terror, fangs gleaming menacingly. It exuded an aura of wickedness; I felt power seep from it, radiating into the air around me.

"This one is special. Save *her* for last, and ensure that any experiments with her genetic material are an indisputable success." My heart fluttered as I stood up, the awareness of our goals being so close at hand nearly overwhelming.

Weaver

"Yes, miss Schillinger. Anything else?" The lid was slid onto the sarcophagus, a large black bird outlined on the cover.
"My company will take care of anything you need. But be careful. I have a feeling you don't have much time before the others find out what's happening to her."
"*Her?*" One of the scientists asked, lifting the coffin into the helicopter and sitting down next to it.
"Yes. I know this one." I said quietly, crouching down and removing the lid. Her cold, empty eyes seethed hatred, glaring at me evilly.
"Don't I, Sorrow?"

Sorrow

Infinite
Krystal

I was empty. No despaired feelings of torment or rage flooded my heart; Rather, I felt hollow, and at peace with the fact that it was wrong. For all the tears I had shed, I was at last drained of all capability to express even the simplest of emotions. Violet sat next to me, assisting me with the disposal of a shared bottle of vodka, abetting the indisputable and irrevocable silence that bound our throats. She swayed slowly, peaceably intoxicated and comfortably anaesthetized.

"Thanks." I muttered, the first word spoken since our return. "For staying." She nodded slowly, her eyes only half-open and swelled with the bloodshot sting of spent pain.

"Alice...felt that it would be better if she took care of Amy." She whispered, her voice long broken from taxing screams. I tilted the bottle against my lips once more, allowing the hot rush of liquid to sear its way down my throat and nauseate my stomach briefly before subsiding.

"Here." Violet continued, holding out her purse for me. I took it warily, blearily leafing through its contents before discovering the item intended for me. Without further question, I removed the plastic cap from the labeled syringe and pressed the metal tip into my veins. The familiar euphoria of warm solidarity slipped its way through my veins and into my heart, setting the wooden bar counter alight in

Weaver

waving, shifting patterns of wooden swirls. "That's...the last one I'm stealing for you, Krystal. You need to quit. I worry about you."
"I know..." I sighed, the air in my lungs frigid, yet frighteningly exhilarated. "Don't worry about me..."

***

"I was so scared." I whispered, brushing a lock of delicate black hair out of her eyes.
"Well, don't be worried. I'm a tough cookie." She said, trying to make light of the situation. I remained serious, unable to see things carelessly. The thought of losing her...
"Kara...If anything happened to you...I don't know what I would do." She smiled.
"Nothing will happen to me." She pulled me in and hugged me, briefly, but sweetly. I moved the bouquet of lilies out of the way so we didn't crush them, turning my head to watch Sonya greet several of her friends.
"I just don't want you to leave me." I said, looking into her eyes and leaning back. My body heat decreased again. It was the same blissful, yet terrified feeling I got every time she returned from an assignment. Her eyes darkened slightly.
"You know I'm not going to, Krystal. I wouldn't leave any of you."
"I know you say that, Kara..."I faltered, scavenging for the right words. It was hard to reason clearly in her presence, every fiber in my body longing to press myself against her and steal away her fear. "I love you." She cupped a hand along the side on my face and smiled, her perfect eyes saturating my heart with perceptions of safety.
"I know." She whispered, failing to return the gesture. I wanted to argue with the thousand things she failed to say; I wanted to scream and cry at the simple fact that she couldn't voice the words I was so sure she meant. There had to be something in her eyes, hidden away

Sorrow

from me. There must have been something she couldn't find the words for, straining against her soul.

"Do you? Truly?" She giggled, nodding.

"I do. I know. You've told me a thousand times." Her happiness was unwarranted, sharply contrasting against the solemn emotion I tried so fervently to justify. There were no more descriptions I could conjure to convey my love for everything she had become, no words to give to her that she would understand. I pulled her face close to mine and pressed my lips eagerly against hers, unleashing every ounce of affection that I could possibly have borne. She flinched, delaying for a passing moment before returning the gesture and gently satisfying my need for her attention. I endured, wrapping my arms around her shoulders and holding her body close to my own before she recoiled, breaking away from my impassioned hold and shaking her head.

"I'm so sorry. I'm cold, aren't I? I'm probably freezing-"

"Krystal, I can't." Her quick words thrust daggers into my throat, effectively cutting it off from speech. "I don't feel love the way you do, Krystal. You mean a lot to me, but maybe it's time to get some distance. It's just not healthy." She took a step back and tried to sound as positive as possible, forcing herself to speak through her harrowing emotions. "I told you not to wait for me. I told you not to waste your time. I'm going to end up hurting you, and not by my choice. I can't promise you I'll be back every time I leave. You...have to stay away from me." I turned around and drew an unsteady breath.

"That's the problem. Just by you being alive, being near me...it's invigorating. It's not unhealthy. It's an addiction, but a good one. I want to be there every time you return just to know you're still here. I can't keep myself away." Her smile faded.

"Krystal, I... you know how I feel about the situation. What else do you want me to say?"

"You mean everything to me, Kara. Why can't you realize that? I've done everything I can for you to make myself better, and you're just...throwing it away." She sighed, frustrated at the situation. I felt horrendous for placing her in the emotional turmoil she was forced into, but I couldn't falter. I didn't want to make her feel this way. But she was so close to realizing that she loved me.

"I'm not ready for love, Krystal. It's not who I am. I'm a warrior. A soldier. I won't ever be a wife or a mother. I'm not capable of it. No one has ever been able to handle...who I am."

"I can, Kara! I always have."

"Everything I have in my past... everything that could ruin my future. You can't help me with everything that haunts me. I'm sorry that you think you can. I know it gives you hope, but it would drag us both into despair." She bowed her head, finished speaking.

"I know that it's just in your nature," I whispered, whirling around to face her, "But you don't have to be made of ice like I am. You can let your feelings show, you just choose not to. The worst part about this is the fact that I saw it coming. All those years ago when I was a teenager and first fell in love with you...when I first started learning who I was. You were a part of that. You're a part of me. I saw that you could feel the same way towards me. But you won't." She seemed to grow angry and lashed out.

"You're right. I can feel, Krystal, and I do choose not to. Because it hurts. I don't want to hurt myself; I don't want to hurt you...Why can't you just accept the fact that I'm gone?"

"Because you're not gone!" I screamed, throwing the flowers aside forcibly. The reunion around us grew silent as frozen lily petals rained around the two of us.

"You are right here in front of me and I can't have you! That's what makes me so...insane!"

"You're already insane." She said forcefully.

"Maybe I am. But it takes a broken child to play with a broken toy."

"That's my point, Krystal. I'm just your toy. That's it. And eventually, all toys get used just one time too much, and they break. I'll never love you

the way you love me. I'm not capable of it." She started walking away, but I spoke once more, almost inaudibly.
"Kara. I promise you...that every day that one of us is alive, I will be in love with you. I will never give up. I don't need your approval. I just need to be there by your side. Even if that means you're trying to push me away." One teardrop trickled down my face, across my quivering lips. She stopped moving, standing for a moment before speaking again.
"Love alters not with his brief hours and weeks-"
"But bears it out even to the edge of doom." I finished. It was from my favorite Shakespeare sonnet, and gave me the small hope that she wasn't giving up. She continued walking, and I continued to shed tears, unsure of my own emotions. Regardless, I had a reason to cry, and for a very long time, I did.

***

The bitter memories I had sustained through years of torment were interrupted by the doors of the nightclub being thrown open in forced aggression, hammering against the walls behind them and falling closed once more. Jalix moved quickly past me, the flair of a well-pressed suit disappearing as he crouched behind the bar and dug through the contents of its underside.
"If you're looking for whiskey, it's behind you." I mumbled, accompanying the statement with a long pull from the bottle in front of me.
"I'm actually not, Krystal. In fact, rather than sitting in my own depression and wallowing in my own guilt, I'm going out to do something about it." Alice's shotgun was withdrawn from its hiding place as Jalix stood and chambered a round into its barrel.
"Why?" The simple question triggered a furious response.
"Because she deserves it, Krystal! They all do! It's Raven's fault that so many people have died. It's Raven's fault that we live in fear. So

Weaver

unless you're going to stop me- which, I'll shoot you if you try- I'm going to kill her." I stood quickly, nearly falling to the floor in my intoxicated stupor. His frame towered against mine in a frenzied rage of vicious energy.
"No, you're staying here. When *we* go to kill her, we're all going." He pressed a hand against my still-damaged ribcage, unremorsefully inflicting pain and knocking me back against my chair.
"Shut up, Krystal. I'm serious; I have no problem with killing you right now. I'm going after her, and that's final."
"Why?" I screamed, recovering and pushing back against his chest. He threw the shotgun onto the bar with a loud clatter, preparing for a fight. "Why do *you* have the right to put us all in danger for your own revenge? What *right* do you have that we don't?"
"She was my wife!" He bellowed, inching his way toward me. "I have the right that no one else does!"
"And what about Jared? And Val? You don't think we loved them, too? You just don't care? You're blinded by her memory, Jalix!"
"Blinded?" He cried, stunned. "You're sitting in the bar drinking your life away! At least I'm doing something!"
"You're going to get us all killed!" I screamed, slamming my fist into the counter. The shotgun was brittle from the bitingly cold energy radiating from my body, and shattered as my hand was driven through it. "If you die, Raven will find all the other families we sent away and kill them! She'll come down here and *murder* all of us! Would you really sacrifice all of our lives just for-"
"Yes, Krystal! I would!" He roared, drawing in a sharp breath. "In a heartbeat! Do you think that this war is over, just because Kara is dead? Do you think Raven is going to stop, now that our leader is gone?" He spun around unexpectedly, fumbling his hands over the bar in the dark and finally finding the remote for the television. He turned it on and flipped through several channels as I waited for his line of reasoning, stopping at a national news station and cranking up

Sorrow

the volume. A reporter collectedly sat behind her desk, mid-sentence in regards to Schillinger's death.

"...found destroyed. The facility suffered the same fate as the laboratory in Salem, but with more dire consequences." The scene changed to Raven's tan figure giving a speech to a crowd of reporters. Seemingly genuine tears streaked her face, but deterred none of her obviously planned dialogue.

"My father was a great man. He was ambitious, and kind. He was what many people would consider a hero for all the things he did for the face of our world. And he was...taken from us, far too soon. Whoever did all of these...terrible things...is nothing less than evil. From the assassination of Gregory Hartman to the murder of my father and the ruthless, terroristic destruction of Jalix Kane's flight, they have proven themselves monsters. Both myself and my company will be providing nothing but the most generous cooperation in finding these criminals...and bringing them to justice." Reporters thrust their microphones forward, begging for more answers. Raven's thin fingers pointed to one specific journalist, prompting her to speak.

"Miss Schillinger, with your father gone and your company under such deliberate attack, what is your plan for your own personal security, and the security of your third and final research facility?" She cleared her throat and answered promptly.

"My own safety is not an issue. I put the lives of the brave men and women I work with far above my own. Our corporate building in Boston will be open later tonight for the Raven's Nest charity gala as planned, with the addition of heightened security for our guests. With our laboratory in Boston, myself and the other executives decided that it would be prudent to add a contingent of security forces that will maintain control of the facility while our work continues." The excitement of the crowd increased again, another reporter singled out for additional questions.

"Raven, if you truly cared about the safety of your workers, why wouldn't you close the lab and discontinue your research?" Her sickening face contorted into a smirk, narrowing my vision to a tunnel as I focused on her deliberate answer.
"My company is on the brink of bringing a discovery to light. This work is far more important than the lives of a few, and my employees agree to the fullest extent. We have recently acquired... some distinct genetic material that will allow us to provide a source of limitless care to those who were previously believed to be hopeless. We will bring salvation to millions."
"Are you talking about a cure for cancer?" Another journalist belted out the question before she was finished speaking.
"While the confidentiality of our research is regarded as the most serious of issues, I cannot answer that. But what I can say...is that our entire world is about to undergo the fastest change it has ever seen. And my father's work will be the catalyst." Jalix clicked the remote once, shutting the television off and turning to me.
"Don't you see? They didn't just *kill* Kara. They're going to use her body for their sick research. She's taunting me, Krystal. Didn't you hear her? Project Catalyst. She made it very clear that she's always needed Kara's body for their project. I'm not going to let her death mean the end of the human race." He pushed past me, stalking past my freezing body as Violet spoke out.
"You're not doing this for the human race, Jalix. This is about Kara." He stopped, turning to advance on her.
"You're goddamn right I am." He growled. "She was the one good thing in my life, and they took her from me. They *don't* have her memories, they *can't* bring her back, and I know she's gone. But there is nothing stopping me from going after the bitch that killed her. Call it whatever you want. Use whatever reasoning makes you feel better. But I'm going after Raven, and I'm going to slaughter her."

Sorrow

"You're not thinking straight!" She argued, grabbing his arm. "We're all suffering through this, Jalix! Kara was like a mother to me! Krystal was in love with her. Just because you cared about her...it doesn't mean that other people didn't. We loved her, too. We loved Val..." Her voice began to break down once again, the hoarse choking of sobs suppressed by her short bursts of speaking. "Jared was my friend, too. I even knew Maddie. She was...she was like my little sister." Beyond comfort or recall, Violet slunk into her chair and cried again, turning away from Jalix as he began to regret his actions. He turned to me, attempting to justify himself.

"Krystal, you have to understand-"

"You don't think I want her dead, too, Jalix?" I started, my eyes stinging with tears as I listened to Violet. "You don't think I've suffered just as much as you? I have. But killing yourself is only going to make *you* feel better. *Look* at her." I pointed aggressively at Violet's slumped figure, the harshness of my words sending a frosty wave of cold that froze the tips of his hair. "If you leave now, and you don't see this through, you'll kill Violet. You'll kill Alice. And I'm sure you don't give a damn about my life, but I can't fight off whatever army they're brewing in those labs. So if you want to leave, fine. My life is over, and I've come to terms with that. But you think about what your decisions have already cost us."

"My decisions?" He rebuked, failing to see my point.

"Yes, Jalix! Who went after Schillinger? You. If you hadn't done that, Kilkovf and Raven wouldn't have needed to become so brutal in their tactics. *You* started all of this, Jalix."

"What, so I'm the reason they're dead?" His voice cracked as he spoke, his anger fading into remorse. "You're saying that if it wasn't for me, Val would still be here? Jared wouldn't have died? And Kara..." He couldn't find the will to speak anymore, shaking his head in silent tears. His personality was always strong and immobile, and seeing him in his state of loss was unforgiving against my already-reddened eyes.

"No, Jalix. But what I *am* saying is that they were ready to trust you. Kara always knew that if things went wrong, you'd be strong enough to take her position. Val considered you enough of a friend to die for. And Jared felt exactly the same. We all do. But you...throwing your life away for revenge?" Knowing that I was the only thing between Jalix and reason, I pushed through my tears and continued. "She deserves better. We all do. We need you. Your daughter needs you." I summoned all the strength I could and gained control over my feelings, focusing on the enduring high from the morphine and washing away the waves of cold that flooded the air around us. I wrapped my arms around his shoulders and leaned in, giving him a moment of support.

"I can't let her get away with it, Krystal. I can't." He croaked, gently stroking my hair.

"And she won't. But we-" The darkness of the room was once again pervaded by the artificial sunset of the main hall, Eric's small frame lingering in the doorway.

"I need you all to hear me out." He said quietly, taking no time to allow us to answer. "You all need to come with me. Jalix, I know about your plan, and I'm going to help you. But *all* of you...need to come with me right now." He stared at me purposefully, indicating that I was not excluded from his instructions. His attitude was strange, a strong departure from his traditionally meek attitude and unexpectedly strong.

"Eric, we're-"

"Now." He asserted, leaving the room. I pulled away from Jalix, giving him a moment to collect himself.

"Let's go see what this is about before you go rogue." I mumbled, lifting Violet from her huddled position on the bar. "Come on, sweetie. You're all right. You should go spend more time with Amy.

Sorrow

You're very good with her, and I think it would be great for you both to bond for a bit." She was leaning into me heavily as we approached the doors, more disheartened than drunk.

"Alright." She whispered. "Thanks for...spending time with me."

"I'll meet you in Alice's room soon. Okay?" I placed a finger under her chin and lifted, ensuring eye contact. She nodded slowly, plodding down the main hall toward Alice's room. I turned to Jalix as we walked, the orange glow of the lights a harsh difference from the darkness of the bar.

"What's this all about?" He asked, sighing deeply.

"I have no idea. He might want to hold a...service...for them. I'm not sure." I shoved aside my preconceptions as we rounded the corner to the living areas, lost in our own thoughts.

"I'm sorry." He said quietly, stopping outside Eric's room. "I...I can't think about all of this right now. If I stop, even for a second...I'm going to break down. And I can't do that. We have too much at risk."

"We *always* have something at risk, Jalix. But it doesn't give you the right to put their lives in danger. If they launch a counterattack-"

"I'm trying to protect them." He raised his voice, firm in his argument, but refraining from anger.

"That's not your job, Jalix. It was...hers. You'll never be able to replace her. So don't try." The hoarseness of my voice was coupled with a stinging in my throat, emotion I was unable to control. "I just...I loved her so much." The well-acquainted dread I was so used to took me once more, angering me beyond belief.

"I did, too, Krystal." He whispered, shaking his head. "I don't know what I'm going to do without her." I waited for him to say more, to affirm his reasoning or give me some idea of his plans for the future. Nothing of the sort followed his statement, a sorrowful silence befalling the two of us. The word *sorrow* was the only term to describe how I felt, but the word itself twisted the knife already buried deep in my heart.

Weaver

I grabbed his arm lightly and dragged the two of us into Eric's room, forcing a change of scenery and what was hopefully, a change of topic. Sonya stood in the corner of the room, her eyes glued to a tablet computer and the glossy reflection of lingering tears sparkling against her face. Eric sat behind a row of computer monitors, somehow devoid of emotion and quietly waiting for our attention.
"I know neither one of you want to be here right now." He started, standing and lifting several stacks of papers from his desk. "But I need you both to hear me out. Trust me when I say that neither of you will regret the five minutes it's going to take."
"Whatever you need, Eric." Jalix assured. "Just try to make it quick."
"Trust me...I'll *have* to be quick." Sonya jumped as he thumped the pile of papers down once again, gesturing almost proudly to the incomprehensible jumble of documents. "This is all data from the hard drive that...Kara recovered when she met with Schillinger." He said her name all too quickly, gingerly avoiding it like a curse. "Over the last few hours I made my way through it, looking for anything we can use. And Jalix, I'll need your help."
"Eric-"
"Just wait, Jalix. Trust me. You get to kill Raven. Tonight." His eyes lifted from the floor, alight with a somber satisfaction at the declaration. "But..." He handed Jalix a wireless headset and a small storage device, much like the one used against Schillinger. "You need to find her personal laptop and plug *this* into it. After you do that, call me. Pair that headset with your phone so I can talk to you when you're ready. We're going to use all of the information she has to plan an attack on the Boston labs." My heart lifted from the desolate place it rested on, sending a spark of hope fluttering across my breast. "No one is going to use Kara for their experiments."
"I'll get it done, Eric. I swear to you." Jalix took a step forward and put his hand on Eric's shoulder. "Thank you. For all of this."

"Don't thank me just yet. I can't help you get into Raven's charity event."

"I'll worry about that. You just make sure you're ready when I call." He turned to leave, stopped by Eric's voice again.

"Jalix." He turned around. "You only get one shot at this...and you're not done here. No suicide mission. No sacrifice. And Raven doesn't make it out alive."

"Trust me..." Jalix faced the door again, tucking the storage device into the breast pocket of his jacket. "You don't need to worry about that." He disappeared around the corner, his footsteps fading into the distance. I looked up at Eric, his mouth open to speak, when Sonya threw her device down onto his desk loudly and stalked after Jalix in a rush.

"Sonya-" I called, to no avail. "Where's she going?" I asked Eric, who was equally as confused as I was.

"I have no idea...but *her*...I was expecting." He pointed, my sister suddenly appearing behind me. Her face was surprisingly unstained of tears, almost glowing with an odd aura of positivity. No smile crossed her face, but no telltale signs of the same deep depression within me manifested itself in her expression.

"I came as quickly as I could, Eric. I had to wait for Violet to take Amy for me."

"Then let's get started." Eric quickly pressed into the keyboard on his desk, his fingers flying between the keys and bringing images of grisly, macabre photographs on his screen. My sister spoke up before I had to chance to ask any questions.

"Krystal, I know your reputation is telling you otherwise, but for the love of all that we hold dear, keep your mouth shut for the next five minutes." She gave a directed look to Eric, who stood abruptly and placed his hands on my shoulders. His grip was odd, as though he was expecting me to fall or run.

Weaver

"Krystal, I lied to Jalix." He waited, ensuring that I was complying with Alice's instructions. "I don't need her laptop for the reasons I told him. I need that laptop because it has a schedule on it."

"A schedule for what?" I asked, biting my tongue as soon as I spoke.

"For their experiments, like the ones in the Salem lab. These." He pointed to one of the images, a greatly decayed human carcass sprawled across a metal table. "Krystal, they don't want Kara as *a* catalyst. They want Kara to be *the* catalyst."

"What are you talking about?" I breathed, my heart racing to an unperceivable rate. Alice spoke up, warming my body with her own as she took Eric's place.

"Krystal...do you remember when we were talking about the lab we rescued Jalix from? Those big towers full of sensors? They don't scan infrared light or radioactivity. They scan for magnetic energy. Like the strip on the back of your credit card, anytime someone walks through them, they...they make a copy. *That's* why they use so much energy and needed their own electrical line. Eric figured it out, Krystal."

"I don't understand." I grew lightheaded and nauseous as my mind started to put together pieces of the puzzle collected over several days. Eric decided to enlighten me, putting things in the simplest terms.

"Krystal, they didn't kill Kara until now for a reason. I have every last detail of their experiments right here. A log of *everything* they've done and it's all part of one...master plan. They lured Kara into a trap when they stole Jalix. As soon as she walked into the lab he was in, her memories were stolen by those sensors and sent to Raven. While Jalix was unconscious, they captured him and tested their memory-implantation machine. Then they lured all of you out into the open and killed her so they could take her body. They're bringing her back, Krystal." Eric whispered, looking up from the computer screen. The room was as silent as death itself as his words settled into my mind.

"She's dead..." I breathed. I didn't want to believe myself, nor did I want to believe in Eric's words for the simple fact either side could fail in its efforts: to either resurrect or rescue Kara. A pained feeling grew in my chest, a throbbing combination of blissful tears and suppressed energy.
We can get her back.
"Now, I need you to keep listening, Krystal. It's not as easy as breaking her out. I need you to absorb *every* detail I'm about to tell you. We have a lot of work to do if we're going to make this happen."
"I'm yours. Tell me what I need to do." Alice put a reassuring, calming hand on my shoulder as he continued, the faintest intimations of a smile sliding its way onto his mouth.
"Her laptop will tell us when they're going to do the experiment, which Jalix is retrieving right now. But listen, Krystal...their experiment isn't to revive Kara with her memories...it's to revive her with Schillinger's." Despair was delayed as he quickly explained, nearly throwing me into a fit between the brief sentences. "But that doesn't mean that those scientists can't or won't do what *we* want. They're basically slaves. If they have a shot at breaking free...at helping them get revenge? They'll do it. We just need to get there at the perfect time."
"What's the perfect time?" I interrupted, ignoring his request for my silence.
"They have to regenerate her body first. That's easy enough for them, now that they have her genetic material to finish perfecting their version of our virus. Then they're going to run tests on her to make sure she's properly formed. And after that, they'll try to implant Schillinger's memories into her body." Alice interrupted this time, catching me by surprise.
"I don't understand. Their project was started before Schillinger died. How did they already know that they wanted to implant *his*

memories in *her* body? Why wouldn't they plan on reviving her own memories?"

"Because Kara is the ultimate huntress. She's the perfectly evolved being. Why would they bring her back with the wrong mindset when they can have two bad guys running around? Can you imagine the destruction they could wreak?" Silence befell the trio as we avoided considering the consequences of failing. Eric continued, ignoring the negative possibilities. "We can do this. But I need everyone here."

"Then why didn't you tell Jalix?"

"Didn't you see him? He's...he's far too emotional right now. I don't want him carrying out some vigilante mission against the lab by himself and destroying our opportunity."

"Yeah...I understand. I'll go grab Violet, and Alice, you can call Sonya." I turned around to leave, euphoric at the thought of bringing Kara back to me.

"Krystal, no." Eric said quietly as I spun around. "I mean *everyone*." I looked at him confusedly, a distinct grimace overcoming his face. "This is going to be an all-out *war*. When we make this last move, when we go to retrieve Kara...there's no turning back. They have all the resources they could possibly ask for, they're armed to the teeth, and they have a whole army waiting for us. The only thing working to our advantage is the fact that the lab is on the docks, so noise isn't going to be too much of an issue. They'll definitely hear gunfire, but it'll be muffled, so we might have a few extra minutes. And...I found the electronic code that governs their self-destruct system. I can deactivate the entire thing without them ever knowing. With that being said...we need to go in with everyone willing to fight, at least a dozen. The rest need to guard the city in case there's a counterattack while we're gone."

"I'll make some phone calls." Alice said, pulling her cell phone from the pocket of her jeans.

"Eric...you need to be straight with me." Alice stood still as I approached Eric, slowly and deliberately. "I will go to the ends of the earth to ensure that these scientist bastards meet their death. But if you're lying to me...just to get me to fight..."

"Kara meant everything to me." He spurted, neither agitated nor at peace. "She gave me a second chance at life. I was paralyzed. Trapped in my own body. She gave me freedom...friends...a home. She gave me life. You may not see it, Krystal, but no one here thinks lightly of her. Kara was..." He gritted his teeth, determined in his resolve. "She *is* a guardian angel. For all of us. And if you think for a second I would ever give you the false hope of getting her back, you're dead wrong."

"So we can actually do this?" A teary smile lashed itself to my face, enraptured by the thought of her life being brought back into my own.

"We can actually do this." He smiled, nodding. "But you need to be ready. And you need to understand that if we fail-"

"We won't."

"Krystal...if we fail...we still secured freedom for our people. We still liberated ourselves. And you need to understand that. Resurrection or not, Kara gave her life for us. Make it count." I looked at my sister, dialing a number on her phone frantically. It was nearly impossible to see her, my blurry vision on the brink of nonexistence. She cleared her throat as someone answered, proudly speaking to them as the voice of hope.

"Elizabeth. You and your husband need to come back to the city. We need you." Realizing I had forgotten my phone in the bar, I slid past her and left the room, hearing the last few words she uttered to her friend. "We're going to war." I contained my energy, focusing on my current train of thought, rather than expending it by racing to the nightclub.

She's coming back to me. I can get her back. I'll see her again.

Weaver

Violet's quietly shuffling feet interrupted my elated state of mind, silently swaying Amy in the middle of the main hall. The child's eyes were closed over her shoulder, either fast asleep or on the edge of a dream.

"Hey..." I whispered, approaching the two of them quietly. Violet stroked the girl's head tenderly, running her fingers over the thin strands of hair that crept from the top of her head.

"Hey." She returned, barely moving her mouth.

"We need to talk, Vi." I whispered, staring at the beautiful child in her arms. "It's important." She nodded, taking a slow step in the direction of the infirmary, its glass doors held open by broken hinges. I remained silent as we walked, avoiding at all costs the awakening of the young Amelia. The city was deadly silent, an absence of waking life apparent across the width of the structure. Visible through the windows of the hospital was a singular room that stood out from the rest. Electrical cords were strung with care along the walls and floor, gingerly avoided as we stepped over them to approach Amy's room. Alice's labor in the area was unmistakable: a careful incubator surrounded with silent monitors littering the walls of the child's domain. Violet tenderly lowered her into the powered crib, warm air washing over the tiny body and sweeping it away into comforting dreams. The suspense tore into me, the will to raise Violet's spirits overpowering as I jerked on her arm and pulled her back into the main hall. She stumbled, and I realized she was still heavily affected by her drinking.

"Violet, I need you to sober up for a minute. This is...you're not going to believe it."

"What." She groaned, speaking the individual word rather than ask me a direct question. Her lack of consideration was nothing short of predominant, my spirits unfaltering in the light of my disposition.

"Violet, they're bringing her back to life. Shift Company, or Raven, or whoever. The scientists led by Schillinger's daughter are bringing her

Sorrow

back." Her eyes widened immediately, lilac-painted fingernails clutching her open mouth.

"Are you serious?"

"We're going to rescue her, Vi!" My voice was a whisper, an endeavor to temper my excitement and avoid waking Amelia.

"How?" She asked incredulously, her already-bloodshot eyes beginning to sparkle with elated tears.

"Eric has all the details; it's too much for me to explain in a few seconds. They're going to bring her back, and we're going to rescue her. That's all that matters. We're getting her back!" She lunged forward and wrapped her arms around me, overjoyed.

"This is amazing, Krystal."

"It really is...but we have a lot of work to do first. You need to call everyone you know and tell them to get back to the city."

"Wait..." She pulled away, a look of concern on her face. "Why?"

"We need a small army to go up against Raven's forces." My feelings of hope faded as she shook her head, taking a further step back.

"No...Krystal, no. What's wrong with you?" Her body radiated with disapproval, a look of disgust staining her face.

"What do you mean? Vi, we *have* to get her back. This is the only way."

"By telling mothers and fathers to go on a suicide mission? To put them in danger for one person? No, Krystal. That's...insane. I love Kara, but...she wouldn't want this." I was stunned, not because her opinion opposed my own, but because there was truth to her words.

"Violet...you have to understand-"

"I understand plenty!" She spat. "You're willing to send innocent people to their deaths in the *hope* that you can bring Kara back!"

"We can!" I pleaded to her, trying to grow closer as she moved away from me. "Vi, I know we can. You have to believe in us."

"I believed in Kara. And she's gone. You need to accept that, Krystal." I began to speak, but was interrupted. "What was your plan before all of this? Were you just *expecting* someone to tell you that everything would be okay? Or were you going to spend the rest of your life drinking and slamming painkillers into your veins? You haven't dealt with this yet, Krystal."

"I have dealt with it!" I defended, recoiling. "I was...destroyed, Vi! I was torn *apart* by her death. How can you even say that?"

"I can say it because it's true! You didn't *confront* it, you just...felt the loss. How were you going to move on?" I stuttered, lacking the answer she desired. "How, Krystal?"

"I don't know! Okay? I'd rather die than live without her!" I unleashed my inner beliefs, hearing them aloud for the first time. "I would hate to live my life without her. I have no purpose here. Not in this city, not with these people. My sole purpose in life was to love her. I am nothing unless she's with me."

"Bringing her back won't make her love you, Krystal." She snarled, pointing to Amy's medical nursery. "That child is all that's left of Kara. You need to find a way to live with that." I bit down, my fangs sinking into my lower lip and driving blood between my teeth.

"There's a fine line between truth and cruelty, Violet." My voice quivered as I made every possible attempt to shy away from regarding her words. "You're young, by anyone's standards. You have a lot to learn about what the truth is, and you haven't begun to scratch the surface. But one day, you're going to find someone that you love unconditionally. And you're going to appreciate them more and more every day...growing just a little bit more attached to them. And you're going to hope and pray that they lie to you...just so you can hold on to that love. Sometimes, Violet...lies are all that hold a person together." Sonya's yelling echoed through the hall, deeply embroiled in a distant argument with Jalix that I ignored. I looked into her chocolate-brown eyes as some form of disgust overcame them, tainting her view of who I was. "And sometimes...it's all that's holding two people together. Sometimes those lies...*become* what we love." She shook her head, clutching fistfuls of matted hair between her fingers.

"That's not true! I heard what Jalix said to Kara, and it wasn't a lie! He said that love is something you do, a gift you give to someone. It's not how you feel. And I *know* I loved you, Krystal. You're the only one I've ever opened up to. Are you saying you've only ever deceived me?"

"No, I-"

"She'll never love you, Krystal! Look at yourself! Face your *own* lies!"

"I'm going to get her back, Violet." I hissed, casting aside everything she said. "What she does with her second chance is up to *her*, and *her* alone. If she doesn't love me...then so be it. But that's the gift I'm going to give to her. It's how much I love her...with my life." Violet took several steps backwards, retreating into the darkness of the infirmary's doorway.

"You're not lying to *me*, Krystal. You're not dishonest to Kara, or to Jalix. Those lies? The ones you're so in love with? They're the ones that you tell to yourself."

I can't lose another friend.

"Violet, please-"

"Go away, Krystal...go find Kara."

Don't let her leave.

"Vi, you're my friend..."

"I thought I was. I'm just one of your lies."

I was...so close to feeling.

"Don't leave me." I whimpered tearfully, watching as she disappeared into the darkness to tend to Amy's cries. "Please come back." My whispered plea went unheard in the resonating echo of the concrete hall.

Weaver

Sorrow

Agony
Jalix

A distinct, struggled effort to avoid my own thoughts was halted by Sonya's voice ringing out across the training room. There was no way to ignore her clearly aggravated temperament.

"Jalix. Where are you going?" I spun around and was taken aback by her ragged appearance. Her thin, tall frame trembled with an intense cold, her eyes blazing with both anger and sadness.

"I'm going to kill Raven. So we can finish this."

"Jalix, where's your daughter?" The clear-cut question caught me off-guard.

"Last I saw, Alice had her."

"Violet is taking care of her, currently." I waited for further explanation that never arrived.

"Okay. Thanks." The door to the city's exit opened with a slow creak, exposing the long darkness of the hallway that lay in front of me.

"That's it?" I stopped once again, exasperated with her efforts to prove some belabored point.

"What do you want, Sonya? I don't have time for this."

"That's exactly my point. You have no time for your own daughter? Jalix, you've seen her *once*. The minute you got back to the city, you gave her to Alice and....disappeared for a few hours. Now, all of the sudden you're leaving, possibly for the last time, and you don't even go to say goodbye?"

"She's an infant, Sonya. She wouldn't remember or understand it if I did."
"That's not the point!" She cried in anguish. "The point is that you are essentially abandoning the last thing Kara gave to this world."
"Abandoning?" I approached her, lowering my voice so she would understand the clarity of my thoughts. "I am *not* abandoning her. I am leaving right now to go remove the only thing that threatens her existence. Can you imagine what they would do with the daughter of Jalix Kane and Karalynn Valencia? The torture she would undergo? You can't. None of us can. And I'm leaving right now to go make sure that none of us ever do."
"No, Jalix, you're leaving because you want revenge."
"I can do two things at once." I said coolly, stepping into the dark hallway as she followed me.
"No, you can't, Jalix. Revenge doesn't require you to come back."
I don't need to come back.
"I'll be fine, Sonya."
"You are ignoring me. And it's not going to work. I'll stop you if I have to." I stopped walking, the door to the basement of the frame shop in view a dozen feet in front of me.
"I...would love...to see you try that." I snarled, turning to see her face only a few feet from my own. "Because unless you kill me, you're not going to stop me."
"I don't want to stop you. I don't have a problem with you going after Raven. In fact, I hope you rip her cold heart out of her chest. What I *do* have a problem with is you forsaking your daughter. Treating her like some object." I shook my head and continued my journey, ducking through the doorway into the dank sublevel of the store.
"I am not forsaking her. I'm protecting her."
"But do you actually care about her? She's a person, Jalix. She's going to be an incredible woman someday. Do you see that? Or do you see an estranged child?"

Sorrow

"I see death!" I bellowed, turning on her. "I see Kara's body lying on the ground, covered in thousand degree flames! I hear her voice telling me that things would be okay, when we both knew she was dying! If I go back to that child, all I'm going to see is Kara's death."
"But you're her father." She protested angrily, digging her fingers into my shoulders as I strode upstairs. "If you don't look after her-"
"Then someone else will. If I'm dead, she'll be better off. She'll have someone to take care of her that isn't broken." An elongated bloodstain marred the tile floor behind the front desk, a telltale sign of where our ally was murdered. "She deserves better than a father that's surrounded by war and death."
"Then you need to cast all that aside!"
"It's not that easy!" I roared, kicking open the glass doors of the storefront. "I *have* to do this. I *have* to protect her! War? War is my only option!" I stopped on the sidewalk, the evening streets of downtown Salem empty of civilization. "Sonya, I need to make the world a better place for her. Not just for her...for all of you. And would I love to be a father to Amy someday? Of course. She...she's all I have left of Kara. But..." I ran a cold hand through my hair, cooling my scalp from the heat of my anger. "I don't know how to be a dad. Kara and I talked about this. We agreed that we weren't ready to be parents, just yet."
"Jalix, parenthood isn't a series of actions. It's not something you read a book on and magically go through the steps. It's a...mindset. It's a journey. Being a proper father is about making the right decisions...about being a supporting figure. Guiding them through the first stage of her life and letting her know that there *is* a future for her. No one else can do that." I suppressed tears at the thought of Amelia's grown life, taking Kara's role as a resilient, independent woman. "You need to think about this, Jalix. That little girl is something *you* created. She's a part of you...and a part of her. If you would give that care to her mother, if you would love her as much as

Kara...then you've already succeeded. She's going to have friends that tell her to do stupid things. She's going to make bad decisions on her own...but when that happens, she's going to ask *why*. *Why* that decision was bad, or wrong, or immoral. A father is someone who tells them why, and shows how much they dislike those decisions. And then...then they love their child anyway. All it is, is love...Jalix."

"I'm not ready for it, Sonya." I whispered, facing her against the bitter night wind. "I don't know how." She smiled, contrasting the tears that rolled down her cheeks.

"You remind me so much of Kara. You always have. She...she said the same thing before she met you. She said that she wasn't ready to love someone. But you came into her life, and...it wasn't even her choice. She *had* to love you. She couldn't pull herself away. And after she realized that she was capable of being what you needed? She didn't want to. She was *hoping* to get pregnant, Jalix. She wanted to share that love with someone else." My throat clenched shut, the thought of her personality washing over my head again. Loss gripped my chest, a hollow echo in the cavity of my heart. "And she did. She gave that to you, Jalix. What are you going to do with it?" I collected myself, wiping the tears from my eyes and sighing, sucking the bitterly cold air into my lungs.

"I'm going to keep her safe." I avowed. "I'm going to execute Raven. I'm going to join you all in obliterating their efforts...and then I'm going to go home. Once and for all." She withdrew a set of keys from the pocket of her yellow sundress, tossing them to me unexpectedly. "This is from Krystal." One of the keys had an ornate, embellished logo wrought in silver with blue undertones. "She said to come back. With...or without her car."

"I will. I promise. But first...I'm going to finish this, Sonya. And..." I hesitated, hating goodbyes. "If I don't make it back...make sure Amy knows I love her."

Sorrow

***

The neon of the city lights flew past my window as I sat in silence. Time in my own head was disconcerting, but there was no escape from it.

"Get in, arrange a private meeting with Raven, kill her, and get out. Don't try to do anything stupid right now. You'll just endanger us." I whispered, a fruitless attempt to hide from the mournful thoughts drowning my focus. Focusing on Raven's death was a tremendous comfort, intimations of closure and justice being a powerful motivator. The thought of leaving her alive, letting her get away with the chance to escape and disappear without paying the price she owed...it was nauseating.

"She'll pay, Kara. For everything she's ever done." I whispered to myself as I saw spotlights, illuminating the skyscraper of a corporate office building and flooding the courtyard with harsh white light. The scene was reminiscent of a celebrity gathering; a full-fledged red carpet and exquisite atmosphere tainted by a frenzied mob of media crews. I gently pulled the imported car up to the entrance, guarded by a colossal duo of guards, and sat for a moment in peace.

You're here. Don't screw it up.

As I had come to learn, there was a disadvantage to having the brainpower associated with being a Vampyre. I could imagine every scenario, every possible ending to the situation played out in my head in a split second. I could calculate the velocity needed to throw her out of an upper-story window or to survive if I jumped myself. The curse was that it didn't go away. I couldn't get rid of it. The flashes of grisly images in my head were exposed in front of my eyes like a small child's imagination, one after the other with no way of ending it. I looked out the tinted window to see cameras flashing all over, aimed directly at the car. I threw on a crooked smile and looked

Weaver

out the window again, amused by the fact that no one could see me. It disappeared when I realized that they didn't know who I was.
They think you're dead.
"Let's prove 'em wrong." I breathed, throwing open the door and taking a confident step onto the concrete walkway of valet parking. Without a singular second's delay, the horde of hungry journalists screeched at me, straining against the barrier of armed guards that stood between us.
"Mister Kane, is it true you were onboard a private aircraft when it crashed-"
"Mister Kane, did you attempt to fake your own death to avoid further attacks by the Russian assassin-"
"What do you know about the attacks against Raven Biopharmaceutical lab, and-"
I strode along the line of reporters, ignoring their banshee cries for my attention and scanning the professional crowd for telltale signs of Raven's presence. Even in the harsh glare of spotlights and camera flashes, adrenaline kept my vision focused to a razor, hunting for my prey.
"Where's Kara?" One of the reporter's screams pierced the veil of monotone voices, faltering me enough that the crowd fell silent and focused on my response. I turned slowly, giving them all a brief moment of clarity.
"I know you all have questions. But to tell the truth, I've just been hiding. There have been a lot of bad things happening to Raven's incredible cause, and I don't want to be in the line of fire. Kara is elsewhere right now, taking a break from the chaos of my life. But I wouldn't expect us to be without each other for long. Thank you for all your support and I hope to continue moving forward with this company." I almost choked on my wording, and it took great effort not to think about it. I used the opportunity of further pandemonium to move to the side and start making my way toward the front doors.

Sorrow

Raven stood by one of them, drinking in my publicity with a saturated look of success. I looked at her and made a quick, polite smile for the cameras, my fist curling into a white ball of hatred.
"Jalix!" She called, stepping out from behind her podium and beginning to walk down the crimson-colored carpet. "Jalix, I'm *so* sorry to hear about you and Kara." With an ordinary human's hearing, it would have sounded sincere, but she rushed her words a little too much to not sound excited. My restraint was remarkable as she continued casually. "Why don't you come inside and we'll get you something to drink. Top-shelf is usually reserved for VIP's, but tonight, you *are* one." She winked at me and held the door open, giving me an incredible view of the room's interior. The lobby had been transformed into a chandelier-lit, modern ballroom. The noise was moderate, fairly loud music blaring and groups of people talking over it with drinks in their hands; nevertheless, it was silent compared to the crowds outside. We approached an intricate bar, taking a seat on lavish chairs and absorbing our surroundings. There were already a million ways to slit her throat, bash in her skull, or otherwise maim her to the point of slow torture. Glass was in no short supply, and usually accompanied with metal hors d'oeuvre utensils.
"Known as a *genius* for your negotiating skills and brokering abilities, I would have thought you could talk Kara into jumping off a bridge for you. The separation is surprising. I'm assuming it was something *she* did?" Raven tried to push salt into the wound as I continued with my violent train of thought.
I'm going back underground anyway. If people see me slaughter her, it won't be a big deal.
"I'd rather not talk about it." I said tersely. Thoughts, ideas, plans, and strategies: Each facet of the situation evolved itself into a highly effective plan to publicly murder and humiliate her. I couldn't

disregard it or stifle the manipulation. I was slowly torturing myself, and there was no way I could do this sober.
"Vodka on the rocks. Actually, a double. And get another one ready." I said over my shoulder to the bartender. He slid me a small glass.
"Ooh, Jalix. Don't have too many of those. Don't forget, we *are* going to be talking business later."
"Doubt it." I mumbled before taking a drink from the glass set in front of me.
Don't lure her away just yet. It'll arouse suspicion.
I looked around briefly, trying to find a familiar face. The only one I saw was the occasional black-and-white photo of Schillinger.
"I'm sorry about your father." I said, taking another drink. I tried to keep my voice low, but she picked up a bitter note of insincerity in my voice.
"Thank you for your condolences. He'll be remembered. I'll make sure of that." I pressed on her words, trying to make her slip up.
"Big plans for *you* or big plans for the *company*, Raven?" She smirked, my words obviously not fazing her.
"It's classified. But I don't want to talk about *me*. We'll take care of that later. How about we talk about you? You've been gone a few days. Presumed dead."
"It's classified. Sorry." I mocked and turned around, knowing the response was agitating to her.
"Has anyone ever told you you're exceptionally difficult to get a read on?"
"Yes, I've heard that before. But I think if you want to get a *read* on me…we should talk someplace quieter." She grinned, flashing her white teeth in my direction.
"I'm not going to make it that easy for you." I nodded slowly, a smirk creeping across my face.
"You won't have to, Raven. I'll be the one to make it simple. We should talk about your *father*."

"He's dead. There's nothing to talk about." She retorted, draining her glass and curling her lips into a snarl.

"Is he?" I leaned in as the shock washed over her face, concern finally falling visible against the mask of her confidence.

"You're lying." She hissed.

"You're right. I came all this way to have a free drink. I'll see you later, Raven." I placed my glass on the counter and stood, stopped by a hand far too strong for a human woman's.

"Okay. Fine." She scowled. "I'm sleeping in a room on the top floor right now. We can take the elevator and go upstairs...I have a key."

"What makes you so sure I want to talk, Raven? I might just be here to gloat that we're torturing your father with everything we have." She shook her head, confident in her answer.

"I don't know what it is, but you want something." She snapped her head to look at me. "What is it?"

"Classified." I mouthed, grinning. She was beginning to fall into despair, the false understanding of her father's capture disrupting her ability to make sound decisions.

"Jalix, please...what do you want?"

"I want my wife back." I hissed, leaning back as I realized I was inches from her face and drawing the attention of a select number of individuals from the crowd. She nodded once, surprising me and standing from her seat.

"If it means the release of my father, I'll...help you. It may not be in the way you want, but I'll help you." Her tone was hushed, avoiding the attraction of eavesdroppers.

"Then let's go talk." I motioned to the bronze elevators doors on the opposing side of the room, cringing as she wrapped her arm around mine and began to make her way through the crowd.

"Is this necessary?" I hissed, waving my free hand at a small group I recognized.

Weaver

"Unless you want my guards to think you're coercing me, yes." She returned, almost satisfied with the fact that she had some small measure of power left over me. Tuxedos and gowns passed by all too slowly, meandering through the herd of brokers and salesmen at a sluggish pace.

"Miss Raven. Leaving?" A tall guard stood by the elevator, his hands tucked idly into his belt and his stance slightly wider than a normal standing position.

The safety on his weapon is off. His dominant foot is to the rear. His eyes are watching my hands and face.

I unexpectedly withdrew my arm from Raven's hold, cracking my knuckles and yawning in a split second. He flinched, his palm grazing the grip of his weapon before tucking it back into his pocket. To a human, we wouldn't have stood out, but the tension in Raven's face was palpable as the guard passed my test.

He's a Vampyre.

"Lucas. We're going upstairs."

"Miss Schillinger, I don't think-"

"I don't pay you to think. Now shut your goddamn mouth and open the door before I use you to test the correlation between pain and insanity."

She reminds me of Krystal.

He reluctantly pressed a button on the control panel, the brass doors sliding open and inviting us inside. Another guard waited within the confines of its cramped walls.

"Out." She snarled, jerking a thumb to point behind her. He hastily abandoned his post and fled to another position, out of sight. We stepped in together, her suntanned fingers pressing the button for the top floor. Slowly, the doors closed and we were left alone.

Not yet. You don't know what's waiting on the top floor.

"You know..." I started. "You're not very intimidating. Not physically, I mean. It's impressive that you get them to obey so easily. It's like they're...brainwashed."

"They're not brainwashed. They're believers." The reply forced confusion, repressed by a brief enlightenment. "They've all been shown what my father and I are capable of. What our research is. Most of them are...enlightened by our endeavors. They believe in our cause."

"They already believed in your cause. They were around long before you, Raven. They used to be called the Pyrates before you got your hands on them."

"I know what they are."

"Then you know they've always believed in their own convictions. It's only a matter of time before they realize that they don't need you."

She was clearly troubled by my words, basking in a brief silence before returning with a question.

"I'm assuming that you're actually telling the truth? About my father, I mean. You could have killed me, here in the elevator, and no one would be the wiser." The elevator slowed to a halt, an automated voice declaring that we had arrived on the top floor. There was a brief pause before the doors opened, giving me a crucial period of time to think.

Faint smell of cologne. Quiet radio static. Metal lightly scraping against metal. The quiet click of a weapon's safety.

The doors slid open quickly, the silenced barrel of a pistol shoved aside by my powerful hands. In a single step, I moved forward, pressing my body against his and placing my hands under his chin and on the side of his head. No look of shock or fear had time to creep across the aggressive visage of his face as it spun around quickly, the satisfying crunch of broken vertebrae muffled in the carpeted space of Raven's personal room. An image of fear, Raven realized quickly that I was no one to be trifled with.

Weaver

"Next time, give me some warning." I remarked calmly, stepping over the guard's body and looking around. "I was almost surprised by that one."

The room was definitely not fashioned for living. It was styled like an office, huge windows overlooking the rest of the city from its towering nest above the other rooftops. The tips of the black bird's wings from the Raven Biomedical emblem were visible just outside the window in both corners of the room. A queen-sized bed was awkwardly thrown in front of the middle window, out of place from everything else. No other indications of security presented themselves.

"Alright, Raven. Time to talk. Help me, and I'll give you back your father. Give me *any* reason, and I'll gouge out your eyes with my fingers." She stepped out of the elevator, pointing to a large mahogany desk a few feet from her bedspread.

"I need to go get my laptop. If you don't mind." Her unassuming statement caught me by surprise. Her compliance was a good sign.

"What? Oh, yeah. Go ahead. I'll wait here." I looked around the room, pretending to take in the furniture and décor.

I can throw her out the window...

I approached the window and gently pushed on it. The glass was bulletproof.

"Damn." I whispered.

"It's a nice view, isn't it?" Raven called, rifling through her desk.

"It's not half bad."

"I love it. I live half an hour away, with city traffic and all. I don't get to see much of the city..." Her voice was a meaningless buzz in my ears as I flitted from object to object, growing increasingly excited about the various murder methods springing to the forefront of my thoughts.

"Know what I mean?" Her footsteps and her voice echoed behind me simultaneously, forcing me to drop the letter opener in my hand and turn around. She held a tablet computer in her hand, busying herself with its contents and glaring into the screen with agitation.

"I'm not here for casual conversation, bitch. How are you going to get my wife back?"

"Always so straight down to business." She made a clicking noise with her tongue and waved a finger at me, as though I was a young child being criticized for an unethical action. Her apathy was clearly a display of defiance. "Do you know what a catalyst is, Jalix?" I was genuinely fixated on her, now, absorbing every word that came out of her mouth.

"Yes, I remember taking high school chemistry. Something that speeds up a chemical reaction."

"Correct. What I'm doing for us, the human race by the way, not just the company, is speeding up evolution." She looked in my eyes again. "Genetic engineering. Chromosome programming, more or less. Altering the virus for children to be perfect before they're born, for dying humans to be revitalized. With a few...snags, I might add. Diet problems, survival rate of the mothers, some other minor birth defects, but nonetheless, it's coming along rather well. Your wife's body might help us hurry the process a bit." She smirked, and I knew in that moment that I was going to kill her soon. I felt it in the twitch that echoed through my arms and hands, and in the clenching of my teeth.

"Don't you dare talk about her like that."

Just another few minutes.

"Jalix, I mean no disrespect. Look, as opposed to *your* kind, my father and I are...civilized. We don't like the fact that we had to kill Karalynn, but it was necessary. We'd never have taken her alive, and we needed her DNA."

"Civilized? Is that what you call it? Murdering families? Children?"

Not yet. Hold on a little longer.

"*That* was not my doing. That was our brutish assistant. I disagreed with his methods. But...he got results."
"You're stalling. How are you going to-"
"Yes, Jalix, I get it. You want her back. It doesn't happen in seconds. Be patient." She snapped, chaotically moving her fingers across the screen of her computer. After several seconds of inactivity, the screen was luminous with an alert, humming with vibration and chirping loudly. She pressed a key on the front of the device and began speaking into it.
"What's your progress?" She demanded, turning and taking several steps toward the window. A male voice echoed on the other end.
"We've broken down her chromosomes and introduced them to Strain Four. It took immediately. We have some work to do, but the virus spreads too fast-"
"Start the project. Use the remains and regenerate a prototype."
"A prototype?" I seethed, glaring at her and advancing.
"Miss, are you-"
"Listen to me!" She barked into the device, unflinching at my aggressiveness. "Regenerate her body. Use whatever other genetic material you need to in order to test its efficacy. Move up the schedule and upload the edits directly to my personal computer. I want this started *tonight*."
"But, ma'am, it's too unstable. We can't-"
"You *can*, and you *will*, unless you want to become the next test subject." She tapped the screen once, throwing the tablet onto her bed and spreading her arms.
"You said to regenerate a *prototype*." I emphasized, pointing to the device. "You didn't say you would bring her *back*."
"Jalix, her memories are going to take time to-"
"You have her memories?" I breathed. Her mouth hung open as she realized her mistake, exposing too many details. "How?" She paused, sighing in a defeated smile and cocking her head.

"The sensors. In our labs. I have copies of all of you. Except for...what's the girl's name...Krystal? Except for her. Allison, yourself, your wife, Valterius. Every one of you that's been detrimental to our efforts."

"Call them back." I growled, picking up the device and thrusting it into her chest forcefully. "I want her memories back in her head. And I want her delivered to me, unharmed."

"Jalix, stop." She sounded sincere in her words, far too thorough to be lying. "Regenerating her body is going to require trials, and *if* we can perfect it, implanting her memories properly will take further efforts."

"It only took a few hours for me." I protested, forcing the tablet into her chest. "And I know damn well it works."

"Because you have thirty-some years of memories!" She snatched the device from me and shook it frantically in my face. "She has *hundreds* of years of detailed memories as a Vampyre! She remembered things from before America was a country! She can recount every day of her life as if it just happened. That takes *time* to implant."

"It doesn't take time." I realized, moving closer to her. She fearfully dropped the laptop and shook her head, backing into the window. "It takes *time* when the memories you're going to implant...aren't hers."

"Jalix...I swear, I'll...I'll bring her back."

"You're going to put your father's memories in her, aren't you?" Her silence was deafening, fearful tears beginning to creep into view.

"I won't. I swear. Just...let me go. Let my father go. We're of no more use to you."

She's right.

Her hand moved quickly to cover her mouth as my eyes set in a bloodthirsty gaze onto her neck.

"No, I...I can help you. The scientists, they...they need my information."

Weaver

"They don't need you anymore." I smiled, the painful sting of my canine teeth growing to extend beyond the edges of my other teeth. Slowly, I placed my hand on her neck as she struggled against me, far inferior in strength and unmatched in desire. "Your father is dead, Raven." I taunted, pressing her throat gently against the glass. She attempted to gasp, her air supply disconnected from her lungs by my prevailing, formidable grasp. "I killed him myself." The sharp enamel points cut into my tongue as I spoke, my face leaning close to look into her eyes. Her hands pathetically pulled at my own, ineffective at getting me to release her. "You're a murderer, Raven!" I slammed her head against the glass, a single crack splitting the material down the center of her window. "And this? This is for that family." I smashed her skull against the glass again, a trickle of blood spurting from her scalp and cracking the window once again.
"This is for Maddie." Her eyes dimmed, blood flow slowing to a halt to her brain as I pulled on her neck quickly, thrusting her head backwards one more time. "For Val...my best friend...my brother. This? This is for Jared." I loosened my grip for a split second, sending a searing pain of consciousness into her eyes before I tightened my hold once more. "And this..." My fingers dug into the tough flesh of her throat's muscle, rippling and breaking into fragments of bloody pulp under her skin. "This is for my wife, you pathetic bitch."

Slowly, I bit down on her neck and waited. The waves of freezing ecstasy washed over her body, a feeling I suffered only once before. I could feel that she was in a paradise, enjoying what she felt without questioning what it was. Her body quietly convulsed as my teeth sank just a little deeper. I felt the veins of her warm tissue pass my fangs and linger just behind my teeth. There was a brief silence as she tried to take a last breath and realized that she couldn't.

I thrashed as hard as I could, ripping the flesh and veins from her neck and pushing her back. She had little time to react and reached up violently, gurgling and choking on what little life she had left.

Sorrow

Moving closer to watch her die, I watched her eyes as she lay on the bed, and was unexpectedly confused by what I saw. I expected her last moment of defiance to be cold and judgmental, portraying rage or hatred for what I had done to her. It wasn't. Her eyes were tormented and antagonized in an unusually primal way. She knew she was going to die. They screamed out at me to help her and to save her: A look I knew all too well from the eyes of my wife.

"Rot." I whispered, emotional closure sewing the wounds in my chest as the final light of existence left her eyes. I stared at her body for far too long, reveling in the sight of her mangled neck. The light from her tablet glistened off the growing pool of blood.

We're going to use all of the information she has to plan an attack on the Boston labs.

I snatched the computer from her bed and dug through the inside pocket of my suit, withdrawing the small black device, as well as the headset Eric gave me and my cell phone. Thrusting the device into a port on its side, I clipped the headset onto my ear and dialed Eric's phone. The wet, pungent smell of spilled blood filled my nostrils as the phone rang briefly.

"Jalix? Are you alright?"

"Eric, they're bringing her back." I blurted, explaining the situation to him frantically. "Raven is dead, but not before she called the lab and told them to revive her. That device you gave me is plugged into her computer. You need to-"

"God...damn it." He whispered, his voice trailing away from his phone. "Jalix, I *knew* they were bringing her back. Tell me you didn't force her to call them." Silence was my succinct reply. "I cannot believe...alright. Jalix, they were *going* to bring her back anyway. It's their master plan. We're all in the city right now gearing up for a massive assault. You might have just taken away some of the time we needed to prepare."

"I'm not going to apologize." I said quietly. "I did the right thing." He sighed, audibly hacking away at his keyboard.
"I don't disagree with you, Jalix. It just makes my job harder." He paused for a moment. "I've got it. I have their schedule. Now, Jalix, you need to get out of there right now. If they find her body, they're going to come after you, and we need you alive for this last push. Especially if you want to see Kara alive again."
Seeing Kara alive again...
"How much time do I have before they start, Eric? How long do I have to get out?"
"Let's see...alright, they're powering up the machines and running diagnostics now. They're going to start in an hour, but I don't know how long-"
"I'll meet you at the lab." I said, my finger hovering over the button to end the call. His frantic voice rung out, yelling for me to wait. "What?" I asked, walking up to the mangled remains of Raven's window.
"Jalix, they're not just going to snap their fingers and have a working plan. I-" The sounds of arguing preceded Alice's peaceful tone floating into my ear.
"Jalix?"
"Alice, you need to hurry, I don't know how much time I have before they come to check on her."
"Come back to the city. I've been running tests on Amy's blood samples, and-"
"You what?"
She's experimenting on my child.
"Jalix, calm down. I do it to all the Vampyre newborns to make sure they're healthy. But while I was testing the samples, I ran some tests. A young, non-DNA-bound virus can only regenerate at a certain rate. Her chromosomes are very capable, but-"

Sorrow

"Get to the point, Alice..." I turned around as the elevator's car began to descend to the ground floor, an indication that someone was on their way up. "I need to go."

"Jalix, we have at least an hour before they start, and another hour before she's fully alive, and if we break in before she's fully healed, we have no chance of bringing her back alive. Eric is going to monitor their research, but you need to get back to the city. Now." She ended the call, doing me a favor by ending the conversation.

"Now what?" I whispered, listening to the elevator grind to a halt several stories below me. "I'm twenty stories up..." I peered out of the window, listening to the howling wind seep through the cracks of the glass. "And nothing to land on. No water, no trees, no...trampoline..." I ran a hand through my hair, turning to see Raven's body slumped messily on her mattress.

You could jump with that.

"Nope." I shook my head violently, searching the room for alternate means of hiding or escape. The elevator began to move again, a dozen distant voices clamoring for information.

You can't fight them all. They have guns.

I shook my head again, my hands beginning to shake as I realized that it was the only option.

"I'm not doing this." I whispered, dragging her limp body onto the floor and tearing the sheets from the bed. "I'm not. There's no way."

The sound of the elevator grew closer as I turned and slammed my fists into the shattered window, freeing the glass and forming a gaping hole that opened up into the night air. The sounds of weapons' safeties clicked distantly as the elevator began to slow. My sweaty hands gripped the sides of the heavy mattress, swinging it over to the window and looking into the black sky.

"If I survive this, it'll be a damn miracle." Grunting, I sprawled out across the mattress and gripped the top corners, feigning some sort of ability to control my fall. I leaned forward as the elevator doors

opened, a barrage of exploding gunfire compelling me to submit myself to the mercy of gravity. I leaned back as the air rushed around me, trying to keep the mattress somewhat level as I fell. The icy wind bit my face as I grated my teeth, the ground below hidden by the piece of cushioning material between us. The breeze fought against me, straining to turn my body sideways against my summoned strength. Falling now was slower than when we had jumped from Krystal's plane, the mattress doing what it could to resist the force of my body. My fingers fought to keep their clutched hold as seconds passed, the windows of nearby buildings passing through my vision in a haze of dark reflections. Impacting, the streetlight of an urban setting whirled around me as I bounced several feet off the ground, my face smashing into the springs of the cushioning and nearly knocking me unconscious. I flew off the mattress finally, landing on the solid asphalt of a city road and rolling to a stop against a concrete curb.
I made it.
"Son...of a bitch..." I moaned, ignoring the pain shooting through my hips and legs. I managed to stagger against a lamppost, shaking my head to clear the haziness from my vision and observe my surroundings. I had apparently landed a block away, the towering vision of Raven's corporate building looming several hundred feet from where I stood.
"Man..." I heard a gruff voice from across the street and blinked hard to expose the image of a homeless man, wrapped in blankets. "I thought *I* had to stop drinkin'. Did you just-"
"Yep." I croaked, doubled over. "It was dumb." I breathed heavily, shaking away the pain that wracked nearly every bone in my body. The adrenaline coursing through my veins began to die, my heart slowing to the rate of a caffeinated racehorse.

It began to increase again as the roar of an exotic engine howled through the road in front of me, a pale blue sports car screeching to a stop mere inches from my feet. Nearly blinded by its headlights, I struggled to see the driver as she rolled down the window and yelled at me.

"Get in, dumbass!" I stumbled forward, throwing open the door and closing it behind me. Krystal's foot drove into the pedal for a second time as we lurched forward and flew past the building from which I had just jumped.

"How did you-"

"I told you I wanted my car back." She said sarcastically, turning to look at me.

"Actually, Sonya said-"

"I know what she said. But I wanted my car back." I sighed, my stomach nauseated by the pace of recent events.

"How did you even...how did you know?" I asked. I rolled down her window and leaned out, expecting to vomit profusely.

"I followed you in Val's truck, then picked up my car from the valet and waited. I kinda figured you had a one-way plan. Didn't expect you to turn into a flying squirrel, though. That was...that was the craziest thing I have ever seen in my-"

"Yeah, can we not talk about it?" I groaned, the image of buildings flying past my eyes encouraging the queasiness in my gut. I sat for a moment, slowly combing over the consequences of the last hour.

You did it. You're going to get her back.

I grinned, ecstasy overcoming my stomach as I closed her window and turned to speak.

"We're going to get her back, Krystal." The corner of her mouth turned upwards, though the rest of her face refused to succumb to positivity. "What's wrong?"

"Nothing." She replied quickly. "I'm glad she's...I'm glad we can do this." She hesitated, turning to me. "But I should warn you...when you say that *we* are going to get her back...you're going to find out exactly what that means."

"What are you talking about? Did some people come back to the city?"
"No. We didn't get a few people to return." She replied quietly, the roar of the engine wailing against the open road. "They *all* came back, Jalix. Every last one."

***

Sonya stood in the doorway to the training room, a light smile gracing her enlightened complexion.
"I made it back." I said quietly, spreading my arms. The muffled echo of a large crowd made its way through the few feet of tunnel I had yet to traverse, sparking a question. "How many are there?"
"A little over five hundred people. Everyone that lived down here...they're back." I raised my eyebrows as I breached the doorway and peered around the corner of the room, absorbing the image of the society that waited in the main hall. "We even had Vampyres that lived on the surface come down to help." Krystal pushed past me quietly, disappearing around the corner.
"What are they doing?" They appeared to be standing idly, consumed in chatter between themselves, despite the fact that they were all congregated into a single area.
"They're waiting for you." My head snapped to look at her.
"Me? Why?"
"Because you're their leader now. *You* need to tell them what's going on. What they need to be ready for."
"Sonya, I can't-"
"You can." She interjected. "I know you're not filled in on the full plan yet, but they don't need to know everything. They just need to hear your voice. They need to know that you're here. Ready to protect them." I looked over her shoulder as Violet approached us, Amy's writhing body struggling against her arms.

Sorrow

"I'm so sorry, Jalix. She won't stop crying, and I have no idea what to do. Alice fed her with some baby formula, but-"
"It's okay, Violet. Let me hold her. I'll see if that helps." Sonya moved aside as I strode into the training room, Alice standing in the corner watching the crowd. Violet gingerly handed me Amy's swaddled body, angry with infant tears.
"Hey...shh...you're okay." I rocked back and forth gently, full of pride at the life I had helped create. Her eyes were clenched shut, her mouth open in blubbered cries. "Shh..." I shushed her quietly, swaying back and forth. Alice turned around, smiling at the sight of her quieting figure.
"She knows, Jalix. She knows you're her daddy."
"I'm her dad..." I breathed, watching her beautiful eyes open and gaze into mine. They looked exactly like Kara's, a bright-mirrored silver iris surrounded by a thin ring of black. "She's so beautiful." I whispered, beaming at Sonya. The three of them crowded around me, watching as Amy grew curious, her eyes darting from person to person.
"She looks just like you guys." Sonya whispered, placing a finger between the tiny digits on my daughter's hand.
"She does..." I affirmed. Holding her in my own arms seemed like a blessed opportunity. Knowing that her little smile was something I helped bring to life, seeing the tiny body that Kara and I were a part of...I was speechless.
This was Kara's gift to you.
"Thanks, Jalix. I'm sorry, again." Violet reached over to hold Amy, but I hesitated, turning her over reluctantly.
"Don't go too far, okay, Violet? I'd...like to spend some time with her after I go talk to the crowd." Sonya's face was alight with excitement at my simple words, overjoyed at the fact that I was proud to be a father. "Alright..." I sighed. "Wish me luck."

Weaver

"I'll save my luck for our rescue mission, if you don't mind." Sonya's playful sarcasm left me chuckling as I stepped into the main hall, the full width of the crowd falling into view. There were easily two dozen people to my front, extending back at least a hundred feet and each of their faces falling silent as I stood in front of them. They watched entrancedly as I looked around, taking in the raw, direct influence that Kara had on each of their lives.

She brought them all together.

I cleared my throat, uneasy at the trust that they placed in my ability to lead. Violet meandered slowly across the hall, Amy's sleeping form cradled in soft blankets as the crowd erupted in hushed gasps. She smiled at me, gazing down at my daughter with the utmost affection. "Everyone..." I started. "I'd like you to meet Amelia. Amelia Lynn Kane." Reactions varied from quiet congratulations to scattered applause throughout the crowd. I held up my hand, silencing their voices for a moment.

"She...is what Kara died for. Not because we were attacked. And not because she was drawn into a trap. She died in childbirth, too far from the city to seek medical care. Even with her last breath...she was trying to show the world that she was human." Tears threatened to well in my eyes as I continued, unwavering in my resolve to make Kara's people feel safe.

Our people.

"I know that many of you, or probably most of you, knew Kara very well. And...I'll never fill the role that she played. In fact, I'm not even going to try." I chuckled, alarming Alice and Sonya. The gathering was worried, concerned that I was abandoning them. I pressed on, immediately stealing their attention.

"I've been here for a week. In that one week, I've done things that amazed me. Things I'd never have thought possible. I became a superhero, or at least that's what I told Kara when she first explained it to me. I led the charge into our enemy's territory, severing the head of the snake. I got married...and I made a lot of good friends. I found someone like a brother to me. I made another friend that thought she'd be my enemy. I've done a hell of a lot of good...and seen a lot of bad." I paused, gritting my teeth.

"And then it all changed. I lost my wife...I lost my friends. I lost my cause. Everything that I was fighting for was taken from me. But in return...I gained a daughter." I took a deep breath, beckoning for Alice and Sonya to join me at the front of the assembly.

"Over the last few days, I went from a hopeless romantic and a bad cook...to a father. I changed from human...to something far more than that. And by now, I'm a far different person than I was when Kara was kind enough to bring me here. I've been changed by loss. Our friend Jared. Our friend Val. My beautiful wife...and others I never had the pleasure of knowing. I watched an entire family...disappear. But through all of that, I learned something. Despite my loss...my sorrows...I had a family here." I took Sonya and Alice's hands in my own, grasping them warmly.

"No matter how dark things looked, I always had something to fight for. And now? Now I think I understand what Kara was trying to become. She couldn't look after all of you. She failed. And it...it cost her...her life. So what I'm about to tell you is going to very different from what Kara would have said. Because... I'll never fill the role that she played here. And I'm not even going to try. But what I *will* tell you all..." I took a step toward the group, looking out at their faces as I paced.

"Is that you are *already* free. No one is going to hunt your families ever again. Raven Schillinger is dead. Her father, Robert Schillinger, is dead. Their puppet, Kilkovf Strevieg is dead. No one will hurt any of you again. We...we won our fight." Dozens of them erupted in applause, cheering for our victory.

"But..." The crowd quieted again. "We're not finished. We have one last task that we owe this world. You see, this war was never *about*

us. This war was never meant to bring us to harm...but we suffered. And we had one person, one woman, one Vampyre that kept you all free. And I think you know who that is." Violet stepped back as I grew louder, keeping Amy out of the way of the noise.
"Kara kept you all safe...she saved you! All of you! And before...before she died...I told her something that I'll never forget." I swallowed the lump in my throat and continued, gritting my teeth. "I told her that love isn't something you feel. It's not a magic emotion or something that happens to you. It's a gift. It's an action that you show to someone that demonstrates how much you care. I know...we all loved Kara. I know *I* love her. And I'm going to give her one last gift, one last display of our love. Together, as a people, to show how much she means to us!" Alice stepped forward, igniting her body in a dancing wrath of orange flames that licked at my skin.
"We aren't going to let those sick bastards *use* her for their experiments! We're not going to stand by while they take the ones that *we* love! Not anymore. So we can mourn...we can cry over her loss. I know I have. But we have another option. We can say our goodbyes, remember her, and tell ourselves that life will go on..." Sonya put a gentle hand on my shoulder, the wisps of her blonde hair grazing against my ear. "Or we can get her back."

Violet rushed my daughter out of the room in a flash as the cavern erupted in violent, passionate chaos. Voices rung out against the concrete wall of our proud city, igniting a spark of hope in their eyes as they renewed their faith in each other. Sonya's head leaned into my shoulder, quivering with tears at the sight of our civilization united once again. I turned to her, wiping away the teardrops that trickled down her cheek.
"We have a lot of work to do, Sonya."
"That we do." She sniffled, smiling and nodding her head. "But we still have a little while before we can leave."

"Yeah." I sighed, shaking my head. "It's the waiting that's killing me." I looked back at the crowd, loudly dissipating into their various places within the city. A flood of Vampyres swarmed the chapel and infirmary, leaving the nightclub untouched in spite of the celebratory mood.

"Would you mind if we went back to my room?" She asked, turning away from the scene.

"Yeah, of course. I have a bunch of questions I'd like to ask, anyway. If you don't mind." We pushed our way through the gathering, making our way into the living areas after several struggled minutes.

"I don't mind, Jalix. I'm surprised you haven't asked earlier."

"Well, it's not like we've had much time to socialize. The only moment we've had for ourselves was the party."

"That's true." She chuckled. "And no offense, but I think Kara needed my attention a bit more than you did."

"I agree. And speaking of which...you two were...I don't really know how to phrase it."

We stepped through the open door of her apartment, stripped of most personal possessions and patterned with a multitude of clothing and toiletries. She seemed to be in a state of haste when she arrived, taking little, if any, time to organize or enjoy her visit.

"With Kara and I, there really *isn't* a way to say it. No one else has the type of relationship we do. We were best friends. Sisters in arms. We shared every secret, every inner feeling. Her diaries from our time together detailed everything we ever did. I still have a lot of problems remembering things, but...I just *know*. Like we were together for so long, it became an instinct to care about her. When Val called...I already knew my answer."

"Yeah, that's another thing. Weren't you...almost dead? I mean, no offense, but are you really in the best position to be here?" She laughed quietly, digging through a pile of her clothes in search of something.

Weaver

"It happened a while ago. Physically, I'm fine. And mentally? Yeah, I'm still trying to recover. But I'll never get better by staying sheltered. Being here? Being around you guys and helping in the fight? It feels right. It feels like I'm supposed to be here. And occasionally, I even get a little...flash of something. Just a glimmer of an old memory. Like an image, I guess. I don't know how to explain it. And my abilities, I'm working on, but they'll take far longer to recover fully."
"Wait. You have abilities, too?" I asked, the thought never having occurred. She nodded slowly, finally removing her wallet from the bottom of her backpack.
"Yeah. I'm not sure if Kara ever told you, but all three of us had the same power at one point. A long time ago."
"The three of you?"
"Schillinger. You know how things just...explode when he wants them to? It's the same ability we have. But Kara didn't want us to use it until we could control it fully. So we practiced, and...perfected it. Instead of an uncontrolled energy, we focused and refined it."
"You evolved your own abilities." I breathed, awestruck at yet another of Kara's accomplishments.
"Yeah. And we were both skilled. Another thing I managed to lose in my injury. I can still..." She paused, lifting her hand and tossing her wallet into the air. It fell several feet before stopping momentarily, hovering in the air before collapsing onto the floor in a mess of credit cards and photographs. "Somewhat use it. Like I said, some things are more instinct than focus. But beyond the easy stuff...I can't." She bent over, hurriedly collecting her belongings and replacing them within her clutch.
"What do you need your wallet for? Plan on going shopping once we're done?"
"Well, first of all, yes. I do. I'm going to go on a spree for furniture. But secondly..." She closed the wallet, a single photograph pinched between her fingers as she gingerly handed it to me. "I wanted you to

have this." I took it from her carefully and inspected the image. Krystal, Alice, Sonya, Val, and Kara were all huddled together with Kara kneeling in the group's center. Their faces were all smiling, with the exception of Kara's. The faintest remnant of a smirk twitched across half of her mouth, but it wasn't very genuine. "This is what we looked like before Kara and I left the States with our mercenary company. This was the happiest she had been in fifty years...knowing that we were trying to chase down Kilkovf."

"So the *terrorist* we were trying to chase down was actually-"

"Yeah, it was him. He was a black market arms dealer in Russia before he started arming its enemies. He took on a few fake names after Schillinger contracted him."

"And Kara wasn't happy to chase him down?"

"She was. That's my point. This is all the happiness she knew. There was a reason I called her Sorrow. She didn't know *how* to be happy. She knew what it was, but...she wasn't capable of feeling that way." I sighed, handing the picture back to her. Looking at Kara's face any further would only have served to provoke the pressing feelings of anxiousness and loss. "Until she met you." She finished.

"That's sweet, Sonya. But it still doesn't explain why you're so dedicated to her. And our daughter. I mean, if I forgot everything I knew, I doubt the first thing-"

"She saved my life, Jalix." She interrupted. "I was dead. For all intents and purposes, I had died. She had no reason to stick with me as long as she did. But...she stayed. I'm alive. She gave me a second chance."

"Yeah...it seems like that's a habit of hers."

"It was a gift." She said pointedly, looking into my eyes. "It was *her* gift. And I plan on returning the favor."

"Sonya. You *have* to be ready for this. I can't lose another friend. None of us can afford that."

Weaver

"I told you, Jalix, I'm in great physical shape. Kind of a badass, to be honest. And I don't need to remember my breakfast from three hundred years ago to save her." I smiled, nodding.

"Alright. Fair enough. I trust you. Think we should go check on the rest of the group?"

"Yeah. We've been talking for too long. They probably think we left without them." She stuffed her wallet in her bag and put a hand on my shoulder, guiding us out of the room. The main hall was still packed with the citizens of the city, pacing across the width of the settlement with building materials and supplies.

"What are they doing?" I asked, unable to see their destination.

"They're rebuilding. A few broken doors. Some shattered walls. They're going to restore everything to the way it should be." I smiled.

"Good." Through the thick mob of Vampyres, I could see Alice waving her hands as she made her way toward us. From several feet away, she began to call to us.

"Eric is waiting for us in the conference room!"

"Come on." I waved my hand at my friend, turning to walk toward the conference room. Alice strode alongside me as she broke through the wall of people.

"Did you mean all of that, Jalix? What you said to everyone?" She asked, a hopeful smile on her lips.

"You're damn right I did. But we need to make good on those promises. Let's go see Eric." She nodded as we approached the glass doors of our meeting place, holding them open for me as I led the pack inside. Krystal was already sitting in the corner, her arms crossed and leaning back in a cocky pose.

"You really like to hear yourself talk, don't you?" She taunted, burying her tongue in her cheek.

"You should have been there. Might've learned something."

Sorrow

"Oh, I could hear you all the way in here. I didn't miss anything, sweet cheeks." Eric strode into the room from a door on the opposite side, his hands surprisingly empty for a change.
"Hey." He smiled. "Dodo bird. You made it."
"Dodo bird? What kind of-"
"It's a flightless bird." Krystal explained, thoroughly amused.
"Yeah, I know what it is, but-"
"It was a reference to you jumping out of a twentieth story window." I nodded, grimacing at the memory.
"Alright, let's focus." Eric said, standing at our front. He roamed his eyes over our assembled crew, nodding in approval. "Our plan isn't like most of the other one's we've come up with. I'll warn you all now."
"Oh, thank God." Krystal sighed ironically. "This plan is actually sane."
"Touché. No, it's still crazy. But it's not a lot to remember. Jalix, Tony is upstairs right now modifying a few of our vehicles. You're going to lead the group to the docks, plow through their fence, and kill off the security that's outside. Afterward, you're going to head into the facility and look for Kara. Once you find her, do what you need to. Find a way to get her memories restored. And then get out." He paused, looking at Krystal. "I already spoke with Krystal, and she's going to split off from the group when you guys get inside. I told her how she could keep the alarms from going off by manipulating some of the circuitry in the control room. I know...it's not going to be easy. But I think it's a lot saner than some of the things we've tried before." He stopped speaking, crossing his arms to hear our thoughts.
"Who's going?" Alice asked. "Just the people in this room?"
"Yeah. It's probably best. There are enough of you. Now that Krystal is healed enough to walk around and move a bit, with Alice we have two people here with very aggressive abilities. Jalix, you're proficient in combat. So is Sonya. I'm going to stay here as usual and watch their security systems. I'll keep the alarms from going off until Krystal gets

there. And Tony is going to stay with the rest of them, keeping them occupied and trying to restore the city...Rebuild, a bit."

"How much time do we have before we leave?" I spoke up, prompting an apologetic glance.

"Yeah...about that. When Raven called them, they were supposed to start getting things together. Apparently, they were already prepared. I...didn't come to the speech because I was watching a live camera feed of their first trial." I launched myself out of my seat and leaned into the conference table, looking directly into his eyes.

"Did it work? Did they bring her back?" He grinned, nodding.

"Yeah. She's brain-dead...but she's alive." Never would I have thought those words to be a reason to celebrate, but nevertheless, I nearly collapsed to my knees as the room erupted in cheer.

She's alive.

Krystal's arms wrapped around my chest from behind me, pulling me into an unwilling and bitterly cold embrace. She said nothing, shaking violently with joyful tears. I reached over my shoulder and stroked her hair, doing the best I could to keep us both calm.

"Hey!" Alice barked, drawing our attention to her hand placed firmly on the door handle. "Stop celebrating, and let's go get her back." We lunged forward through the doorway, sprinting into the main hall. The crowd was still present, cheering us on as we raced into the training room and disappeared from their sight. I distinctly heard chanting as we forced our way through the narrow tunnel, echoing off the stone walls and ringing in my ears.

"Sorrow! Sorrow! Sorrow!" The sound became more distant as we moved forward, approaching the basement of the frame shop.

"How many vehicles are we taking?" I looked at Krystal as I spoke, assuming she knew more in regards to the situation than I.

"Eric said two, when we were talking. Hopefully Tony is already done." The doorway to the basement crackled in a blaze of heat as

Alice pushed it open, moving quickly up the stairs and into the storefront.

"Did he say at *all* in what way he was...modifying our cars?" She shook her head at the question, pushing her way to the front and opening the metal doors for the group.

"No, he didn't. He just said that he was making them safer to plow through the fencing. More durable, or something like that." I shook my head, grinning like an idiot at the trivial questions I found myself asking.

One last push. One final effort.

The group strode side-by-side as we rounded the corner to the hidden parking lot, freezing at the same moment and equally as shocked.

"What the hell..." Alice's mouth was hung open, her eyes roaming over the scene of haphazard engineering and backwards industrial work. Tony looked up from his place in the driver's seat of my SUV, beaming with pride.

"Hey, guys. I, uh...I made sure you were ready for a war."

"That's an understatement." Krystal mumbled, running her hands over the work appreciatively.

"Tony, I thought you said this would be *safer*."

"Well...safer for *you*. Not so much anyone that gets in your way."

I stepped toward my no-longer-familiar vehicle, running my hands over the sharpened helicopter blades that protruded from its front. Pieces of the disassembled aircraft were bolted or welded onto the frame, either creating massive protrusions of twisted metal, or reinforcing the sides with plated protection. Alice stood in front of her own car, fashioned in much the same way.

"Four of you, huh?" He continued, scratching his chin. "You sure you can handle everything on your own?" I chuckled, placing my hand firmly on his shoulder.

Weaver

"Tony...you're forgetting something." I beckoned to the three women, each of them in awe at the level of destruction of which we were now capable. "In some way or another, we all owe our lives to Kara. And there's not a damn thing that's going to stand in the way of us returning the favor."

Sorrow

Reclamation
Jalix

The folder slid across the desk, too easily and too quickly. I prayed it would have taken forever to open, or that it would suddenly catch fire or fall to the floor.
"I'm sorry, Captain." The Colonel said with too much sympathy.
"I'm not a Captain anymore, sir." I said politely, inferring that such manners were out of place and only adding to the weight of what was happening.
"Then you don't have to call me 'sir' anymore, Jalix." It was a fair rebuttal, and something I focused my attention on, rather than the wretched file in front of me. With a trembling hand, I flipped the cover open, avoiding the pictures with all of the strength I had left. The mission report was compiled as usual. Generic header. Classification: Secret. Their deaths weren't even substantial enough to maintain a Top Secret clearance.
"I am sorry, Jalix. I know what they meant to you. I was in your command at one point. The same unit. The same training. The same missions-"
"The same brothers." I whispered. I flipped through the pages of condolence letters, stopping at the last one. Captain Reed Walters. My replacement. My blood boiled to a rage at the thought of his failure, but was quickly overcome by the grief that had already overwhelmed me.
"It's not your fault-"

Weaver

"The hell it isn't, sir." I looked at him, accepting full responsibility for something I knew I hadn't done. He sighed and ran a hand through his short, graying hair.

"Jalix, you retired. Your last mission ended with a Purple Heart. Frag to the knee, bullet to the shoulder, and one too many days left stranded in the heat. You were done, and I can live with that. I've never been through that kind of shit. I was a lucky one. You did, and realized that there was more to life than getting shot at."

"Not more than letting these men die!" I yelled, throwing the folder across the desk and letting it hit the wall before falling to the floor. "I knew every one of these men! Staff Sergeant William Hawes, Special Forces Weapons Sergeant, married with two daughters. Sergeant First Class Antonio Warren, my Medical Sergeant, divorced with his son waiting for him to come back home. And the one son of a bitch I never knew let them all die!"

"At ease, Jalix. It wasn't his fault. No one knew the kind of trouble they walked into. The building wasn't sound, and your men knew it. But they spent every second uploading the data we needed before those charges went off. Data that might have saved this country. They thought it was worth dying for, Jalix. Your Captain, your replacement, was trying to drag them out of there. And every one of them refused." I shook my head, knowing that they would have done that without a second thought.

"Jalix, you got lucky with them. The shit you've pulled, disobeying orders to stay behind and defend a landing zone, leaving without orders to track down a terrorist, I don't need to continue. If your official orders weren't already in a moral grey area, you would have been court-martialed. Or killed. You always got lucky. Every time you came back alive."

"No, sir." I gritted my teeth, trying to contain my anger. "I was good at what I did. I listened to my men. I took the time to train with them and learn every last detail about how they operated. I was just that good. It never came down to luck. And we knew there was no coming back, after every mission we went on. But we defied it."

"Because they had someone that they looked up to, Jalix. This isn't your fault."

"I never should have left..." I sighed, leaning back in my chair.

"That's something I wanted to talk to you about..." He added, opening the filing cabinet behind him and reaching for another folder. I shot up, alarmed. This time, he handed it to me personally rather than letting it sit on the desk. I took it from him and opened it quickly, searching through the pages.

"Major Jalix Kane..." I muttered, reading the important points aloud. "One hundred thousand dollar bonus...promotion...leadership over a new squad?" I shook my head and put it back down in front of him, standing up to leave.

"Sir, I am never coming back. I can't go through this again. And I won't." He spoke as my fist tightened around the door handle, preparing to walk away from the only lifestyle I had ever known.

"Jalix. We need you. There isn't a damn soldier out there like you. You need to lead again. It's in your blood, son." I turned around, standing for a moment in silence. Pictures of my fallen squad mates lay on the floor behind him, already forgotten by him.

"Sir. If I was lucky, it's run out. If I was good at what I did...I'm not anymore."

***

Alice was kind enough to dial the phone for me as I drove, despite the fact that my attention to the road wasn't required in any significant capacity. My headlights, shadowed by the massive helicopter rotors that protruded from the front, illuminated the empty road in front of us.

Weaver

"Yeah?" Krystal's voice answered the call, traces of Sonya's hushed words slipping through the line.
"We're almost there. We have about three minutes. Any cops yet?" I looked over my shoulder, Krystal's vehicle a few hundred feet behind my own.
"No, surprisingly. And if there aren't any by now..."
"Then there won't be. Good. How are you two doing?"
"Just fine, Jalix. What about you guys?" Sonya answered.
"We're good. Nervous...but good." Alice responded, placing the phone on my dashboard.
"Well...we all know the plan. I won't go over it again. But in case anything happens, I want you guys to understand that...despite Kara not giving me a choice about being a Vampyre...I'm glad I was. I made all the right decisions, you know? I stayed in the city with you all. I helped you fight. And I'm proud to call all of you my friends."
"Thanks, Jalix."
"Thanks, dumbass." Sonya and Krystal both replied, audibly anxious in regards to what lay ahead. Alice smiled at me, rubbing my shoulder gently.
"Alright." I continued. "Another half-mile, we're going to make a left turn, and that's going to aim us straight at the pier. You can't miss it; they're between the water and us. As soon as you get around the corner up here, throttle it."
"Will do, Jalix. And hey, I have a question." Krystal's voice went quiet, waiting for a reply.
"Yes, Krystal?"
"Who's faster?" She ended the call and I grinned, pleased that she was supportive of our borderline-suicidal plot. "Your sister is crazy, Alice."
"She's psychotic. But hey, I'll take brains over beauty any day."
"So...you *do* admit that she's the hot one?" I teased, turning the wheel and coming to a slow crawl as we fell into view of the lab. "And by the

way, I had a question." She looked at me with curiosity as I continued. "Why don't your clothes burn off when you...catch fire? I mean, not to say I mind, exactly, but...I mean, what gives? Are they magic?" She chuckled and shook her head.
"No, they're not magic. Just flame retardant. Val made them for me."
"You said retard-*ent*, right? Not –"
"Yes, Jalix. That's what I said."
"Okay. Because I used to wonder about him sometimes. He was a little...damaged. But hell, do I miss him."
Floodlights engulfed the building's courtyard in a white fluorescent glow, outlining the edge of a chain-link fence. Krystal's car pulled up next to mine as she rolled down the window.
"What do you think, about a quarter mile away?" She called, a simple nod as a reply. "How many do you see? I count...ten on the outside."
"I see ten." I confirmed, skipping my eyes over the exterior walls of the building. We sat in silence for a moment, enjoying our last seconds of peace.
"I can do...fifteen seconds." She said quietly, her familiarly cocky smirk faintly visible.
"I think I can keep up." I returned.
"What, in that thing? Not likely." She rolled up her window, gripping the steering wheel tightly as her face fell into a somber grimace. Sonya said something to her, inaudible, before kissing her on the cheek.
"We'll be alright, Jalix." Alice whispered reassuringly.
"I know." I pressed my foot into the brake pedal and shifted into drive. "They won't." I released my hold on the brakes, slamming my foot down into the gas as the engine roared to life and lurched forward. Krystal's car followed half a second later, remaining close to my side.
One last push. One final rescue.

Weaver

The growling scream of our engines apparently captured the attention of the guards keeping watch over the lab, scrambling to various points of defense. Four of them, two on either side, gripped the bars on the fence's gate and began to pull it shut.
Seven seconds.
Krystal's car edged past my own, gaining the lead by only a few feet. Sonya's tongue was stuck out teasingly at me as we passed. The gate has an opening of only a few feet, growing closed more quickly than we could travel.
Three seconds.
I leaned backwards, forcing my skull into the headrest of my seat as Alice did the same, bracing for the inevitable impact. As I had come to find familiar, my energy skyrocketed as the gate grew to only an arm's length away, sharpening my vision to pinpoint focus and allowing an extraordinary clarity of thought. Every piece of shrapnel from the shredded gate was calculated in front of me, collapsing the helicopter's rotor into a mangled pile of scrap on the grill of my SUV. Krystal's vehicle tore through more easily, having an advantage of roughly thirty feet and a lack of resistance from the gate I destroyed.

    Across both of our vehicles, the unlucky bodies of the four guards were strewn in bloody heaps, a sign that they didn't believe we would break through. The resistance and extra weight between the bodies and crushed pile of fencing took its toll on the vehicle, sputtering as the engine was fatally damaged. Nearing the wall of the facility, I spun the wheel to my left, frantically rotating the vehicle on its front wheels and slowing to a hissing stop mere inches from the cement face of the building. Wasting no time, I withdrew the pistol from my suit jacket, kicking open my crumpled door and striding into the open courtyard. Krystal was already well at work, two mercenaries by the door already slaughtered by thick spikes of ice.
That's six already.

Sorrow

One of the sentries stood on the roof of the structure, his rifle falling to aim in my direction. He failed in his endeavor, my reflexes far faster than his own as I squeezed off a shot that ripped through his skull.

"Alice, to your right!" Sonya spun around, firing a shot from her pistol and killing one of the three men that advanced on Alice. Armed with only stun guns, they stood little chance against the torrent of fire than blazed from her palms, igniting them in a brief inferno before they fell still and silent.

That's all ten.

"Come on." I said, taking a position outside of the door. Sonya joined behind me, Alice and Krystal on the opposing side.

"I told you." Krystal whispered, peering through the small window on the secured door.

"Told me what?" I hissed.

"Your SUV sucks."

"It's fuel efficient!" I condemned, driving my foot into the lock of the door. It crumpled inwards, giving way to the force of my kick and lazily hanging from its hinges. Alice and I rounded the corner first, peering down the long hall that lay to our front with equal confusion.

"This...isn't like the other ones." Alice groaned, keeping a watchful eye on any movement that came from the hallway.

"No, it's not. Eric said this one's different. Go down this hall, then turn left. It's the room all the way at the end." Krystal stepped backwards as she spoke, entering a separate hallway to our right.

"Where are you going?" I demanded, knowing that she was the only one familiar with the place.

"I have to keep the alarms off. I'm the only one that knows how. Just go. If it doesn't work, and the alarm trips, I'll meet you all at my car. It's still running." I wanted to argue, but as she ran down the hall to her destination, I knew that it was our best shot at getting Kara out of here.

Weaver

"Come on." I repeated, moving slowly with Sonya and Alice. Closed doors lined our left and right flanks, no hints as to what lay behind them.
"Why aren't there more guards? And why is it that every time there aren't any, something worse is waiting for us?" Neither of them had a reply. We crawled our way past the empty rooms, Alice's hands ablaze and pistols in the hands of Sonya and me.
Keep moving. Just keep going.
I let the memories of Kara's presence encourage my bravery, eradicating any thoughts of giving up. The hallway culminated in a three-way intersection, the right side far longer than the left.
"That looks like an operating room." Alice whispered, pointing to the red cross painted on the glass doors. I looked down the corridor to my left, silently agreeing with her.
She has to be in there. She has to be.
"Alright. The door has a keypad on it. Alice, you melt the glass. Sonya and I will go in first and take care of security. Follow us inside and watch our backs." She nodded once, staying an arm's length away as we moved together toward the enigmatic medical room.
"This one doesn't have any doors..." Sonya lowered her handgun as we walked, gesturing to the solid cement walls.
"I noticed. This place must have been..." I almost tripped over my own feet as I realized why the facility was structured oddly. "This place was built for Kara." I blurted. They stopped, their heads snapping to me and expecting further explanation. "That's why all the guards were outside. That's why it was fenced in. It's the same reason everything is so closed-off. They're not trying to keep people *out*."
"They knew they'd have to keep *her* inside." Alice breathed, growing infuriated at the thought of them keeping Kara trapped like an animal. We halted, leaning against the glass doors and searching for a view of the room's interior. Our perspective was blocked by a mint-

Sorrow

green curtain strewn across the width of the opening, effectively eliminating any forward planning.

"Ready?" I whispered. They both nodded slightly. I moved to the side, pinning Sonya and myself against the wall as the glass melted into a puddle at our feet. Adrenaline and fear taking hold on my chest, I pushed inside, knocking down the curtain and slowing to a stop as I grasped our situation. A large, observatory-style window was pressed into the cement in front of us, casting a clear view on the scene several feet below. Surgical tables supported a dozen bodies, all covered in white sheets and hidden from our view. Muffled, I could hear a doctor's voice as he dragged one of the bodies into a large, tubular machine.

"Be careful. They want her unharmed." Tears flooded my eyes as one of the three personnel pulled back the sheet, exposing Kara's jet-black hair and flawless face. Her breathing was slow, but visible through the thin cotton sheet.

"How do we get down there?" I asked frantically, spinning around to look at my surroundings. No door or staircase gave clues to a way onto their level, the window to my front and the door behind me the only visible means of entering or exiting the observing room.

"Jalix, what are all those bodies?" Alice pointed, distracting me from my search.

"Alice, I don't have time for this. I need a way down there." I pressed my fingertips against the glass, pressing to determine its thickness. Looking at its edges, I could tell that it was easily six inches thick. "I need a way down there!" I shouted, pointing to Kara's body as it was slid into the machine.

"Why don't they hear us?" Sonya cried, troubled.

"Because this goddamn glass is six inches thick and the rest of the room is concrete! Now help me get through it! Alice, do something!" The machine began to whir with a low hum, the interior wrought with a white glow as it powered on.

Weaver

"Get back, Jalix." Alice spread her arms, a band of flame circling her hands and collecting until a white-hot stream of fire raced its way around her fingertips. Grunting, she pushed against the glass, the belt of raw heat searing its way through the material. It crackled and hissed as she forced her hands further into it, finally breaking through. The glass was unmoved, but loosened in its place on the wall as a thin band of melted glass outlined a large rectangle.

"Move." Sonya commanded, stepping toward the window. Avoiding its surface, she lifted her hands and placed them in the center of the weak point, closing her eyes. She pushed slowly, the barrier between her hands and the glass nearly diminished. Clenching her hands into tight fists, she grunted, the brick of glass exploding in a fine mist of powder and allowing several surrounding chunks of glass to fall onto the floor below. Two of the scientists screamed, taking cover underneath the row of metal tables as I launched myself through the opening, narrowly missing the scorching hot wall of boiling glass.

"Don't move!" I bellowed, drawing my weapon and leveling it between the eyes of the doctor. A tense silence ensued for several seconds. His surgical mask hid his expression, though he responded coolly and quietly.

"What do you want?"

"I want my wife back!" I screamed, pointing to the machine. "I want Kara's memories restored! Now!"

"I can't do that." He responded softly. I pressed the metal barrel of my pistol against his skull, inflicting an intense pain on his temple.

"You're going to." I growled, seething with wrath.

"I'm not. And you're not going to kill me. Because I'm the only one capable of restoring her memories. My assistants are here to observe the process. They don't have the knowledge to-"

"I don't care!" I screamed, grabbing a fistful of his hair and slamming his head into the control panel of the machine. "Do it!" He remained still and quiet, refusing to acknowledge me. I released my grip on his head and reached under the nearest table, grasping a fistful of hair. Screaming, the assistant resisted my struggle and I pulled her from underneath the table and wrapped my arm around her throat, pressing my gun to her chin.

"How about now?" I barked. He shook his head slowly as he stood.

"I'll not condone murder. But furthermore, I will not allow you to free this…monster…and have her slaughter dozens more."

"Monster?" I asked incredulously. "Your boss was the monster! Raven and Kilkovf, they were monsters!" He shook his head again as the assistant began to sob, wailing pitifully against me.

"They are trying to bring order."

"They're dead! Your cause is over! Okay? Just…just give me my wife back…" I pleaded, staring as the device continued to hum quietly.

"What's your name?" I hissed, pulling the assistant closer. My violence didn't seem to affect the doctor as he stood stoically.

"M-Madison…my friends c-call me M-Maddie." Cold crept over my chest as I released her, allowing her to cower in the corner of the room. The pistol fell from my hand, striking the ground with a defeated clatter.

"I can't." I whispered, tearfully looking into the doctor's eyes. "I can't do it. I can't be…as cold as you. But please. Help me. Bring her back to me." He stared at me for several long seconds, finally cocking his head and asking a simple question.

"Why?" There was no hesitation in my reply.

"Because I love her. She's my wife, and-"

"No." He interrupted, looking over at the young woman huddling in the corner. "Why…didn't you kill her?" I sighed, placing my hands on top of my head and breathing heavily.

"Because I…knew a little girl named Maddie. Your boss slaughtered her. In cold blood." I shook my head, glaring at him. "She was twelve." I whispered.

Weaver

"What...purpose did it serve?" He reached over to the desk behind him as he spoke, picking up one of a dozen hard drives, labeled with a long number.

"None." I hissed. "He did it because he was a cold-blooded bastard. He wanted to *prove* something to Kara, that...that her efforts didn't matter. That her emotions made her weak." The doctor finally showed a sign of emotion, scoffing.

"Weak?" He muttered, placing the drive into a slot on the side of the device. "Her emotions...her lack of ability to fully embrace the cold-bloodedness of her species...is why we were bringing her back. It's why we were waiting for her DNA."

"What are you doing with that?" I demanded, watching him adjust a series of controls on the side of the device.

"Mister Kane...emotion is a weakness, but it's one that we all share. I know full well that my employers...my captors...lacked such a quality. But never did I believe that they would go to such lengths to deceive me." He turned a large dial on the side of the machine, increasing the volume of its humming resonance. He continued speaking, unmoving from his position. "I see truth in your words, Mister Kane. And regardless of *what* you are telling the truth about...I will not deprive you of love." The machine snapped loudly, an earsplitting crackle echoing off the walls of the small room. He shouted over the volume, his hands raised in a show of compliance.

"We have only tested this twice, Mister Kane! I am unsure if the machine works!" He fell silent, turning to watch the device perform its task.

"We're going to find out, aren't we?" I said quietly, taking a step closer. Kara's legs thrashed violently, in obvious pain or turmoil. The doctor took his place beside his assistant, beckoning for the one in hiding to approach him. She rushed out, the three of them huddled in an embrace. I looked up, staring through the hole Alice and Sonya had

Sorrow

created. Their hands were joined, leaning into each other for support as they watched, praying that she would come out alive.
Please...I miss her so much.
The machine popped once more, jerking to the side for a brief moment.
All I want is to love her again.
The noise quieted, a steady, loud hum nearly matching the ringing in my ears.
My daughter needs her. We all need her.
After an eternity, the vibration slowed to a low buzz. The lingering noise quickly subsiding, falling completely silent has her legs ceased their movement. I spun around, pleadingly staring at the doctor. Unmoved, he watched, nodding slowly.
"Kara." I whispered, taking a step forward. No sign of consciousness gave an indication of success. "Kara? It's me." I waited again for a long moment, biting my lower lip until blood trickled down my chin. "Kara?" A loud thump jerked the device to its side as her legs moved inward, cringing.
"Ow! Goddamn it! Where the hell am I?"
She's alive. She's with me again.
I reached down, grabbing her ankles and jerking her body out of the device. She fell to her knees, her beautiful, mirror-grey eyes meeting mine as she looked upward.
"Jalix?" She asked. I lifted her up and pulled her body as close to mine as I was able, stroking her hair with one hand and clutching her bare back with the other. I didn't resist the emotion that fought its way into my eyes; I had no reservations sniffling pathetically into her shoulder.
"Jalix, what's going on? Where are we?"
"I rescued you." I whispered, turning so she could see Sonya and Alice standing in the observatory. Sonya was weak from the use of her

abilities, heavily leaning into Alice as they stood together. "*We* rescued you."
"Jalix, I was rescuing *you*. Five seconds ago. I don't-"
"I know. I have a lot to catch you up on. You were...you were asleep for a while."
"Asleep? Jalix, I don't-"
"We need to get you out of here, we really don't have time to talk right now." I looked at the doctor, his eyes set in a soft smile. "Thank you." I said quietly. The room illuminated in a flood of red light, an all-too familiar alarm sounding through the laboratory.
"Jalix?" I swept Kara into my arms, sprinting to the window and crouching, gathering all the strength I had available in my legs. I leapt, barely making it over the edge and setting her down on the cold floor.
"Can you walk?" I asked frantically as she stumbled into Sonya's arms. She clutched the white sheet to her chest, nodding. "Good. Let's go."
"Wait!" The doctor called out from the operating room, gathering my attention for a brief moment. "One of your friends is alive!" I peered down into the lab, shouting back at him.
"What are you talking about?"
"Room one-twelve, on your way out! He was our test subject!" I nodded once, turning to sprint down the long hall we came through.
"What did he say?" Alice panted, struggling to keep Kara upright.
"We need to make a stop. Room one-twelve." She didn't ask questions, sprinting past the long line of closed doors before we found the one the doctor mentioned. "Hello?" I called, pressing my ear to the door. A muffled reply came through, indiscernible against the blare of the alarm. I rammed my shoulder into the frame, repeatedly striking it until I fell through, dropping to the floor. I looked up quickly, a lumbering figure amicably extending a hand.
"Val?" I grinned as he heaved on my arm.

"Alive and in the flesh."

"Stop coming back to life. You're pissing me off." I grabbed his arm and flung the two of us into the hallway, hurling toward the door at immeasurable speed. Without warning, one of the closed doors flew open and exploded in a hail of deafening gunfire. I shielded Kara's body with my own as we ducked, allowing Alice an opportunity to send a torrid inferno echoing down the hall. The men screamed as Kara and I stood again, briefly watching them flail and thrash on the floor. There were four of them, and their body armor had begun to melt into their skin, sizzling and searing its way through their flesh. Sonya lifted her hand slowly, flicking her wrist and ending their pain with a quick snap of their necks.

"Thanks." I panted, moving forward once more.

"Every one of you owes me an explanation." Val complained as the group rounded its final corner, nearing the exit to our personal hell.

"The last thing I remember is sneaking into the lab to get Jalix back."

"Val, not now buddy!" I called over the alarm. "There's a time and a place, and this isn't it!"

"Where's Krystal?" Sonya yelled, our group breaking the barrier between the harsh alarm and the chilled night air. Her voice was faint, the struggle to stay upright clearly visible against her thin frame.

"Anyone want to tell me why I'm almost naked?"

"Not now, Val."

"She said she'd wait for us here." I looked around, waiting for a sign to present itself. "I'll go back." I lunged toward the door again, stopped by Alice's burning hand.

"No, Jalix, we can't lose someone else."

"We will if you don't let me go back for her!" I bellowed, tearing my arm away from her grip and rushing back into the building.

Krystal owes me one for this.

Weaver

Poison
Krystal

I was not surprised to see him, but the thought of him dying alongside me was frightening.

"Jalix, get the hell out of here." I said calmly, resetting the timer on the alarm. It skipped a beat, a resounding silence befalling the room for a brief moment before echoing through the complex with its previous blaring tones.

"What?" He looked at me with his mouth open, not understanding what I was trying to tell him.

"I have to make sure this thing goes off and takes this place down. It's all that's left of Raven's research, and I'm not going to leave it intact."

"That's a chance I have to take, Krystal. She's alive! Val, too! You're coming with us; I'm not losing someone again."

"I can't. More guards are on their way from the lower levels, and...I can't let this place survive." I looked him in the eyes and let the realization of what I was doing sink in. "Jalix...Let me do this. She'll never want me the way I want her. She'll never love me the way that I want her to. It's time to let me go. Let me do this for her."

"Krystal..." He frantically looked around, knowing he only had about a minute left. "Please. At least *be* there in her life." I sighed, gritting my teeth and fighting back against the emotional turmoil that raged within me.

Weaver

"It will hurt her less knowing that I'm gone than knowing I can still hurt her....knowing that she has to see me in pain. I need this, Jalix. I'm sorry. Let me go." A rumble deep underneath the facility shook the ground, and I fought to regain my balance.

"Jalix, those were the lower levels. You need to go, now!"

"Krystal..." He groaned, unsure of what to say, if there was anything left to say at all. "Please!" He begged, pointing to the door. "You don't need to do this! They won't be able to turn it off!"

"They *can*, Jalix! And there's no way in hell I'm leaving this place without knowing for sure it's leveled. Once the guards get here, we won't be able to fight them off! They'll shut the alarm off, lock this place down, and they'll just make another Kara! They'll make another Schillinger! Hack *told* me that there were other bodies, Jalix!" He shook his head, glaring at me.

"Krystal..."

"Jalix, go!" I yelled, slamming my fist into the wall.

"She loves you. Know that, Krystal." He looked down at me one last time before turning away and running toward his escape. I let out a breath, quivering with tears. The red lights flashed around me as I twirled my hands in elegant circles, conjuring all the ice I could gather. I let memories of Kara flow into my thoughts, fueling the frost consuming the walls of the room. I let it overpower me and take control of me, dominating my thoughts.

Her long black hair draped over my face as the smell of rose petals crawled over my body.

The ice became thicker, closing in and making the room substantially smaller. It became a prison, sealing the door closed and barring me from any hope of freedom.

She smiled at me after a dark joke, the sexy, seductive laugh ringing in my ears.

The first layer of frost came in contact with my skin, indifferent in temperature against my flesh. My movements become more and

more subtle, the smile on my lips wider and wider, as the ice conformed to the shape of my body. The cavity of the room was lessened to a crawlspace, a dozen feet of solid ice encasing my body and sealing me inside its powerful surface. It wasn't enough to protect me. But it was enough to make me feel warm one last time. The explosion echoed through the halls before entering the engineering room and consuming me.
Her pale skin pressed against mine.
Her lips on my cheek.
The flames penetrated the ice and hissed at my skin.
Her beautiful silver eyes locking with mine.
Her fingertips tracing the outline of my face.
I felt a comforting warmth creep over my skin, numbing my pain.
"I love you." *I whispered, cradling her hunched body against my own. For the first time in forever, I felt warm. Not from the heat of the fireplace, or the heat from Kara's body, but from something in my chest I had no way of describing.*
"I know." *She replied quietly, gazing into the dying embers of my fireplace.* "And I love you, too."

Weaver

Sorrow

Phoenix
Kara

I laid the folded paper next to the bed of flowers and closed my eyes, the particularly neutral temperature of the wooden coffin grazing my fingertips. Tears stung my already reddened eyelids as I fought to maintain my composure in front of my friends.
"Come on, Kara. Let's step outside for a moment." Jalix's voice whispered from behind me; it echoed the loose grip he maintained on my shoulder. I looked down at the empty coffin for the thousandth time, weakly letting my eyes roam over the picture next to the bouquet. I wanted nothing more than to crawl inside the coffin and be left alone. Refusing to think, I mumbled an agreement and took a step away.
"Come on, baby. Just for a minute." He continued. I turned around and embraced him tightly; a typical, frequent act on my behalf. Ever since my resurrection, I hadn't been able to keep my hands off him. I pulled away and turned around, letting my feet drag the rest of my body outside into the vibrant, lively world outside. The spring breeze warmed away a degree of the emotion, allowing a free moment to wipe away my tears and run a hand through my hair.
I couldn't feel the true depth of the loss that I had believed existed within me, the feeling I repeatedly told myself was coming. I wasn't beyond recall or broken. I simply missed her, and I was heartbroken that she was gone.

Weaver

"She did it to save you." Jalix offered for the hundredth time. It wasn't annoying, but I had heard it before, and the statement offered me no comfort.
"I know, Jalix. But that would imply that her life was lesser in comparison to mine. And it wasn't. She had a lot to offer the world."
"She gave the world the greatest gift that she could have. A future free from slavery....from prosecution and hunting. She gave us freedom." His words rung true in my heart, but felt hollow in my mind.
I wish I could have said goodbye.
"Kara, sweetie." Alice opened the door slightly and called to her. "It's time for the eulogy." Alice was maintaining her composure far healthier than I was; it was remarkable for losing a sibling.
"I'm coming." I took Jalix by the hand and walked back inside. The earthy tones of her mansion's walls set a tone of tranquility, a comforting ease in a time of mourning. Moving slowly, I stepped toward the podium, my blue dress chasing my ankles lightheartedly. I had worn it for Krystal's sake, a gift from long ago. I cleared my throat and looked into the small gathering in front of me. Val had a lily neatly tucked into his suit pocket, and Alice had an arm wrapped around his own. Sonya had a somber smile on her face, nodding to me faintly for encouragement. I took a deep, shaky breath and spoke.
"I...fought alongside Krystal for nearly three hundred years. But I only truly knew her for a short time." I looked at the casket to my right, carefully arranged on a table decorated with flowers. "You guys know more than anyone that...we're a family. All of us. And it goes beyond blood and genetics. Krystal was...Like my sister. My apprentice. My friend. She was a lot of things that make someone a great ally. And she made some poor choices. She had her moments of darkness and of doubt, but who doesn't?" A somber, hoarse chuckle came from the back of my throat. Amelia gurgled from the crowd, held fragilely by Violet. "She was an amazing human being...more

Sorrow

than human by her genetics, but in her sacrifices and in the ideals she resembled, she was a person. And...I know I'm going to miss her." I wiped my eyes and discreetly checked my hands for mascara as I stepped down. I couldn't tell if the pain in my stomach was because I needed blood or if it was just sadness, but I ignored it as I walked by the table and put my hand on the coffin. It was a brief moment, as I knew the coffin was empty and only symbolic.

"Here, mommy. I think she needs a diaper change, and...while I don't mind doing it, I'm not skilled. At all." As the crowd broke away from their chairs, approaching the memorial to pay their respects, Violet approached me, holding my beautiful baby girl in her arms. Amy was gurgling quietly, carrying on a mystical conversation with herself. "Come here, sweetie." I lifted her gently, freeing Violet from her much-appreciated babysitting duties. "Thank you so much for your help recently, Vi."

"You know I don't mind, Kara. She's the easiest baby I've ever taken care of. Besides Krystal." She chuckled, the smile quickly vanishing as she resisted the urge to cry.

"I know it's hard, Vi." Jalix offered his support gently, floating his hand through the crimped strands of her hair. "But things will get easier. Kara and I are here whenever you want to talk, and you know that you can always come to us."

"I know, and thank you. The last few weeks have been hell, you know? After Jared's funeral, and trying to...wait for Krystal. It got easier the last few days, but...today?" She watched as Alice laid a wreath over the ebony casket. "Today is hard."

"It is for all of us." I placed a light hand on her shoulder cradling Amy against my chest. "But we'll get through it. We're going to be busy making sure that people remember her. Every person that returned back to the city is going to know what she did for us." My attention was averted away from Violet as Tony made his way through the crowd, his hand over the speaker of his cell phone.

"We can go now, but we only have two hours." He said softly, returning to his call. "Thank you. We'll be there shortly."
"Okay, thank you so much, Tony. We'll take Alice, and go by ourselves first. You guys can go after we get back." I turned to Jalix, already holding Amy's diaper bag and our car keys. "Let's go." He opened the door to Krystal's mansion gingerly, as if he was afraid of disturbing anything that used to belong to her. Amy burbled quietly in my arms, bothered by the difference in environment.
"It's okay, my darling. Go back to sleep." I kissed her forehead, leaving a faint smudge of red lipstick.
"Do you want me to keep her busy during the drive?" Jalix asked, opening the car door for me. I ducked down, cradling her in my arms and placing the tiny body into the car seat.
"That would be amazing. She's been quiet today, but I'd like to keep it that way."
"She's been quiet because she's busy filling her diapers." He grumbled, sliding into the seat next to her. I grinned, kissing his forehead before closing the door and taking my place in the passenger seat. Alice started the car and pulled out of Krystal's long driveway.
"I don't know how I feel about this, guys." Alice whispered, wiping the remaining wetness from her cheeks.
"It'll be healthy, Alice. We'll get to truly say goodbye." I heard Amelia giggle from the backseat, and I turned around to see Jalix making faces at her, lightly touching her nose and hiding behind her blanket. I sighed blissfully, still struggling with the suppression of my guilt.
"And once we're done, we can start helping make the city a safer place."
"I think Val has that handled." Alice responded confidently. "He's been...passionate about everything since he came back."
"Yeah. He's been doing very well. I'm proud of him." I responded, nodding. "And I'm definitely glad to have him back."

"What's the plan once we get there?" Jalix asked quietly.
"Tony was talking directly with the foreman dealing with the site. I can go talk to him and let him know that we won't be any trouble."
"That sounds great." I agreed with Alice's plan quietly as she turned onto the highway.
"How's Sonya doing?" She asked, taking her eyes off the road for a brief moment to gauge my reaction.
"She's doing great. I sat with her the other day and we talked for a long time. Her memories are really starting to come back. She has some minor lapses, but all in all, she's doing very well."
"Good." She whispered. "Almost everything is the way it should be." I nodded, the familiar tightness of pain clenching my throat shut.
"Almost."

***

My hand gripped the handle of the baby stroller tighter than it should have, as though it were going to suddenly fly away from me. Jalix made faces at Amelia as she giggled; it was the image of perfect bliss, and one that I never expected to have. Fatherhood suited him well, it seemed. In only the brief weeks that we had been parents, he adapted to every need she seemed to have. With no preparation or warning, he became a father, and did so in the most perfect of ways. I still, despite Jalix's recounting of the events repeatedly, couldn't believe that I was a mother. Despite my wildest hopes and dreams, it was something I was sure would have never happened.

I nervously cringed as the construction equipment beeped loudly and served as a possible trigger for Amy's crying fits. It went unnoticed, thanks to Jalix's extraordinary distraction skills. He gently floated her rattle away from her, keeping it just out of reach, then putting it back just in time for her to realize that it was a game. I smiled, the sight almost too adorable.

"He's so cute. Look at you, daddy." Alice said from behind me. I hadn't realized that she was back already.
"What did they say? Will they let us in?" I asked nervously.
"Yeah, they said it's perfectly safe. They have the story that it was a gas leak that caught on fire. They even told me where the engineering part used to be before it..." She didn't finish the sentence, but looked at the rubble of the facility for a long moment. "I told the construction foreman that we had friends that died here, and he said as long as we get out of here within the hour, we can visit where it happened."

I nodded as she handed me the flowers and took the baby stroller from my hands.
"I'll push her so you can lay the flowers down." She said gently, putting a hand on my back.
"Thanks, Alice." I held Jalix's hand as we walked towards the area that Alice beckoned to. The concrete chunks and copper pipe made an almost flat surface; it was easier to walk on than I would have thought. It seemed like the very air around me chilled as we got closer and closer until the marker designating the end of the engineering wing was finally reached. I took a deep breath, unsure of what to say, if there was anything left to say at all.
"Thank you, Krystal. You gave me my life back. My baby. My husband. You kept it free from a dark world and free from bad people. And I can't tell you how much I appreciate it. I'll never forget what you did. You might not be with me anymore, but the consequences of your actions are something that I have the privilege of living with for the rest of my life." I laid the flowers on the ground and turned away, hugging Jalix for a moment. "I don't know what else to say." I whispered, feeling inadequate at the short farewell.
"You said what was important. And that's all that matters." I nodded, wiping tears from my eyes and turning to Alice.
"Give me the stroller, Alice. I'll let you say goodbye." I took it from her gently and kissed her cheek. "Just let me know when you're ready.

We're going to wait at the car." She nodded and looked down, thinking of something to say. The gravel and debris crunched under my footsteps as we began walking away.

"Kara, I know it's hard. But if you want to talk, I'm here..." He offered sweetly. I nodded and smiled, making my way towards the opening we were allowed to come through.

"Kara..." Alice called. Her voice was odd, and something about it caught our attention. "Kara!" She sounded panicked now, and we walked back to her with haste. I put a reassuring hand on her back in an attempt to bring her comfort.

"It's okay, Alice. I know it's hard-"

"Jalix, look." She stepped away from the flowers and pointed at them as if they were possessed.

"What's wrong, Alice..." His voice trailed off as we both realized what was occurring. Despite the warm air of summer and the immaculate sun illuminating the grave of my fallen friend, a thin layer of white frost crept over the petals.

Weaver

Sorrow

"I am Sorrow"

It's only after my death that I've realized both who I am, and who I had become. After each pale reflection in my shadowy mirror, I've seen who is looking back at me. An angel, trapped within the reaches of what lie beyond my touch. The slivers of that shadow are all that's left. The mirror is shattered, and she is lost. But not forgotten. The somber, bitter realization has come to me slowly that it is who I was. But it is not who I choose to be. I choose a different path. I choose to leave her behind, and everything she made me. Now, I am a mother. A wife. A friend. The specter that shadowed my path is banished to my past and kept there by an icy guardian, colder than the depths of the darkest winter. And my future is kept bright and warm by something I could never have claimed as Sorrow. In all my vast power and infinite strength, it is a singular object I could not find, and an extraordinary feeling I could not possess.

Love.

CPSIA information can be obtained
at www.ICGtesting.com
Printed in the USA
BVOW03s2201070617
486359BV00001B/6/P